WHEN WAS THE FIRST ___
THE FIRST FANTASTICAL TALE SPUN?

Now you can find out how and when the careers of some of your favorite fantasy writers began with the sixteen "first" stories collected here. From Andre Norton, Peter Beagle, and Ursula K. Le Guin to Mickey Zucker Reichert, Mercedes Lackey, and Tanya Huff, MAGICAL BEGINNINGS offers an enchanting journey through time to recapture those special moments when would-be writers became published authors. Some of the stories will bring back fond memories, others may be new discoveries for you. But all of these stories—and the authors own introductions to them—will offer a treasure chest of gems that any knight would quest to find and any dragon would eagerly hoard.

MAGICAL BEGINNINGS

MAGICAL BEGINNINGS

edited by

Steven H. Silver
and
Martin H. Greenberg

DAW BOOKS, INC.
DONALD A. WOLLHEIM, FOUNDER
375 Hudson Street, New York, NY 10014
ELIZABETH R. WOLLHEIM
SHEILA E. GILBERT
PUBLISHERS
www.dawbooks.com

First Printing, February 2003
1   2   3   4   5   6   7   8

DAW TRADEMARK REGISTERED

U.S. PAT. OFF. AND FOREIGN COUNTRIES

—MARCA REGISTRADA.

HECHO EN U.S.A.

PRINTED IN THE U.S.A.

ACKNOWLEDGMENTS

Introduction © 2003 by Steven H. Silver.

Introduction to "People of the Crater," copyright © 2003 by Andre Norton.

"People of the Crater" by Andre Norton, copyright © 1947 by Andre Norton. First published in *Fantasy Book #1*. Reprinted by permission of the author.

Introduction to "My Daughter's Name Is Sarah" by Peter S. Beagle. Copyright © 2003 by Peter S. Beagle.

"My Daughter's Name Is Sarah" by Peter S. Beagle, copyright © 1959 by Peter Beagle. First published in *Overture*. Reprinted by permission of the author.

Introduction to "April in Paris," copyright © 2003 by Ursula K. Le Guin.

"April in Paris" by Ursula K. Le Guin, copyright © 1962 by Ursula K. Le Guin. First published in *Fantastic*, September 1962. Reprinted by permission of the author and her agents, the Virginia Kidd Literary Agency, Inc.

"To Light a Fire," copyright © 2003 by Susan Shwartz.

"The Fires of Her Vengeance" by Susan Shwartz, copyright © 1978 by Susan Shwartz. First published in *The Keeper's Price*. Reprinted by permission of the author.

Introduction to "The Fane of the Grey Rose," copyright © 2003 by Charles de Lint.

"The Fane of the Grey Rose" by Charles de Lint, copyright © 1979 by Charles de Lint. First published in *Swords Against Darkness IV*. Reprinted by permission of the author.

Introduction to "Bones for Dulath," copyright © 2003 by Megan Lindholm.

To Elaine for being there
and Pat for pushing and searching

CONTENTS

INTRODUCTION

Steven Silver

THERE is a certain magic in receiving that first letter from an editor letting you know that something you have written is not only worthy of being read, but worthy of payment. The knowledge that a publishing company is willing to take a chance on a new voice with the belief that people will have an interest in the stories which have sprung from your mind and fingertips ranks with the most arcane magical knowledge.

These magical beginnings are momentous events in the life of the author, the author's family, and perhaps a few friends. All too often, the sudden appearance of a new author is greeted with little, if any, fanfare: perhaps one line in a magazine noting a first sale. All authors begin with this first sale. Many authors continue to make sales and build up their readers, some casual, some fanatic. Many of those readers, however, will never have a chance to read the author's debut story, capturing the moment when magic struck for the author.

There is a certain magic to discovering a new author. The thrill of knowing that there is someone out there who shares your sensitivities and point of view, or perhaps who can make you think about issues in a new and entertaining manner. This magic is even more pronounced when the author is newly published and you can combine your sense of discovery with the belief that only a few others are aware of the author's existence.

These stories often show the author's talents in their most

raw state. The prose isn't necessarily as polished as their later, more famous, works, but frequently the ideas within the stories demonstrate the most innovative ideas. These are stories which are bursting to be told and have to find their own way to the page. Occasionally, the author will have the opportunity to rewrite and expand these early stories as his or her career progresses. More often, these stories become rarities, lost to most readers, existing only as a sort of Holy Grail for the most dedicated fans.

Magical Beginnings is intended to provide assistance to those readers who want to enjoy the earliest published stories by their favorite authors. The authors included range from grand masters and stalwarts of the field to up and comers whose careers should provide plenty of magic in the future.

When Andre Norton began publishing with "People of the Crater," she published under the masculine pseudonym "Andrew North." Many other female authors who published in the forties, fifties, sixties, and even into the seventies, felt the need to hide their gender behind a pseudonym or initials. Their careers, however, made it easier for women to publish under their own names.

Megan Lindholm's first story, "Bones for Dulath," was published under her own name. Two decades later, she has adopted a pseudonym, Robin Hobb. In her case, magic struck twice for people who had the opportunity to discover her as a new author under her own name and later when they discovered Robin Hobb and thought that they had made another discovery.

Some authors take their original story and expand it to novel length. Charles de Lint's professional career began with the story "The Fane of the Grey Rose." Even before it was published, in a shorter version than he originally wrote, de Lint was working on expanding it to form the novel *The Harp of the Grey Rose*. In this way, de Lint's readers could regain the magic of his story.

In these pages, you'll be able to read the magical words that launched these writers' professional careers. These authors have managed to sustain the magic they introduced into the world with their first stories and subsequent stories and novels. *Magical Beginnings* rekindles the first spells they wove, giving their fans, and new readers, the opportunity to achieve the magic that comes with the discovery of a new author, or at least one who is new to you.

INTRODUCTION TO "PEOPLE OF THE CRATER"

by Andre Norton

From the time I could understand what was being read, it was always fantastic tales that drew me more than any other kind. My mother herself read, and told, stories, and they never concerned everyday experiences. When I was very young, I would bring my little chair to where she was ironing, settle myself comfortably, and order: "Tell me about Uncle Wiggily and the Boy Scouts!" Having absorbed all the available *Uncle Wiggily* books, I wanted that dauntless rabbit to enter another field of endeavor, and Mother obligingly spun for me a whole series of new adventures.

At the age of seven, I came down with the measles and, according to the medical protocol of the day, I was imprisoned in a very dark room in order to preserve my sight. But a vision of a whole new world was opened at that time to the eyes of my imagination, for the second Oz book was just then being serialized in the Cleveland paper, and my mother read each installment to me while seated in the hall under a light. Then daydreams about the country "over the rainbow" began.

When I was in my teens, *A Princess of Mars* fell into my hands—a literary encounter that proved a significant influence on my writing career. At that time, one could buy Burroughs' works in hardcover editions for the sum of seventy-five cents, and I had his titles on my permanent Christmas list for some years there-after.

However, the major "find" for me in imaginative fiction was the discovery of *The Face in the Abyss*. Merritt covered, superbly, all the points I enjoyed most in a story. His exotic backgrounds and characters—what reader could ever forget the Snake Mother?—were visited with delight over and over. I longed to create my own Abyss, but some quirk of fate defeated me.

In that era, the only market for speculative tales was for short stories. Unfortunately, my pattern of thought has always made it difficult for me to compose brief tales; my efforts generally read like outlines for novels. So for the time being I kept to my familiar field of adventure, spy, or historical books. But my imagination constantly groped after the fantastic. *Witch World*, for example, grew out of an attempt to write a historical tale about the Knights of Outremer.

With the advent of the atomic age in 1945, science fiction— heretofore symbolized in the minds of the reading public by "pulps" with jackets depicting the flight of scantily-clad maidens from monsters of varying vileness—became not only respectable but sought after. New publishing houses were actually founded that were dedicated to the genre.

"Hard science" stories were those most officially approved, but publications such as *Weird Tales* wanted Merritt's type of fantasy. I therefore ventured to work out "People of the Crater," a piece in the tradition of *The Face in the Abyss*. I still did not believe I had written anything that was marketable, but William Crawford, a beginning publisher, took the novella for his *Fantasy Book* magazine. Later, with the addition of extra material, it was offered as a full-length novel.

For a long while thereafter, *Crater* and two other shorter stories—"The Gifts of Asti" and "All Cats are Gray"—were my only achievements in the field of fantasy. To my continuing surprise, the latter two tales have been, and still are, reprinted from time to time in anthologies. "People of the Crater" has, as I noted, also made a second appearance, expanded as *Garan the Eternal*.

The kinship of the latter piece with the work of Merritt is very apparent; it also contains foreshadowings of the *Witch World* to come. I can read it even now with some small pride. It has always been my contention that I write stories to amuse and, hopefully, to excite wonder; and I believe that, dated and naive though this tale may be, it does a little of both.

PEOPLE OF THE CRATER

by Andre Norton

CHAPTER ONE

Through the Blue Haze

SIX months and three days after the Peace of Shanghai was signed and the great War of 1965–1970 declared at an end by an exhausted world, a young man huddled on a park bench in New York, staring miserably at the gravel beneath his badly-worn shoes. He had been trained to fill the pilot's seat in the control cabin of a fighting plane and for nothing else. The search for a niche in civilian life had cost him both health and ambition.

A newcomer dropped down on the other end of the bench. The flier studied him bitterly. *He* had decent shoes, a warm coat, and the air of satisfaction with the world that is the result of economic security. Although he was well into middle age, the man had a compact grace of movement and an air of alertness.

"Aren't you Captain Garin Featherstone?"

Startled, the flier nodded dumbly.

From a plump billfold the man drew a clipping and waved it toward his seatmate. Two years before, Captain

Garin Featherstone of the United Democratic Forces had led a perilous bombing raid into the wilds of Siberia to wipe out the vast expeditionary army secretly gathering there. It had been a spectacular affair and had brought the survivors some fleeting fame.

"You're the sort of chap I've been looking for," the stranger folded the clipping again, "a flier with courage, initiative, and brains. The man who led that raid is worth investing in."

"What's the proposition?" asked Featherstone a little wearily. He no longer believed in luck.

"I'm Gregory Farson," the other returned as if that should answer the question.

"The Antarctic man!"

"Just so. As you have probably heard, I was halted on the eve of my last expedition by the spread of war to this country. Now I am preparing to sail south again."

"But I don't see—"

"How you can help me? Very simple, Captain Featherstone. I need pilots. Unfortunately, the war has disposed of most of them. I'm lucky to contact one such as yourself—"

And it was as simple as that. But Garin didn't really believe that it was more than a dream until they touched the glacial shores of the polar continent some months later. As they brought ashore the three large planes, he began to wonder at the driving motive behind Farson's vague plans.

When the supply ship sailed, not to return for a year, Farson called them together. Three of the company were pilots, all war veterans, and two were engineers who spent most of their waking hours engrossed in the maps Farson produced.

"Tomorrow," the leader glanced from face to face, "we start inland. Here—" On a map spread before him, he indicated a line marked in purple.

"Ten years ago, I was a member of the Verdane expedition. Once, when flying due south, our plane was caught by some freakish air current and drawn off its course. When we were totally off our map, we saw in the distance a thick bluish haze. It seemed to rise in a straight line from the ice plain to the sky. Unfortunately, our fuel was low, and we dared not risk a closer investigation. So we fought our way back to the base.

"Verdane, however, had little interest in our report, and we did not investigate it. Three years ago, that Kattack expedition hunting oil deposits by the order of the Dictator reported seeing the same haze. This time we are going to explore it!"

"Why," Garin asked curiously, "are you so eager to penetrate this haze? I gather that's what we're going to do—"

Farson hesitated before answering. "It has often been suggested that beneath the ice sheeting of this continent may be hidden mineral wealth. I believe that the haze is caused by some form of volcanic activity, and perhaps a break in the ice crust."

Garin frowned at the map. He wasn't so sure about that explanation, but Farson was paying the bills. The flier shrugged away his uneasiness. Much could be forgiven a man who allowed one to eat regularly again.

Four days later they set out. Helmly, one of the engineers, Rawlson, a pilot, and Farson occupied the first plane. The other engineer and pilot were in the second, and Garin, with the extra supplies, was alone in the third.

He was content to be alone as they took off across the blue-white waste. His ship, because of its load, was logy, so he did not attempt to follow the other two into the higher lane. They were in communication by radio, and Garin, as he snapped on his earphones, remembered something Farson had said that morning:

"The haze affects radio. On our trip near it, the static was very bad. Almost," with a laugh, "like speech in some foreign tongue."

As they roared over the ice, Garin wondered if it might have been speech—from, perhaps, a secret enemy expedition, such as the Kattack one.

In his sealed cockpit, he did not feel the bite of the frost, and the ship rode smoothly. With a little sigh of content, he settled back against the cushions, keeping to the course set by the planes ahead of and above him.

Some five hours after they left the base, Garin caught

sight of a dark shadow far ahead. At the same time, Farson's voice chattered in his earphones.

"That's it. Set course straight ahead."

The shadow grew until it became a wall of purple-blue from earth to sky. The first plane was quite close to it, diving down into the vapor. Suddenly the ship rocked violently and swung earthward as if out of control. Then it straightened and turned back. Garin could hear Farson demanding to know what was the matter. But from the first plane there was no reply.

As Farson's plane kept going, Garin throttled down. The actions of the first ship indicated trouble. What if that haze were a toxic gas?

"Close up, Featherstone!" barked Farson suddenly.

He obediently drew ahead until they flew wing to wing. The haze was just before them, and now Garin could see movement in it—oily, impenetrable billows. The motors bit into it. There was clammy, foggy moisture on the windows.

Abruptly, Garin sensed that he was no longer alone. Somewhere in the empty cabin behind him was another intelligence, a measuring power. He fought furiously against it—against the very idea of it. But, after a long, terrifying moment while it seemed to study him, it took control. His hands and feet still manipulated the ship, but *it* flew!

On the ship hurtled through the thickening mist. He lost sight of Farson's plane. And, though he was still fighting against the will that overrode his, his struggles grew weaker. Then came the order to dive into the dark heart of the purple mists.

Down they whirled. Once, as the haze opened, Garin caught a glimpse of tortured gray rock seamed with yellow. Farson had been right: here the ice crust was broken.

Down and down. If his instruments were correct, the plane was below sea level now. The haze thinned and was gone. Below spread a plain cloaked in vivid green. Here and there reared clumps of what might be trees. He saw, too, the waters of a yellow stream.

But there was something terrifyingly alien about that landscape. Even as he circled above it, Garin wrestled to break the grip of the will that had brought him there. There came a crackle of sound in his earphones and, at that moment, the Presence withdrew.

The nose of the plane went up in obedience to his own desire. Frantically, he climbed away from the green land. Again the haze absorbed him. He watched the moisture bead on the windows. Another hundred feet or so, and he would be free of it—and that unbelievable world beneath.

Then, with an ominous sputter, the port engine conked out. The plane lurched and slipped into a dive. Down it whirled again into the steady light of the green land.

Trees came out of the ground, huge fernlike plants with crimson-scaled trunks. Toward a clump of these the plane swooped.

Frantically, Garin fought the controls. The ship steadied, and the dive became a fast glide. He looked for an open space to land. Then he felt the landing gear scrape some surface. Directly ahead loomed one of the fern trees. The plane sped toward the long fronds. There came a ripping crash, the splintering of metal and wood. The scarlet cloud gathering before Garin's eyes turned black.

CHAPTER TWO

The Folk of Tav

GARIN returned to consciousness through a mist of pain. He was pinned in the crumpled mass of metal that had once been the cabin. Through a rent in the wall close to his head thrust a long spike of green; shredded leaves still clung to it. He lay and watched it, not daring to move lest the pain prove more than he could bear.

It was then that he heard the pattering sound outside. It seemed as if soft hands were pushing and pulling at the wreck. The tree branch shook, and a portion of the cabin wall dropped away with a clang.

Garin turned his head slowly. Through the aperture was clambering a goblin figure.

It stood about five feet tall, and it walked upon its hind

legs in human fashion, but the legs were short and stumpy, ending in feet with five toes of equal length. Slender, shapely arms possessed small hands with only four digits. The creature had a high, well-rounded forehead but no chin, the face being distinctly lizardlike in contour. The skin was a dull black, with a velvety surface. About its loins it wore a short kilt of metallic cloth, the garment being supported by a jeweled belt of exquisite workmanship.

For a long moment the apparition eyed Garin. And it was those golden eyes, fixed unwinkingly on his, which banished the flier's fear. There was nothing but great pity in their depths.

The lizard-man stooped and brushed the sweat-dampened hair from Garin's forehead. Then he fingered the bonds of metal that held the flier, as if estimating their strength. Having done so, he turned to the opening and apparently gave an order, returning again to squat by Garin.

Two more of his kind appeared to tear away the ruins of the cockpit. Though they were very careful, Garin fainted twice before they had freed him. He was placed on a litter swung between two clumsy beasts that might have been small elephants, except that they lacked trunks and possessed four tusks each.

They crossed the plain to the towering mouth of a huge cavern where the litter was taken up by four of the lizard-folk. The flier lay staring up at the roof of the cavern. In the black stone had been carved fronds and flowers in bewildering profusion. Shining motes, giving off faint light, sifted through the air. At times as they advanced, these gathered in clusters, and the light grew brighter.

Midway down a long corridor the bearers halted, while their leader pulled upon a knob on the wall. An oval door swung back and the party passed through.

They came into a round room, the walls of which had been fashioned of creamy quartz veined with violet. At the highest point in the ceiling a large globe of the motes hung, furnishing soft light below.

Two lizard-men, clad in long robes, conferred with the leader of the flier's party before coming in to stand over Garin. One of the robed ones shook his head at the sight of the flier's twisted body and waved the litter on into an inner chamber.

Here the walls were dull blue, and in the exact center was a long block of quartz. Beside this the litter was put down, and the bearers disappeared. With sharp knives the robed men cut away furs and leather to expose Garin's broken body.

They lifted him to the quartz table and there made him fast with metal bonds. Then one of them went to the wall and pulled a gleaming rod. From the dome of the roof shot an eerie blue light to beat upon Garin's helpless body. There followed a tingling through every muscle and joint, a prickling sensation in his skin, but soon his pain vanished as if it had never been.

The light flashed off, and the three lizard-men gathered around him. He was wrapped in a soft robe and carried to another room. This, too, was circular, shaped like half of a giant bubble. The floor sloped toward the center, where there was a depression filled with cushions. There they laid Garin. At the top of the bubble, a pinkish cloud formed. He watched it drowsily until he fell asleep.

Something warm stirred against his bare shoulder. He opened his eyes, for a moment unable to remember where he was. There was a plucking at the robe twisted about him and he looked down.

If the lizard-folk had been goblin in their grotesqueness, this visitor was elfin. It was about three feet high, its monkeylike body completely covered with silky white hair. The tiny hands were human in shape and hairless, but its feet were much like a cat's paws. From either side of the small round head branched large fan-shaped ears. The face was furred and boasted stiff cat whiskers on the upper lip. These *Anas*, as Garin learned later, were happy little creatures, each one choosing some mistress or master among the Folk, as this one had come to him. They were content to follow their big protector, speechless with delight at trifling gifts. Loyal and brave, they could do simple tasks or carry written messages for their chosen friend, and they remained with him until death. They were neither beast nor human but were rumored to be the result of some experiment carried out eons ago by the Ancient Ones.

After patting Garin's shoulder, the Ana touched the flier's hair wonderingly, comparing the bronze lengths with its own white fur. Since the Folk were hairless, hair was a strange sight in the Caverns. With a contented purr, it rubbed its head against his hand.

A door in the wall opened with a sudden click. The Ana got to its feet and ran to greet the newcomers. The chieftain of the Folk, he who had first discovered Garin, entered, followed by several of his fellows. The flier sat up. Not only was the pain gone, but he felt stronger and younger than he had for weary months. Exultingly, he stretched wide his arms and grinned at the lizard beings, who murmured happily in return.

Lizard-men busied themselves about Garin, girding on him the short kilt and jewel-set belt that were the only clothing of the Caverns. When they were finished, the chieftain took his hand and drew him to the door.

They traversed a hallway whose walls were carved and inlaid with glittering stones and metalwork, coming, at last, into a huge cavern, the outer walls of which were hidden by shadows. On a dais stood three tall thrones, and Garin was conducted to the foot of these.

The highest throne was of rose crystal. On its right was one of green jade, worn smooth by centuries of time. At the left was the third, carved of a single block of jet. The rose throne and that of jet were unoccupied, but in the seat of jade reposed one of the Folk. He was taller than his fellows, and in his eyes, as he stared at Garin, was wisdom—and a brooding sadness.

"It is well!" The words resounded in the flier's head. "We have chosen wisely. This youth is fit to mate with the Daughter. But he will be tried, as fire tries metal. He must win the Daughter forth and strive with the Kepta—"

A hissing murmur echoed through the hall. Garin guessed that hundreds of the Folk must be gathered there.

"Urg!" the being on the throne commanded.

The chieftain moved a step toward the dais.

"Do you take this youth and instruct him. And then will I

speak with him again. For—" sadness colored the words now, "—we would have the Rose Throne filled again and the black one blasted into dust. Time moves swiftly."

The chieftain led a wondering Garin away.

CHAPTER THREE

Garin Hears of the Black Ones

URG brought the flier into one of the bubble-shaped rooms that contained a low, cushioned bench facing a metal screen, and here they seated themselves.

What followed was a language lesson. On the screen appeared objects which Urg would name, to have his sibilant uttering repeated by Garin. As the American later learned, the ray treatment he had undergone had quickened his mental powers, and in an incredibly short time he had a working vocabulary.

Judging by the pictures, the lizard-folk were the rulers of the crater world, although other forms of life also dwelt there. The elephantlike *Tand* was a beast of burden, while the squirrellike *Eron* lived underground and carried on a crude agriculture in small clearings, coming shyly twice a year to exchange grain for a liquid rubber produced by the Folk.

Then there was the Gibi, a monstrous bee, also friendly to the lizard-people. It supplied the cavern dwellers with wax, and in return the Folk gave the Gibi colonies shelter during the unhealthful times of the Great Mists.

Highly civilized were the Folk. They did no work by hand, except the finer kinds of jewel setting and carving. Machines wove their metal cloth, and machines prepared their food, harvested their fields, hollowed out new dwellings.

Freed from manual labor, they had turned to acquiring knowledge. Urg projected onto the screen pictures of vast laboratories and great libraries of scientific lore. But all they knew in the beginning they had learned from the Ancient

Ones, a race unlike themselves, which had preceded them in sovereignty over *Tav*. Even the Folk themselves were the result of constant forced evolution and experimentation carried on by these Ancient Ones.

All this wisdom was guarded most carefully, but against what or whom, Urg could not tell, although he insisted that the danger was very real. Something within the blue wall of the crater disputed the rule of the Folk.

As Garin tried to probe further, a gong sounded. Urg arose.

"It is the hour of eating," he announced. "Let us go."

They came to a large room where a heavy table of white stone stretched along three walls, with benches before it. Urg seated himself and pressed a knob on the table, motioning Garin to do likewise. The wall facing them opened, and two trays slid out. There was a platter of hot meat covered with rich sauce, a stone bowl of grain porridge, and a cluster of fruit, still fastened to a leafy branch. This the Ana eyed so wistfully that Garin gave it to the creature.

The Folk ate silently and arose quietly when they had finished, their trays vanishing back through the wall. Garin noticed only males in the room and recalled that he had, as yet, seen no females among the Folk. He ventured a question.

Urg chuckled. "So, you think there are no women in the Caverns? Well, we shall go to the Hall of Women that you may see."

To the Hall of Women they went. It was breathtaking in its richness, with stones worth a nation's ransom sparkling from its domed roof and painted walls. Here were the matrons and maidens of the Folk, their black forms veiled in robes of silver net, each cross-strand of which was set with a tiny gem, so that they appeared to be wrapped in glittering scales.

There were not many of them—a hundred, perhaps. And a few led by the hand smaller editions of themselves, who stared at Garin with round yellow eyes and chewed black fingertips shyly.

The women were entrusted with the finest jewel work, and with pride they showed the stranger their handiwork. At the far end of the hall was a wondrous thing in the making.

One of the silver nets that were the foundations of their robes was fastened there, and three of the women were putting small rose jewels into each microscopic setting. Here and there they had varied the pattern with tiny emeralds or flaming opals so that the finished portion was a rainbow.

One of the workers smoothed the robe and glanced up at Garin, a gentle teasing in her voice as she explained:

"This is for the Daughter when she comes to her throne."

The Daughter! What had the Lord of the Folk said? *"This youth is fit to mate with the Daughter."* But Urg had said that the Ancient Ones had gone from Tav.

"Who is the Daughter?" he demanded.

"Thrala of the Light."

"Where is she?"

The woman shivered, and there was fear in her eyes. "Thrala lies in the Caves of Darkness."

"The Caves of Darkness!" Did she mean Thrala was dead? Was he, Garin Featherstone, to be the victim of some rite of sacrifice that was designed to unite him with the dead?

Urg touched his arm. "Not so. Thrala has not yet entered the Place of Ancestors."

"You know my thoughts?"

Urg laughed. "Thoughts are easy to read. Thrala lives. Sera served the Daughter as handmaiden while she was yet among us. Sera, do you show us Thrala as she was."

The woman crossed to a wall where there was a mirror such as Urg had used for his language lesson. She gazed into it and then beckoned for the flier to stand beside her.

The mirror misted, and then he was looking, as if through a window, into a room with walls and ceiling of rose quartz. On the floor were thick rugs of silver rose, and a great heap of cushions made a low couch in the center.

"The inner chamber of the Daughter," Sera announced.

A circular panel in the wall opened, and a woman slipped through. She was very young, little more than a girl. There were happy curves in her full crimson lips, joyous lights in her violet eyes.

She was human of shape, but her beauty was unearthly. Her skin was pearl white, yet other colors seemed to play faintly upon it, so that it reminded Garin of mother-of-pearl with its lights and shadows. The hair that veiled her as a cloud was blue-black and reached below her knees. She was robed in the silver net of the Folk, and she wore a heavy girdle of rose-shaded jewels about her slender waist.

"That was Thrala before the Black Ones took her," said Sera.

Garin uttered a cry of disappointment as the picture vanished. Urg laughed.

"What care you for shadows, when the Daughter herself waits for you? You have but to bring her from the Caves of Darkness—"

"Where are these Caves—" Garin's question was interrupted by the pealing of the Cavern gong. Sera cried out:

"The Black Ones!"

Urg shrugged. "When they spared not the Ancient Ones, how could we hope to escape? Come, we must go to the Hall of Thrones."

Before the jade throne of the Lord of the Folk stood a small group of the lizard-men beside two litters. As Garin entered, the Lord spoke.

"Let the outlander come hither that he may see the work of the Black Ones."

Garin advanced unwillingly, coming to stand by those struggling things that gasped their message between moans and screams of agony. They were men of the Folk, but their black skins were green with rot.

The Lord leaned forward on his throne. "It is well," he said. "You may depart."

As if obeying his command, the tortured things let go of the life to which they had clung, and were still.

"Look upon the work of the Black Ones," the ruler said to Garin. "Jiv and Betv were captured while on a mission to the Gibi of the Cliff. It seems that the Black Ones needed material for their laboratories. They seek even to give the Daughter to their workers of horror!"

A terrible cry of hatred arose from the hall, and Garin's jaw set. To give that fair vision he had just seen to such a death as this—!

"Jiv and Betv were imprisoned close to the Daughter, and

they heard the threats of Kepta. Our brothers, stricken with foul disease, were sent forth to carry the plague to us, but they swam through the pool of boiling mud. They have died, but the evil died with them. And I think that while we breed such as they, the Black Ones shall not rest easy. Listen now, outlander, to the story of the Black Ones and the Caves of Darkness, of how the Ancient Ones brought the Folk up from the slime of a long-dried sea and made them great, and of how the Ancient Ones at last went down to their destruction."

CHAPTER FOUR

The Defeat of the Ancient Ones

"IN the days before the lands of the outer world were born of the Sea, before even the Land of Sun, Mu, and the Land of Sea, Atlantis, arose from molten rock and sand, there was land here in the far south. It was a sere land of rock plains and swamps where slimy life mated, lived, and died.

"Then came the Ancient Ones from beyond the stars. Their race was already older than this earth. Their wise men had watched its birth-rending from the sun. And when their world perished, taking most of their blood into nothingness, a handful fled hither. But when they climbed from their spaceship, it was into hell, for they had gained, in place of their loved home, bare rock and stinking slime.

"They blasted out this Tav and entered into it with the treasures of their flying ships and also certain living creatures captured in the swamps. From these, they produced the Folk, the Gibi, the Tand, and the land-tending Eron. Among these, the Folk were eager for wisdom and climbed high. But still the learning of the Ancient Ones remained beyond their grasp.

"During the eons the Ancient Ones dwelt within their protecting wall of haze, the outer world changed. Cold came to the north and south; the Land of Sun and the Land of Sea arose to bear the foot of true man. On their mirrors of see-ing, the Ancient Ones watched man-life spread across the world. They had the power of prolonging life, but still the race was dying; from without must come new blood. So certain men were summoned from the Land of Sun. Then the race flourished for a space.

"The Ancient Ones decided to leave Tav for the outer world, but the sea swallowed the Land of Sun. Again in the time of the Land of Sea the stock within Tav was replenished and the Ancient Ones prepared for exodus; again the sea cheated them.

"Those men left in the outer world reverted to savagery. Since the Ancient Ones would not mingle their blood with that of almost-beasts, they built the haze wall stronger and remained. But a handful of them were attracted by the forbidden, and secretly they summoned the beast-men. Of that monstrous mating came the Black Ones. They live but for the evil they may do, and the power which they acquired is debased and used to forward cruelty.

"At first the sin was not discovered. When it was, the others would have slain the offspring but for the law which forbids them to kill—they must use their power for good, or it departs from them. So they drove the Black Ones to the southern end of Tav and gave them the Caves of Darkness. Never were the Black Ones to come north of the River of Gold—nor were the Ancient Ones to go south of it.

· "For perhaps two thousand years the Black Ones kept the law. But they worked, building powers of destruction. While matters rested thus, the Ancient Ones searched the world, seeking men by whom they could renew the race. Once there came men from an island far to the north. Six lived to penetrate the mists and take wives among the Daughters. Again, they called the yellow-haired men of another breed, great sea-rovers.

"But the Black Ones called, too. As the Ancient Ones searched for the best, the Black Ones brought in great workers of evil. And, at last, they succeeded in shutting off the channels of sending thought so that the Ancient Ones could call no more.

"Then did the Black Ones cross the River of Gold and

enter the land of the Ancient Ones. Thran, Dweller in the Light and Lord of the Caverns, summoned the Folk to him.

" 'There will come one to aid you,' he told us. 'Try the summoning again after the Black Ones have seemed to win. Thrala, Daughter of the Light, will not enter into the Room of Pleasant Death with the rest of the women but will give herself into the hands of the Black Ones, that they may think themselves truly victorious. You of the Folk withdraw into the Place of Reptiles until the Black Ones are gone. Nor will all the Ancient Ones perish—more will be saved, but the manner of their preservation I dare not tell. When the sun-haired youth comes from the outer world, send him into the Caves of Darkness to rescue Thrala and put an end to evil.'

"And then the Lady Thrala arose and said softly, 'As the Lord Thran has said, so let it be. I shall deliver myself into the hands of the Black Ones that their doom may come upon them.'

"Lord Thran smiled upon her as he said: 'So will happiness be your portion. After the Great Mists, does not light come again?'

"The women of the Ancient Ones then took their leave and passed into the Place of Pleasant Death while the men made ready for battle with the Black Ones. For three days they fought, but a new weapon of the Black Ones won the day, and the chief of the Black Ones set up this throne of jet as proof of his power. Since, however, the Black Ones were not happy in the Caverns, longing for the darkness of their caves, they soon withdrew and we, the Folk, came forth again.

"But now the time has come when the dark ones will sacrifice the Daughter to their evil. If you can win her free, outlander, they shall perish as if they had not been."

"What of the Ancient Ones?" asked Garin, "those others Thran said would be saved?"

"Of those we know nothing save that, when we bore the bodies of the fallen to the Place of Ancestors, there were some missing. That you may see the truth of this story, Urg will take you to the gallery above the Place of Pleasant Death, and you may look upon those who sleep there."

With Urg guiding, Garin climbed a steep ramp leading

from the Hall of Thrones. This led to a narrow balcony, one side of which was clear crystal. Urg pointed down.

They were above a long room whose walls were tinted jade green. On the polished floor were scattered piles of cushions. Each was occupied by a sleeping woman, and several of these clasped a child in their arms. Their long hair rippled to the floor, while curved lashes made dark shadows on pale faces.

"But they are sleeping!" protested Garin.

Urg shook his head. "It is the sleep of death. Twice each ten hours, vapors rise from the floor. Those breathing them do not wake again, and if they are undisturbed they will lie thus for a thousand years. Look there—"

He pointed to the closed double doors of the room. There lay the first men of the Ancient Ones whom Garin had seen. They, too, seemed but asleep, their handsome heads pillowed on their arms.

"Thran ordered those who remained after the last battle in the Hall of Thrones to enter the Place of Pleasant Death that the Black Ones might not torture them for their beastly pleasures. Thran himself remained behind to close the door, and so died."

There were no aged among the sleepers. None of the men seemed to count more than thirty years, and many of them appeared younger. Garin remarked upon this.

"The Ancient Ones appeared thus until the day of their death, though many lived twice a hundred years. The light rays kept them so. Even we of the Folk can hold back age. But come now, our Lord Trar would speak with you again."

CHAPTER FIVE

Into the Caves of Darkness

AGAIN Garin stood before the Jade Throne of Trar and heard the stirring of the multitude of the Folk in the shadows. Trar was turning a small rod of glittering, greenish metal around in his soft hands.

"Listen well, outlander," he began, "for little time remains to us. Within seven days the Great Mists will be upon us. Then no living thing may venture forth from shelter and escape death. And before that time Thrala must be out of the Caves. This rod will be your weapon; the Black Ones have not its secret. Watch."

Two of the Folk dragged an ingot of metal before him. He touched it with the rod. Great flakes of rust appeared, to spread across the entire surface. It crumbled away, and one of the Folk trod upon the pile of dust where it had been.

"Thrala lies in the heart of the Caves, but Kepta's men have grown careless with the years. Enter boldly and trust to fortune. They know nothing of your coming or of Thran's words concerning you."

Urg stood forward and held out his hands in appeal.

"What would you, Urg?"

"Lord, I would go with the outlander. He knows nothing of the Forest of the Morgels or of the Pool of Mud. It is easy to go astray in the woodland—"

Trar shook his head. "That may not be. He must go alone, even as Thran said."

The Ana, which had followed in Garin's shadow all day, whistled shrilly and stood on tiptoe to tug at his hand. Trar smiled. "That one may go; its eyes may serve you well. Urg will guide you to the outer portal of the Place of Ancestors and set you upon the road to the Caves. Farewell, outlander, and may the spirits of the Ancient Ones be with you."

Garin bowed to the ruler of the Folk and turned to follow Urg. Near the door stood a small group of women. Sera pressed forward from them, holding out a small bag.

"Outlander," she said hurriedly, "when you look upon the Daughter, speak to her of Sera, for I have awaited her many years."

He smiled. "That I will."

"If you remember, outlander. I am a great lady among the Folk and have my share of suitors, yet I think I could envy the Daughter. Nay, I shall not explain that," she laughed mockingly. "You will understand in due time. Here is a packet of food. Now go swiftly that we may have you among us again before the Mists."

So a woman's farewell sped them on their way. Urg
chose a ramp that led downward. At its foot was a niche in
the rock, above which a rose light burned dimly. Urg
reached within the hollow and drew out a pair of high
buskins, which he aided Garin to lace on. They were a good
fit, having been fashioned for a man of the Ancient Ones.

The passage before them was narrow and crooked. Dust
lay in a thick carpet underfoot, patterned by the prints of the
Folk. They rounded a corner, and a tall door loomed out of
the gloom. Urg pressed the surface, a click sounded, and the
stone rolled back.

"This is the Place of Ancestors," he announced as he
stepped within.

They stood at the end of a colossal hall whose domed
roof disappeared into shadows. Thick pillars of gleaming
crystal divided it into aisles, all of which led inward to a
raised dais of oval shape. Filling the aisles were couches,
and each soft nest held its sleeper. Near to the door lay the
men and women of the Folk, but closer to the dais were the
Ancient Ones. Here and there a couch bore a double burden,
when upon the shoulder of a man was pillowed the drooping
head of a woman. Urg stopped beside such a one.

"See, outlander, here was one who was called from your
world. Marena of the House of Light looked with favor upon
him, and their days of happiness were many."

The man on the couch had red-gold hair, and on his upper
arm was a heavy band of gold whose mate Garin had once
seen in a museum. A son of pre-Norman Ireland. Urg traced
with a crooked finger the archaic lettering carved upon the
stone base of the couch.

"Lovers in the Light sleep sweetly. The Light returns on
the appointed day."

"Who lies there?" Garin motioned to the dais.

"The first Ancient Ones. Come, look upon those who
made this Tav."

On the dais the couches were arranged in two rows, and
between them, in the center, was a single couch raised above
the others. Fifty men and women lay as if merely resting for
the hour, smiles on their peaceful faces but weary shadows

beneath their eyes. They had an unhuman quality about them that was lacking in their descendants.

Urg advanced to the high couch and beckoned Garin to join him. A man and a woman lay there, the woman's head upon the man's breast. There was that in their faces which made Garin turn away. He felt as if he had intruded roughly where no man should go.

"Here lies Thran, Son of Light, first Lord of the Caverns, and his lady Thrala, Dweller in the Light. So have they lain a thousand thousand years, and so will they lie until this planet rots to dust beneath them. They led the Folk out of the slime and made Tav. Such as they we shall never see again."

They passed silently down the aisles of the dead. Once Garin caught sight of another fair-haired man, perhaps another outlander, since the Ancient Ones were all dark of hair. Urg paused once more before they left the hall. He stood by the couch of a man, wrapped in a long robe, whose face was ravaged with marks of agony.

Urg spoke a single name: "Thran."

So this was the last Lord of the Caverns. Garin leaned closer to study the dead face, but Urg seemed to have lost his patience. He hurried his charge on to a panel-door.

"This is the southern portal of the Caverns," he explained. "Trust to the Ana to guide you, and beware of the boiling mud. Should the morgels scent you, kill quickly, for they are the servants of the Black Ones. May fortune favor you, outlander."

The door was open, and Garin looked out upon Tav. The soft blue light was as strong as it had been when he had first seen it. With the Ana perched on his shoulder, the green rod and the bag of food in his hands, he stepped out onto the moss sod.

Urg raised his hand in salute, and the door clicked into place. Garin stood alone, pledged to bring the Daughter out of the Caves of Darkness.

There is no night or day in Tav, since the blue light is steady; but the Folk divide their time by artificial means. However, Garin, newly come from the rays of healing, felt no fatigue. As he hesitated, the Ana chattered and pointed confidently ahead.

Before them was a dense wood of fern trees. It was quiet in the forest as Garin made his way into its gloom, and for the first time he noted a peculiarity of Tav: there were no birds.

The portion of the woodland they had to traverse was but a spur of the forest to the west. After an hour of travel, they came out upon the bank of a sluggish river. The turbid waters of the stream were a dull saffron color. This, Garin thought, must be the River of Gold, the boundary of the lands of the Black Ones.

He rounded a bend to come upon a bridge, so old that time itself had worn its stone angles into curves. The bridge gave on a wide plain where tall grass grew sere and yellow. From the left came a hissing and bubbling, and a huge wave of boiling mud arose in the air. Garin choked in a wind thick with chemicals that blew from it. He smelled and tasted the sulphur-tainted air all across the plain.

And he was glad enough to plunge into a small fern grove that half-concealed a spring. There he bathed his head and arms while the Ana pulled open Sera's food bag.

Together they ate the cakes of grain and the dried fruit. When they were done, the Ana tugged at Garin's hand and pointed on.

Cautiously, Garin wormed his way through the thick underbrush, until at last he looked out into a clearing and, at its edge, the entrance of the Black Ones' Caves. Two tall pillars, carved into the likeness of foul monsters, guarded a rough-edged hole. A fine greenish mist whirled and danced in its mouth.

The flier studied the entrance. There was no life to be seen. He gripped the destroying rod and inched forward. Before the green mist he braced himself and then stepped within.

CHAPTER SIX

Kepta's Second Prisoner

THE green mist enveloped Garin. He drew into his lungs hot moist air faintly tinged with a scent of sickly sweetness as from some hidden corruption. Green motes in the air gave forth little light and seemed to cling to the intruder.

With the Ana pattering before him, the American started down a steep ramp, the soft soles of his buskins making no sound. At regular intervals along the wall, niches held small statues, and about the head of each perverted figure was a crown of green motes.

The Ana stopped, its large ears outspread as if to catch the faintest murmur of sound. From somewhere under the earth came the howls of a maddened dog. The Ana shivered, creeping closer to Garin.

Down led the ramp, growing narrower and steeper, and louder sounded the insane, coughing howls of the dog. Then the passage was abruptly barred by a grille of black stone. Garin peered through its bars at a flight of stairs leading down into a pit. From the pit arose snarling laughter.

Padding back and forth were things that might have been conceived by demons. They were sleek, ratlike creatures, hairless and large as ponies. Red saliva dripped from the corners of their sharp jaws. But in the eyes, which they raised now and then toward the grille, there was intelligence. These were the morgels, watchdogs and slaves of the Black Ones.

From a second pair of stairs directly across the pit arose a moaning call. A door opened, and two men came down the steps. The morgels surged forward but fell back when whips were cracked over their heads.

The masters of the morgels were human in appearance. Black loincloths were twisted about them, and long, wing-shaped cloaks hung from their shoulders. On their heads, completely masking their hair, were cloth caps that bore ragged crests not unlike cockscombs. As far as Garin could see, they were unarmed except for their whips.

A second party was coming down the steps. Between two

of the Black Ones struggled a prisoner. He made a desperate and hopeless fight of it, but they dragged him to the edge of the pit before they halted. The morgels, intent upon their promised prey, crouched before them.

Five steps above were two figures to whom the guards looked for instructions. One was a man of their race, of slender, handsome body and evil, beautiful face. His hand lay possessively upon the arm of his companion.

It was Thrala who stood beside him, her head proudly erect. The laughter-curves were gone from her lips; only sorrow and resignation were to be read there now. But her spirit burned like a white flame in her eyes.

"Look!" her warder ordered. "Does not Kepta keep his promises? Shall we give Dandtan into the jaws of our slaves, or will you unsay certain words of yours, Lady Thrala?"

The prisoner answered for her. "Kepta, son of vileness, Thrala is not for you. Remember, beloved one," he spoke to the Daughter, "the day of deliverance is at hand—"

Garin felt a sudden emptiness. The prisoner had called Thrala "beloved" with the ease of one who had the right.

"I await Thrala's answer," Kepta returned evenly. And her answer he got.

"Beast among beasts, you may send Dandtan to his death, you may heap all manner of insult and evil upon me, but still I say the Daughter is not for your touch. Rather will I cut the line of my life with my own hands, taking upon me the punishment of the Elder Ones. To Dandtan," she smiled down upon the prisoner, "I say farewell. We shall meet again beyond the Curtain of Time." She held out her hands to him.

"Thrala, dear one—!" One of his guards slapped a hand over the prisoner's mouth, putting an end to his words.

But now Thrala was looking beyond him, straight at the grille that sheltered Garin. Kepta pulled at her arm to gain her attention. "Watch! Thus do my enemies die. To the pit with him!"

The guards twisted their prisoner around, and the morgels crept closer, their eyes fixed upon that young, writhing body. Garin knew that he must take a hand in the game. The Ana was tugging him to the right, where there was an open archway that led to a balcony running around the side of the pit.

Those below were too entranced by the coming sport to notice the invader. But Thrala glanced up, and Garin thought that she sighted him. Something in her attitude attracted Kepta, and he, too, looked up. For a moment he stared in stark amazement; then he thrust the Daughter through the door behind him.

"Ho, outlander! Welcome to the Caves. So the Folk have meddled—"

"Greeting, Kepta." Garin hardly knew whence came the words that fell so easily from his tongue. "I have come as was promised, to remain until the Black Throne is no more."

"Not even the morgels boast before their prey lies limp in their jaws," flashed Kepta. "What manner of beast are you?"

"A clean beast, Kepta, which you are not. Bid your two-legged morgels loose the youth, lest I grow impatient." The flier swung the green rod into view.

Kepta's eyes narrowed but his smile did not fade. "I have heard of old that the Ancient Ones do not destroy—"

"As an outlander I am not bound by their limits," returned Garin, "as you will learn if you do not call off your stinking pack."

The master of the Caves laughed. "You are as the Tand, a fool without a brain. Never shall you see the Caverns again—"

"You shall own me master yet, Kepta."

The Black Chief seemed to consider. Then he waved to his men. "Release him," he ordered. "Outlander, you are braver than I thought. We might bargain—"

"Thrala goes forth from the Caves, and the black throne is dust. Those are the terms of the Caverns."

"And if we do not accept?"

"Then Thrala goes forth, the throne is dust, and Tav shall have a day of judging such as it has never seen before."

"You challenge me?"

Again, words that seemed to have their origin elsewhere came to him. "As in Yu-lac, I shall take—"

Before Kepta could reply, there was trouble in the pit. Dandtan, freed by his guards, was crossing the floor in running leaps. Garin threw himself belly-down on the balcony and dropped the jeweled strap of his belt over the lip.

A moment later, it snapped taut, and he stiffened to an upward pull. Already Dandtan's heels were above the snapping jaws of a morgel. The flier caught the youth around the shoulders and heaved, and they rolled together against the wall.

"They are gone! All of them!" Dandtan cried as he regained his feet. He was right: the morgels howled below, but Kepta and his men had vanished.

"Thrala!" Garin exclaimed.

Dandtan nodded. "They have taken her back to the cells. They believe her safe there."

"Then they think wrong." Garin stopped to pick up the green rod. His companion laughed.

"We'd best start before they get prepared for us."

Garin picked up the Ana. "Which way?"

Dandtan showed him a passage leading from behind the other door. Then he dodged into a side chamber, to return with two of the wing cloaks and cloth hoods, so that they might pass as Black Ones.

They went by the mouths of three side tunnels, all deserted. None disputed their going; all the Black Ones had withdrawn from this part of the Caves.

Dandtan sniffed uneasily. "All is not well. I fear a trap."

"While we can pass, let us."

The passage curved to the right, and they came into an oval room. Again Dandtan shook his head but ventured no protest. Instead he flung open a door and hurried down a short hall.

It seemed to Garin that there were strange rustlings and squeakings in the dark corners. Then Dandtan stopped so short that the flier ran into him.

"Here is the guardroom—and it is empty!"

Garin looked over his shoulder into a large room. Racks of strange weapons hung on the walls, and the sleeping pallets of the guards were stacked evenly, but the men were nowhere to be seen.

They crossed the room and passed beneath an archway.

"Even the bars are not down," observed Dandtan. He

pointed overhead; there hung a portcullis of stone. Garin studied it apprehensively, but Dandtan drew him on into a narrow corridor where were barred doors.

"The cells," he explained, and drew back a bar from across one door. The portal swung back, and they pushed within.

CHAPTER SEVEN

Kepta's Trap

THRALA arose to face them. Forgetting the disguise he wore, Garin drew back, chilled by her icy demeanor; but Dandtan sprang forward and caught her in his arms. She struggled madly until she saw the face beneath her captor's hood; then she gave a cry of delight, and her arms were about his neck.

"Dandtan!"

He smiled. "Even so. But it is the outlander's doing."

She came to the American, studying his face. "Outlander? So cold a name is not for you, when you have served us so." She offered him her hands, and he raised them to his lips.

"And how are you named?"

Dandtan laughed. "Thus the eternal curiosity of women!"

"Garin."

"Garin," she repeated. "How like—" A faint rose glowed beneath her pearl flesh.

Dandtan's hand fell lightly upon his rescuer's shoulder. "Indeed he is like him. From this day let him bear that other's name: Garan, son of light."

"Why not?" she returned calmly. "After all—"

"The reward that might have been Garan's may be his? Tell him the story of his namesake when we are again in the Caverns—"

Dandtan was interrupted by a frightened squeak from the Ana. Then came a mocking voice.

"So the prey has entered the trap of its own will. How many hunters may boast the same?"

Kepta leaned against the door, the light of vicious mischief dancing in his eyes. Garin dropped his cloak to the floor, but Dandtan must have read what was in the flier's mind, for he caught him by the arm.

"On your life, touch him not!"

"So you have learned that much wisdom while you have dwelt among us, Dandtan? Would that Thrala had done the same. But fair women find me weak." He eyed her proud body in a way that would have sent Garin at his throat had Dandtan not held him. "So shall Thrala have a second chance. How would you like to see these men in the Room of Instruments, Lady?"

"I do not fear you," she returned. "Thran once made a prophecy, and he never spoke idly. We shall win free—"

"That will be as fate would have it. Meanwhile, I leave you to each other." He whipped around the door and slammed it to behind him. They heard the grating of the bar he slid into place; then his footsteps died away.

"There goes evil," murmured Thrala softly. "Perhaps it would have been better if Garin had killed him as he thought to do. We must get away . . ."

Garin drew the rod from his belt. The green light-motes gathered and clung about its polished length.

"Touch not the door," Thrala advised, "only its hinges."

Beneath the tip of the rod, the stone became spongy and flaked away. Dandtan and the flier caught the door and eased it to the floor. With one quick movement, Thrala caught up Garin's cloak and swirled it about her, hiding the glitter of her gem-encrusted robe.

There was a curious cold lifelessness about the air of the corridor; the light-bearing motes were vanishing as if blown out.

"Hurry!" the Daughter urged. "Kepta is withdrawing the living light, so that we will have to wander in the dark."

When they had reached the end of the hall, the light was quite gone, and Garin bruised his hands against the stone portcullis which had been lowered. From somewhere on the other side of the barrier came rippling laughter.

"Oh, outlander," called Kepta mockingly, "you will get through easily enough when you remember your weapon.

But the dark you cannot conquer so easily, nor that which runs the halls."

Garin was already busy with the rod. Within five minutes their way was clear again, but Thrala stopped them when they would have gone through. "Kepta has loosed the hunters."

"The hunters?"

"The morgels and—others," explained Dandtan. "The Black Ones have withdrawn, and only death comes this way. And the morgels see in the dark . . ."

"So does the Ana."

"Well thought of," agreed the son of the Ancient Ones. "It will lead us out."

As if in answer, there came a tug on Garin's belt. Reaching back, he caught Thrala's hand and knew that she had taken Dandtan's. So linked, they crossed the guardroom. Then the Ana paused for a long time, as if listening. There was nothing to see but the darkness that hung about them like the smothering folds of a curtain.

"Something follows us," whispered Dandtan.

"Nothing to fear," stated Thrala. "It dare not attack. It is, I think, of Kepta's fashioning. And that which has not true life dreads death above all things. It is going—"

There came sounds of something crawling slowly away.

"Kepta will not try that again," continued the Daughter disdainfully. "He knew that his monstrosities would not attack. Only in the light are they to be dreaded—and then only because of the horror of their forms."

Again the Ana tugged at its master's belt. They shuffled into the narrow passage beyond. But there remained the sense of things about them in the dark, things that Thrala continued to insist were harmless, yet which filled Garin with loathing.

Then they entered the far corridor into which led the three halls and which ended in the morgel pit. Here, Garin believed, was the greatest danger from the morgels.

The Ana stopped short, dropping back against Garin's thigh. In the blackness appeared two yellow disks, sparks of saffron in their depths. Garin thrust the rod into Thrala's hands.

"What do you?" she demanded.

"I'm going to clear the way. It's too dark to use the rod against moving creatures . . ." He flung the words over his shoulder as he moved toward the unwinking eyes.

CHAPTER EIGHT

Escape from the Caves

KEEPING his eyes upon those soulless yellow disks, Garin snatched off his hood, wadding it into a ball. Then he sprang. His fingers slipped on smooth hide as sharp fangs ripped his forearm, blunt nails scraped his ribs. A foul breath puffed into his face, and warm slaver trickled down his neck and chest. But his plan succeeded.

The cap was wedged into the morgel's throat, and the beast was slowly choking. Blood dripped from the flier's torn flesh, but he held on grimly until he saw the light fade from those yellow eyes. The dying morgel made a last mad plunge for freedom, dragging his attacker along the rock floor.; then Garin felt the heaving body rest limply against his own. He staggered against the wall, panting.

"Garin!" cried Thrala. Her questing hand touched his shoulder and crept to his face. "It is well with you?"

"Yes," he gasped. "Let us go on."

Thrala's fingers had lingered on his arm, and now she walked beside him, her cloak making whispering sounds as it brushed against the wall and floor.

"Wait," she cautioned suddenly. "The morgel pit . . ."

Dandtan slipped by them. "1 will try the door."

In a moment he was back. "It is open," he whispered.

"Kepta believes," mused Thrala, "that we will keep to the safety of the gallery. Therefore, let us go through the pit. The morgels will be gone to better hunting grounds."

Through the pit they went. A choking stench arose from underfoot, and they trod very carefully. They climbed the stairs on the far side unchallenged, Dandtan leading.

"The rod here, Garin," he called. "This door is barred."

Garin pressed the weapon into the other's hand and leaned against the rock. He was sick and dizzy. The long, deep wounds on his arm and shoulder were stiffening and ached with a biting throb.

When they went on, he panted with effort. They still moved in darkness, however, and his distress went unnoticed.

"This is wrong," he muttered, half to himself. "We go too easily—"

And he was answered out of the blackness. "Well noted, outlander. But you go free for the moment, as do Thrala and Dandtan. Our full accounting is not yet. And now, farewell, until we meet again in the Hall of Thrones. I could find it in me to applaud your courage, outlander. Perhaps you will come to serve me yet."

Garin turned and threw himself toward the voice, bringing up with bruising force against rock wall. Kepta laughed.

"Not with the skill of the bull Tand will you capture me."

Kepta's second laugh was cut cleanly off, as if a door had been closed. In silence the three hurried up the ramp. Then, as through a curtain, they came into the light of Tav.

Thrala let fall her drab cloak, stood with arms outstretched in the crater land. Her sparkling robe sheathed her in glory, and she sang softly, rapt in her own delight. Then Dandtan put his arm about her; she clung to him, staring about as might a beauty-bewildered child.

Garin wondered dully how he would be able to make the journey back to the Caverns when his arm and shoulder were eaten with a consuming fire. The Ana crept closer to him, peering into his white face.

They were aroused by a howl from the Caves. Thrala cried out, and Dandtan answered her unspoken question. "They have set the morgels on our trail!"

The howl from the Caves was echoed from the forest. Morgels before and behind them! Garin might set himself against one, Dandtan another, and Thrala could defend herself with the rod, but in the end the pack would kill them.

"We shall claim protection from the Gibi of the Cliff—by the law, they must give us aid," said Thrala, as, turning up her long robe, she began to run lightly. Garin picked up her

cloak and drew it across his shoulder to hide his welts.
When he could no longer hold her pace, she must not guess
the reason for his falling behind.

Of that flight through the forest the flier afterward remembered little. At last, the gurgle of water broke upon his
pounding ears, as he stumbled a good ten lengths behind his
companions. They had come to the edge of the wood along
the banks of the river.

Without hesitation, Thrala and Dandtan plunged into the
oily flood, swimming easily for the other side. Garin
dropped the cloak, wondering if, once he stepped into the
yellow stream, he would ever be able to struggle out again.
Already the Ana was in, paddling in circles near the shore
and pleading with him to follow. Weaily, Garin waded out.

The water, which washed the blood and sweat from his
aching body, was faintly brackish and stung his wounds to
life. He could not fight the sluggish current, and it bore him
downstream, well away from where the others landed.

But at last he managed to win free, crawling out near
where a smaller stream joined the river. There he lay panting, facedown upon the moss. And there they found him,
water dripping from his bedraggled finery, the Ana stroking
his muddied hair. Thrala cried out with concern and pillowed his head on her knees while Dandtan examined his
wounds.

"Why did you not tell us?" demanded Thrala.

He did not try to answer, content to lie there, her arms
supporting him. Dandtan disappeared into the forest, returning soon, his hands filled with a mass of crushed leaves.
With these he plastered Garin's wounds.

"You'd better go on," Garin warned.

Dandtan shook his head. "The morgels cannot swim. If
they cross, they must go to the bridge, and that is half the
crater away."

The Ana dropped into their midst, its small hands filled
with clusters of purple fruit. And so they feasted, Garin at
ease on a fern couch, accepting food from Thrala's hand.

There seemed to be some virtue in Dandtan's leaf plaster
for, after a short rest, Garin was able to get to his feet with
no more than a twinge or two in his wounds. But they started

on at a more sober pace. Through mossy glens and sunlit glades, where strange flowers made perfume, the trail led. The stream they followed branched twice before, on the edge of meadowland, they struck away from the guiding water toward the crater wall.

Suddenly Thrala threw back her head and gave a shrill, sweet whistle. Out of the air dropped a yellow and black insect, as large as a hawk. Twice it circled her head and then perched itself on her outstretched wrist.

Its swollen body was jet black, its curving legs, three to a side, chrome yellow. The round head ended in a sharp beak, and it had large, many-faceted eyes. The wings, which lazily tested the air, were black and touched with gold.

Thrala rubbed the round head while the insect nuzzled affectionately at her cheek. Then she held out her wrist again, and it was gone.

"We shall be expected now and may pass unmolested."

Shortly they became aware of a murmuring sound. The crater wall loomed ahead, dwarfing the trees at its base.

"There is the city of the Gibi," remarked Dandtan.

Clinging to the rock were the towers and turrets of many eight-sided cells.

"They are preparing for the Mists," observed Thrala. "We shall have company on our journey to the Caverns."

They passed the trees and reached the foot of the wax skyscrapers which towered dizzily above their heads. A great cloud of the Gibi hovered about them. Garin felt the soft brush of their wings against his body. And they crowded each other jealously to be near Thrala.

The soft hush-hush of their wings filled the clearing as one large Gibi of outstanding beauty approached. The commoners fluttered off, and Thrala greeted the Queen of the cells as an equal. Then she turned to her companions with the information the Gibi Queen had to offer.

"We are just in time. Tomorrow the Gibi leave. The morgels have crossed the river and are out of control. Instead of hunting us, they have gone to ravage the forest lands. All Tav has been warned against them. But they may be caught by the Mist and so destroyed. We are to rest in the cliff hollows, and one shall come for us when it is time to leave."

The Gibi withdrew to the cell-combs after conducting their guests to the rock-hollows.

CHAPTER NINE

Days of Preparation

GARIN was awakened by a loud murmuring. Dandtan knelt beside him.

"We must go. Even now the Gibi seal the last of the cells."

They ate hurriedly of cakes of grain and honey, and, as they feasted, the Queen again visited them. The first of the swarm were already winging eastward.

With the Gibi nation hanging like a storm cloud above them, the three started off across the meadow. The purple-blue haze was thickening, and, here and there, curious formations like the dust devils of the desert arose and danced and disappeared again. The tropic heat of Tav increased; it was as if the ground itself were steaming.

"The Mists draw close; we must hurry," panted Dandtan.

They traversed the tongue of forest that bordered the meadow and came to the cental plain of Tav. Brooding stillness hung there. The Ana, perched on Garin's shoulder, shivered.

Their walk became a trot; the Gibi bunched together. Once Thrala caught her breath in a half sob.

"They are flying slowly because of us. And it's so far—"

"Look!" Dandtan pointed at the plain. "The morgels!"

The morgel pack, driven by fear, ran in leaping bounds. They passed within a hundred yards of the three yet did not turn from their course, though several snarled at them.

"They are already dead," observed Dandtan. "There is no time for them to reach the shelter of the Caves."

Splashing through a shallow brook, the three began to run. For the first time, Thrala faltered and broke pace. Garin thrust the Ana into Dandtan's hands, and before she could protest, swept the girl up in his arms.

The haze was denser now, settling upon them as a curtain. Black hair, finer than silk, whipped across Garin's throat. Thrala's head was on his shoulder, her heaving breast arching as she gasped the sultry air.

"They—keep—watch . . . !" shouted Dandtan.

Piercing the gloom were pinpoints of light. A dark shape grazed Garin's head—one of the Gibi Queen's guards.

Then abruptly they stumbled into a throng of the Folk, one of whom reached for Thrala with a crooning cry. It was Sera welcoming her mistress. Thrala was borne away by the women, leaving Garin with a feeling of desolation.

"The Mists, outlander." It was Urg, pointing toward the Cavern mouth. Two of the Folk swung their weight on a lever. Across the opening a sheet of crystal clicked into place. The Caverns were sealed.

The haze was now inky black outside, and billows of it beat against the protecting barrier. It might have been the middle of the most starless night.

"So will it be for forty days. What is without—dies," said Urg.

"Then we have forty days in which to prepare," Garin spoke his thought aloud. Dandtan's keen face lightened.

"Well said, Garin. Forty days before Kepta may seek us. And we have much to do. But first, let us pay our respects to the Lord of the Folk."

Together they went to the Hall of Thrones where, when he saw Dandtan, Trar arose and held out his jade-tipped rod of office. The son of the Ancient Ones touched it.

"Hail! Dweller in the Light, and Outlander who has fulfilled the promise of Thran. Thrala is once more within the Caverns. Now send you to dust this black throne . . ."

Garin, nothing loath, drew the destroying rod from his belt, but Dandtan shook his head. "The time is not yet, Trar. Kepta must finish the pattern he began. Forty days have we, and then the Black Ones come."

Trar considered thoughtfully. "So that be the way of it. Thran did not see another war . . ."

"But he saw an end to Kepta!"

Trar straightened as if some burden had rolled from his thin shoulders. "Well do you speak, Lord. When there is one to sit upon the Rose Throne, what have we to fear? Listen, oh, ye Folk, the Light has returned to the Caverns!"

His cry was echoed by the gathering of the Folk.

"And now, Lord—" he turned to Dandtan with deference, "what are your commands?"

"For the space of one sleep I shall enter the Chamber of Renewing with this outlander, who is no longer an outlander but one, Garin, accepted by the Daughter according to the Law. And while we rest let all be made ready . . ."

"The Dweller in the Light has spoken!" Trar himself escorted them from the Hall.

They came, through many winding passages, to a deep pool of water, in the depths of which lurked odd purple shadows. Dandtan stripped and plunged in, Garin following his example. The water was tinglingly alive, and they did not linger in it long. From it, they went to a bubble room such as the one Garin had rested in after the bath of light rays, and on the cushions in its center they stretched their tired bodies.

When Garin awoke, he experienced the same exultation he had felt before. Dandtan regarded him with a smile. "Now to work," he said, as he reached out to press a knob set in the wall.

Two of the Folk appeared, bringing with them clean trappings. After they dressed and broke their fast, Dandtan started for the laboratories. Garin would have gone with him, but Sera intercepted them.

"There is one would speak with Lord Garin . . ."

Dandtan laughed. "Go," he ordered the American. "Thrala's commands may not be slighted."

The Hall of Women was deserted. And the corridor beyond, roofed and walled with slabs of rose-shot crystal, was as empty. Sera drew aside a golden curtain, and they were in the audience chamber of the Daughter.

A semicircular dais of the clearest crystal, heaped with rose and gold cushions, faced them. Before it, a fountain, in the form of a flower nodding on a curved stem, sent a spray of water into a shallow basin. The walls of the room were divided into alcoves by marble pillars, each one curved in the semblance of a fern frond. From the domed ceiling, on chains of twisted gold, seven lamps, each wrought from a single yellow sapphire, gave soft light. The floor was a mosaic of gold and crystal.

Two small Anas, who had been playing among the cushions, pattered up to exchange greetings with Garin's. Of the mistress of the chamber, however, there was no sign. Garin turned to Sera, but before he could phrase his question, she asked mockingly:

"Who is the Lord Garin that he cannot wait with patience?" But she left in search of the Daughter.

Garin glanced uneasily about the room. This jeweled chamber was no place for him. He had started toward the door when Thrala stepped within.

"Greetings to the Daughter." His voice sounded formal and cold, even to himself.

Her hands, which had been outheld in welcome, dropped to her sides. A ghost of a frown dimmed her beauty.

"Greetings, Garin," she returned slowly.

"You sent for me—" he prompted, eager to escape from this jewel box and the unattainable treasure it held.

"Yes." The coldness of her tone was an order of exile. "I would know how you fared and whether your wounds yet troubled you."

He looked down at his own smooth flesh, cleanly healed by the wisdom of the Folk. "I am myself again and eager to be at such work as Dandtan can find for me . . ."

Her robe seemed to hiss across the floor as she turned upon him. "Then go!" she ordered. "Go quickly!"

And blindly he obeyed. She had spoken as if to a servant, one whom she could summon and dismiss at whim. Even if Dandtan held her love, she might have extended him her friendship. But he knew within him that friendship would be a poor crumb beside the feast his pulses pounded for.

There came hurrying feet behind him. So, she would call him back! His pride sent him on. But it was Sera. Her head thrust forward until she truly resembled a reptile.

"Fool! Morgel!" she spat. "Even the Black Ones did not

treat her so. Get you out of the Place of Women lest they divide your skin among them!"

Garin broke free, not heeding her torrent of reproach. Then he seized upon one of the Folk as a guide and sought the laboratories.

Far beneath the surface of Tav, where the light-motes shone ghostly in the gloom, they came into a place of ceaseless activity, where there were tables crowded with instruments, coils of glass and metal tubing, and other equipment and supplies. These were the focusing-point for ceaseless streams of the Folk. On a platform at the far end, Garin saw the tall son of the Ancient Ones laboring over a framework of metal and shining crystal.

He glanced up as Garin joined him. "You are late," he accused. "But your excuse is a good one. Now get you to work. Hold this here—and here—while I fasten these clamps."

So Garin became extra hands and feet for Dandtan, and they strove feverishly to build against the lifting of the Mists. There was no day or night in the laboratories. They worked steadily, without rest and without feeling fatigue.

Twice they went to the Chamber of Renewing but, except for these trips to the upper ways, they were not out of the laboratories through all those days. Of Thrala there was no sign, nor did anyone speak of her.

The Cavern dwellers were depending upon two defenses: an evil green liquid, to be thrown in frail glass globes, and a screen charged with energy. Shortly before the lifting of the Mists, these arms were transported to the entrance and installed there. Dandtan and Garin made a last inspection.

"Kepta makes the mistake of underrating his enemies," Dandtan reflected, feeling the edge of the screen caressingly. "When I was captured, on the day my people died, I was sent to the Black Ones' laboratories so that their seekers-after-knowledge might learn the secrets of the Ancient Ones. But I proved a better pupil than teacher, and I discovered the defense against the Black Fire. After I had learned that, Kepta grew impatient with my supposed stupidity and tried to use me to force Thrala to his will. For that, as for other things, shall he pay—and the paying will not be in coin of his own striking. Let us think of that . . ." He turned to greet Urg and Trar and the other leaders of the Folk, who had approached unnoticed.

Among them stood Thrala, her gaze fixed upon the crystal wall between them and the thinning Mist. She noticed Garin no more than she did the Anas playing with her train and the women whispering behind her. But Garin stepped back into the shadows—and what he saw was not weapons of war, but cloudy black hair and graceful white limbs veiled in splendor.

Urg and one of the other chieftains bore down upon the door lever. With a protesting squeak, the glass wall disappeared into the rock. The green of Tav beckoned them out to walk in its freshness; it was renewed with lusty life. But in all that expanse of meadow and forest there was a strange stillness.

"Post sentries," ordered Dandtan. "The Black Ones will come soon."

He beckoned Garin forward as he spoke to Thrala:

"Let us go to the Hall of Thrones."

But the Daughter did not answer his smile. "It is not meet that we should spend time in idle talk. Let us go instead to call upon the help of those who have gone before us." So speaking, she darted a glance at Garin as chill as the arctic lands beyond the lip of Tav, and then swept away with Sera bearing her train.

Dandtan stared at Garin. "What has happened between you two?"

The flier shook his head. "I don't know. No man is born with an understanding of women—"

"But she is angered with you. What has happened?"

For a moment Garin was tempted to tell the truth: that he dared not break any barrier she chose to raise, lest he seize what in honor was none of his. But he shook his head mutely. Neither of them saw Thrala again until Death entered the Caverns.

CHAPTER TEN

Battle and Victory

GARIN stood with Dandtan looking out into the plain of Tav. Some distance away were two slender, steel-tipped towers, which were in reality but hollow tubes filled with the Black Fire. Before these, dark-clad figures were busy.

"They seem to believe us already defeated. Let them think so," commented Dandtan, touching the screen they had erected before the Cavern entrance.

As he spoke, Kepta swaggered through the tall grass to call a greeting:

"Ho, rock dweller, I would speak with you—"

Dandtan edged around the screen, Garin a pace behind.

"I see you, Kepta."

"Good. I trust that your ears will serve you as well as your eyes. These are my terms: give Thrala to me to dwell in my chamber and the outlander to provide sport for my captains. Make no resistance, but throw open the Caverns so that I may take my rightful place in the Hall of Thrones. Do this, and we shall be at peace . . ."

"And this is our reply." Dandtan stood unmovingly before the screen. "Return to the Caves; break down the bridge between your land and ours. Let no Black One come hither again, ever . . ."

Kepta laughed. "So, that be the way of it! Then this shall we do: take Thrala, to be mine for a space, and then to go to my captains—"

Garin hurled himself forward, felt Kepta's lips mash beneath his fist; his fingers were closing about the other's throat as Dandtan, who was trying to pull him away from his prey, shouted a warning: "Watch out!"

A morgel had leaped from the grass, its teeth snapping about Garin's wrist, forcing him to drop Kepta. Then Dandtan laid it senseless by a sharp blow with his belt.

On hands and knees, Kepta crawled back to his men. The lower part of his face was a red-dripping smear. He screamed an order with savage fury.

Dandtan drew the still-raging flier behind the screen. "Be

a little prudent," he panted, "Kepta can be dealt with in other ways than with bare hands."

The towers were swinging their tips toward the entrance. Dandtan ordered the screen wedged tightly into place.

Outside, the morgel Dandtan had stunned got groggily to its feet. When it had limped half the distance back to its master, Kepta gave the order to fire. The broad beam of black light from the tip of the nearest tower caught the beast head-on. There was a chilling scream of agony, and where the morgel had stood, gray ashes drifted on the wind.

A hideous crackling arose as the black beam struck the screen. The grass beneath seared away, leaving only parched earth and naked blue soil. Those within the Cavern crouched behind their frail protection, half-blinded by the light from the seared grass, coughing from the chemical-ridden fumes that curled about the cracks of the rock.

Then the beam faded out. Thin smoke plumed from the tips of the towers; steam arose from the blackened ground. Dandtan drew a deep breath.

"It held!" he cried, betraying at last the fear that had ridden him.

Men of the Folk dragged engines of tubing before the screen, while others brought forth the globes of green liquid. Dandtan stood aside, as if this matter were the business of the Folk alone, and Garin recalled that the Ancient Ones were opposed to the taking of life.

Trar was in command now. At his orders, the globes were poised on spoon-shaped holders. Loopholes in the screen clicked open. Trar brought his hand down in signal. The globes arose lazily, sliding through the loopholes and floating out toward the towers.

One, aimed short, struck the ground where the fire had burned it bare, and broke. The liquid came forth, sluggishly, forming a gray-green gas as the air struck it. Another spiral of the gas arose almost at the foot of one of the towers—and then another . . . and another.

There followed a tortured screaming, which soon dwindled to a weak yammering. They could see shapes, no longer human or animal, staggering about in the fog.

Dandtan turned away, his face white with horror. Garin's hands were over his ears to shut out that crying.

At last it was quiet; there was no more movement by the towers. Urg placed a sphere of rosy light upon the nearest machine and flipped it out into the camp of the enemy. As if it were a magnet, it drew the green tendrils of gas, to leave the air clear. Here and there lay shrunken, livid shapes, the towers brooding over them.

One of the Folk burst into their midst—a woman of Thrala's following.

"Haste!" She clawed at Garin. "Kepta takes Thrala!"

She ran wildly back the way she had come, with the American pounding at her heels. They burst into the Hall of Thrones and saw a struggling group before the dais.

Garin heard someone howl like an animal, then became aware that the sound issued from his own throat. For the second time his fist found its mark on Kepta's face. With a shriek of rage, the Black One threw Thrala from him and sprang at Garin, his nails tearing gashes in the flier's face. Twice the American twisted free and sent bone-crushing blows into the other's ribs. Then he got the grip he wanted, and his fingers closed around Kepta's throat. In spite of the Black One's struggles, he held on until a limp body rolled beneath him.

Panting, the American pulled himself up from the blood-stained floor and grabbed the arm of the Jade Throne for support.

"Garin!" Thrala's arms were about him, her pitying fingers on his wounds. And in that moment he forgot Dandtan, forgot everything he had steeled himself to remember. Nor was she unresponsive, but yielded, as a flower yields to the wind.

"Garin!" she whispered softly. Then, almost shyly, she broke from his hold. Beyond her stood Dandtan, his face white, his mouth set. Garin remembered and, a little mad with pain and longing, he dropped his eyes, trying not to see the loveliness that was Thrala.

"So, Outlander, Thrala flies to your arms—"

Garin whirled about. Kepta was hunched on the broad seat of the Jet Throne.

"No, I am not dead, Outlander—nor shall you kill me, as you think to do. I go now, but I shall return. We have met and hated, fought and died, before—you and I. You were a certain Garan, Marshal of the air fleet of Yu-Lac on a vanished world, and I was Lord of Koom. That was in the days before the Ancient Ones pioneered space. You and I and Thrala, we are bound together, and even fate cannot break those bonds. Farewell, Garin. And do you, Thrala, remember the ending of that other Garan. It was not an easy one."

With a last malicious chuckle, he leaned back in the throne. His battered body slumped. Then the sharp lines of the throne blurred; it shimmered in the light. Abruptly, both it and its occupant were gone. They were staring at empty space, above which loomed the Rose Throne of the Ancient Ones.

"He spoke true," murmured Thrala. "We have had other lives, other meetings—so will we meet again. But for the present he returns to the darkness that sent him forth. It is finished."

Without warning, a low rumbling filled the Cavern; the walls rocked and swayed. Lizard and human, they huddled together until the swaying stopped. Finally, a runner appeared with the news that one of the Gibi had ventured forth and discovered that the Caves of Darkness had been sealed by an underground quake. The menace of the Black Ones was definitely at an end.

CHAPTER ELEVEN

Thrala's Mate

ALTHOUGH there were falls of rock within the Caverns and some of the passages were closed, few of the Folk suffered injury. Gibi scouts reported that the land about the entrance to the Caves had sunk and that the River of Gold, thrown out of its bed, was fast filling this basin to form a lake.

As far as they could discover, none of the Black Ones had

survived the battle and the sealing of the Caves. But they could not be sure that there was not a handful of outlaws somewhere within the confines of Tav.

The Crater itself was changed. A series of raw hills had appeared in the central plain. The pool of boiling mud had vanished, and trees in the forest lay flat, as if cut by a giant scythe.

Upon their return to the cliff city, the Gibi found most of their wax skyscrapers in ruins, but they set about rebuilding without complaint. The squirrel-farmers emerged from their burrows and were again busy in the fields.

Garin felt out of place in all the activity that filled the caverns. More than ever, he was the outlander with no true roots in Tav. Restlessly, he explored the Caverns, spending many hours in the Place of Ancestors, where he studied those men of the outer world who had preceded him into this weird land.

One night when he came back to his chamber, he found Dandtan and Trar awaiting him. There was a curious hardness in Dandtan's attitude, a somber sobriety in Trar's carriage.

"Have you sought the Hall of Women since the battle?" demanded the son of the Ancient Ones abruptly.

"No," retorted Garin shortly. Did Dandtan accuse him of double-dealing?

"Have you sent a message to Thrala?"

Garin held back his rising temper. "I have not ventured where I cannot."

Dandtan nodded to Trar as if his suspicions had been confirmed. "You see how it stands, Trar."

Trar shook his head slowly. "But never has the summoning been at fault—"

"You forget," Dandtan reminded him sharply. "It was, once—and the penalty was exacted. So shall it be again."

Garin looked from one to the other, confused. Dandtan seemed possessed of a certain ruthless anger, but Trar was manifestly unhappy.

"It must come after Council, the Daughter willing," the Lord of the Folk said.

Dandtan strode toward the door. "Thrala is not to know.

Assemble the Council tonight. Meanwhile, see that he—" he jerked his thumb toward Garin, "—does not leave this room."

Thus Garin became a prisoner under the guard of the Folk, unable to discover of what Dandtan accused him, or how he had earned the hatred of the Cavern ruler. Perhaps Dandtan's jealousy had been aroused, and he was determined to rid himself of a rival.

Believing this, the flier went willingly to the chamber where the judges waited. Dandtan sat at the head of a long table, Trar at his right hand and lesser nobles of the Folk beyond.

"You know the charge," Dandtan's words were tipped with venom as Garin came to stand before him. "Out of his own mouth has this outlander condemned himself. Therefore I ask that you decree for him the fate of that outlander of the second calling who rebelled against the summoning."

"The outlander has admitted his fault?" questioned one of the Folk.

Trar inclined his head sadly. "He did."

As Garin opened his mouth to demand a stating of the charge against him, Dandtan spoke again.

"What say you, Lords?"

For a long moment they sat in silence and then they bobbed their lizard heads in assent. "Do as you desire, Dweller in the Light."

Dandtan smiled without mirth. "Look, outlander." He passed his hand over the glass of the seeing-mirror set in the tabletop. "This is the fate of him who rebels—"

In the shining surface, Garin saw pictured a break in Tav's wall. At its foot stood a group of men of the Ancient Ones, and in their midst struggled a prisoner. They were forcing him to climb the crater wall. Garin watched him reach the lip and crawl over, to stagger across the steaming rock, dodging the scalding vapor of hot springs, until he pitched facedown in the slimy mud.

"Such was his ending, and so will you end—"

The calm brutality of that statement aroused Garin's anger. "Rather would I die that way than linger in this den," he cried hotly. "You, who owe your life to me, would send me to such a death without even telling me of what I am accused. Little is there to choose between you and Kepta, after all—except that he was an open enemy!"

Dandtan sprang to his feet, but Trar caught his arm.

"He speaks fairly. Ask him why he will not fulfill the summoning."

While Dandtan hesitated, Garin leaned across the table, flinging his words, weaponlike, straight into that cold face.

"I'll admit that I love Thrala—have loved her since that moment when I saw her on the steps of the morgel pit in the Caves. Since when has it become a crime to love that which may not be yours—if you do not try to take it?"

Trar released Dandtan, his golden eyes gleaming.

"If you love her, claim her. It is your right."

"Do I not know," Garin turned to him, "that she is Dandtan's? Thran had no idea of Dandtan's survival when he laid his will upon her. Shall I stoop to holding her to an unwelcome bargain? Let her go to the one she loves . . ."

Dandtan's face was livid, and his hands, resting on the table, trembled. One by one the lords of the Folk slipped away, leaving the two face-to-face.

"And I thought to order you to your death." Dandtan's whisper was husky as it emerged from between dry lips. "Garin, we thought you knew—and, knowing, had refused her."

"Knew what?"

"That I am Thran's son—and Thrala's brother."

The floor swung beneath Garin's unsteady feet. Dandtan's hands were warm on his shoulders.

"I am a fool," said the American slowly.

Dandtan smiled. "A very honorable fool! Now get you to Thrala, who deserves to hear the full of this tangle."

So it was that, with Dandtan by his side, Garin walked for the second time down that hallway, to pass the golden curtains and stand in the presence of the Daughter. She came straight from her cushions into his arms when she read what was in his face. They needed no words.

And in that hour began Garin's life in Tav.

INTRODUCTION TO "MY DAUGHTER'S NAME IS SARAH"

by Peter S. Beagle

"My Daughter's Name Is Sarah" isn't the first story I ever wrote, nor the first I ever published; but I feel it's the first one that made some attempt at dealing believably with believable human beings, instead of the ghosts, demons, and displaced Greek gods that populated most of my juvenilia. It has its origins in a story my mother once told me about her older sister, my Aunt Fanny, whom I loved, and who died far too young. The narrator, Elias Reiner, is an imagining of my maternal grandfather, Avrom Soyer. I never knew him—he died himself when I was ten months old. He was a writer and teacher (two collections of his stories have been published in English), and was, by all accounts, as gentle and thoughtful a man as I tried to portray. I was eighteen or nineteen, a student at the University of Pittsburgh, when I wrote the story.

I'm sixty-two now—probably Elias' age—and it's more than a little strange to look back and realize how deeply and easily I identified with older people all those years ago. "Sarah" isn't a great story, but I'm proud of it still, in a special, personal way.

MY DAUGHTER'S NAME IS SARAH

by Peter S. Beagle

MY name is Elias Reiner and I have a daughter named Sarah and we live in an apartment on Batterman Street. That sounds a little like the jump rope game the children play in the afternoons. I have seen Sarah do it, jumping up and down while two other girls turn the rope, her eyes closed with concentration, chanting, "My-name-is-Sarah-and-my-father-is-Elias-and-we-live-on-Batterman-Street." She is very fond of jumping rope, and I know that if ever I want to buy her a present and can't think of anything, a jump rope is always good. Other girls just use lengths of clothesline, but Sarah has three jump ropes with handles.

The street is very quiet now in the sun. Schwartz's fruit truck went by ten minutes ago. Schwartz leaned out the window and yelled, *"Hoyaaaaa—peaches! Hoyaaaaa—peaches!"* but no one came out to buy. The old women sit in the sun and talk about their children. A boy goes past on a bicycle and the women's eyes follow him. "Why isn't he in school?" they say, and "Since when do they get out so early, all of a sudden?" and "I know that boy. His mother is a *yenta*." The boy hunches over the handlebars and disappears around the corner.

It is a lovely day, so beautiful I am a little sad. I get a glass of milk out of the icebox and sit down at the window to watch for Sarah, when she comes home from school. I have just gotten home myself, from Queens College where I teach two courses in Hebrew. It is a good job, and I am happy in it. I still speak with an accent, but the students do not mind. Many of them speak Hebrew very well, and sometimes I conduct the whole class in Hebrew.

It is two-thirty now. At three o'clock the children will come home. They will run up the street, calling to each other, snatching the girls' caps and tossing them back and forth, swinging their books held together by old skate straps. They will come, beautiful and laughing, and as inexorable, in their way, as army ants. And somewhere in the middle of them will be Sarah. When I see her from the window it will be a little hard to breathe for a moment, and I will want to go down and meet her and walk the rest of the way with her.

She wouldn't like that, though. She would not like it if she knew that I sit at the window every day to watch her come home. She would look patient and say, "Papa, *nobody* does that anymore. Not in the sixth grade." And she would be right, of course.

When I see her coming, I will go to the icebox again and get a glass of milk for her, and some cookies. She likes one kind of cookie very much; it is all marshmallow and chocolate. Moise, down on Tremont, always saves a box or two for her. She will come flying down the hall, drop her books on a chair, call, "Papa, I'm home," and sit down immediately at the table. I will come out of the living room—I always go there just before she comes, and look busy—and say, "Hello, Sarah."

"Hello, Papa," she will say, with her mouth full of cookies.

"Have a good day?" I will ask casually.

"It was all right." She will look up. "Harry Spector got in trouble again."

This is not news to me. I have never met Harry Spector but, according to Sarah, if he does not get into trouble in class it is because he is not feeling well.

"His mother has to come to class," Sarah will say.

"She must live there."

Sarah will giggle. "I got 87 on the geography test."

"Wonderful. Did you remember about Australia?"

"Uh-huh. Can I have another cookie?"

I will give her one, and she will dip it in the milk. "Marilyn said the funniest thing today," and she will tell me what Marilyn Fine, her best friend, said. Then she will go out to play, and I will watch her in the street until she turns the corner. I will start to make supper.

No, I had forgotten. Today will be different. I slap my forehead. How can one man be so stupid? Today is the last day of school, and Sarah's class is having a party to celebrate and say good-bye. How could I have forgotten, with

Sarah talking about nothing else for two weeks? It's a good thing I remembered before she came home.

I bought her a dress for the party. Children can be cruel to a poorly dressed child. Sarah does not know that. She is not cruel herself, and no one has ever been cruel to her. It's a nice dress, dark blue with a sort of white trimming to set off Sarah's black hair. I bought it at Klein's to surprise her. I was afraid she would want to wear it every day and spoil it for the party, but she put it away in the closet until today. "I want Eddie to see me in a brand-new dress," she explained. "I want him to know that I wore it specially for him."

There is a boy named Eddie Liebowitz in Sarah's class, and she loves him. I do not question this for a moment. As much as an eleven-year-old girl can love, my daughter Sarah loves Eddie Liebowitz. I do not think he knows she loves him. I saw them walking home together once. Eddie walked looking straight ahead, talking to Sarah without turning his head. He is a good-looking boy, dark-haired and slim, with an easy way of walking. Sarah walked with her eyes on the ground, kicking a pebble in front of her, occasionally looking at Eddie and looking away again very quickly. On the corner of Batterman some friends called Eddie and he ran off to join them. Sarah stood on the corner and looked after him. The children pressed around her and jostled her and stepped on her feet, but she stood there and would not move until he was out of sight.

She has talked a great deal about Eddie all year. "He's not like any other boy in the class, Papa," she said once. "They're all creeps except Eddie."

"Creep?" I said. "What is a creep?"

I know what *creep* means, and Sarah knows I know. I tease her sometimes, about her friends and their customs and fads and slang. When I see her with them, going to the movies or sitting on a stoop in the spring afternoons, I often feel very far away from her. So I make a joke out of it and make her laugh.

That particular time, she talked so much about Eddie that I finally said, "You must like him very much." She looked down at her cereal, said, "Uh-huh" in a small voice, and

began to eat very fast. I do not tease her about Eddie anymore, and I never bring him up unless she wants to talk
about him.

I look out the window and think about the party in
Sarah's class. It must be almost over now. "We all chipped
in a quarter," Sarah said this morning, "and Mrs. Glazer
bought a lot of jelly beans and Tootsie Rolls and potato
chips and stuff. And some Coca-Cola," she added, "because
potato chips make you thirsty."

"Will you do anything at this party," I asked, "besides
eat?"

Sarah brushed some bread crumbs into her left hand with
the edge of her right hand and swallowed them. "Uh-huh.
We're going to dance."

I pretended to be shocked. "So? Since when do you
dance in school, where you're supposed to get an educa-
tion?"

"Oh, *Papa!*" Sarah has a wonderful laugh. It is whole-
hearted and without fear. "It's not a *real* dance. I mean, it is,
but—look, I'll show you." She pushed her chair back and
got up. "Come on, I'll show you. Mrs. Glazer taught us."

"In your bathrobe?" I was ironing her party dress.

"Come *on*, Papa." She stamped her foot lightly.

I unplugged the iron. "All right. So show your poor father
where his taxes are going. What do I do?"

"The girls stand against the wall," Sarah said, "and Mrs.
Glazer puts on a record that goes *dee-dum-dum, dee-dum-
dum, dum-dee-dee-dum-dee-dum-dee-dum.* Then the boys
pick out partners—" she held out her hands and I took them,
"—and we dance." We waltzed around in a circle at arm's
length. Sarah's eyes were half-shut, and she was *dum-dee-
dumming* happily until I stepped on her foot. She yelped and
broke away.

I dropped to one knee. "Are you all right? Let me see."

"I'm all right. You have big feet."

We laughed together, and I got up. "Well, you won't be
dancing with me. Whom will you dance with, Sarala?"

"Eddie," said Sarah, softly but clearly. "I'm going to
dance with Eddie."

"What Eddie," I teased her. "Eddie who?"

"*Papa!* Eddie Liebowitz!"

"Oh, *that* Eddie. Will he pick you out?"

"Of course he will." Oh, she was so calm and sure.

I began to iron her dress again. "Finish your breakfast. You'll be late." Sarah looked at the clock and began to gulp her milk. "Slow, slow! You will burp right in the middle of the dance and wouldn't that be lovely?"

Sarah began to laugh and choked over her milk. I handed her a napkin and she wiped her face and got up. I finished ironing and gave her the dress. She went into her bedroom, and I heard her singing as she dressed. I put the dishes in the sink and cleaned off the table.

I went into the hall and called into Sarah's bedroom. "You know, Sarala, this dance your Mrs. Glazer taught you would be very popular in Samoa."

"Where?" Sarah's voice was muffled.

"Samoa. It is like a tribal dance the boys and girls do there. There is a picture of it in the College—I'll bring it home."

Sarah appeared in the bedroom doorway suddenly. She was wearing the new dress and her best shoes. She had brushed her hair without my reminding her, and she was wearing a necklace of little white beads that I bought her one afternoon, coming home from the College.

"Do I look nice?" she asked.

"Mmmmmm." I squinted my eyes and tilted my head to the side. "Passable, passable." And then I held her close and told her how beautiful she was until she twisted away and said, "Papa, you'll wrinkle my dress."

"God forbid," I said. I took her by the shoulders and looked down at her. "Sarah, Sarala—if anything goes wrong—don't be disappointed." It sounded foolish immediately.

"What do you mean, Papa?"

"Well, I mean—if Eddie does not dance with you—" Sarah began to laugh.

"Papa, who else would he dance with?"

You can never protect the unhurt. You cannot tell them that everyone must be a little afraid to be safe.

"No one, Sarah. I was being silly." I turned back to the kitchen. "Go to school now."

She pattered after me and caught my arm. "There is a girl in the class who'd like Eddie to dance with her. Her name is Tilly Hofberg, and she's a *nebbish*."

Nebbish is a favorite word of ours. We use it to describe a mousy, colorless sort of person. We even have degrees of *nebbishes*. "What kind of a *nebbish* is Tilly Hofberg?"

"A first-class, A-number-one, triple-distilled *nebbish*."

"Triple-distilled?"

"Triple-distilled. She looks at Eddie all day and tries to get close to him in fire drill. Once she even followed him home." She laughed with a sort of cheerful contempt.

"Does he like her?"

"He used to, but he doesn't anymore. Eleanor Frankel told Marilyn and Marilyn told me. Do you think Eddie'll like the necklace?"

"He will love it," I said. "Go now, or you will be late." Sarah kissed me and ran down the hall.

"Your books," I called after her. "You left your books."

"I don't need them," she called over her shoulder as she ran out the door. "I don't need them."

I went to the window and saw her as she crossed the street with Marilyn Fine. They had their arms around each other and they were talking. Sarah's blue dress shone in the sun.

It is almost three o'clock now. In a few minutes the children will be coming home. The old women talk to each other and move their wooden folding chairs to keep in the shade. Engel the junkman goes by, his cart pulled by his old white horse. The children love that horse and call him "Silver." I rest my elbow on the windowsill and wait.

Suddenly the street is full of children. They run up the long street singing and shouting, because this is the last day of school. There are so many children. I know some of them by sight now, particularly one fat boy who keeps bumping into the other children. I do not think he means to, but he is clumsy and cannot help himself. I asked Sarah about him once, and she said that he was a fifth grader and once cried at recess when the children teased him.

I see Sarah. She is walking with Marilyn still. They are talking and I see Sarah laugh. My stomach seems to relax—I did not realize that I had been so worried about her. The party has gone well, and now it is over, and Sarah is coming home. I turn away from the window to get Sarah's milk and cookies. I set them on the table.

I will not ask her about the party. This is something private, and if she wants to tell me, she may. This belongs to her. I go into the living room and take a book from the shelf. I do not open it, although it is poetry. The door opens. I hear Sarah's footsteps in the hall.

She turns into the kitchen and then turns to the living room. She stands in the doorway, smiling. "Hello, Papa."

"Hello, Sarah."

Silence. She is still smiling. "Papa?"

I look at my beautiful daughter. "So?"

Suddenly the smile is gone, and it is like watching the winter come. Sarah's face is pale, and her mouth is trembling. "Papa," she says, and her voice breaks. "Oh, Papa—he went to Tilly!"

Then she is in my arms and crying as I have never heard her cry. Her whole body is shaking as if a wind had passed over her and her face and hands are so cold. Over and over, "Tilly—he went to Tilly!"

What do you do, what do you do? What am I to tell her, after all? I hold her very tight and say, "Sarah, Sarah, Sarala—this is not the end. Sarah, darling, this is not the end." And I know that it is not the end, because I am grown, and therefore wise. But my daughter Sarah cries as though it were.

INTRODUCTION TO "APRIL IN PARIS"

by Ursula K. Le Guin

I was over thirty; I had been writing stories ever since I was ten, and submitting them to magazines for the past five or six years. All the stories always came back to me in their little manila jackets, looking dirty, looking sad. At times I too looked sad, if not dirty. Helpful people told me, "What you need to do is write about what you know about!" That seemed hopeless, because I never felt I really knew anything. I only imagined things.

But perhaps they were right. So I asked myself: What *do* I know about? There was a long silence. Finally I thought: I know quite a lot about Late Medieval and Early Renaissance French Literature.

It didn't seem wildly promising as subject matter for fiction. But I always did like it for its own sake; and so my mind wandered off on familiar paths, imagining the Paris of four or five hundred years ago . . . and wondering what happened to the poet François Villon, who disappeared into the darkness of the fifteenth century . . . and suddenly my mind came upon Professor Barry Pennywither sitting at his table staring at a book and bread crust. He was thinking about Villon, too.

So I followed him into that dim, cold attic room in Paris, and found my story waiting for me there.

APRIL IN PARIS

by Ursula K. LeGuin

PROFESSOR Barry Pennywither sat in a cold, shadowy garret and stared at the table in front of him, on which lay a book and a bread crust. The bread had been his dinner, the book had been his lifework. Both were dry. Dr. Pennywither sighed, and then shivered. Though the lower-floor apartments of the old house were quite elegant, the heat was turned off on April 1st, come what may; it was now April 2nd, and sleeting. If Dr. Pennywither raised his head a little he could see from his window the two square towers of Notre Dame de Paris, vague and soaring in the dusk, almost near enough to touch: for the Island of Saint-Louis, where he lived, is like a little barge being towed downstream behind the Island of the City, where Notre Dame stands. But he did not raise his head. He was too cold.

The great towers sank into darkness. Dr. Pennywither sank into gloom. He stared with loathing at his book. It had won him a year in Paris—publish or perish, said the Dean of Faculties, and he had published, and been rewarded with a year's leave from teaching, without pay. Munson College could not afford to pay unteaching teachers. So on his scraped-up savings he had come back to Paris, to live again as a student in a garret, to read fifteenth-century manuscripts at the Library, to see the chestnuts flower along the avenues. But it hadn't worked. He was forty, too old for lonely garrets. The sleet would blight the budding chestnut flowers. And he was sick of his work. Who cared about his theory, the Pennywither Theory, concerning the mysterious disappearance of the poet François Villon in 1463? Nobody. For after all his Theory about poor Villon, the greatest juvenile delinquent of all time, was only a theory and could never be proved, not across the gulf of five hundred years. Nothing could be proved. And besides, what did it matter if Villon died on Montfaucon gallows or (as Pennywither thought) in a Lyons brothel on the way to Italy? Nobody cared. Nobody else loved Villon enough. Nobody loved Dr. Pennywither,

either; not even Dr. Pennywither. Why should he? An unso-
cial, unmarried, underpaid pedant, sitting here alone in an
unheated attic in an unrestored tenement trying to write another unreadable book. "I'm unrealistic," he said aloud with
another sigh and another shiver. He got up and took the
blanket off his bed, wrapped himself in it, sat down thus
bundled at the table, and tried to light a Gauloise Bleue. His
lighter snapped vainly. He sighed once more, got up, fetched
a can of vile-smelling French lighter fluid, sat down,
rewrapped his cocoon, filled the lighter, and snapped it. The
fluid had spilled around a good bit. The lighter lit, so did Dr.
Pennywither, from the wrists down. "Oh hell!" he cried,
blue flames leaping from his knuckles, and jumped up bat-
ting his arms wildly, shouting "Hell!" and raging against
Destiny. Nothing ever went right. What was the use? It was
then 8:12 on the night of April 2nd, 1961.

A man sat hunched at a table in a cold, high room.
Through the window behind him the two square towers of
Notre Dame loomed in the Spring dusk. In front of him on
the table lay a hunk of cheese and a huge, iron-latched,
handwritten book. The book was called (in Latin) *On the
Primacy of the Element Fire over the Other Three Elements.*
Its author stared at it with loathing. Nearby on a small iron
stove a small alembic simmered. Jehan Lenoir mechanically
inched his chair nearer the stove now and then, for warmth,
but his thoughts were on deeper problems. "Hell!" he said
finally (in Late Medieval French), slammed the book shut,
and got up. What if his theory was wrong? What if water
were the primal element? How could you prove these
things? There must be some way—some method—so that
one could be sure, absolutely sure, of one single fact! But
each fact led into others, a monstrous tangle, and the Au-
thorities conflicted, and anyway no one would read his
book, not even the wretched pedants at the Sorbonne. They
smelled heresy. What was the use? What good this life spent
in poverty and alone, when he had learned nothing, merely
guessed and theorized? He strode about the garret, raging,
and then stood still. "All right!" he said to Destiny. "Very
good! You've given me nothing, so I'll take what I want!"
He went to one of the stacks of books that covered most of

the floor space, yanked out a bottom volume (scarring the leather and bruising his knuckles when the overlying folios avalanched), slapped it on the table and began to study one page of it. Then, still with a set cold look of rebellion, he got things ready: sulfur, silver, chalk. . . . Though the room was dusty and littered, his little workbench was neatly and handily arranged. He was soon ready. Then he paused. "This is ridiculous," he muttered, glancing out the window into the darkness where now one could only guess at the two square towers. A watchman passed below calling out the hour, eight o'clock of a cold clear night. It was so still he could hear the lapping of the Seine. He shrugged, frowned, took up the chalk and drew a neat pentagram on the floor near his table, then took up the book and began to read in a clear but self-conscious voice: "Haere, haere, audi me . . ." It was a long spell, and mostly nonsense. His voice sank. He stood bored and embarrassed. He hurried through the last words, shut the book, and then fell backwards against the door, gap-mouthed, staring at the enormous, shapeless figure that stood within the pentagram, lit only by the blue flicker of its waving, fiery claws.

Barry Pennywither finally got control of himself and put out the fire by burying his hands in the folds of the blanket wrapped around him. Unburned but upset, he sat down again. He looked at his book. Then he stared at it. It was no longer thin and gray and titled *The Last Years of Villon: an Investigation of Possibilities.* It was thick and brown and titled *Incantatoria Magna.* On his table? A priceless manuscript dating from 1407 of which the only extant undamaged copy was in the Ambrosian Library in Milan. He looked slowly around. His mouth dropped slowly open. He observed a stove, a chemist's workbench, two or three dozen heaps of unbelievable leatherbound books, the window, the door. His window, his door. But crouching against his door was a little creature, black and shapeless, from which came a dry rattling sound.

Barry Pennywither was not a very brave man, but he was rational. He thought he had lost his mind, and so he said quite steadily, "Are you the Devil?"

The creature shuddered and rattled.

Experimentally, with a glance at invisible Notre Dame, the professor made the sign of the Cross.

At this the creature twitched; not a flinch, a twitch. Then it said something, feebly, but in perfectly good English—no, in perfectly good French—no, in rather odd French: "Mais vous estes de Dieu," it said.

Barry got up and peered at it. "Who are you?" he demanded, and it lifted up a quite human face and answered meekly, "Jehan Lenoir."

"What are you doing in my room?"

There was a pause. Lenoir got up from his knees and stood straight, all five foot two of him. "This is *my* room," he said at last, though very politely.

Barry looked around at the books and alembics. There was another pause. "Then how did I get here?"

"I brought you."

"Are you a doctor?"

Lenoir nodded, with pride. His whole air had changed. "Yes, I'm a doctor," he said. "Yes, I brought you here. If Nature will yield me no knowledge, then I can conquer Nature herself, I can work a miracle! To the Devil with science, then. I was a scientist—" he glared at Barry. "No longer! They call me a fool, a heretic, well, by God, I'm worse! I'm a sorcerer, a black magician, Jehan the Black! Magic works, does it? Then science is a waste of time. Ha!" he said, but he did not really look triumphant. "I wish it hadn't worked," he said more quietly, pacing up and down between folios.

"So do I," said the guest.

"Who are you?" Lenoir looked up challengingly at Barry, though there was nearly a foot difference in their heights.

"Barry A. Pennywither, I'm a professor of French at Munson College, Indiana, on leave in Paris to pursue my studies of Late Medieval Fr—" He stopped. He had just realized what kind of accent Lenoir had. "What year is this? What century? Please, Dr. Lenoir—" The Frenchman looked confused. The meanings of words change, as well as their pronunciations. "Who rules this country?" Barry shouted.

Lenoir gave a shrug, a French shrug (some things never

change). "Louis is king," he said. "Louis the Eleventh. The dirty old spider."

They stood staring at each other like wooden Indians for some time. Lenoir spoke first. "Then you're a man?"

"Yes. Look, Lenoir, I think you—your spell—you must have muffed it a bit."

"Evidently," said the alchemist, "Are you French?"

"No."

"Are you English?" Lenoir glared. "Are you a filthy Goddam?"

"No. No. I'm from America. I'm from the—from your future. From the twentieth century A.D." Barry blushed. It sounded silly, and he was a modest man. But he knew this was no illusion. The room he stood in, his room, was new. Not five centuries old. Unswept, but new. And the copy of Albertus Magnus by his knee was new, bound in soft supple calfskin, the gold lettering gleaming. And there stood Lenoir in his black gown, not in costume, at home. . . .

"Please sit down, sir," Lenoir was saying. And he added, with the fine though absent courtesy of the poor scholar, "Are you tired from the journey? I have bread and cheese, if you'll honor me by sharing it."

They sat at the table munching bread and cheese. At first Lenoir tried to explain why he had tried black magic. "I was fed up," he said. "Fed up! I've slaved in solitude since I was twenty, for what? For knowledge. To learn some of Nature's secrets. They are not to be learned." He drove his knife half an inch into the table, and Barry jumped. Lenoir was a thin little fellow, but evidently a passionate one. It was a fine face, though pale and lean: intelligent, alert, vivid. Barry was reminded of the face of a famous atomic physicist, seen in newspaper pictures up until 1953. Somehow this likeness prompted him to say, "Some are, Lenoir; we've learned a good bit; here and there. . . ."

"What?" said the alchemist, skeptical but curious.

"Well, I'm no scientist—"

"Can you make gold?" He grinned as he asked.

"No, I don't think so, but they do make diamonds."

"How?"

"Carbon—coal, you know—under great heat and pressure, I believe. Coal and diamond are both carbon, you know, the same element."

"Element?"

"Now as I say, I'm no—"

"Which is the primal element?" Lenoir shouted, his eyes fiery, the knife poised in his hand.

"There are about a hundred elements," Barry said coldly, hiding his alarm.

Two hours later, having squeezed out of Barry every dribble of the remnants of his college chemistry course, Lenoir rushed out into the night and reappeared shortly with a bottle. "O my master," he cried, "to think I offered you only bread and cheese!" It was a pleasant burgundy, vintage 1477, a good year. After they had drunk a glass together Lenoir said, "If somehow I could repay you . . ."

"You can. Do you know the name of the poet François Villon?"

"Yes," Lenoir said with some surprise, "but he wrote only French trash, you know, not in Latin."

"Do you know how or when he died?"

"Oh, yes; hanged at Montfaucon here in '64 or '65, with a crew of no-goods like himself. Why?"

Two hours later the bottle was dry, their throats were dry, and the watchman had called three o'clock of a cold clear morning. "Jehan, I'm worn out," Barry said, "you'd better send me back." The alchemist was too polite, too grateful, and perhaps also too tired to argue. Barry stood stiffly inside the pentagram, a tall bony figure muffled in a brown blanket, smoking a Gauloise Bleue. "Adieu," Lenoir said sadly. "Au revoir," Barry replied. Lenoir began to read the spell backwards. The candle flickered, his voice softened. "Me audi, haere, haere," he read, sighed, and looked up. The pentagram was empty. The candle flickered. "But I learned so little!" Lenoir cried out to the empty room. Then he beat the open book with his fists and said, "And a friend like that— a real friend—" He smoked one of the cigarettes Barry had left him—he had taken to tobacco at once. He slept, sitting at his table, for a couple of hours. When he woke he brooded a while, relit his candle, smoked the other cigarette, then opened the *Incantatoria* and began to read aloud: "Haere, haere . . ."

"Oh, thank God," Barry said, stepping quickly out of the pentagram and grasping Lenoir's hand. "Listen, I got back there—this room, this same room, Jehan! but old, horribly old, and empty, you weren't there—I thought, my God, what have I done? I'd sell my soul to get back there, to him— What can I do with what I've learned? Who'll believe it? How can I prove it? And who the devil could I tell it to anyhow? Who cares? I couldn't sleep, I sat and cried for an hour—"

"Will you stay?"

"Yes. Look, I brought these—in case you did invoke me." Sheepishly he exhibited eight packs of Gauloises, several books, and a gold watch. "It might fetch a price," he explained. "I knew paper francs wouldn't do much good."

At sight of the printed books Lenoir's eyes gleamed with curiosity, but he stood still. "My friend," he said, "you said you'd sell your soul . . . you know . . . so would I. Yet we haven't. How—after all—how did this happen? That we're both men. No devils. No pacts in blood. Two men who've lived in this room . . ."

"I don't know," said Barry. "We'll think that out later. Can I stay with you, Jehan?"

"Consider this your home," Lenoir said with a gracious gesture around the room, the stacks of books, the alembics, the candle growing pale. Outside the window, gray on gray, rose up the two great towers of Notre Dame. It was the dawn of April 3rd.

After breakfast (bread crusts and cheese rinds) they went out and climbed the south tower. The cathedral looked the same as always, though cleaner than in 1961, but the view was rather a shock to Barry. He looked down upon a little town. Two small islands covered with houses; on the right bank more houses crowded inside a fortified wall; on the left bank a few streets twisting around the college; and that was all. Pigeons chortled on the sun-warmed stone between gargoyles. Lenoir, who had seen the view before, was carving the date (in Roman numerals) on a parapet. "Let's celebrate," he said. "Let's go out into the country. I haven't been out of the city for two years. Let's go clear over there—" he pointed to a misty green hill on which a few huts and a windmill were just visible, "—to Montmartre, eh? There are some good bars there, I'm told."

Their life soon settled into an easy routine. At first Barry was a little nervous in the crowded streets, but, in a spare black gown of Lenoir's, he was not noticed as outlandish except for his height. He was probably the tallest man in fifteenth-century France. Living standards were low and lice were unavoidable, but Barry had never valued comfort much; the only thing he really missed was coffee at breakfast. When they had bought a bed and a razor—Barry had forgotten his—and introduced him to the landlord, as M. Barrie, a cousin of Lenoir's from the Auvergne, their housekeeping arrangements were complete. Barry's watch brought a tremendous price, four gold pieces, enough to live on for a year. They sold it as a wondrous new timepiece from Illyria, and the buyer, a Court chamberlain looking for a nice present to give the king, looked at the inscription— Hamilton Bros., New Haven, 1881—and nodded sagely. Unfortunately, he was shut up in one of King Louis' cages for naughty courtiers at Tours before he had presented his gift, and the watch may still be there behind some brick in the ruins of Plessis; but this did not affect the two scholars. Mornings they wandered about sightseeing the Bastille and the churches, or visiting various minor poets in whom Barry was interested; after lunch they discussed electricity, the atomic theory, physiology, and other matters in which Lenoir was interested, and performed minor chemical and anatomical experiments, usually unsuccessfully; after supper they merely talked. Endless, easy talks that ranged over the centuries but always ended here, in the shadowy room with its window open to the Spring night, in their friendship. After two weeks they might have known each other all their lives. They were perfectly happy. They knew they would do nothing with what they had learned from each other. In 1961 how could Barry ever prove his knowledge of old Paris, in 1482 how could Lenoir ever prove the validity of the scientific method? It did not bother them. They had never really expected to be listened to. They had merely wanted to learn.

So they were happy for the first time in their lives; so happy, in fact, that certain desires always before subjugated to the desire for knowledge, began to awaken. "I don't suppose," Barry said one night across the table, "that you ever thought much about marrying?"

"Well, no," his friend answered, doubtfully. "That is, I'm in minor orders . . . and it seemed irrelevant. . . ."

"And expensive. Besides, in my time, no self-respecting woman would want to share my kind of life. American women are so damned poised and efficient and glamorous, terrifying creatures. . . ."

"And women here are little and dark, like beetles, with bad teeth," Lenoir said morosely.

They said no more about women that night. But the next night they did; and the next; and on the next, celebrating the successful dissection of the main nervous system of a pregnant frog, they drank two bottles of Montrachet '74 and got soused. "Let's invoke a woman, Jehan," Barry said in a lascivious bass, grinning like a gargoyle.

"What if I raised a devil this time?"

"Is there really much difference?"

They laughed wildly, and drew a pentagram. "Haere, haere," Lenoir began; when he got the hiccups, Barry took over. He read the last words. There was a rush of cold, marshy-smelling air, and in the pentagram stood a wild-eyed being with long black hair, stark naked, screaming.

"Woman, by God," said Barry.

"Is it?"

It was. "Here, take my cloak," Barry said, for the poor thing now stood gawping and shivering. He put the cloak over her shoulders. Mechanically she pulled it round her, muttering, "Gratias ago, domine."

"Latin!" Lenoir shouted. "A woman speaking Latin?" It took him longer to get over that shock than it did Bota to get over hers. She was, it seemed, a slave in the household of the Sub-Prefect of North Gaul, who lived on the smaller island of the muddy island town called Lutetia. She spoke Latin with a thick Celtic brogue, and did not even know who was emperor in Rome in her day. A real barbarian, Lenoir said with scorn. So she was, an ignorant, taciturn, humble barbarian with tangled hair, white skin, and clear gray eyes. She had been waked from a sound sleep. When they convinced her that she was not dreaming, she evidently assumed that this was some prank of her foreign and all-powerful master the Sub-Prefect, and accepted the situation without further question. "Am I to serve you, my masters?" she inquired timidly but without sullenness, looking from one to the other.

"Not me," Lenoir growled, and added in French to Barry, "Go on; I'll sleep in the storeroom." He departed.

Bota looked up at Barry. No Gauls, and few Romans, were so magnificently tall; no Gauls and no Romans ever spoke so kindly. "Your lamp" (it was a candle, but she had never seen a candle) "is nearly burnt out," she said. "Shall I blow it out?"

For an additional two sols a year the landlord let them use the storeroom as a second bedroom, and Lenoir now slept alone again in the main room of the garret. He observed his friend's idyll with a brooding, unjealous interest. The professor and the slave-girl loved each other with delight and tenderness. Their pleasure overlapped Lenoir in waves of protective joy. Bota had led a brutal life, treated always as a woman but never as a human. In one short week she bloomed, she came alive, evincing beneath her gentle passiveness a cheerful, clever nature. "You're turning out a regular Parisienne," he heard Barry accuse her one night (the attic walls were thin). She replied, "If you knew what it is for me not to be always defending myself, always afraid, always alone . . ."

Lenoir sat up on his cot and brooded. About midnight, when all was quiet, he rose and noiselessly prepared the pinches of sulfur and silver, drew the pentagram, opened the book. Very softly be read the spell. His face was apprehensive.

In the pentagram appeared a small white dog. It cowered and hung its tail, then came shyly forward, sniffed Lenoir's hand, looked up at him with liquid eyes and gave a modest, pleading whine. A lost puppy . . . Lenoir stroked it. It licked his hands and jumped all over him, wild with relief. On its white leather collar was a silver plaque engraved, "Jolie. Dupont, 36 rue de Seine, Paris VIe."

Jolie went to sleep, after gnawing a crust, curled up under Lenoir's chair. And the alchemist opened the book again and read, still softly, but this time without self-consciousness, without fear, knowing what would happen.

Emerging from his storeroom-bedroom-honeymoon in the morning, Barry stopped short in the doorway. Lenoir was sitting up in bed, petting a white puppy, and deep in conversation with the person sitting on the foot of the bed, a tall red-haired woman dressed in silver. The puppy barked. Lenoir said, "Good morning!" The woman smiled wondrously.

"Jumping Jesus," Barry muttered (in English). Then he said, "Good morning. When are you from?" The effect was Rita Hayworth, sublimated—Hayworth plus the Mona Lisa, perhaps?

"From Altair, about seven thousand years from now," she said, smiling still more wondrously. Her French accent was worse than that of a football-scholarship freshman. "I'm an archaeologist. I was excavating the ruins of Paris III. I'm sorry I speak the language so badly; of course we know it only from inscriptions."

"From Altair? The star? But you're human—I think—"

"Our planet was colonized from Earth about four thousand years ago—that is, three thousand years from now." She laughed, most wondrously, and glanced at Lenoir. "Jehan explained it all to me, but I still get confused."

"It was a dangerous thing to try it again, Jehan!" Barry accused him. "We've been awfully lucky, you know."

"No," said the Frenchman. "Not lucky."

"But after all it's black magic you're playing with— Listen—I don't know your name, madame."

"Kislk," she said.

"Listen, Kislk," Barry said without even a stumble, "your science must be fantastically advanced—is there any magic? Does it exist? Can the laws of Nature really be broken, as we seem to be doing?"

"I've never seen nor heard of an authenticated case of magic."

"Then what goes on?" Barry roared. "Why does that stupid old spell work for Jehan, for us, that one spell, and here, nowhere else, for nobody else, in five—no, eight—no, fifteen thousand years of recorded history? Why? Why? And where did that damn puppy come from?"

"The puppy was lost," Lenoir said, his dark face grave. "Somewhere near this house, on the Ile Saint-Louis."

"And I was sorting potsherds," Kislk said, also gravely, "in a house-site, Island 2, Pit 4, Section D. A lovely Spring day, and I hated it. Loathed it. The day, the work, the people around me." Again she looked at the gaunt little alchemist, a long, quiet look. "I tried to explain it to Jehan last night. We have improved the race, you see. We're all very tall, healthy, and beautiful. No fillings in our teeth. All skulls from Early America have fillings in the teeth. . . . Some of us are brown, some white, some gold-skinned. But all beautiful, and healthy, and well-adjusted, and aggressive, and successful. Our professions and degree of success are preplanned for us in the State Pre-School Homes. But there's an occasional genetic flaw. Me, for instance. I was trained as an archaeologist because the Teachers saw that I really didn't like people, live people. People bored me. All like me on the outside, all alien to me on the inside. When everything's alike, which place is home? . . . But now I've seen an unhygienic room with insufficient heating. Now I've seen a cathedral not in ruins. Now I've met a living man who's shorter than me, with bad teeth and a short temper. Now I'm home, I'm where I can be myself, I'm no longer alone!"

"Alone," Lenoir said gently to Barry. "Loneliness, eh? Loneliness is the spell, loneliness is stronger. . . . Really, it doesn't seem unnatural."

Bota was peering round the doorway, her face flushed between the black tangles of her hair. She smiled shyly and said a polite Latin good morning to the newcomer.

"Kislk doesn't know Latin," Lenoir said with immense satisfaction. "We must teach Bota some French. French is the language of love, anyway, eh? Come along, let's go out and buy some bread. I'm hungry."

   Kislk hid her silver tunic under the useful and anony-
mous cloak, while Lenoir pulled on his moth-eaten black
gown. Bota combed her hair, while Barry thoughtfully
scratched a louse-bite on his neck. Then they set forth to get
breakfast. The alchemist and the interstellar archaeologist
went first, speaking French; the Gaulish slave and the professor from Indiana followed, speaking Latin, and holding
hands. The narrow streets were crowded, bright with sun-
shine. Above them Notre Dame reared its two square towers
against the sky. Beside them the Seine rippled softly. It was
April in Paris, and on the banks of the river the chestnuts
were in bloom.

TO LIGHT A FIRE

Introduction by Susan Shwartz

What needs to be said first of all is that I'm one of the many writers whom the late Marion Zimmer Bradley encouraged, and I miss her.

I've been astonishingly fortunate in the way that science fiction and fantasy writers of vast seniority have advised me so that here I am, more than twenty years after answering a DAW ad about the Friends of Darkover, writing about my first story sale like a kid clattering about in my elders' shoes.

I'm about to do Too Much Sharing. Marion always said that every one of her Free Amazons had a story, and it was always a tragedy. I'm not a Free Amazon, and my story's hardly tragic, though it resembles a soap opera, down to the designer clothes and the Park Avenue day job.

Back up to 1978 when I replied to that ad, sending money, as I recall, "in the currency of the *Terranan*" and apologizing for the lack of negotiable copper. I was astonished to get a note back from Marion herself thanking me for my "delightful" letter. At the time, I'd completed the first of two seriously bad trunk novels. I was a newly minted Ph.D teaching English at Ithaca College, in Marion's own upstate New York, which really is as cold as the Hellers. I was broke, had run afoul of the NIMBY (not in my backyard) Marxism of the provincial *lumpenprofessoriat*—my life was definitely a mixed bag. I'd gotten an agent I couldn't keep. I'd turned down, silly me, a slot in New York University's pilot program to retrain PhDs for business in favor of a grant from the National Endowment for the Humanities to study medieval literature up at Dartmouth. I was getting badmouthed by my department chair, who's now a college president and, I'm not surprised to learn, a superb fund raiser.

I entered the first Darkover-fiction contest with a remarkably melodramatic story from Lew Alton's point of view. It placed third, behind a second-placer I forget and Mary Frey's well-constructed and well-balanced story of the founding of a Tower. My story had no plot to speak of, but strong characterization and enough passionate intensity to stand me in good stead when Marion announced a professional anthology.

Although she bought "The Fires of Her Vengeance," she told me that someone—possibly Don Wollheim, she never said—recommended passing on it. Well it *was* an account of the rape of the Keeper Marelie Hastur, and it was emotionally raw enough that two rape victims wrote, saying I'd captured what they'd felt.

Marion bought the story anyway, because, as this person also said about me, "I don't know what it is, but she's got *something*."

So I cried and drank a bottle of cheap champagne in celebration. A couple weeks later, I sold a second story to *Analog* right before having my wisdom teeth out. There's got to be a connection.

The *Analog* story, "The Struldbrugg Solution," was a satire on academics. Write what you know: I left teaching a year later. But it was "The Fires of Her Vengeance" that set the pattern for my writing. I like tackling major themes, I go for the jugular, my plots don't shrink from violence, and my characters tend to be passionate, even operatic.

That was something I had in common with Marion: we both saw music and writing as not only related, but part of the way we worked. I remember one wild discussion in an elevator, while other writers swirled bemused about us as she told me I was crazy for enjoying Renata Scotto's performance in Bellini's *Norma*, but absolutely on target for saying Tatiana Troyanos was incredible as Adalgisa. I had no idea at the time that Marion had her eyes—and ears—on that opera, which is set in Roman Britain and which became a kind of leitmotif in *Mists of Avalon* and its sequels. *Mists* was a subversive, revisionist story that changed the focus of Arthurian literature and, instead of T.H. White, became the mark at which subsequent Arthurian writers aimed—and I say this both as the Arthurian scholar I was trained to be and the novelist I've become.

Diana Paxson, her sister-in-law, used Wagner's *Tristan und Isolde* for *The White Raven*. Some years later, I adapted Wagner's *Parsifal* into *The Grail of Hearts*, taking a fundamentally anti-Semitic work and turning it on its ear.

Marion, you see, didn't just teach her writers to write, she made them want to sing. Loudly and in their own voices and for years to come.

THE FIRES OF HER VENGEANCE

by Susan M. Shwartz

"*M*ARELIE, Marelie! Woe if you cannot kill! And woe, woe, if you should ever wish to!"

"Cleindori!" Marelie cried. The name husked from between lips bitten and fouled with sickness. "Don't leave me."

But the apparition of the old *leronis* who'd trained her guttered out. There were only trees and the snow, clouds and the savage light of the bloody sun. Blood defiled the snow. Hers: well had Cleindori predicted that Marelie Esyllt, princess of Hastur and Lady of Arilinn, could not kill, not even to save herself when *he*, the black-bearded one,

dragged her away from the rest of the Kilghard bandit pack
and . . . and . . .

"Now show yourself to the *Hali'imyn* as a sign of their
doom!" he had shouted.

*The Keeper who could not, or would not defend herself
against rape,* people would whisper. *Keeper now no longer.*

Marelie retched dryly, tasted blood, dirt, and snow. Her
eyes burned with unshed tears and her cheeks felt feverish
with an outrage beyond humiliation. Still, she lay facedown
on the icy ground. Her groin ached. Each muscle felt
strained from the fight she had put up (though she had
quailed from summoning the lightnings), a fight ending
when a blow to her jaw had knocked her senseless. And
once she was safely unconscious, he had raped her.

Merciful Evanda, forgive me. How could I use laran *to
kill?*

Contemptuously someone had flung a cloak over her before the bandits had retreated to their Kilghard *forst* and the
war leader who had been raiding Arilinn. Zandru wither
their manhood! Marelie loathed owing her life to their charity. But why not? Rape the Keeper and the woman is disarmed. No need for her to freeze to death.

Only a dawn ago Marelie had ridden with an escort of
City Guardsmen toward the ashes that once had been a village sworn to Hastur. Survivors, so badly burned that their
flesh charred from their dying limbs, moaned of flames
leaping from nowhere to ignite their homes. Then the bandits had attacked, bandits who grinned as they forced children trying to flee back into the flames. And over the
crackling of the flames and the wail of the dying had come
the mad, damned laughter, "Like Naotalba, *vai leronis,* as
she twists in Zandru's arms!"

This was no common war. Someone possessed one of the
giant artificial matrices and a matrix circle skilled and perverted enough to misuse it so. Most of the matrices tenth-
level or stronger had been destroyed; a few, monitored and
largely idle, remained insulated in the Towers. Still, the
Comyn had always feared this: an illegal matrix surviving
the Ages of Chaos and falling into the power of a *laranzu*
mad enough to use it for war. Marelie, sworn to defend the

Domains with her life against such attack, rode out to investigate.

The bandits had lain in ambush, as if their leader had ordered them to expect her. Brandishing knives and torches, they pounced. The torches spooked the *chervines*, seared her guardsmen. As they writhed on the ground, the bandits had stabbed them. Several others had overpowered her own mount and flung her to the ground to await the pack's captain.

Screams, burning, burning her ears, and shrieking over them the mad damned laughter . . .

Someone had known that the ravaged village and the abuse of *laran* would draw her. And without her, Arilinn—well, Janna, its other Keeper, had nowhere near her strength. Arilinn lay as vulnerable as she had after the beastmind of her attacker had flamed into rage and his hard fist cracked against her jaw.

Who could wish to destroy Arilinn? Marelie thought in desperation. *The Lords were at peace; it must be a madman, an outcast, Zandru savage him! But could even a madman wish to level the Towers and lord it over devastation?*

Aldones! Were the Ages of Chaos come again?

Such a man was one Marelie wished to kill. Even more, however, she wished to flee back to Arilinn.

With one rigid arm, she levered herself up. It was the hardest thing she had ever done. She studied the hills, the beaten track which ran through the forest. Arilinn lay *that* way. In fact, she realized, just over that rise loomed the city gates. Oh, the bandits had been sure, sure that they had disarmed and destroyed her.

Marelie forced herself to sit. She coiled her legs under her, the throbbing ache in her torn flesh making her a little dizzy. As she had mastered other pain in the long discipline of her training, she mastered it. The wind blew and she shuddered. Despite her revulsion, she forced herself to pull the cloak they'd left her—heavy, colorless wool bordered with shabby fur—over shivering shoulders. She would need its warmth in order to walk to Arilinn. And she craved its concealment: it was not fitting that the Lady of Arilinn walk abroad in her Domain with bodice torn and skirts bloodied.

But was she Keeper any longer?

Ah, she exulted, her enemy's ignorance would destroy him yet! A time of seclusion, time to heal, to forget a little, and once more Marelie, Lady of Arilinn would twist to her will the energon rings. Janna the Underkeeper, and Felizia, her cousin and Arilinn's *rikhi*, would restore her to herself.

Anguish caught her in the belly, doubled her over. Air forced itself in a tiny keen through tightened lips. The burning, the burning! So many bodies had lain unburied in that village. With trembling, fumbling fingers Marelie drew her matrix (*praise Avarra they'd not taken it or she'd have died in shock*!) from the tatters of her robes. Almost afraid to look into its flickering depths, she cupped her fingers about it. The starstone warmed, pulsed to her touch with the rhythms of her heartbeats. She gazed into it, seeking to visualize her desire. Arilinn.

The Tower—besieged! Shaken as she was, she could not penetrate the locked screens of its defense. So far then, Arilinn stood. But now for herself. She scanned her body quickly, suppressed a gasp of dismay as she watched the nerve channels and nodes in her pelvic region pulse red and sluggishly. Once clear as befitted the purity of a virgin Keeper, her channels were now tainted. It was not fair. She had not consented, but still her channels were overloaded from the trauma of the rape. The world, she sighed, went as it would, not as she would have it. Nevertheless, Arilinn stood. Soon she would be home.

Marelie Esyllt, Keeper and Lady, compelled herself to her feet. How odd her steps felt on the frozen ground. They jarred her ravaged body, but she forced herself to walk. As befitted sorceress and princess she held her head high as she entered the gates of Arilinn. The bloody sun glowered lower on the horizon, touching the distant peaks with flame. A guard shouted, and she flung the noisome cloak's hood back from her face: carven, pale features under the lambent fire of her tangled hair. The challenge died on the man's lips. On she walked.

I am Marelie Hastur, I am not shamed, she chanted to herself. Gladly she would have sobbed like a wounded child in the arms of her foster mother, but she was Keeper and

Keepers do not weep. Arilinn's Veil, the rainbow haze so deadly to enemies, shivered before her and she passed through it, feeling the hair on her arms prickle in fear lest the Veil should turn against her, a Keeper no longer virgin, crisp her with its lightnings.

Footsteps echoed, firm, rapid, deliberate on the stairs of the Tower. A man's footsteps. Despite her knowledge that a man in Arilinn Tower could only be her kinsman, sworn to her, Marelie shrank into a corner. The man's *laran*, however, betrayed her presence to him.

"Marelie! Oh, thank the Lord of Light you're safe!" Amaury Ridenow-Elhalyn, son of a prince, strode toward her, hands outstretched as if to embrace her. She was Keeper: no man might touch her. As she backed against the wall, he remembered and stopped. Marelie raised her hand, touched his fingertips.

"Bandits kidnapped me," she said softly, the crystalline tones of Keeper addressing technician. "My guard was killed, but I managed to escape."

Evanda, let him not doubt the word of a Hastur. Amaury was a technician, ranking just below herself, Janna, and young Felizia. Let him just scan her and he would know instantly. She must distract him.

"They have an unmonitored matrix, tenth-level or stronger," she told him. "Have they used it against the Tower?"

"Oh, gods, you could not have known," Amaury groaned. His face went pale. "We fought, how we fought. Janna—you would have been proud of her. But Janna's . . . she's dead, burned herself out and we couldn't restore. . . ."

Then there could be no seclusion, no Keeper's aid for Marelie. What Marelie required Felizia alone could not supply. And in conscience Marelie could not withdraw her from the circle in order to try and fail to heal herself: against a tenth-level matrix circle, Arilinn needed its Keeper.

"Avarra grant her peace," Marelie murmured. She saw the fatigue that shadowed Amaury's eyes. "But the others— Felizia, Damon, Arnaud—"

"When Janna collapsed, Arnaud took a lethal back-flow

trying to save her," Amaury reported. "The monitors tried to pull him clear: they're still unconscious. We hope they'll survive. But the gods help us tonight if they attack again. I'm, I'm *afraid* that they will."

Prince's son, technician, proud like all the Elhalyn, Amaury *looked* at Marelie. *Be strong, oh, be Keeper and protect us*, the gray eyes begged. They were reddened, burning. . . .

Marelie glanced aside, politely ignoring his self-betrayal.

"The city. Tell me," she demanded. Soon she could retreat to the sanctuary of her own rooms, rid herself of the stained robes she wore, bathe, and rest. But her first responsibility was to those sworn to her, circle and city.

"Captain Marius died in the first onslaught. The bandits attacked while we were . . . distracted by the enemy circle. Duvic, *teniente* of the Guard, commands now," Amaury reported. His eyes flashed; he too had been a guardsman once, warrior before he'd turned warlock. "He speaks of *geilt*. . . ."

The word from an obscure Heller dialect was new to Marelie. Amaury translated. "Berserk. They fear nothing, feel no wound, no pain. Hack off the sword hand and they draw dagger with their right. The men are almost unnerved, but Duvic's trying to rally them for an attack again tonight."

He shook his head, dashed a hand through the long copper-gilt hair. "Until you returned, Janna being . . . gone, we hadn't much hope of maintaining the Veil or Arilinn itself." His voice faltered. "It was like a challenge between Towers, lady. Aldones, are the Ages of Chaos come again?"

Marelie, shrinking even from the fingertip touch required, brushed his shoulder. She too had asked that question. But Amaury looked to her to answer it. "I pray not, kinsman," she said. "We will hold them here. No bandits rule in the Domains."

At a run Damon entered the room, his face lighting like the sun when it strikes the pass at Scaravel after a blizzard. Two men in the room! Marelie held herself rigid, suppressed fear and then the relief she felt as Felizia entered after him.

The girl, her brother's eldest daughter, gasped and would have run to her.

"Hold, child!" Marelie commanded. "A Keeper controls herself." Felizia's mouth worked, her face twisted as she attempted to check her panic and relief. They were too much for her, and she burst into half-hysterical sobs. No one touched her: Keeper, sacrosanct.

"Kinswoman, the Guard must know of your return," said Damon, a mechanic with the sturdiness of an Alton backing his trained skill. "The men will fight the better. 'Higher our thoughts, our hearts more keen, our courage sterner as our strength lessens,'" he half-hummed, half-quoted from his favorite ballad. "May I tell . . ."

"Yes," said Marelie. She drew herself up, a tall, slender woman, imperial with the *presence* that made the children of Hastur, son of Aldones who is the Lord of Light, seem more than human. "Say to Duvic and our brave Guardsmen that Marelie Esyllt, Lady of Arilinn—" she breathed deeply despite the sobs that would cramp her throat, "—sees them and blesses them. They shall not be overcome, this I vow!" She raised a grimy hand. "The gods witness it, and the holy things at Hali!"

"Your words brighten the sky, *vai leronis*," Damon whispered the ritual response, bowed deeply, and left.

Do I have a choice? she thought. *I am sworn to defend the Tower and the Domains with my life. And now my life is no longer than a candle's span.*

"Go, Amaury," she said. "Ready the circle. When Liriel rises in the sky, we will gather for war in the matrix chamber. Felizia, *chiya*, retire to your room to meditate and calm yourself. With Janna dead, I must rely upon you."

"But you are tired," Felizia dared to protest. "See— you're limping."

Marelie paused on her way to her rooms. "I need neither your assistance now nor your disobedience," she told the girl. "The *kyrri* will supply what I require."

Someone—probably Amaury—tried to touch her mind. She blocked contact, remembering the brutishness and the pain, the explosion in her jaw that had shattered her consciousness. Nothing showed in her face; the damage, she knew, lay deeper. Her channels were contaminated, and, burning in her heart, twisting in her belly like a firedrake, smoldered the urge to kill.

Though the room was now empty, Marelie seemed to feel in it the *presence* of Cleindori, so long dead, who had ruled Arilinn before her, and to hear her words:

"Woe, Marelie, should you wish to kill!"

The *kyrri* pattered out into the Garden of Fragrance where Marelie stood under a tree. Snow and the violet petals from its blossoms drifted down onto her disheveled hair. The nonhuman indicated that her bath was ready.

"Thank you." With the high empathic rating of its kind, the *kyrri* stared at her, something like concern in its green eyes, before it turned away.

Marelie drew one dirty hand to her mouth. A blossom lay upon it and she touched it gently. *Nevermore to see, to smell her garden in flower. . . .*

She had promised to assemble a circle of war in the matrix chamber. Keeper, but no virgin: her channels tainted, but no chance, no time, to clear them. Not with Janna dead and Amaury—she could not expose to Amaury what that beast-bandit had done to her. She was alone and very much afraid. The power of the energon rings generated by the matrices of her circle flowed through her into the screens and relays, power that she alone must forge into a weapon. Using *laran* to kill was dangerous at any time, but now especially . . . now she thought she understood Cleindori's prophecy.

Marelie wanted to kill. But it would mean her death. Only a virgin's channels could handle the energy a Keeper must wield. Oh, certainly, there were stories, fragments from the Ages of Chaos, myths to while away the long nights before Midwinter Festival, of Keepers who turned from their lovers to their work in the circle. But the ritual virginity of the Keeper had been sacrosanct since women, centuries ago, had replaced the *tenerézuin* of Varzil the Good's time: no one thought of disbelieving it. The unchaste Keeper was no Keeper at all. Marelie, despite her resolution, was terrified.

And she was so cold, so dirty.

She entered her rooms and undressed, hastily throwing

cloak, torn crimson garments, and her underlinen into a bundle.

"Burn these," she told the *kyrri*, and watched it leave.

The bathwater was warm, delicately scented; and infinitely welcome to her battered body. It even soothed the pain between her legs. She lay full-length in the tub, scrubbing and soaking as if she could remove memory as well as dirt. The *kyrri* came in to attend her, but she waved it away. Naked was vulnerable. In the few hours left to her, Marelie, princess of Hastur, refused to be vulnerable again. Her starstone, freed from its silk and leather sac, lay between her breasts under the water, and she stared at it.

Fire, fire in its depths.

What else could she expect? A battle and victory: but she desired to live and face no woman's pity, no man's whisper. Nor would she leave the Tower she had saved. Hasturs took oath lifelong. Marelie had sworn to be Lady of Arilinn unto death.

After a time she rose and dried herself on the heavy, warmed towels the *kyrri* had left for her. She wrapped herself in a robe, and found food waiting on a small table by the fire. Mechanically she sat and ate. Hunger kindled, and she savored the food as she had not for years. Bathing, eating, and resting, propped against pillows for an hour of meditation, assumed almost ritual significance.

For each, the last time. . . .

The bloody sun was an ember behind the Kilghards when Marelie Esyllt began to dress. Sweet, perfumed oil on her chafed skin, fresh linen, and, over it, the crimson robes of the Keeper. Red for blood, red for fire. The copper and gilt of the embroideries and ornaments at neck and waist glinted like sparks; the gem on her brow flamed. She allowed her starstone to blaze at her throat.

I am fire and air, she whispered to her reflection in the silver mirror. The gray eyes burned back at her as she brushed her long hair. Static made it crackle about the brush; it drifted in red clouds over her slim shoulders. Bodies were of importance to Keepers only as the means of sustaining and accomplishing their work, but Marelie, outraged, going to her death, looked upon herself.

She was beautiful. Beautiful as the Flamehair before the son of Hastur had chained her. Now she, Hastur's daughter, must invoke the burning.

She brushed her hair back, pinned it, and rose. Liriel glowed over her quiet, sealed garden. It was time.

Marelie Hastur's slippered footsteps echoed in the silence of the vaulted matrix chamber.

"I set the dampers to guard us," she heard Felizia say. "But with Arnaud dead, there are no fit monitors, and we can spare are no one from the circle."

"Then we shall not have monitors," Marelie said. A monitor would detect the turmoil in her channels, know what had been done to her, stop her, pity her: she would not bear it. She dared not allow it, not with Arilinn to be protected. She raised a hand, quelling protest.

"Damon, the Guard?"

"Duvic can hold the gates against the bandits for a little time if no sorcery is sent against him."

"We shall relieve him quickly."

The violet night shone through the clerestory beneath the ancient wooden vault. Below it only the eldritch flickers of the matrix screens and lattices lit the room, embers in the dark that Marelie's circle must fan to violent life. She raised a hand and the overlight glimmered from her six fingertips, danced madly in the giant artificial starstone she unveiled and set upon the massive table.

She took her raised seat, watched the others join their hands, then convulsively looked away. The werelight of matrices and lattices glanced over the dark woodwork of the cupboards, throwing the figures carved on them into high relief. Marelie found herself studying the figures intently and wrenched her eyes away.

"Begin," she commanded.

The circle's nine survivors, a pathetically small group to master the great matrix, fell into rapport like the layers of a crystal struck by flint to produce sparks. In what had always been the only intimacy of her life, Marelie touched each mind.

She raised her left hand. Her mind expanded, focused to receive and seize the energon flows from the rapport circle.

Deep within the giant crystal the blue flame began to quiver and pulsate. The ancient screens awoke to violent life.

Then Marelie's mind soared from her body like sparks from a resin tree in flame.

Below her teniente *Duvic fought. His sword was notched, reddened to the hilt. He stumbled and fell. In an instant, bandits heedless of their wounds leaped upon him and the white-lipped cadet who bestrode his body. . . .*

Flying above the battle, Marelie stretched forth a "hand." From it leaped the lightning, the lightning. Bandits shrieked as they burned. Again! And the men lurking in reserve jerked and yammered as the lightning consumed them too.

Then Marelie was flying over the gates and the forests. Past the accursed place where she had lain—she suppressed memory before Felizia could detect it—*into the foothills. Past the charnel remnant of the village the mad matrix had burned.* She suppressed a moan of anguish at the charred bodies, the smoking roofs below her. A bolt of blue flame obliterated them. Soon the snow would cover the place.

She sought for direction. *To the east.* The bandits—her attacker and their *laranzu*—had a *forst* in the eastern crags. She aimed her thought-self east, felt her "body" grow warm as it rushed through the unresisting night air.

Not yet! she prayed.

Question troubled the circle and she flashed it reassurance.

Again she skimmed over hills. Beyond the foothills towered the Kilghards; stunted trees and, looming over them, crags and peaks. There the kyorebni *wheeled and the banshees screamed in terror of the blue-lit* forst *that glowered beside an abyss. Marelie's eyes maddened and she hurled her lightnings. Again and again. She laughed, the fiery hair of her thought-self shaking in the wind. Now who would laugh last, herself or her enemy?*

Walls shattered. In the forst's *inmost keep the outlaw circle clasped hands about a great jagged matrix. Keeper in the circle was a flame-haired* emmasca. *Even through the trance of concentration with which the* emmasca *sought to defend his circle and destroy the Domains, Marelie saw hate and madness etched into his face like acid burning, burning. . . .*

Pressed near him among a throng of entranced followers who loaned him their strength, their belief, stood a man, bulky with muscle, his bearded jaw blue in the matrix fire. Marelie recognized him. Marelie demanded his death.

Briefly she returned to her body in the circle at Arilinn. Lightnings crackled and flashed from matrices to screens, screens to lattices. Ozone and alarm sharpened the air, threatening the calm of matrix trance. She scanned herself, saw the damage the energon flows left as they seared through her body, ravaged her nerves. Her neural ganglia looked like hot coals. She could not live long.

No matter, no matter.

No! It was Amaury's thought.

Yes! she commanded him. *We must end this.*

Woe, woe, a mental voice keened in the heart scalding coronach. Cleindori's voice again, or Amaury? She looked at the technician. In his mind was a truth she had never before noticed. *No time now.*

Again Marelie exploded from her throbbing nerves and body, extended her hands over her enemy First the laranzu, *then the others. First of them, her rapist. Then, one by one, slowly, all the others, wasters of her Domain. . . .*

Flame speared the *laranzu*'s chair. Blackjaw screamed, his clothes afire. He plunged for the outside and the safety of a snowbank, but fell over the cliff. Marelie felt the speed of his fall as if it were her own. She heard him scream against the cold and she exulted. *Was this what Sharra had felt in the instant before Hastur's son bound her with burning chains?*

Marelie laughed, a beautiful savage sound that echoed in the matrix chamber. The fires of her vengeance seemed to glow on the rapt faces of her circle. How still, how beautiful they were! Her laughter rang with triumph; she, defiled, defeated, she had saved them. Satisfaction tossed her consciousness, like a spark in an updraft, high above Arilinn. All around the old city, soldiers straightened, content to be alive. Marelie laughed as she drifted down toward her body.

Then her flesh knew the agony of the burning; but even in the last seconds of exultation, she knew that Arilinn was safe.

INTRODUCTION TO "THE FANE OF THE GREY ROSE"

by Charles de Lint

"The Fane of the Grey Rose" wasn't the first story I wrote, nor even the first I had published. But it was the first longer piece I managed to finish, and it was my first professional sale.

Like many new writers, I would begin longer projects, but then abandon them as soon as a more intriguing idea came along. Nothing wrong with that, if one is simply writing for a hobby, but if you want to be published and reach a wider audience, the first rule is to actually finish the story.

"The Fane of the Grey Rose" I managed to finish.

(In fact, not so long after I'd written "The Fane of the Grey Rose," and after far too many drafts of another novel I'd been working on, I expanded it into my novel *The Harp of the Grey Rose*, only revising the ending somewhat to open the story up so that the longer version flowed organically out of what I'd already written. But I digress.)

I sent "The Fane of the Grey Rose" to Andrew J. Offutt, a writer with whom I'd been having a correspondence in the late seventies, sending it for the same reason that so many unpublished writers pass their stories around: you want to be read. Imagine my surprise when, sometime later, Andy wrote back to tell me he'd like to use it in an anthology series he was editing for Zebra Books called *Swords Against Darkness*.

The only catch was, it had to be a lot shorter to get into the book.

So "The Fane of the Grey Rose" also gave me my second lesson on the road to becoming a professional writer: listen to the editor.

By that I don't mean slavishly do whatever he or she might suggest simply to make the almighty sale. But it is important to consider their input. After all, a good editor is only interested in making the story you're telling the best it can be. Good editors don't ask for arbitrary changes. There are always viable reasons behind their requests. Some might be artistic, some commercial (as the case was here—my story was simply too long for the collection as it stood). It's the writer's job to consider the requested changes and decide whether or not they'll improve the story. Or at least whether you can live with them.

I could. So in 1978 I made my first professional sale, and a year later "The Fane of the Grey Rose" appeared in *Swords Against Darkness VI*. Let me tell you, it was a serious thrill to be in the same anthology as authors I'd long admired such as Manly Wade Wellman, Ardath Mayhar, Poul Anderson, Tanith Lee, and Orson Scott Card, as well as some of my talented peers: Charles R. Saunders, Gordon Linzner, Diana L. Paxson, and others.

By the time the book came out, it would still be another four years before I finally sold a novel, but this was the sale that made it all seem possible to the young hopeful writer I was at the time. And while I've thanked him before, I'd like to take this opportunity to thank Andy again for all his support and interest in my writing at that early point in my career when it seems you're only writing for the four walls of your study.

Andy's own books aren't as available now as they should be, but with the wonders of the Internet, you can at least download *The Long Dark Road to Wizardry*, one of his collaborations with Richard K. Lyon, at the Pulp and Dagger website at: www.geocities.com/ area51/crater/1908/pulpmag/contents.html.

And you can find out more about my work at www.charlesdelint.com.

THE FANE OF THE GREY ROSE

by Charles de Lint

> *The fateful slumber floats and flows*
> *About the tangle of the rose;*
> *But lo! the fated hand and heart*
> *To rend the slumberous curse apart!*
> *—William Morris*

I REMEMBER well the day I first set eyes on her, the maid I named the Grey Rose for the blossom she wore in her rust-brown hair. It was the hue of twilight, as gray as the mists upon the downs, and seemed fresh-plucked, with traces of morning dew clinging to its fragile petals. It was at eventide that she first came to Wran Cheaping, yet that rose spoke of the morning sun to me. In my mind's eye I envisaged the first beams of light washing over briars and dew-laden blossoms. I could see tiny mists rising from petals as their moisture faded in the summer heat. That evening, though, the sun was slipping steadily westward to settle at last in the bosom of the low hills that girded the town. Yet the rose was wet with morning dew; and it was gray.

It was during the midsummer of my twentieth year that this befell. I had taken myself from Farmer Heyre's fields, earlier than was my wont, to stand bemusedly amidst the bustle of the closing market. The chapmen were busily securing their shops against the approaching night while the husbandmen and their goodwives were loading their wagons with unsold wares, when she swept by me, her mantle rustling like windblown leaves.

Oak-green was the mantle. 'Neath it she wore a rust smock and a cream-white blouse. Stars seemed to glisten in her dusky eyes and there was a breath of autumn wrapped about her, filling the air with a sweet and heady scent. Though she was not tall, something about her lent her the appearance of height, and she walked with a loose, easy stride. Here she bought a sack of grains, there a handful of fresh sprouts and greens—all carried in a wicker basket upon her arm.

I longed to speak with her but was shamed at my appearance—suddenly very aware of my rough woolens and shabby cloak, of the dirt of the fields that clung to my skin. As she reached the far side of the market, I turned as if to go. In that moment she stole a glance my way, her eyes catching mine in such a way that we seemed to share a secret that only we two might partake of. She smiled and I cast my gaze to the ground, feeling a flush 'neath my collar. When I lifted my eyes once more, she was gone.

Slowly I wandered to the stable I called my home, my thoughts on this maid of the Grey Rose. Once there, I busied myself with sweeping the floor.

When the last chore was done, I crept to my corner at the rear of the stable and drew forth a rudely-carved harp from 'neath my straw pallet. It was not the work of a skilled craftsman, for I had laboriously fashioned it myself. The supports and soundbox were cut from weatherworn barnwood, and it was strong with cow gut I pilfered from the back of Ralen's meat-mart. For all its looks, though, it had a pleasing tone and I could coax tunes from it to fill the long hours that I spent on my own.

That evening I tuned it while troubled of heart. The one smile from the lips of the Grey Rose had woken a discontent in me. I thought of my life in Wran Cheaping with sudden displeasure. My mother Eithne was a Harper of the old school, revered and respected until she was cast from the halls of Wistlore for wedding an outlaw from the Grassfields of Kohr. Not often was a woman taken into the Harper's Guild. So skilled had Eithne been that not only was she of the Guild, she bore high rank therein as well. Until she met Windlane—outlawed from his tribe and as wild as the Grassfields themselves.

The Guild forbade their wedding. When she set herself against them, she was banished from the hallowed Halls of

Wistlore, where the Harpers have ever held sovereign with the Loremasters, Wyslings, and other wizard folk. Whither they were bound when the sickness took them here in Wran Cheaping, I fear I'll never know. To the Southern Kingdoms, more likely than not, where the Guild holds no sway. I was four when the sickness took them both and orphaned me here.

I was taken in by Farmer Heyre. As soon as I turned eight, I was set to work in the fields. Ah, but my mother's blood ran strong through my veins so that, though I labored in fields of corn and barley, I resolved that I would one day master the minstrel craft and earn my living with the harp rather than the hoe.

When I reached my fifteenth year I left the farm to move to this stable in town. I called it my home, poor though it was. At morn and eve I would clean it to pay for my lodgings. For my toil in his fields, Farmer Heyre paid me three good coppers a week so that I might feed myself. Hidden in my pallet, in a small leather pouch, I had thirty coppers saved. With those—and my heart set a-longing for new lands and faces from that brief glimpse of the fair maid in the market placed—I was determined to make my own way out into the world at summer's end. All the days of my short life I had dwelt in Wran Cheaping, whose folk had never made me feel overwelcome.

My thoughts came full circle and I thought on the maid of the Grey Rose once more. As I spoke her name to myself, a thrilling filled my heart. The one smile was all it took. Possibilities opened before my eyes. Here I was a farm laborer, nothing more. In the world beyond I could make my dreams become real. Perhaps I could make a name for myself and return to show the folk of Wran Cheaping what sort of a man I could be. Aye, and if that maid, that maid of the Grey Rose, dwelt here yet, perchance I'd go a-courting her, with a fine harp strapped to my shoulder and tales worth the telling to delight her ears.

I laughed softly at my fancies. The courage at least to try, though, had been stirred awake. So bemused, with my fingers trailing quiet melodies on my harp, I felt a weariness come over me. I played the last tune, arose to store my harp safely in the straw, and readied my bed.

Another week passed before I had a day free from the fields. I arose early on that morn and, with my harp in a burlap sack over my shoulder, I made for the Golden Wood that lies north of Wran Cheaping on the edge of the downs. There was a loaf of bread and a slab of cheese in my wallet, a lightness in my heart.

The sun was bright overhead and far from the nooning when at last I reached the Wood's trembling shade. Soft-footed, I wandered 'neath the summer-rich boughs of the beech and elms. Pushing my way through stands of thin maple and silver birch, I came to the banks of a brook filled with clear, bubbling water. I cast my clothes on the cat's-tail and watercress that ridged the stream. Plunging in, I let the cool waters wash the dirt of my week's toil from me and refresh my limbs.

When I tired of the sport I clambered up the bank and caught hold of my clothes to give them a good scrubbing. Soon I was sitting in the sun, my clothes drying on a black-thorn bush anigh, while I dreamed lazily of the world outside the West Downs. 'Twas said that the muryan dwelt in those hills, that aelves made their homes in the dark glades deep within the Golden Wood. At least so I'd heard in the tales of the folk that once held these lands, in elder days. Folk unlike man they were, in a time before man's coming. I often thought of the folk from these tales and longed to meet an aelf or any sort of magical being.

I rose with a sigh, clad myself, and fared deeper into the wood. I'd walked for perhaps two hours, full of dreams and dreamy thoughts, when I came to a dale as sweet as ever there was. Orchids and red campions, light blue columbines and other wildflowers shimmered in the grass underfoot. A hawkfinch rose chittering before and swept into the canopy of tall oaks and elm that encompassed the dell. There were mushrooms growing in their shade. I picked a few to eat later with my bread and cheese.

When I had a pocketful, I sat down. Taking my harp from its rude sack, I tuned it. Soon I was deep into a new tune, losing myself to the wealth of harmonies I could imagine within its measure. Aye, here the tumbling breathy timbre of a flute might add a trill, there the lift and lilt of a fiddle's tone could strengthen the flow. This was for the maid of the Grey Rose, I decided, as the tune took firm hold of me. I began to hum until words came spilling from my tongue— ill-shaped perhaps by a true Harper's standard, but fair sounding to me.

I sang, then . . . and imagine my surprise when I heard another voice, low and sweet, join mine in the refrain. I stopped in mid-tune and glanced about to see that self-same maid of my new song standing by my side. She was clad in a short, white kirtle that briefly outlined the sweet shape of her form and contrasted sharply against the sun-brown of her slender limbs. I scrambled to my feet, hot with embarrassment, my harp falling to the grass with a discordant ring.

"Wh-what do you here?" I asked. I wished I hadn't spoken as I stumbled over the words.

A low chuckle escaped her throat and she favored me with a smile. "Why, I'm picking mushrooms for my supper, Harper." She brushed a willful lock of rust hair from her brow. "That was a brave tune you were playing. How is it named?"

For a moment I thought she was mocking me. My only thought was to flee the glen. Yet her face seemed to hold no guile and her words were so generous that I gathered my courage.

"M'lady, 'tis but a new tune that I've begun to shape today. When 'tis done, I thought to name it for you . . . for the Grey Rose."

I could feel my cheeks redden. The maid smiled again and gracefully settled herself on the sward, her slim legs tucked 'neath her kirtle.

"You honor me, Harper. Will you play it again?"

Numbly, I nodded and sat down beside her. I picked up my harp. Nervously I strummed the opening chords until, haltingly and with many false starts, I began the tune again. Though I dared not sing the half-formed words I had sung earlier, I strove to play the air as best I could. When I came to a complex sequence, I suddenly forgot my shyness, for the tune took hold of me once more and I played with an assurance and confidence unknown to me, save when alone in my corner of the stable or in some secluded wood or field.

Again she hummed the air and my fingers fairly flew over the strings as her voice set my spirit all atremble. All too soon, the moment passed and the last strains of our music faded into the quickening day. She sighed.

"How are you named, Harper?"

"Cerin," I replied. Though I longed to, I dared not ask her the same. When she made no reply, I added, "I am no Harper."

She looked quizzically at me. "You've not the look of one, that's true enough. You've a husbandman's raiment and your hands are callused from work in the fields. And yet, who's to say what a Harper should look like? You've a touch as light and fresh as any I've heard." She stood suddenly. "I've barley-bowl and mushrooms awaiting us upon my supper table. Will you come and share my meager meal with me?"

Right gladly I agreed, my heart thumping in my breast. I gathered up my harp and wallet to follow her through the woods to her home. Her slight form slipped through the trees with an aelfin grace.

We came at last to another glade, bounded by gnarled ash trees and thickets of birch and young oaks. In its midst nestled a tiny cottage, vine-draped and built of stone, with a garden of wildflowers before it and a well to one side. As she went within to fetch us some refreshment, I stood in the sun and gazed about myself, marveling. I had been to this glade before—aye, perhaps three months past when the spring was in the air—and though this cottage had been here true enough, it had been all in ruin and the glade itself overgrown with weeds and brush.

I puzzled over this. Yet when she came without, balancing a tray laden with two mugs of steaming tea and a platter of fresh-baked bannocks, I soon forgot the riddle, forsaking it for the victuals and her company.

That afternoon and the even that followed will ever be among my fondest memories. We dined on simple fare, 'tis true, and talked long into the night. Ah, that conversation in her company was better to me than all the meat and drink of a noble's table might ever be.

When first I had seen her in the market, this maid of the Grey Rose, I yearned for her as any man might yearn for a maid that warms his heart.

As the evening slipped away though, I realized we could never be lovers. There was something in her manner, some mystery, that made me aware of this. Yet the thought did not sadden me, for here in the Golden Wood, I had met one with whom I could share my innermost thoughts without fear of ridicule. It was as if we were old friends, sundered for a time, and now come together again. I would never cease to long for her, as a man longs for a maid. I would strive to keep my yearnings to myself, though, for if I had lost a lover, I gained a speech-friend that was thrice as dear.

We sang many a song that eve, ones that I knew and strange wistful tales and airs that the maid taught to me. It was much later, after I laid my harp aside, that I asked her how long she had dwelt here and from what land she was come. She was quiet and a long silence wrapped itself about us. Glancing at the shadows playing on the walls of the cottage—born from the dim glow of the hearth fire—she said at last:

"I am from a place that is near, yet far from here. There is a geas upon me that drives me like a leaf before the wind throughout many lands, aye, and there is a shade of the dark that follows me and strives to undo all my deeds and make me its own. Long roads have I wended until, at the waxing of the Dyad Moon, I came to this wood, weary from wandering and yearning to rest for a spell. But not for long, no, not for long . . ."

Her voice trailed off and she lapsed into a thoughtful silence. I, for my part, felt a tremor of fear stir my heart at her words. I wondered again at who she might be and how she had raised this cottage from a ruin. Her dark talk of a geas and the threatening shade confused me and made me anxious for her sake. I was about to offer her my aid, for what it was worth, when she smiled suddenly and our conversation and my thoughts turned away from the puzzle to fare on to other things.

When it was well past moonrise, I rose reluctantly to begin my journey homeward. The maid accompanied me to her threshold. There she bade me a good eve.

"Will you come again, Cerin?" she asked.

I said I would readily enough.

I was very thoughtful on my return to Wran Cheaping, walking through the darkened Golden Wood. There was a mournful wind upon the West Downs, with a chill in its breath. As I bore the afterglow of the maid's company warm in my breast, and my thoughts were on her and when next I might have a free day to see her, the chill I minded not.

So passed the summer. I worked in Farmer Heyre's fields by day, dreaming of the Grey Rose, and at night I sat writing tunes for her, or adding airs to the tales she told me, sometimes setting them to rhyme. Aye, and oft I would fare to that glade in the Golden Wood to spend an eve or a day with her. At summer's end, though I had thirty-nine coppers saved, there was no wish in me to leave Wran Cheaping. The Grey Rose made my life fuller than I had deemed it possible. I would not have this joy come to an end.

There came a day, upon the edge of autumn when the countryside was filled with the glory of the leaf-fall, that my idyll came to an end. I walked from Wran Cheaping that day with a new tune at my fingers, basking in the wonder of the season. All the world seemed a-hum with the autumn. Seas of rusts and golds, browns and singing reds, swept across the Downs and the Golden Wood was so bright that I must needs almost turn my eyes from it.

Underfoot, bright melyonen bloomed violet amidst the fallen leaves and nuts. The bushes hung heavy with berries, thick splashes of color against the growing somber attire of the hedges. My heart was light and I hummed merrily to myself as I strode along. A quickening confidence had blossomed within me, along with the maturing of the barley and corn in their fields, and I harvested it more eagerly than ever the farmers might their crops. This was my gift from the Grey Rose. She sowed this sureness of spirit within me. Aye, had she not been my speech-friend, yet would I have blessed her thrice over for this.

I came at last to the glen wherein her cottage stood and paused in midstep. Although I could not define it, some subtle change had come about that went beyond the simple turning of the seasons. It was as though a malevolent shadow overhung the glade; a brooding darkness fashioned in some nether region beyond mortal kenning.

Hurriedly, I crossed the glade. When I came to the door, it stood ajar. I peered through to see the Grey Rose sitting disconsolately at her kitchen table, a half-packed journeysack set upon it before her. I stepped within.

"What betides?" I asked. My heart fell as I spoke for I knew well enough by the looks of things that she was making ready her departure. She had spoken of it oft enough. I had taken no heed of it, deeming that the day would never truly come. She looked up at the sound of my voice and tried a brave smile.

"Ah, Cerin, I must away. Too long have I tarried here. I have a geas that is overdue in its fulfilling, aye, and a bane that will soon come a-knocking on my door. I fear I've not the strength to flee any longer."

"What do you mean?" My thoughts fled back to our first evening together and her strange speech that she was repeating now. We had not spoken of that since. "What befalls? Can I aid you?" The words spilled from me in a jumble. I tried uselessly to still the thudding of my heart.

"I fear not, kind friend," she said. She sighed and took my hand. "Sit you down, Cerin, and I will tell you the tale of my life. Aye, and the sorry end it comes to."

Her words filled me with foreboding. What did she speak of? It seemed that the time for answers to the many riddles surrounding her had come. Now, curious as I once was, I wished this time had never come.

"Have you ever heard tell of the Cradle of the Kings?" she asked.

"Aye. 'Twas a great city in the elder days, though now it lies in ruins. I've heard of it, of the bright lords that ruled there and sought the wisdoms of the world. More revered than Wistlore it was. Now naught remains but fallen towers and the shades of the dead. It lies just above the western entrance to Holme's Way, on the edge of the Perilous Mountains, and fell in some great war. 'Twas another name for it as well."

"Banlore," said the maid.

"That was it. But what has that haunt of daemons to do with you?"

"I am hand-fasted to one therein that you might well name a daemon. Yarac Stone-slayer he is named. A Waster, a child of the Daketh, the Dark Gods, is what I am to wed."

I was stricken with horror at her words. As I opened my mouth to speak, she tightened her grip on my hand.

"No, list first to my tale, Cerin, ere you voice your protests. Long ago it was that I pledged my hand to him. In return for that pledge, I gained the promise that no harm could come to the Hill Lords, those who reigned in the Trembling Lands at the end of the Elder Days. It was a cruel war that seemed to rage for longer than long is. This was its only ending, for the Hill Lords were pitiful in number by then. They would soon have fallen had we not this offer to make the Waster. I am of their kin, you see. It was my will that this be, hateful as it might prove to me.

"Then, on the eve of our wedding, Yarac sent a plague of were-riders and yargs into the Trembling Lands. They slew nigh all the Hill Lords, Yarac never deeming that I would learn of it until too late; until my power was his, my body his. Word came nevertheless. I flew from Banlore—for so was it named when Yarac wrought its ruin—and he pursued me.

"Yarac met with us, myself and the remnants of the Hill Lords—on the hills nigh the city. They were slain, but I escaped, aye, and I flee yet. Three year-turnings past, he stole my spirit's shadow and so gained a control over me. There is a hollowness within me, a weakening of my strengths, Cerin. I cannot live longer without it. I fear he is leagued with others of the Dark now, but I cannot be sure. Tonight, though, I know he will come for me and there is naught I may do to stop him from taking me."

I shook my head in bewilderment. I knew the tales of the Wasters, aye, and shuddered at their telling. I knew as well of wars in the Trembling Lands that had touched even the West Downs and the Golden Wood, yet the time of their waging was ages past. There had been no strife in these lands within living memory. That she might speak of these things as though they were yesterday . . . for that she must needs be ten score ten years herself and this could not be. The undying dwelt only in tales . . .

My scalp prickled and I felt the cold sweat of fear upon me.

"Who are you?" I asked her, almost loath to hear her answer.

"To you," she said with a sad smile, "I would e'er be the Grey Rose."

It was no answer. I was about to say as much when she continued.

"They are all gone . . . the Hill Lords and their people, aye, and the were-beasts and their riders, the yargs and goblins . . . all gone, save for Yarac. He and I, we are the last players that remain from that ancient struggle. I would know where he gained this new strength, though, when my own is waning . . ." She shook her head slowly and fell into a brooding silence.

"I like it not . . ." I began.

She glared at me.

"And do you think I do?" Her voice was laced with bitterness. "Do you think I welcome the honoring of a broken pledge? To have that creature foul my flesh as he beds me?" Her eyes flashed fire from their dusky depths and I drew back from her. She sighed, saying in a gentler tone: "But no, Cerin. I wrong you. You should not feel the brunt of my anger. That I will save for when the Stone-slayer comes for me this eve, little good that it might do."

"I will aid you," I said. "I know not how, but I will stop him."

"'Tis bravely spoken, Cerin, but better it were if you were not here when he comes. To face him could mean your death, perhaps worse."

"I will not leave."

I marveled at my courage. Had this been the early summer, I would never have dreamed that such things might betide. Aye, or that I would be facing them! I gathered strength from the fact that this maid I loved was in need. Fearful I was, indeed, yet not so fearful that I would not try.

We sat at the table and the day slowly wore by. As the long shadows of dusk darkened the room, the Grey Rose stood from the table to light a candle. Wearily, she finished packing her journeysack by its light and the wan light that yet caught the glade without in its grasp. When she was done, she sat again, gazing out of the still open door.

It pained me to see her so, she who had always given me strength when I needed it. Even the rose in her hair seemed unwell to my eyes. Quietly I arose and closed the door, dropping an oak bar the width of my thigh across it. Returning to the table, I saw tears glistening in her eyes.

"Cerin, Cerin," she said. "I would not have you die. Flee now, I beg you. You cannot know what you will be facing. This is no tale to be told before a roaring fire, with mugs of hot tea in hand and a harp plucked softly behind the telling. There is more to the world than the ways of humankind. North of the Perilous Mountains there are wide rolling lands, hills and downs; aye, and long tracks of unbroken woods and dark moors where the old ways are not forgotten. There are aelves in those woods—as there once were in this forest—muryan in the moors, dwarves in the mountains. And where there are beings of Light, there are the minions of the Dark as well.

"Yarac Stone-slayer is real. If you bide here with me, he could slay you as easily as he can crush stone."

"That may be," I said, "but still will I stay. I am not as the folk are here. My mother was a Harper and my father a warrior from the great Grasslands of Kohr. My kin are from those northern lands. Though I may not have the knowledge of magical power, I have yet the strength of my limbs. There may not be much meat to my frame, but the long hours I have toiled in the fields have not left me a weakling. I will face this Stone-slayer. Perhaps I will fall, but I will not flee."

The darkness had grown as we spoke. A look of despair came into the maid's eyes when she realized that my resolve was hardened, that I could not be swayed to leave. Without the cottage I could hear the wind rising, rattling a loose shutter and tearing at the autumn-dried vines. For all my brave words, I felt the cold hand of terror upon me. I prayed that my courage would not forsake me.

It was almost fully dark. The wind became like a thing alive, howling about the cottage. Nothing but an autumn storm, I thought, a common enough thing. My thoughts hovered around the maid's words of the Waster. Foreboding set my heart a-pounding as the growing storm seemed less and less natural. Soon it would be moonrise, the rise of the Blood Moon. As the wind still howled, I wondered at the ill omen of this moon's naming.

Suddenly, the Grey Rose stood—so swiftly that her chair fell with a clatter to the floor behind her.

"He calls," she said in a strained voice. "Oh, Cerin. He calls and I am afraid."

I stood beside her, striving to hear that call. All that came to my ears was the raging of the wind. She groaned and took a step toward the door. I put out a hand to stop her. No sooner had I touched the sleeve of her gown than the door burst asunder, whipping shards of wood about us. Something was there, something darker than night that shook my very soul. The candle blew out as the wind tore into the cottage, yet I had no need of its light to see the maid moving toward the threshold where the intruder awaited her.

"No!" I cried.

Pushing her aside, I caught up my chair two-handedly and leaped at the thing, putting all my strength into that assault. The chair crashed resoundingly against the huge dark form, yet the hard wood splintered into kindling and I was flung from him to the floor, the wind screaming in my ears. A flash of lightning ripped across the heavens outside and I saw the Waster clearly silhouetted against the sudden light.

He was shaped like a man, yet stood nigh eight feet in height, towering like a monolith over me. His flesh had felt like living iron. Coals of red fire smoldered in his eyes. He picked me up from the floor with one huge hand and, as my fists struck futile blows against his massive chest, he hurled me across the room. I landed with a jarring crash. The breath was struck from me and a pain stitched through my body as though each and every one of my bones had shattered from the impact.

I sought to rise and found that I could not. Helplessly, I watched him take up the maid of the Grey Rose and turn from the threshold. Her eyes were wide with terror, her scream silent. Raging and gnashing my teeth, I managed to crawl across the litter-strewn floor. My body shrieked in agony at each movement I made. Ages seemed to pass before I reached the threshold. I glared out into the ensorcelled night. The wind whipped the trees into a frenzy. As I watched, a sheet of rain erupted from above and I could see no farther than my hand. Before it fell, though, I saw that the glen was empty. Both the maid and her abductor were gone. Bitter tears laced my cheek as I realized my failure. I fell forward. A darkness washed over me and I knew no more.

I regained my senses just before moonset. The glen and wood beyond were as silent as a held breath. My clothing was soaked from the rain that fell upon me while I lay unconscious. I shivered with a chill and ached from a thousand bruises, though I could feel no broken bones. Cautiously, I stood and made my way from the threshold. In a corner I found the candle where it had blown from the table. I lit it with unsteady hands. Dragging a chair to the table, I slumped in it and sat dejectedly there, trying to gather my thoughts.

I awoke with a start to realize that I had slept through the remainder of the night. In the bright morning light, the stump of the candle seemed to stare at me, mocking me for my failure. Brave words they were that I spoke last eve, but only words. What had I done to aid her, and she my friend, this maid of the Grey Rose?

I must follow them. She had spoken of the Cradle of the Kings, the ruined city that was now named Banlore. To there I must go. First I needed knowledge. To defeat the Waster I must know his weaknesses, be there any; I must learn how to destroy him. There was only one I knew of that might have such knowledge stored away within her: Old Tess.

To Wran Cheaping and Old Tess I would return then, for though the townsfolk named her mad and shunned her company, she was my friend. All my tales and songs of old I had from her. The old wisdoms were hers; learnings and knowledge that even the Wyslings in Wistlore might yearn for were locked away in her mind. She would aid me if she could.

I drew myself up from the table to hobble to the door. I leaned against the twisted remains of its frame for a moment to draw deeply into my lungs the crisp autumn air, before I made for the woodpile on the far side of the cottage. There I searched through the unchopped wood and kindling for a length of wood that might serve me for a cane. After much prying and scrabbling, I came upon a thick staff cut from a rowan tree. This I strove to break into a suitable length for my cane. Either my strength was more depleted from my encounter with the Waster than I had thought, or the wood was especially resilient. I could not break it.

I glared at it, as though my gaze might serve where my limbs could not. Then I realized that it would serve me admirably as a staff, just as it was.

Leaning heavily on the length of its white wood, I returned to Wran Cheaping and a meeting with Old Tess.

Though I fretted for each moment wasted, it was still a week before my strength returned sufficiently for me to hazard the journey to Banlore. Always my thoughts were on the Grey Rose. It grieved my heart sore that she should be in the clutches of that fiend, Yarac Stone-slayer. Yet the week served me well. My limbs soon felt as hardy as ever. Still, I turned more in my sleep than was my wont. Partly from stiffness this was, and partly from unfamiliar and dark dreams that took hold of my sleep-bemused spirit and filled it with shadowed omens.

On another clear day, with the autumn well in hand, I left Wran Cheaping once more. This time it was for good. Whether my quest went well or ill, I would not be returning. As I walked my way across the downs to the Grey Rose's cottage in the Golden Wood, my purse with its thirty-nine coppers jingled at my belt and I thought on what old Tess had told me.

"It's Heart's-sure ye must be carrying in your belt, Cerin. And when ye face him, it's a deft thrust with a dead king's sword, a sword of shadows. Ah! And how would I be knowing where ye might get such a sword? Search a barrow, lad; search a barrow! And mind ye be sure ye've the dead one's blessing, or it's more sorrow ye'll be reaping than sowing. Aye, so say the old tales . . . Heart's-sure and a dead king's sword. And was there another thing? I can't recall . . ."

I shook my head as I strode along. Riddles, always riddles. First, the maid herself. That riddle I had forsaken, for sweet was her company and I had been loath to spoil it with prying questions. Then there was the Waster, the city of ruins, of ruins, those tales of old wars . . . and now yet more riddles, these from Old Tess. Heart's-sure I knew of. It grew along the mountain slopes and I would be passing that way. But a dead king's sword! I knew of no barrows in these lands, though the downs were said to be hollowed in places and there were hills that might harbor a barrow nigh the Cradle of the Kings itself. Mayhap, if luck favored me, I would find one along my way, and if it was not a king's barrow and there was no sword in it . . . I would have to face the Waster empty-handed. What else had she said, Old Tess? She had called me back, just as I was leaving . . .

"And, Cerin! Look for aid along yer way, and in strange guises. Mark this rede of mine, for the lands beyond the Mountains—aye, and those Mountains themselves—are filled with queer folk, unlike us, and there's one or two might treat ye kindly. Go with caution, Cerin."

I was soon come to the cottage, planning to stop only long enough to gather my harp. I went through the maid's journeysack, setting aside the food that was spoiled. I added the fresh produce and breads that were in my own wallet. I looked around then for something of the maid's that I might bring with me as my token. By the door—having fallen from her hair as she'd struggled in the Waster's arms, no doubt— was the Grey Rose she'd always worn. It was still flourishing, though no way near as healthy as I remembered it.

It was sorcery, surely, that kept it so; a sorcery that was fading. I knew I must familiarize myself with magics, aye, and as this was the maid's, I had no fear of it. Still, I felt a strange tingle run up my spine when I took it in my hand to place it inside my tunic where it lay cool against my skin.

I took up her journeysack and shouldered it with my

harp. So burdened, and with my staff in hand, I set my steps westward for the Perilous Mountains.

That night I camped in the midst of the West Downs and watched twilight settle over the gaunt hills. Silence hung heavy on the air, broken only by a lean whispering wind that was subtle as a moth's flight, aye, and gentle as its touch. The dusk poised upon the land for another moment before the deep night swept over all. Before moonrise, I fell into a dreamless sleep that lasted till the dawn.

I lay awake for a few instants, savoring my new freedom. No more toil in Farmer Heyre's fields was there for me now, no more of any of Wran Cheaping. A thought of the Grey Rose and her plight intruded into my musing and I scrambled to my feet. To my right, the sidehills of the mountains began their clambering rise, ending at last in heights that towered and glistened in the morning sun. Along their base, my path led through the foothills until I came to Holme's Way. I resolved to make that pass before the nooning was upon me.

The sky became overcast by the time I came to the cleft that marked Holme's Way. I took shelter 'neath a ledge to break my fast before I essayed the pass itself. As the morning had gone by, the gorse and heather-topped hills gave way to a rough land, strewn with granite outcrops and patches of shale over which I slid at times, breaking sure falls with my staff. Finally, even that was left behind. The land was now like one solid root of the mountains. Only the hardiest weed and brush grew in the patches of soil that were clumped in rills and folds of the rock.

Rising from my meal, I took the leftward side of the pass, stepping briskly for I was trying to outdistance the growing storm that I could see gathering itself over the downs. I fared for no longer than an hour, when I heard a rumbling that I took to be thunder from the storm behind me. I paused to listen more closely. The sound came from before me, not my rear. Then it took on a clearer meaning. It was the sound of horses' hooves.

Now, no matter what Old Tess said, I looked to meet none in these lands that I might call friend. I cast about in search of a refuge. The sheer walls of the canyon met my frantic gaze, too high and steep to scale. I felt trapped until I saw an opening in the wall some hundred paces ahead on the right side of the pass. Taking a firm hold of harp, staff and journeysack, I sped for it, heedless of the rubble strewn in my path. I just reached the mouth of the opening—it proved to be a cave, I soon found—when I slipped on the loose rocks and fell in a tangle of limbs.

The breath was knocked from me. Still I had sense enough to gather my belongings and scramble the last few yards. Once within I turned to peer cautiously without, hoping for a view of the oncoming riders so that I might know what manner of men they might be. No sooner did I cast my gaze in the direction of the hooves' rumbling than five riders came thundering from around a turn in the pass. I saw them clear enough then.

Bright mail glittered, even in the dull light of the approaching storm. I could see they were well-weaponed, what with swords, spears and two bearing great axes. It might be wrong to judge a man by first sight—aye, it's not as if I, myself, didn't look a ruffian in my travel-stained clothes and rude equipment—yet I felt that I would not be far off my judgment in deeming these men to be outlaws, or brigands of some sort. I was congratulating myself on my good sense, when disaster struck.

You did well to hide yourself from the likes of them, manling.

To this day I can still recall my shock when that gruff voice resounded within my mind. Sick with dread, I twisted about. My eyes went wide with shock as I beheld the dim outline of the huge humped form that had so addressed me. I backed from it, only to stumble once more. This time I fell out of the opening, in plain view of the approaching riders.

I cursed myself for a blunderer, but it was too late. Already they saw me, while from the opening shuffled the figure I had seen within, the thing that mind-spoke to me. Disbelief ran through me, for by all that is holy, it was a bear. Nigh ten feet high it stood upon its hind legs, all grizzled brown fur topped with a shock of steel-gray hair above its dark eyes. Its two immense forepaws cut the air before it as it neared me. I felt that my doom was upon me.

By my hand lay my staff. I reached for it before I stood. Slowly I backed away from the bear. Behind me, I could hear the riders pulling up. I knew not which was the worst I must face. Mayhap the riders would aid me against this beast, I thought. Yet the bear had not threatened me. What to do? One of the riders spoke mockingly as I was puzzling this out, thereby making my decision for me.

"Ho! Here's sport, indeed. A youth and a beast to feed our blades, comrades. What say you to that?"

As his companions joined him in his laughter, I turned to them, my staff raised chest-high and held loosely in my hands—much as I had seen the lads of Wran Cheaping prepare their quarterstaves for mock combat. Yet this was no play fight, and I was ill prepared for battle. With my death sure upon me, my thoughts turned to the maid of the Grey Rose. I grieved that she should have no champion now. A poor enough one I made, it's true, yet I was all she had.

Behind me, manling.

Again that voice spoke in my mind. I glanced over my shoulder to see the bear almost upon me. His blazing eyes were for the riders only. Our aggressors shifted in their saddles until one broke from the rest to charge us. The bear swept by me on all fours, rising to his full height just as the rider was nigh him. One sweep of those terrible paws and the man was thrown from his frenzied steed, a great gash across his chest. A wail of anger was throated by the others. As one, they bore down upon us.

I can remember little of that short battle. One moment there were four riders storming toward us; in the next two more men were hurled to their deaths at our feet while the others fled, following the lead of the three empty-saddled horses. I had wielded my staff, striking one man a glancing blow. But the bear had been a whirlwind of motion, and our attackers had soon lost their lust for killing. As I watched their figures rapidly dwindling in the distance, I wondered what they had hoped to gain from a beast and a poor traveler such as I. They spoke of sport before they struck at us. If that had been their reason, I felt no guilt in having had a hand in the slaying of three of them.

I was still breathless in the afterglow of the skirmish,

when the bear turned to me with his head cocked, peering thoughtfully. The silence grew uncomfortable between us. At last I drew upon my courage.

"My thanks for your aid, Master . . . ah . . . bear . . ."

My voice trailed off. I felt foolish 'neath his penetrating gaze. A beast that might speak—this was something that could only be in a tale! Still, in this last week or so, I had come to appreciate that the old tales held more truth than ever I thought they might.

Your thanks is accepted, manling, came his voice echoing within my mind again, *though I was as much to blame for startling you. I am named Hickathrift, lately come from Wistlore, where I was given the mantle of Loremaster by William Marrow himself. And you? A Harper, by the looks of that sack, and not a rich one. Still, when has there been a rich Harper, save in the days of Minstrel Raven-dear? Those days are long past now, I fear.*

I was amazed at how swiftly I accepted this mind-speech, aye, and from a bear at that. My heart leaped when he spoke of Wistlore, and that with such familiarity. Though my mother had been cast from those halls, I held a longing to look upon them myself.

"I am named Cerin," I told him.

He shook his head thoughtfully. *The name is unfamiliar. Is it listed in the record scrolls in the Harper's Hall?*

"I'd think not. I've never been in the northlands, though my mother, and father too, were from that land. My mother was a Harper; Eithne was her name. My father was Wind-lane. Have you heard tell of them?"

Hickathrift thought a moment. *Aye. Their tale is writ in the lore books, though what became of them has not been recorded. Nor is it mentioned that they had a child.* He shot me a piercing look. *They were not well-loved at their leave-taking. Did you know of that?*

"I knew."

There must have come a look to my face that showed my displeasure with those who would send from them one of their own, solely because she had found a love that they frowned on. Aye, and had that not occurred, I might have been raised in other lands, far from Wran Cheaping. I might have been a Harper in truth, taught the old ways at my mother's knee.

I was bitter, though not toward my parents. The blame lay not with them. Should I ever reach the Halls of Wistlore, that was one matter that I longed to confront those elders with. Had my parents not been banished, they would never have died from the sickness. Still, had I not dwelt in the West Downs, would I have met with the maid of the Grey Rose? I felt the rose cool and tingly against my skin. Aye, and my parents . . . the sickness could have taken them anywhere. It had not raged solely in Wran Cheaping.

But what of yourself? asked Hickathrift, breaking into my thoughts with his gruff mindvoice. *Are you bound for Wistlore then?*

"In time."

I told him a little of what had befallen me, dwelling longer upon the fate of the Grey Rose and the words of Old Tess than on the rest of my tale. Hickathrift was quiet while I spoke, stopping me only once or twice when my words ran ahead of themselves. Then I must backtrack to explain some matter. When the telling was done, he shook his head gravely.

I would like to meet this Old Tess of whom you speak, aye, and the maid you name the Grey Rose. The lore books are largely silent as to that war between the Stone-slayer and the Hill Lords of the Trembling Lands. To all accounts, it was a dread time. Northward, there was none who knew its ending, or the brave sacrifice of this maid. I think that I would accompany you upon this quest, if you will have my companionship.

This I had not imagined. If I could have his aid . . . ah, with his aid I might have an actual chance of success. I said as much to him. He laughed, deep and throaty.

Do not think too highly of me, Cerin, for I have not the power to stand up against a Waster. Yet I will try. And there are other things I can assist you with. You know of Heart's-sure. As to a dead king's sword . . . there is a barrow not far from the very outskirts of the Cradle of the Kings, hidden in the sidehills. I was within it and explored it to a small extent. I saw no sword within. Still, mayhap you will find something where I saw naught. I was searching for written records. Aye, and how are sword and bloom to be used against the Stone-slayer?

I shrugged my shoulders. I knew not and had worried about that often.

No matter . . . for now. First we have a need to gather those things. When the time for their use is nigh, let us hope that the knowledge will become apparent. He lifted his muzzle to sniff the air. Overhead, dark clouds were gathering, roiling and scudding in a turmoil. *We have yet an hour or so ere the storm strikes. What say you that we leave this place of death and fare onward for that hour? I passed other caves, further on up the pass. Within one of them we can spend the night and take further rede as to this coming struggle.*

We left the dead brigands as they lay, though I took a sword from one. I knew nothing of the art of swordplay, yet I felt a little more confident with such a weapon tucked into my belt. We fared on down the pass and came to the caves. Soon, I was sharing my victuals with him by a fire set just far enough back from the opening of the cave that its glow and reflection might not be seen from without. Therein, while the storm howled the night through, we slept deeply, not heeding the wind and rain.

The next morn, we arose with the sun to fare the remaining length of Holme's Way without further mishap. We stood in a jumble of strewn rock and boulders that marked the western gate of the pass. Hickathrift cast his gaze about, searching for a landmark. Once found, he led a winding way through the rough foothills. With much scrambling upon my part, we came to the barrow where it lay half-hidden in a small gully choked with brush and thick-bladed grasses.

The dusk grows, came Hickathrift's mind-speech.

We stood before a dark opening, flanked by two weathered stones with strange runes running up and down their length. I could not read them. My knowledge was limited to what Old Tess had taught me and she stored her learning in her mind, scorning books and writing. When I asked Hickathrift as to their meaning, he shook his head.

Though the runes are familiar enough, they spell words

in a tongue that I have no knowledge of. I was bound for the Trembling Lands when I came upon this place and meant to make copies of them upon my return so that the Wyslings might puzzle over them. But now—he made a motion to a narrow cleft at the side of the gully with his paw—*let us take our rest there and essay this barrow on the morrow. There are spirits that inhabit barrows that waken when the sun sets. They do not care to be disturbed.*

I shook my head at his counsel. I had tallied the days since the Grey Rose was stolen. That tally was too high.

"No," I said.

I fell to searching for a length of wood to serve me as a torch. There was nothing nigh, so I gathered an armful of the tall grass and sat down to twist their tough fibers into a serviceable torch.

"Time runs out," I said as I worked on it. "I feel that even now it might be too late. Haste is all that remains . . . a need for haste."

So be it, replied Hickathrift. obviously displeased. *On your head be it. That haste may well lead you into ruin. The counsels of the wise are specific in their warnings. If you will not heed them, you must take the risk alone. Tomorrow, I would have gone with you. Now I will await without to guard you from mortal foes. I will not chance a curse of the dead's.*

I shrugged, though I was not feeling overly brave myself. A desperation of sorts had set itself upon my spirit, swamping my own feelings of fear—aye, and the counsels of the wise as well. This was a deed I must do. I had failed her once, my Grey Rose. I could not chance failure again, whatever the risks.

My torch was ready. I lit its end with flint and steel. When it had caught flame, I turned again to the barrow's entrance. With a dead outlaw's blade bared in my hand, in search of a dead king's sword, I entered.

Luck go with you, came Hickathrift's thoughts. Then there was silence, save for the scuff of my boots upon the stone floor and my own breathing.

Within, the passage was narrow. I soon felt cloistered, for the walls seemed to press in upon me. It was an unpleasant feeling, treading this dark confined space with only the light of a torch of twisted grasses. I glanced at my torch and saw that it was burning swiftly, perhaps too swiftly. I felt that its illumination would not last for as long as I had hoped. It flickered and burned unevenly, sending strange shadows scurrying ahead of me down that narrow passageway. I thought of returning to twist a few more. Instead, I pressed on. Ahead I could see that the passage was opening up into a large space of some sort.

When I stepped within, my torch was half-burned, lighting an empty chamber. To the left, I saw the threshold of another passage; on the floor, I could make out the prints of Hickathrift's heavy paws etched in dust. To the opening I went, hurriedly crossing the chamber. Soon I was in another corridor and this was a little wider. Still, my heart was thumping in my breast as I walked. The weight of the rock about me seemed to bear down with renewed strength. An oppression crept in upon me so that I glanced nervously about, with many a look over my shoulder.

When this passageway came to an end, I stood in the heart-room of the barrow. All about was a litter of broken rock, shards of what must once have been weapons and other finery. The stone slab, where the inhabitant of the barrow should have lain, was chipped and empty. Peering closer, I could see a snarl of bones by its side, the remnants of age-rotted cloth and rusted armor. My torch spluttered. I looked about for something that I might replenish my dwindling light with. In one wall was set a torch, blackened with tar. To this I touched mine of twisted grasses. The tarred wood took fire readily and the whole chamber was lit with a brighter illumination.

The minutes slipped by as I took stock of the barrow's holdings. Weapons there were, or at least the heads of axes and spears, their shafts broken and lying in a tangle. Of riches there were none. There were plenty of clay bowls and dishes shaped of stone and rough metal. Some of them were painted with colors that were now fading, though once they must have been fair.

I shook my head despairingly. Nowhere saw I a sword— nor even a dagger. Silence hung leadenly in the stuffy air.

Then came a sound. I thought it was Hickathrift, come to aid me after all, until I realized that it came from the wall that faced the passageway. All my fears rose within me in an overwhelming wave. As I turned to run back to the outside and safety, a keening wail resounded throughout the chamber, freezing my limbs.

As suddenly as the keening rose, it fell. Silence once more encompassed the barrow. Then a voice broke that silence, a voice so loud that the stones of the burial chamber rumbled. I covered my ears to lessen the din.

"WHAT DO YE IN MY BARROW, MORTAL?"

With shaking knees, I turned to face the owner of that voice.

"ARE YE SO WEARY OF LIFE THAT YE HAVE COME TO JOIN ME IN THESE COLD HALLS OF THE DEAD?"

No matter that the torch cast its light about the chamber. I could see nothing before me save a darkness etched against the already black shadows that shrouded that end of the barrow.

"N–no . . ." I managed at last, my throat tight with fear. I struggled to overcome my terror while I backed away from the darkness toward the threshold of the corridor behind me. "I sought but a sword. There is a geas of sorts upon me . . . the sword of a dead king I must have to fulfill it."

"A SWORD?" said that bodiless voice. I caught a hideous chuckle behind its words. "AND WHAT WOULD YE GIVE ME IN EXCHANGE FOR A SWORD? WHAT DO YE HOLD MOST PRECIOUS IN ALL THE WORLD BEYOND THESE WALLS?"

I was dumbfounded and stopped my backward movement to peer closer into that darkness. Was there a sword here? Would this spirit bargain with me and mayhap allow me to flee the barrow with it? I racked my mind, seeking for something that I possessed that might please this shade of the dead. There was little I had, save my harp, the brigand's sword and the clothes on my back. Then I thought of the rose that was cool against my skin, hidden within my tunic. Loath was I to give it up, but to save the maid . . . Slowly I pulled it forth to lay it upon the burial slab.

"I have this."

The torchlight caught its petals, still damp with glistening dew. Though it was not nearly as fair as it had been, I still marveled at its flourishing.

"WHERE GAT YE THIS?" the voice boomed with anger.

I saw the darkness move away from the wall toward me. The force of its anger tore into my mind and I staggered 'neath its brutal attack. Through the twisting horrors that lapped on the boundaries of my consciousness, I tried to form words to explain how the blossom came into my possession.

"WHERE GAT YE THIS?" the voice boomed again. "THIS WAS MY DAUGHTER'S OF OLD, ERE THE WARRING FELL, UPON US. LAST WAS I TO FALL, HERE SO CLOSE TO HIS CURSED HOLD; LAST AND TO NO AVAIL. HOW DARE YE STEAL THE GREY ROSE FROM HER AND OFFER IT TO ME? I WILL SLAY THEE. I WILL REND THEE! SPEAK, MORTAL! WHERE GAT YE HER POWER FROM HER?"

The darkness was upon me. Babbling, I told of what had befallen the maid of the Grey Rose and what I meant to do to aid her. Rapidly I spoke, my heart thumping in my breast. I was on my knees for there was no longer the strength in me to stand. I held the dead bandit's blade uselessly before me, as though I might fend off the shade's wrath with it.

The darkness lashed me. I felt an unfamiliar mind probing my own, weighing my words for their truth. Not gentle was that unspoken questioning. The shade of the dead Hill Lord tore my memories from me. I writhed in my terror, striving to break away, to retain my sanity. Suddenly the horror fell from me and the voice of the shade resounded throughout the chamber.

"YE SPEAK THE TRUTH AND I THANK THEE FOR WHAT YE WOULD DO FOR THE CHILD OF MY FLESH. TAKE YE THE ROSE THAT YE MAY RETURN IT TO HER. I WILL GIVE THEE A SWORD, AYE, A SWORD AS NE'ER THE WORLD HAS KNOWN SINCE THE FALL OF THE LAST OF THE HILL LORDS. BATHE IT IN SMOKE, MORTAL, THE SMOKE OF

HEART'S-SURE BURNING IN A FIRE OF ROWAN WOOD. BLOOD RED FLOWER AND WHITE WOOD . . . THAT IS HIS BANE. HAD I BUT KNOWN IT IN MY TIME, 'TIS HE WOULD BE LYING IN THIS THRICE-DAMNED TOMB, AND I, I WOULD BE FREE.

"GO, MORTAL. LAY HIM LOW. WITH HIS DEATH, MAYHAP I WILL KEN PEACE AT LAST. TAKE THE SWORD AND GO!"

My ears were still pounding with the volume of his voice and I lay prostrate upon the floor, when I realized that he was gone. I rose to my feet, shaking my head numbly. Looking about, I saw the rose lying on the slab. I picked it up, thrust it into my tunic and searched for the sword that the Hill Lord's shade said he had left me. There was none to be found. Unbelieving, I looked again and again, tearing at the rubble strewn over the floor in vain. When I gave up at last, I saw it. Reflected on a wall was the shadow of a sword. With a cry of triumph, I spun about, albeit wobbly, to where the blade that cast the shadow must be. There was nothing there.

I shook my head in bewilderment. Riddles, always riddles. Yet there must be a solution at hand, could I only find it. Then I recalled my talk with Old Tess. What had she said? Slowly, the words returned to me.

. . . a dead king's sword, a sword of shadows . . .

Uncertainly, I approached the wall and put out my hand to the hilt of the shadow-blade. It was solid beneath my fingers! Filled with wonder, I grasped it, drawing my hand back from the wall. The sword came with it. Here was magic as strong as any that the Stone-slayer might wield.

I retraced my steps to where Hickathrift awaited me outside the barrow. I bore no torch, only the shadow-blade in my hand. Yet I stumbled not and made my way without the fears that had plagued me earlier when first I strode down this passageway. When I stepped from the entrance, Hickathrift stared with disbelief at the dim outline of the sword I held.

By my ancestors, you have it! I thought you were slain when I heard those muffled sounds and a cry as though a spirit were being rent from its body.

I could not recall that scream. It must have been torn from my throat when the shade of the Hill Lord entered my mind. I told Hickathrift of what befell me within. He nodded his heavy head calmly as I spoke, though I could see excitement gleaming in his eyes.

A Hill Lord's barrow! he said when I was done. *I should have guessed it by the unfamiliar runes. Now I will do my part and search out a stand of Heart's-sure while you take some rest. But rowan wood . . . where we will find that, your guess is as good as mine. I saw none when I passed through these hills just before we met . . .*

The thought struck us both at the same time. Rowan wood . . . why, my staff was cut from the wood of a rowan. We shared a smile, the bear and I.

"So now I have a chance, indeed," I said to myself as Hickathrift padded off in search of the Heart's-sure. "I only pray that we are not already too late." The words were scarcely spoken before sleep washed over me. I welcomed its embrace with weary gratitude, the shadow-sword clasped firmly in one hand.

By midafternoon of the following day, we came to a rounded hillock overlooking the ruined city of Banlore—the Cradle of the Kings. We laid a fire with the broken shards of my staff of rowan, Hickathrift soon breaking it where my strength had failed before. With flint and steel I set the kindling smoldering. Hickathrift had gathered the Heart's-sure while I slept. When the fire was burning well, I dropped them one by one into its heart.

Do you see that spire, or at least what remains of one? Hickathrift pointed to the northernmost part of the city. *That was the Lord's Tower in elder days. That is where he'll be. And that is where we must go.*

The flames lapped around the Heart's-sure as I dropped them in. Smoke bellowed richly from those flames. I drew the shadow-sword from my belt and held its blade in the smoke. In awe, we watched gray runes forming upon the dark blade.

"What do they say?" I asked.

Hickathrift knew little more than I.

They are writ in the tongue of the Hill Lords. They alone would know the kenning.

I held the blade in the smoke until the Heart's-sure was gone and only coals remained of the rowan wood. When I withdrew it, I held it aloft. We gazed at it for a long while. The sun caught the runes and seemed to turn them into fire so that the whole of the blade glowed. The flames were red like the red of the Heart's-sure, their hearts white. Yet still the blade was a shadow. The paradox of dark and light bewildered me.

Caryaln, said Hickathrift; *the shadow-death. Legend has it that there remained but one. That was in the shape of a spear, though. I wonder where the Hill Lords got this blade . . .*

"Who can say?" I slipped the blade back into my belt, leaving the sword of the dead brigand lying by the fire. As we made ready to start for the ruins below, a long howl broke the still air. I looked about in surprise. "What . . . ?"

An answering cry filled the air, followed by another.

Wolves! came Hickathrift's thought. *Yarac must have set them as guards and they have caught our scent. Swift! We must make for the city!*

I gathered up my harp and journeysack and bolted for the ruins. Hickathrift loped at my side. Howls rent the air again, many of them. They came from all sides, now. Glancing back, I saw dark forms on the hilltop. The beasts were larger than I had imagined wolves to be. They stood silhouetted against the sky with their muzzles lifted in the air. New howls were still echoing when they quit the hill to come speeding toward us.

From the right and left, more dark forms ringed us about. My heart sank. There were at least a score of the beasts in this pack. I saw no hope for us to outrun them, aye, or even outfight them. We could not make the ruins in time; this I knew. I stopped my mad flight to stand panting. Hickathrift brought himself up short beside me.

What do you? We must make for the ruins!

"We'll not reach them in time. We must stand them off here, rather than have them pull us down from behind as we flee."

Then if they must be faced here, let it be me that faces them and you go on with our quest.

"No. We succeed or fall together."

Fool! His gruff voice roared in my mind. *Think of the maid. Think of your Grey Rose.*

Aye, I thought of the Grey Rose, but already the wolves were closing in. I could hear their snarls and growls as they prepared to charge. The hackles were risen along Hickathrift's back and a low warning rumble issued from his throat. The wolves came nearer, almost ringing us in. Their mottled gray pelts seemed to shift and spin in the sun, making me dizzy, accentuating my fear.

I held the shadow-sword in my fist. With a low cry, I leaped forward and swung it at the nearest beast. The wolf dodged my blow with a deft sidling movement. Its head darted for me as I stumbled off-balance. I heard the snapping of its teeth too close for comfort, when a blow from Hickathrift's claws sent the creature reeling backwards, dead before it fell. They were all upon us in the next moment and we were kept busy against their insane bloodlust.

My harp and journeysack I had dropped at the beginning of this onslaught. As the wolves struck now, I backed from them and put my foot through the soundbox of my harp. It splintered 'neath my weight. I cried out at the sound, for poorly crafted it might have been, yet it had been my only solace through long lonely years. I returned to the fray with renewed fury.

The sheer number of them was overwhelming us. Already Hickathrift's magnificent coat was torn from dozens of cuts, for he was taking the brunt of the attack, and my sword arm was weary, so weary. The blade seemed to fight on its own, for I certainly had no skill in its use. Still, it was my arm that bore it, my muscles that ached. I soon felt as though I could scarce lift it any longer.

There came a lull in the struggle. We stood breathing heavily as the wolves regrouped for another attack. Hickathrift turned to me and mind-spoke, the force of his words stinging like a blow.

Go now. I will hold them off.

I shook my head, to say that I would not leave him. He bared his teeth.

Go! he roared.

I backed away from him, my heart filled with worry. Overriding that, though, was the thought of the Grey Rose in the clutches of Yarac Stone-slayer. Cursing, I spun and ran for the city. The wolves sent up a howl and made for me, but Hickathrift threw himself upon them. When I was at the edge of the city, I turned to see him borne down beneath their numbers. Then I ran on, in among the ruined buildings, with tears stinging my eyes. I would have vengeance, I vowed. Aye, I would avenge the death of proud Hickathrift. In the short while we were together, he had become very dear to me. First though, so that his sacrifice might not be in vain, I would deal with the one who was the cause for all my grief. Aye, Yarac would pay. The blade in my hand hummed his death dirge in my mind. A hint of gold appeared amidst the blood red of its runes.

On I sped. My thoughts twisted from anger to sorrow as I made for the crumbling tower we had spied from the hillock outside the city. The day was beginning to fail now and a wan light pervaded the deserted streets. The buildings, all ruined as they were, cast strange shadows across my way, their darkly weathered stones brooding and filled with dim secrets.

My footsteps seemed to slow, the nearer I came to the tower. Curiously, though time passed as I fared onward, the twilight yet wrapped these still streets, as though the night were to be held at bay indefinitely by the half-lit gray of dusk. The maid's rose grew even colder against my skin; the red runes that ran along the shadow-sword's blade glowed with a golden hue. Soon they were too bright to look upon with comfort. The sword itself tugged me in the direction of the tower. Aye, and still, though the night should be well upon the city by now, the twilight held sway.

My movements became so sluggish that I could scarce walk. It was as if I was forcing myself through water, or through the full drifts of winter. I felt tendrils of thought touch the boundaries of my mind. They were much like those of the Hill Lord's, save that they were tainted with a foulness that brought bile up into my throat and made me bolster all my inner strength to draw back from their questing.

Ever onward I fared, yet at a slower and slower pace so that it seemed I scarce moved. The mind-touches grew stronger and more foul, washing into my brain with a steadfastness that grew ever harder to break. It became so bad that I could only win free by concentrating all of my might on forcing them from me. As those moments passed, I would find that I had not moved. Then I would set one foot laboriously before the other, and so go on.

How long that hellish journey lasted, I have no way of knowing. Throughout it all the unnatural twilight soaked the avenues of the ruined city. Mostly the city was fallen down. In places some walls still reared; in others I must clamber over the heaps of rubble that blocked my path. Ever the mind-touches battered away at my consciousness. After one, I found myself lying prostrate upon the ground when at last I forced it from me. All that kept me going was the thought of the Grey Rose trapped in the clutches of the Waster. That and Hickathrift's sacrifice, for my courage was spent and nigh fled from me.

As I reached the end of my strength, I came to the base of the tumbled structure that was all that remained of a once-proud tower in the elder days, when this had been the Cradle of the Kings. I stepped through its portal and a blast of power struck me so that I staggered back to fall to my knees, a scream of pain wresting itself from my throat. Tears blinded my eyes as I struggled to my feet and fought the evil from me. At a snail's pace, I lurched through the doorway. There I gagged as a foul stench hit my nostrils.

Within, all was dark. I crept across the debris-strewn floor, fighting the mind-power each step of the way. The shadow-sword pulled me forward till I came to another door. I entered what I took to be another chamber, when an over-bright glare lit the inside of the tower, dispelling the utter shadow I was forcing my way through. It was a sickly ocher, as foul to my eyes as the stench was to my nose. I lifted my gaze to where a ravaged dais still stood at the far end of a long room. There they stood: the Grey Rose and her tormentor, Yarac Stone-slayer.

I moved forward, the shadow-sword slippery in my sweating palm. The power that had pounded my mind was gone. The silence seemed ominous, but nothing hindered my approach. They stood like images carved of stone, like the pieces of a knar board—gray queen and yarg warlord. When I stood before the dais, elation lifted my heart. Was he defeated already? Had the shadow-sword stripped him of his power? Ah, my thoughts leaped joyfully, only to be dashed in the next moment. From beside the still form of the Waster, the Grey Rose spoke. As I turned my gaze to her, I stepped back at the hate reflected in her eyes.

"Scum," she cried, her voice laced with venom. "Did you not think that if I wanted your presence, I would have bided with you? How dare you follow me here? How dare you profane this place with your farmer's body? Harper!" She laughed at the word. The sound of that laughter sent a chill of horror down my spine. "You would be a Harper, would you? Why not try your tunes on the wolves without the city? They have a need for dinner music, I should think."

A rage awoke in my heart that she should speak thus of Hickathrift. I held the sword before me and stepped nearer. Standing before her, I shivered 'neath her withering gaze. Hell-fires burned in those once dusky eyes, eyes that had looked upon me with friendship. Against my breast, the rose was like ice. I ignored the Waster then, for I saw that all I had striven for was of no avail. There was no need of rescue. She was his willing bride.

"I loved you," I said, the words spilling from my heart. "As a man loves a maid, as a companion loves his speech-friend, I loved you. There was a fane in my heart where once you dwelled, but now its foundations crumble. All that was holy therein, is like a dead thing. I had thought . . ."

"Go!" she cried, breaking into my words. She pointed to the door. "Go, or my mate will break his patience and slay you at my command. You live now only for what was between us once. That is no more; it means nothing. Go!"

I looked on her with pity. Without a glance at her companion, I turned to go, the shadow-sword trembling in my hands. Suddenly, I whirled about to plunge it into her breast. A scream tore that chamber, a scream so fearful and filled with pain that the walls themselves began to crumble and fall in upon us. The ocher light flared to a blinding brilliance. Stark against it was the darkness of the shadow-sword buried to its hilt in the chest of Yarac Stone-slayer.

"No!" he howled. "How could you have known . . ."

There was another flare of light and the room plunged into darkness. Swiftly I sped to where the form of Yarac had first appeared to stand when I entered the chamber. 'Neath my questing hands I found the still body of the maid I knew as the Grey Rose.

I lifted her in my arms and bore her from the tower as it fell to pieces about us. Once outside, I saw that the night had finally come. In the star-flecked sky overhead, the proud vessel of the moon rode the heavens. When we were some distance from the tower, I laid the maid down gently upon the stones. With shaking hands, I reached into my tunic and drew forth her rose. Though she lay as one dead, I remembered that the shade of the Hill Lord had spoken of the rose as though it held some power. I only prayed that it held what was needed to revive her.

I placed the blossom upon her breast and took up her body again to bear it outside the walls of the city. From behind, there came a deafening roar as the Waster's tower fell in upon itself, burying the monster in his death, aye, and so becoming a tomb that he did not even deserve.

The morning sun was rising over the hills. I stood nigh the ruined walls of the city once named the Cradle of the Kings, lost in thought as I had been for most of the night. A low familiar voice broke into my musing.

"Cerin?"

I turned to see the Grey Rose attempting to sit up and hastened to her side. She pushed aside my protesting hand and stood, albeit shakily. Taking a deep breath, she stretched her limbs with obvious joy.

"Ah, sweet life!" she said, smiling to me. "How did you free me, Cerin? How did you best Yarac the Waster?"

I sat down on the grass and she lowered herself by my

side. I told her of all that had befallen me since that night she was taken. There was a deep silence when my telling was done. At last she spoke.

"And Yarac? How knew you that the form you slew was not mine?"

"Because," said I with a laugh, "when Yarac was berating me, I glanced at the form I thought was his and saw that it had your eyes."

She laughed with me, saying, "So much for his trickery!"

"One thing puzzles me," I said when I had caught my breath. "Why did he not slay me out of hand? Why the guile? How could I best him so easily when you have fled before him for uncounted years; when all the might of the Hill Lords could not lay him low?"

"The High Born of the Daketh fear but one thing," she said, her voice serious, "and that is the caryaln, the shadow-death. What cause had Yarac to fear anything else? Surely not you. He knew you for what you were: an innocent lad, brought up in a backward land. What could you know of the caryaln? That was his folly, that he could not measure the courage in your heart, Cerin. And when you appeared in Banlore with a caryaln in your fist—he panicked. He sought to deceive you into leaving so he could deal with you at a later date. So fall even the strongest . . ."

Silence slipped over us once more. My struggling for her sake had rewoken desires within me; the closeness of her body and the sweet heady scent that seemed ever to follow her set my pulse a-thumping.

"Who are you in truth?" I asked, suddenly breaking the silence.

She took my hand. "Look into my eyes, Cerin, if you would know me for what I am."

Hesitantly, I lifted my gaze to hers and was lost to the swirling depths locked within the dusky lights of her eyes. All the shades of gray were therein, light and dark mingled in perfect harmony. As I lowered my gaze, she whispered:

"My father was the Hill Lord whose shade you met— Wendweir an Kasaar he was named. But my mother was of the Tuathan, the eldest race. I am a spirit of the Twilight, the Dark that is Light. My name is *Mar wel na frey Meana.*"

She rose with a graceful motion and lifted me to her side. There was a strength in her arms that belied her earlier helplessness. "I have another journey to make, Cerin, and I fear I must leave you once more. When Yarac held me in his power he told me of the ills that he and his kind have brought to pass over all our lords. I must bring this knowledge to my people so that we may take rede as to how they may be stopped."

"Let me aid you. I have proved my worth."

"Aye," she said, "and thrice over. But I walk paths that you cannot, and swiftness is what is needed now. Fear not, dear friend. We will meet once more, in unlooked for places and perhaps in fairer times. You have proved true to me, Cerin, and you will always wear my thanks for what you have done. This now I will foretell: your life will be long, longer than any of your kind has ever known. In those days to come, you will be the most renowned of the Harpers. Today I name you Songweaver. For now, though, I must bid you farewell. We will meet again . . ."

As she spoke her form began to shimmer, to fade from my sight. Sadness welled in my heart at this parting. I longed for something I might say, something I might do to hold her to me. My mind remained empty and numb.

"Cerin?" came her voice from her fading form.

I looked up expectantly.

"There is one waiting for you on the hillside, aye, and a parting token from me as well. Ne'er let the fane within you die, my friend, for it would grieve me sore. Fare ever well . . ."

"Farewell," I said and she was gone.

Slowly I walked up the hillside, and then I saw him. I'd only half listened to her parting words, so filled with grief had I been.

"Hickathrift!"

I fairly flew over the remaining distance between us. He was battered and cut from so many wounds that I feared for his life. His fur was matted with dried blood. Scarce could he lift his head at my approach. He managed a toothy grin at my worried look, and mind-spoke.

Gaze around you, Cerin. The others fared not half so well as I.

He spoke the truth. The hillside was littered with the corpses of the wolves that had attacked us. And there was something else. By Hickathrift's side was a leather bag. Eagerly I made for it and loosened the bindings, already guessing its contents from its shape.

As the leather fell away, I saw the Grey Rose's parting gift: a harp. A harp so glorious that my heart nigh stood still for its beauty. It was carved from the wood of the rowan, with decorations all along its sides that appeared to live and breathe, so skilled and true were their crafting. Its strings were of a glistening metal that I could put no name to and at its top, where the curving wood met the soundbox, was set a gray rose. Though it was carven from wood, it had the appearance of being fresh-plucked, with dew yet damp upon its petals.

I touched a string and a clear note rang forth to echo and re-echo over the hillside. With a smile, I replaced it within the leather bag—though I dearly longed to play it and do naught else. There were Hickathrift's wounds to be seen to.

Once his hurts were healed, I would fare north to Wistlore with him. There was a world to see, a long road to wend through it, and somewhere I looked to meet once more the maid of the Grey Rose. I had a song to finish before that day, a song that once I'd begun so long ago in the Golden Wood. I had a name for it as well, now. I would call it "The Fane of the Grey Rose."

INTRODUCTION TO "BONES FOR DULATH"

by Megan Lindholm

"Bones for Dulath" first appeared in the DAW anthology *AMAZONS!* The anthology was edited by Jessica Amanda Salmonson, and went on to win a World Fantasy Award for Best Anthology. "Bones for Dulath" was a first in a number of ways for me. It was my first commercially published fantasy story for adults, the first story to feature the characters Ki and Vandien, and the first time that my byline appeared as Megan Lindholm.

At the time I wrote this story, I was living in a mobile home set up on the cliffs of Spruce Cape on Kodiak Island in Alaska. When the tide was out, a rocky beach appeared at the base of the cliffs, but when the tide came in and a storm hit, the waves pounded the cliffs and sent shock waves up through the trailer. It also pelted our not-very-tight windows with salt spray and occasional festoons of seaweed. If the storm was bad, I could look forward to water running off the windows, down the inside walls, and across the kitchen floor.

Amazing, what one can come to accept as "normal" living conditions. As the saying goes, "the cabin doesn't leak when it doesn't rain." And when the sun does come out on Kodiak Island, and the whole world is green and silver and dripping, one can forgive the island for anything. The black shale cliffs and the abrupt mountains remain a landscape that figures predominantly in my writing to this day.

At that time, most of my writing effort was devoted to freelancing for the local papers, and making submissions to children's magazines. Rejection slips for my fiction still outnumbered acceptance letters, but I felt I was on the right track. I had also begun to attempt breaking in to my favorite genre. I had always known I wanted to write fantasy, eventually, when I was "good enough." It seemed to me that the time had come to stop procrastinating and start actually submitting some of the stories I had been hammering on for years.

At about the same time that I was sending "Bones for Dulath" to Jessica Salmonson's small magazine *Fantasy and Terror*, I was also submitting to other fanzines such as *Copper Toadstool*, *Dandelion Wine*, and *Space and Time*. Gordon Linzner, editor of *Space and Time*, accepted a story at just about this same time, and I believe that it actually appeared before "Bones for Dulath." That Jessica chose "Bones" for inclusion in her DAW anthology rather than her magazine remains one of the greatest strokes of good fortune that I've had in my career. It exposed the story to a far wider readership than it would otherwise have reached, including one Terri Windling at Ace Books.

I think that I created the characters Ki and Vandien largely in response to reading a vast amount of Swords and Sorcery. Most of what I encountered featured the lone, bold swordsman making his way through the world, or more rarely a loose alliance between a couple of men, such as Fritz Leiber's Fafhrd and the Grey Mouser. I think that Leiber's characters impressed me the most, for their good-natured give-and-take, the rivalry that masked the deep friendship, and for the remarkable growth and change that the characters underwent during the years of their adventures. Ki and Vandien were my attempt to create a similar camaraderie that included but was not limited to a romantic relationship. I wanted there to be not just an accepted equality to the partnership, but also the sense that each brought something unique to the pact, that together they were more than they would have been as individuals. My fascination, not just with character, but with the interplay between characters and the impact that relationships have on story lines, is another factor that continues to influence my writing to this day.

As for the new byline, that came about in a way that still amuses me. I submitted the story to Jessica Amanda Salmonson with the name I had previously used on all my professional writing: M. Lindholm. It was not an especially magnetic byline, but I was content with it. I had not put a great deal of thought into it. The Lindholm reflected that I had begun writing before I was married, and saw no sense in changing the surname, and the M. that I had never felt any great fondness or attachment to the name Margaret. Jessica, as I recall, felt differently. She felt that for too long, many female writers had hidden their gender behind initials and pseudonyms. She encouraged me to use my full name. I wrote back and explained my dearth of affection for the name Margaret and my lack of identity with it or any of its variants: Marge, Maggie, Peggy, etc. Megan, I added, was not too bad, but M fit me better. And I thought we had settled the matter with that. I believe that Jessica sincerely thought I had offered Megan as an acceptable alternative to M. At any rate, when my contributor's copies of *AMAZONS!* arrived, there was my story, with the by-line Megan Lindholm. A few years later, when my first novel-length work featured again the characters Ki and Vandien, it was judged best to continue with the same byline.

I wrote four Ki-and-Vandien books for Terri Windling at Ace: *Harpy's Flight*, *The Windsingers*, *The Limbreth Gate*, and *Luck of the Wheels*. I still have, somewhere, the sketchy outline and notes that would have continued their adventures through two or three more books. Although I found myself experimenting in other areas of the genre, I always intended to come back to those two and finish their saga. It was not, however, meant to be. Ace and I came to a mutually amicable parting of the ways, and I moved on to write other books that were more immediately compelling to me.

I still look back on these two characters with a great deal of fondness. In the course of writing them, I learned a great deal, not just about constructing characters, but how to listen to them after they had taken on lives of their own. "Bones for Dulath" was their first appearance in print, and an important milestone for my career.

BONES FOR DULATH

by Megan Lindholm

KI set the wheel brake, wrapped the reins about the handle, and leaped from the wagon box in one fluid motion. She dashed forward past the team, caught herself, and proceeded more cautiously. She was not certain where the edge of the concealed pit began. A wild thrashing came from its unseen depths.

"Vandien?"

A muffled curse and the shriek of a trapped animal were the reply.

"Vandien!" Ki called, more urgently.

"WHAT?" he demanded angrily through the sounds of struggle. Still unsure of her footing, Ki stretched out on the snowy ground. Now she could peer into the pit which had abruptly swallowed her companion. She saw a tangle of horse and man thrashing about below.

"Are you all right?" she asked anxiously.

"NO! Will you shut up? This beast is trying to kill me!"

"Cut its throat!" Ki suggested helpfully.

"No! It cost me fifty dru, and I'm not letting my money go so easily." Vandien was breathless with the effort of staying on top away from stamping hooves.

The yellow horse heaved and squealed again, slamming

Vandien's leg once more into the side of the pit. Ki could see its problem. One of its legs had been broken by the fall. Additionally, it was impaled on the ugly spikes set in the bottom of the pit.

"Kill it before it kills you, Vandien. The pain is driving it mad. We'll never get it out of there alive. Besides, it was never worth fifty dru in the first place. I told you that when you bought it."

"No! And shut up!"

"Vandien." Ki chided softly. "The beast is suffering."

She saw the flash of drawn blade, heard a sudden spattering of blood. Gradually the thrashing stilled.

"Damn," came Vandien's voice ruefully. "Ki, you owe me a horse."

"What?" Her voice was distant.

Vandien looked up. She had disappeared. He had a lovely view of an overcast sky. Lips compressed, he drew his leg with difficulty from where the dying horse had trapped it against the side of the pit. It tingled strangely. Was that horse blood down his thigh, or his own? He had been buffeted about so much it was difficult to separate any one pain.

"Ki!" he called in sudden alarm. "Ki, where in damnation are you? Get me out of here!"

A rope came snaking down. "It's tied to the wagon. Can you climb up or shall I haul you out?"

"I can't climb. I've hurt my leg."

Her slim figure was outlined against the sky. Tall boots dug into the side of the pit as she lowered herself. Fur vest and breeches gave her a feline appearance accented by her lithe movement. She rappelled down to land with a light thump on the hindquarters of the dead mount. Vandien gasped lightly in pain from the jolt.

"Where are you hurt?" Ki asked gently. She squeezed his shoulder reassuringly. "Vandien, you're shaking!"

"In my place, you'd shake too. I took one of those spikes in my leg. I fear it was poisoned. My whole leg hums."

Ki moved about to stare at the long gash in his leggings that bared his skin, and the long gash in his skin that bared meat and oozed blood. Carefully she touched one of the spikes. Her finger came away daubed with a dark substance.

"Those spikes aren't wood," Vandien noted. "More like something's old toenails."

"Gah!" Ki wrinkled her nose in distaste. "Vandien, you have a way with words. Let's get you out and clean that gash."

"Don't forget my saddle and gear," he cautioned.

"I won't," she replied, looping the rope under his arms.

Out of the pit, Vandien sat in the snow and looked queasily at his wound. The strange tinging had stopped. He touched the edge of the gash cautiously. Nothing.

"Ki!" He could hear her struggling to uncinch his saddle. "Ki, you owe me a horse!"

"How in damnation do you figure that?" Ki demanded.

"You were the one who wanted to use Old Pass instead of Marner's Road. If we hadn't come this way, I'd still have a horse under me."

"It cut six days off our time, didn't it? Besides, I don't recall pressing you to join me on this haul."

"You owe me a horse," Vandien asserted firmly. "Ki, I can't feel my leg," he added plaintively.

"I'll be right there."

She scrambled out of the pit and hauled up his gear. She knelt beside him in the snow to consider the wound. Ki shook her head in bafflement.

"I'll clean and bind it, and then we had best find who set that trap and what poison they used. And what they were hoping to catch in it. If there's game big enough to warrant a trap that size in this pass, I doubt I shall want to use it again. Come."

She slipped her arm about him and helped him to stand. Leaning heavily on Ki, Vandien limped toward the wagon. The two huge gray horses eyed him with mild reproof. It took most of his strength to mount the box and clamber into the enclosed sleeping area in the front half of the wagon.

"I'll toss your gear in back with the freight."

Vandien nodded and lay still, listening to his heart pump poison through his body.

"Who sets pit traps in Old Pass?"

Ki had wormed her way through the motley crowd in the

tap room of the inn. She stood at the Innmaster's elbow. He glanced at her angry face, and his eyes slid away.

"My patrons call for ale. I must serve them."

One of Ki's hands snagged the Innmaster's sleeve as the other settled on the hilt of a broadsword, incongruously large on her. The Innmaster caught her meaning, for he abruptly plopped down on a stool next to her, wiping his sweaty face on his apron.

"Dulath sets pit traps in Old Pass," the Innmaster admitted reluctantly. "He is not for talk with strangers. The god's traps are why Old Pass has not been used much lately. What did you lose to him?"

"A good friend. Nearly." Ki glared at a listener who swiftly looked away. "I hauled him out, but he is poisoned by a gash from a spike. Even now he sweats and turns on my bed-skins. I must see this Dulath and ask him what poison he used. And I should like to know what he hopes to trap with his pits in the middle of wagon paths."

The Innmaster's hands had become claws on the table edge. He licked dry lips. "You left his pit empty?"

Ki noticed several sets of eyes flicker toward her at his question. "Aye, or nearly so. There's a yellow nag in the bottom, such as it was. Dulath is welcome to such game if he relishes it. Innmaster, I need a room for my friend to rest in while I seek Dulath."

The Innmaster heaved to his feet. "No room. Sorry." He turned away.

Ki's browned hand shot out, seized the Innmaster's large wrist. With surprising strength, her fingers bit into the tender area between wrist and hand, causing the Innmaster to yelp in sudden pain.

"He needs a room. It is cold in the wagon, and he is in pain." She sounded very reasonable.

The Innmaster attempted to twist out of her grip; he gasped when her fingers only tightened.

"A room," Ki reminded him pleasantly. Abruptly she loosed her hold on the Innmaster's wrist and rose to keep a knife from piercing her. Simultaneously, she felt a hand seize both collar and hair.

"This way," came a voice at her ear. Ki complied. Out in the frosty air, the grip loosened, but did not let go.

"That your wagon?"

Ki nodded, unable to speak for the thought of the knife.

"Get on it."

The point of the knife followed her ribs up onto the box, only moving away when she seated herself and gathered the traces. Ki glared down at her antagonist. His face was without malice. He was, in fact, but a youth, younger than Ki, but taller by more than a head. He shrugged, not unkindly.

"My father means no ill to you. But if your friend has taken Dulath's poison, he is a dying man. And we let no rooms to the dead. Now be on your way."

"Be on my way where?" Ki demanded angrily. "The boneyard? Or shall I let him stiffen first?"

The youth's face softened. "Try Rindol. His cottage is back that way, the one of wood chinked with moss. He is skilled in herbs, and takes in the sick and weary. I have heard, though I do not credit it, that once he healed a man of Dulath's poison. But that was not in my lifetime, nor yours. Try there, stranger. And bear us no malice for what must be."

Ki made no reply, but merely shook the reins. The grays stirred; the wagon moved off.

"Ki?"

She did not glance back at the door that led into the wagon. "Shut the door, Vandien. It will do no good to chill yourself."

"No wind could chill me now, Ki. My blood burns within me. My left side is gone numb."

"Save your strength. We go to find a healer. Now shut the door." Ki's face was white, and the team wondered at the trembling of the reins.

At Rindol's cottage, Vandien swayed over Ki, a doll stuffed with sand, as she half dragged, half helped him from the wagon. She straightened under his weight, his arm across her shoulders. She glanced down at his leg, appalled at the swelling that threatened to burst the bandaging. Then she felt part of his weight taken off her, as a wizened old man, disfigured by pox, took Vandien's other arm.

"This way, this way," he shouted cheerfully, in spite of their proximity. "Rindol can always tell who comes to call on him. The lame, the diseased, and the maimed. And the poisoned!" he added shrewdly. "Where got he this pretty token?"

"In a pit trap this morning," Ki said as they maneuvered Vandien through the low door. "A pit trap of one called Dulath. I am told you can heal him. How much will it cost?"

"In this way, and onto that pallet. Pull the skins about him so. No, man, do not fight us. You may feel warm, but your body is chilled to the bone. Let an old man who knows have his way. So. Now, woman, stand aside. There is hot tea on the hearth. Warm yourself. You can do no more here. Let me see the damage now."

Ki wandered across the room to the hearth and poured herself a mug of tea. Her forehead was creased in thought. Now they would surely lose the time they had gained by using Old Pass. And she didn't like the way the old man had sidestepped the question of fee. She had little enough coin, and Vandien's had gone for his ill-fated horse. She had no hope of money until she delivered her freight to Yuri, days and miles away. Damn the man! What call did he have to go plunging himself into pit traps anyway?

Vandien cried out wordlessly under Rindol's probing fingers. Ki winced in sympathy, knowing such sounds were not wrung from his easily.

"At least there is still some feeling!" she observed aloud.

"Save your breath, woman," the old man advised. "The pain has chased his mind out of his body. And his soul soon to follow. I can ease his passing; Waters of Kiev will keep him from feeling the worst. And later, cutting the tendons prevents the body from twisting up as badly as it might. Or, if you wish, I can make his passing more swift. Which shall it be?"

Ki stared at him in consternation. "Cut his tendons? Waters of Kiev? Gods, man, that's the same kind of healing we practiced on his horse earlier today. If that's what I wished, I would do it myself with a blade. Many's the time he's tempted me to." she added softly. "But I am of no mind for that now. No, Rindol, I wish him cured, not killed."

"If the poison be Dulath's, that be impossible. They all die, that take that poison, if they be not already dead when they meet it. That be our custom now. The villagers throw their dead into his traps, to stave him off their livestock. Before the eggs hatch, they return, to burn both bodies and spawn. A tidy method don't you agree?"

Ki rubbed her forehead wearily. A madman. The youth at the inn had sent her to a madman. Or at best an eccentric, his mind under the weight of many years. Best to seek her answers in simple questions.

"Then all die who take Dulath's poison?" she asked.

"Aye . . . or almost. There was a one, upon a time. A hero. He set forth to slay Dulath, paid well by the village. But during the battle, he fell into Dulath's pit. His squire pulled him out and brought him here. The hero did not die, but it was none of my doing. He claimed the credit himself, saying he lived because he had lapped Dulath's fresh blood from his blade. That's as may be, I suppose. Never paid me, either. Left in the middle of the night, and the whole village saying I was to. . . ."

Ki waved him to silence, tried to sift his scrambled words for a thought that might help.

Across the room Vandien lay pale and still unconscious. He could be dying. He probably was, for that seemed the only thing the citizens of this cursed town could agree on. Still, what hunter would use a poison with no cure? She must see Dulath.

"Where can I find this Dulath? I would have words with him," she asked abruptly.

Rindol looked up from slurping hot tea. "Dulath? She will be in the higher peaks today, or mayhap she has returned to her trap to partake of her catch."

"She?" exploded Ki. "Whence comes this 'she'? I would speak to Dulath!"

Rindol continued to eye her mildly. "She, he, it is all one to that kind. As for speaking to him, well, the mouth that leaves such gaps in his prey is not for talking. For Waters of Kiev and tendon slitting, I ask but five measures of grain. My goats fancy it."

Ki's mind was reeling. She sorted her thoughts frantically. "I'll find Dulath at the pit trap?" she asked. The old man nodded. "Waters of Kiev will make Vandien a dribbling idiot. Give him none of that, and do no tendon slitting. I'll give you three measures of oats to keep him here, warm and dry, and ease his pain in any way that will not do him harm. I go to find Dulath. I'll pay you on my return, provided Vandien is intact."

Ki gestured Rindol to silence before he could further confuse her. She rose and, with a strange reluctance, crossed the room to Vandien.

She rested a cautious hand on his hair, but he did not stir. The scent of him rose up to her, a scent like herbs and moss crushed underfoot on a damp morning. She brushed the dark curls back from his forehead. His skin appeared drained of blood, and his face was cool, too cool to her touch.

"Keep him alive for me!" she told Rindol brusquely, and turned to leave.

"Ki!"

She turned back instantly. Vandien's eyes were dull but intelligent.

"Take the rapier from my gear. Use it, if you have need."

"I have my broadsword. I know it, but your rapier is still strange to me."

"Take it. That clubbish sword of yours does not even frighten anyone. Take the rapier."

"I am a child with it. You yourself say I have no skill with it in spite of your lessons."

"You are better with it than many who believe themselves skilled. Take it. I shall not tell you again."

She nodded once, and departed.

Evening became night without warning. Ki had no hours to waste awaiting daylight. She had paused but once, to kindle the torch she now carried. It billowed about her hand uncomfortably. She cursed herself for not bringing an extra one. And she cursed the yellow horse for being dead. Even its bony frame would have made a better mount than broad gray Sigurd. Her hips ached from bestraddling him. But her trip was near an end. She slowed Sigurd. The torch was small help to pierce the night. She had no wish to land in a pit on top of a dead yellow horse.

She need not have worried. Wise Sigurd halted of his own, snorting in disgust at the smell of his dead comrade. Ki slid from his back gratefully. She could trust him to stand.

She advanced cautiously to the edge of the pit. Where would this Dulath be? She peered in.

The yellow horse was not alone. Added to him was the ribby body of an aged man and the corpse of a young woman. Ki gagged, then swallowed convulsively. She backed away from the sight. She gasped in cold air to regain herself. There had been truth in the old man's babblings. The villagers threw their dead into Dulath's pits. Who then, or what, was Dulath, to be appeased by such thoughtfulness? Ki felt no curiousity.

Snow crunched, not on the trail, but above, up the side of the pass. Ki was not alone. She held her ground, uncertain if flight was necessary or wise.

Dulath was white. At first she could not separate him from the snow. It was as if he materialized in one piece within the circle of her torchlight. He paused once, perhaps noticing her, but almost immediately moved on, deeming her of no consequence.

Dulath had no head; he had no front, nor back, nor sides, by any standards Ki knew. His body was roughly ellipsoidal, fringed by dangling orbs that could have been eyes, though they ignored the light of the torch. Beneath each orb hung a spike like a fleshy icicle. Ki had seen those spikes before. His back was smooth, and at least as broad as Sigurd's. He moved on a multitude of skinny jointed legs, some of which ended in fingerlike appendages. He entered the pit with the ease of a caterpillar crawling down a twig. The scuttling of legs in the snow was the only sound.

Ki was shaking. The whites showed all around Sigurd's eyes. "Stand," Ki whispered to him. Suppressing her fear she advanced to the pit.

Within the pit Dulath feasted. He perched lopsidedly on the tangled frozen bodies. Ki watched in nausea as a great parrotlike bill on the underside of Dulath's body closed with a crunch on the plump buttock of the dead woman.

It made no chewing motions or feeding sounds. There was only the rattling of its spidery legs, and the crunch of the great bill nipping off hunks of frozen flesh. Eventually, it had its fill. Dulath then squatted busily. A questing ovipositor descended from its now sagging underbody. With blinding speed, it punched into the bodies of the dead, leaving a neat depression and a glistening white egg. Soon the bodies were specked with the shiny orbs. Ki seemed to come out of a trance as the torch scorched her fingers. Her hand jerked, the torch fell. It streaked into the pit, to fall next to Dulath and his nursery.

Ki heard an angry rattling of castanets. The white body of Dulath surged up over the edge of the pit and at her. She had threatened the nest.

In the stingy light of a waning moon, some of the appendages rose off the ground to become weapons. Opposed claws clicked at her. Ki dragged her rapier free of its sheath and fell into the stance Vandien had schooled her to.

"Present the narrowest target possible," she seemed to hear him say. "Get behind your blade." Dulath came on, clicking. He struck suddenly for her face, and she parried it wildly. Her darting blade thrust his appendage aside. She lunged then in an automatic riposte. Her blade rang against Dulath's hard back, and she retreated hastily.

"Fingers and wrist, fingers and wrist," cautioned Vandien. "Are you a reaper of wheat or a reaper of men?"

She backed away from Dulath, and he, encouraged, struck again. Her blade reacted before her mind, whistling in to strike at the questing appendage. With a snick a segment of it flew away into the snow. Ki felt Dulath squeal in a voice above her hearing level. Heartened, she lunged, but again her rapier only skittered off Dulath's back. Ki fell back, then attacked again. Her rapier tasted air. Dulath had wearied suddenly of this game, especially with a foe that fought back. Scuttling backward, he disappeared into his pit-nest.

Ki fought a sudden trembling. The icy air froze the sweat that damped her hair. In sudden hope she examined the blade of her rapier; no trace of blood. The legend of Dulath's blood curing his poison was now her only chance. But that blood was not easily shed. Her blade would not pierce his back armor and hewing off his appendages would not gain her a drop. Getting at his soft underbelly was a possibility. Still mulling on that, she clambered onto Sigurd and turned his head back to Rindol's. She would need a vessel in which to catch the blood. How she would get the blood she did not know.

Ki stepped into Rindol's hut blinking the night from her eyes and shaking the cold from her clothes. Vandien lay as she had last seen him. She unfastened her cloak and shed it as she moved to his side. He did not stir.

His lashes lay on his cheeks, veiling his dark eyes. The ruddiness of his wind-weathered face contrasted strangely with the pallor of his poisoned body.

"Vandien?" Ki called him softly, as if he wandered in some immeasurable distance.

"Ki?" he mumbled, and turned his face to search for her, but his eyes did not open.

She lifted the coverings and looked at his leg. Rindol had removed the useless bandagings. There was no bleeding. The gash gaped wide and raw amidst the swelling of his thigh. She lay a hand on it softly as if to cure him with a touch.

Vandien stirred and his hand moved to her breast. Startled, Ki jerked away. His eyes opened, and, though sunken in his face, seemed to laugh at her. The gentleness of the cuff she gave him made it almost a caress.

"Do you think of nothing else, even when you're poisoned?"

"Even when I'm dying. Besides, what's a man to do when a woman sends her hand creeping up his thigh?" He tried to laugh and groaned instead.

"You're not dying," Ki asserted without sympathy. "Where's Rindol? I have need of him."

Vandien nodded toward a curtained door. His eyes closed. Even as Ki turned toward the door, Rindol parted the hangings.

"Not a widow yet!" he greeted her cheerfully.

"We are but friends. But I do not expect to lose him. I

have questions, old man. Answer, but please do not chatter at me. How long do those poisoned by Dulath live?"

"It depends," the old man shrugged. "A child or a goat, seldom more than a day. But a man such as he may last, oh, four perhaps. Why, he has not even begun to arch yet. I remember one fellow, took close to a week. . . ."

"Enough! Dulath has laid her eggs and fed. How soon before he digs his next pit?" Ki scowled as she found herself using the mixed pronouns of the old man.

"That too depends. The villagers will burn the pit tomorrow, to keep the eggs from hatching. One god is enough, it seems. Dulath will wait a day, at most two, before digging again. But do not fret; there will be a pit for your man when he goes. . . ."

Ki was hard put to refrain from striking him. Instead she made an abrupt gesture for silence.

"I'll sleep, then, for a while. Rindol, might I buy a goat from you?"

"It depends," the old man began shrewdly. Then, marking the look Ki gave him, he became direct. "Twenty dru."

Ki hefted the purse at her belt, frowning.

"Five dru. And this ring," she pulled it from her hand, "for the goat. Now I sleep."

Ki slapped the ring and coins into his hand before he could object. Then she went out the door, to return with her bedding. She dumped it on the floor next to Vandien. He stirred slightly and opened his eyes.

"Ki, you owe me a horse."

"Shut up," said Ki, without malice, and went to unfastening her boots.

Vandien awoke to the dim light of dawn coming in the open door. A gust of wind carried in a few flakes of snow, and the pocked old man. Rindol shuffled across the room, and tumbled an armful of wood to the hearth.

"You be awake!" he informed Vandien. Rindol ran a pale tongue over his remaining teeth, and leaned unpleasantly close over Vandien. "How does the leg feel?"

"It doesn't." Vandien was appalled at the weakness of his own voice. Yesterday he would have sworn that no man could feel worse than he did. Today he knew better. Once, during the night, he had awakened, and turned his eyes down to his wound. He would not look again. Surely that blackening leg, so immensely swollen it resembled a rotting log, could not be his. Surely Fate would not visit this upon Vandien, her favored child. Surely it could not be himself lying here in a madman's hut, watching his body rot away from him.

Rindol looked about cautiously, then leaned his whiskery face closer. "I have Waters of Kiev. It would give you respite. Why should you not slip away in the memories of love thrusts and swordplay? When you died, you wouldn't even know it!"

"No." Vandien wished he didn't have to speak. Why couldn't the old wretch leave him alone?

"So says the woman. But a poor wife she is to you, sir! Does she sew a shroud or make you death song? No! She sits outside and makes pot meat of a goat!"

"What?" Vandien struggled to understand, his mind slipping.

"Aye! She squats in the snow, to skin and bone a goat. What wife thinks of filling her stomach when her husband is dying? I'd beat her for you myself, were I a younger man!"

"Not wife. Friend. Go away." Vandien tried to turn his face away. He couldn't.

"She will buy no Waters of Kiev for you! Yet she finds coins to buy a goat. Still, I would not see you suffer. You wear a ring, sir. A simple one, true, but I am a man of charity. Give it me, and the Waters of Kiev are yours. Waters of peace, of wondrous dreams, of youth, remembered with the clarity of each passing moment! Waters of Kiev, to ease your passing. What say you?"

"Vab freeze you," muttered Vandien, and sank into darkness.

A thin smoke rose from Dulath's pit. The smells of roasting meat would have been appetizing, had Ki not known what meats were roasting. A small group of villagers kept vigil over their smoldering relatives. Ki and Sigurd paused.

"What do you seek, woman?" asked one.

"The new pit of Dulath. A man is dying." Ki shuddered inwardly at the implications the villagers would give her words.

"Farther up the pass where it is narrowed by a slide. She has dug there, so none may pass unless they pay her toll. Praise Dulath! He cares for our dead! They live in her!"

Ki set her heels to Sigurd and cantered past. She did not trust her tongue to reply.

She found the pit fresh and empty. Her knowing eyes could see the marks of the many scrabbling legs that had dug it. In the bottom there bristled a profusion of the spikes. This pit Dulath had not covered, trusting to its location.

It was a barren area; nothing but the wall of the pass and the jumble of loose stone. Ki led Sigurd behind a tangle of boulders and settled to her watching. Now time might betray her. For wait she must, to be sure her gift to Dulath would be on the top of the pile, to be certain he would eat of it and not merely choose it for eggs. How long before Dulath would return to feed? For Vandien's sake, she hoped it would be soon.

Ki was still crouching among the boulders and snow when the colors of the day faded. By twilight, what was not black was gray. There had been but one visitor to the pit, some petty official of the village who had unceremoniously tumbled in the rags and bones of a beggar. He had not seen Ki.

The wind was rising. Ki pulled her cloak tighter. The wind stealthily ran icy fingers up her back. Ki's legs ached from crouching. But she needed the cold. If she was to succeed, her bundles must remain tightly frozen until she used them.

The sound could have been the rattle of small stones stirred by the wind. But Ki knew what it was. On stiff legs she stumbled to the edge of the pit with her bundles. From each she took a roll of goat meat tied with soft twine. She tossed them gently into the pit so that they landed atop the bony body. Surely Dulath would choose them for his meal. Ki was gambling Vandien's life on it.

She had scarcely regained her hiding place before Dulath came into view. Ki lit no torch; she would risk no chance of disturbing him before he fed. Dulath scuttled out of the snowy hills, pale creature, native of some far world. He moved through the moonlight on his clicking legs, undulating around boulders. He flowed into the pit.

For one chill moment, Ki knew remorse. This was no creature of evil, no demon or god. It was only a beast, following the dictates of its instincts. It alone of its kind remained in this perpetually frozen pass, seeking only to feed and reproduce in its own way. Whence it had come from Ki would never know. Of its beginnings, none would ever speak. Its end would be all she could witness. Then she heard the crisping sound of its feeding. Vandien came to mind. The poison had overwhelmed the left side of his body. His sword arm lay motionless and swollen on the bed skins. A desperate sleep possessed him, seeming to exhaust him more than the most frantic bout of sword. Which of these two would she choose to live? Remorse died within her, replaced by a cold watchfulness. Her chance would be brief; she must not miss it.

The feeding sounds ceased. Now Dulath would be implanting her eggs in the frozen corpse. Ki sent up a prayer, to what god she hardly knew, that Dulath had consumed the parcels of meat. Now would come another waiting. How long would Dulath remain guarding her nest? And how long would it be before Dulath's body heat freed the gifts Ki had worked into the meat?

She had learned from the Pelashi, a woefully poor tribe of the Northern Stretches. They subsisted by trapping food and hides. Each animal furnished the means to capture the next. The supple bones of each were saved, bent and tied in an arch, and frozen. The ends were sharpened. Once frozen, the ties that held the bone could be removed, and the bone buried in a chunk of meat. Left on a game path or near a den, the frozen chunks of meat with their hidden bones were swallowed up by the predator. The heat of the animal's body did the rest. As the bones thawed they straightened, piercing the animal from within.

There were times when it did not work. If the animal chewed the meat, the bones were broken or discarded. But Ki could not afford to consider that chance; Vandien would die if Dulath refused the bones. Dulath must swallow the bones whole. Ki willed it.

There was a scrabbling from the pit. Dulath came bounding over the edge, arching and twisting in an effort to dislodge the bones within. Again Ki felt rather than heard his high scream. He scuttled into darkness.

Ki followed hastily. She must be close when be died, to harvest the blood. Thonged about her neck was the squat vessel with its tight stopper.

She followed the sounds of his flight. She caught a glimpse of him dodging crazily among the scattered boulders of the slide. Ki drew Vandien's rapier as she ran. She could not let Dulath go far. Once she had the blood, she must make all haste to Rindol's. Ki scrambled through the loose stone.

Dulath reared up! From behind a boulder he rose to meet her. A pincer darted at her face. Ki leaped back as it snicked through a fold of her heavy cloak. The rapier's blade flashed through the pincer. But tonight Dulath was in pain. He would not flee. Two new pincers rose to challenge her blade. Ki parried the thrust of one, but did not sever it. The other seized a fold of her cloak and drew her nearer. She struck at it, severing it at a joint. But two other pincers had already risen to replace it. She felt her cloak seized in two, then three places. As swiftly as she struck the claws away, others seized her.

The claws gave a sudden twitch, jerking her onto her knees. She tried to catch herself on one hand, gripping her rapier with the other. She skidded over frozen ground to find herself under the pale body of Dulath.

The parrot beak gaped at her, snapped. Ki twisted aside, struck upward with her blade. But the claws retained their grip on her cloak and limited her movements. She saw the underbody of Dulath loom, heard the snap of his beak. A fold of her jerkin ripped away.

Panic came to her aid. With a strength not her own, she tore her arm free from her crippling cloak. She jabbed deep and tore through the bulging underbody. Ki pulled her rapier free of tangling entrails and stabbed again. Dulath's pincers clattered together as he screamed piercingly. Blood rained down upon Ki.

Ki jabbed up again, to keep the pale body from settling upon her in death. With her free hand she tore loose the vessel, pulled the stopper with her teeth. She waved it frantically to catch the wildly spattering blood. Ki had expected it to be red and warm. It was a creamy white and hot enough to scald her. A gout of it spashed her hand and she felt the vessel grow heavy.

A final jabbing slash lifted Dulath's body high. Ki butted her way through a wall of spiny legs. A single flying pincer snatched a lock of hair from her head. She had no time for pain. Vessel clutched in one hand, rapier in the other, Ki raced for her horse.

Sigurd snorted at the foul smell as Ki threw herself on his back. That he kept his footing coming down out of the boulders was to his credit alone. Ki gave him no directions except her battering heels. Sigurd's great feathered hooves struck sparks from stones. Behind the scrabbling of pincers faded. Sigurd's hooves beating on snow and stone and the hammering of Ki's heart filled her ears.

There were the lights of the cottage, its dark shape, and finally its door. Sigurd halted after he realized Ki had left his back. He sent a rebuking whinny after her. Why was he being treated so ill? But the slam of the door was his only answer.

The poison had begun its work on Vandien's muscles. His heels and head were attempting to meet behind his back. Vandien's eyes stared into hell. Rindol bent over him, tugging at the ring on his unresisting hand. A clear flask with water of the palest rose rested on the table.

Then Rindol was flung aside, to crash against the table and send precious Waters of Kiev trickling down cracks in the floor. Vandien's dark eyes did not change as Ki bent over him.

Ki pulled the stopper from her flask, held it to his mouth, only to discover that the muscles of his jaw were no longer his to control. Madness came into her green eyes as she pressed the hinge of his jaw between her thumbs. Squeezing forced his mouth to open. She shoved gloved fingers between his teeth to hold it and dumped the contents of the flask down his throat. Vandien swallowed convulsively, choked, and swallowed again. Ki released him and stood up.

"That's all I can do, friend. Now we wait." With a venomous look at Rindol, she seated herself and took Vandien's swollen hand in hers.

Sigurd shook his head until his gray mane flew. Even staid Sigmund snorted restlessly. Ki glared impatiently at the inn door. Vandien emerged. The bruises on his jaw were fading, but his limp was still pronounced. He swung up onto the wagon seat next to Ki, grunting as he settled his stiff leg.

"It takes you that long to get a jug?" Ki asked acidly. She shook the reins and the grays stepped out.

"I paused to hear the sage words of a holy man," Vandien explained innocently. Ki glanced across at his wryly pursed mouth.

"What caught your religious fancy?"

"Certain villagers are disturbed. Their homes grow noisome with the dead. Dulath has been lax in his grave digging. They ask the holy man what they must do with their dead."

"And?" prodded Ki.

"He bids them take their dead as gifts and go to seek their god in the pass. He fears they may have displeased him. They plan to seek out his last pit and track him from there, bearing their fragrant offerings."

Ki shook the reins and the grays stepped up their pace. "I fear this village may not be a healthful place for us when Dulath is found, my friend."

"You could be right." For a moment they traveled in silence. Then Vandien rose slightly on the seat, to gesture at a horse trader leading his string of weary wares into the village.

"You do owe me a horse, Ki," he reminded her, nodding appreciatively at a bay.

"Go to hell, Vandien," Ki replied affably.

INTRODUCTION TO "THE UNICORN MASQUE"

by Ellen Kushner

There was so much I wanted to do when I wrote "The Unicorn Masque."

I wanted to continue a sequence of stories I'd begun in college, experimental pieces designed to play like a dolphin with the writers' tricks I'd been learning about in Edward Tayler's Shakespeare class, about symbol and metaphor, meaning, identity, and disguise.

I wanted to grapple with the impact that Dorothy Dunnett's *Lymond* chronicles were having on me: simultaneously loving and querying the fictional existence of a man so appealing that only a woman could have invented him. (I had my theory all worked out: only a woman writer knows what women find attractive, and thus only a woman can create the perfect romantic hero. He must possess the virtues we most value in ourselves: verbal quickness, acute sensitivity, and, of course, a killer clothing sense. Mr. Darcy has them, too, and Peter Wimsey.)

And I wanted to write a decent short story. Stories were hard for me, and still are: my mind doesn't run that way. As friends have pointed out, most of my stories read like chapters of a novel!

In the end, of course, it can all be blamed on Terri Windling, as much of modern mythic fantasy can. Terri and I met when I was a fantasy editor at Pocket Books, about to quit my job to write. Terri knew I had written a series of "Lazarus" stories. When she became the fantasy editor at Ace Books, she was hoping I'd connect the dots and turn them into a novel for her. To show good faith—and see if I really could make anything of them—I decided to tackle "The Unicorn Masque" first as a short story for her *Elsewhere* anthology series.

I sat down with my flawed first draft, and began to rewrite. I sweated. I suffered. I strained myself to the ends of my fledgling abilities, and nearly gave up. But Terri was waiting, and I didn't want to let her down. And when I finally held in my hands the work you now have in yours, I knew that I had actually done something close to what I wanted it to be.

This is the story that taught me one of a writer's most valuable lessons: that once a story leaves your hands, you no longer control it. When I wrote "The Unicorn Masque," I believed with all my heart that if a writer really does the job right, the reader will see and feel and even think exactly what the writer intends them to (give or take a comma). But shortly after this story was published, out of the blue I got a phone call from an older writer, a woman I really admired. "I loved your story," she told me; "it made me cry." It was all I could do to suppress my snort of amusement. Cry? But this was a comical story, rife with irony and human folly! What did she mean, cry?

And yet, and yet. This woman was no fool. And she had loved it. That was not something to argue about. Could it still be a good story, even if it had caused a feeling I hadn't intended?

You don't control the vertical and the horizontal, I now tell my writing students. *You and the reader are in a partnership. You give them your work, and they take it and make it their own.*

What do I think of the story now? Well, now I am roughly the age of that author when she made that kind phone call. And now I read the ending and it makes me want to cry. I've heard that the most enduring art can be enjoyed on different levels at different times in one's life. And I believe that, oddly enough, the arrogant, insecure young girl who wrote that story carried in her the seeds of the knowledge that I, a mature woman, possess, and put them into her work without really knowing or understanding the fruit that they would someday bear.

(*What about the other Lazarus stories?* the reader wants to know. Well, I pulled out and rewrote the next one, "The Hunt of the Unicorn," about fifteen years later for Peter S. Beagle's *Immortal Unicorns* anthology [and Terri picked it up for her *Year's Best Fantasy & Horror* collection for 1995]. What comes next, only the musty college notebooks at the bottom of my old desk drawer know . . . and my partner, Delia Sherman, who says I really need to pull them out and finish the novel someday!)

THE UNICORN MASQUE

by Ellen Kushner

I

A T the age of thirty-two, the queen was a dried rose. Although in her day she had numbered among the most valuable princesses on the marriage market, she had also been the most educated and the least beautiful. Contract after contract was dissolved before it could be consummated. Her younger sisters were married away to foreign powers, while she stayed at home to see her brother ascend the throne on their father's death, and descend it off the back of a rearing horse. The first five years of her reign had been marked by academic policies in council and dionysian splendors at court. It was in the dances, the gallant offerings of verse and song, that she found the attention and admiration denied her as a princess by all the marriage tokens courtesy had demanded be returned: the betrothal rings taken

from her young hands, the portraits of foreign princes
packed away.

After five years, though, the queen had begun to recon-
sider her state. Might the brilliant, posing revelry she delighted in be, not splendor, but merest frivolity? Frivolity
lead to weakness—indeed, the mirror of history held it up as
an early symptom of decay. It was true that she was surrounded by able counselors, but their wisdom would not live
forever. She suddenly saw that she had been wrong to rush
headlong into pleasure, leading the whole court with her as
it was prone to do. So she curtailed the late-night revels that
she might rise each morning at dawn to complete nine lines
of translation before breakfast. Her constant entourage of
beautiful, perfumed young men gave way to the ancient
learned.

The court was amazed to find its favorite pastimes pro-
hibited, its chiefest virtues in disgrace overnight. Its senior
members took it in stride; they had lived through the rapid
succession of three very different monarchs, and knew how
to adapt. The country kept running much as before; only the
fashions of whom to have to dinner changed: musicians were
out, scholars were in. Soon books were replacing trinkets in
the soft jeweled hands of courtiers. When the queen put off
the gaudy gowns that had always outshone her, her faithful
court appareled itself with like sobriety. On this summer's
royal progress through the north counties, though, the at-
mosphere relaxed as many of the younger set succumbed to
bright and fanciful dress once more: time enough for drab-
ness, they said, when school was called again in the fall.

Now the queen sat in her blue silk pavilion, shielded
from the rays of the summer sun by three billowing walls
weighted with her arms embroidered in gold. The fourth
side was looped back, open to what breezes stirred the air. It
was the queen's pleasure to keep this August's court on the
broad summer lawns of her great lords' houses; there her ret-
inue of nobles disported themselves at country pastimes
while she assessed her lands and displayed her traditional
right to beggar whom she chose in entertaining her. Despite
her recent strictures, she continued to permit her liege lords
to pay lavish tribute; they called her Divine Virgin, the

Queen of Field and Grove, and presented musical masques, harvest fruits and their well-groomed children to her. It was one of these she awaited now: childless Lord Andreas' chosen heir, a youth reared abroad and newly come home to his guardian's estates. He was bound to be green; she only hoped he would not stammer, or trip.

They knew that he would not. There was less of chance involved than anyone could imagine in the young gentleman about to be presented to Her Grace. His noble patron put a final fret in the sober white frills around his neck, and stepped back for a look at their creation.

"Perfect," he wheezed, staring frankly at the poised and slender figure gilded like a confection by the shaft of sun coming through the mullion panes of the manor house.

The young man returned the look with a smile intended to make the marrow of any one's bones run quicksilver, and said, "Your servant, sir." If not the smile, then surely the voice; perfect, perfect, infinitely precious with the sense that either could be shattered with the proper blow—if one were wise enough to see past the sterling perfection, and fool enough to want to destroy it.

"It is time," said the tall lean man who had always been there, standing in his dark robes amongst the shadows by the window. "He doesn't need to be fussed over, I've promised you that. And you've had all summer to admire him; now let be."

"Yes," breathed the fleshy lord, squeezing his fat, ringed fingers together in such sinister anticipation that the fair young man threw back his head and laughed. The tall man's eyes slid to his employer's, meeting unquenchable satisfaction there. This arrogance suited him: nothing had been left to chance.

He walked across the green lawns past the clusters of nobles knowing all eyes were on him. The silk of the pavilion fluttered fitfully in the hot summer air. Inside it the Queen sat riffling the pages of a book, formally oblivious to his approach until the bodyguard's pikes clashed together and apart to let the young man enter and kneel at her feet.

She was stunned at first by the blistering aureole over his bent head; then she realized that her eyes were only dazzled by the sun coming in the open tent-way, illuminating hair as light as mirrors.

He waited, head bowed before her, observing the court ways they had taught him with all their ancient formality, until he heard the queen say, "You are welcome." Then he raised his face to her.

The silk shaded her in a bath of color pure as cerulean moonlight. Slowly his eyes adjusted to distinguish her features. Her nose was sharp, her unpainted mouth small and pursed, like her father the king's. Narrow eyes of watery blue surveyed him under heavy half-moon lids. The jeweled clasps pinning her straight colorless hair flat on either side of her head only accentuated the harshness of her face. The only softness was in her cheeks, surprisingly full and round, and in the weakness of her chin. Against the sober, extravagant blue of her skirt, her pale hands, weighted with rings, restlessly toyed with a small book on her lap. Amber leather, stamped in gold. Quickly his eyes returned to his sovereign's face.

The queen caught her breath, then gave a small cough to cover it. She extended her hand for him to take; his limber fingers were smooth, with bones so fine she felt they might be hollow, like a bird's. The sculpted ridges of his lips touched the back of her hand, and then his eyes were again full on her.

"Sir, you are welcome," she said again; "I pray you rise and be seated."

He was modestly dressed in sober black, with white linen shirt ruffles crisp at wrist and throat. She watched him seat himself on a low stool across from her; his movements were lithe, his body as slender and tempered as wire.

He bore the queen's scrutiny calmly, with pride. He understood her expression, the cool reserve sheltering almost awed approval; understood and sympathized. He was flawless. Lord Pudge-Rings and his lean friend would have nothing but praise for him tonight.

"I am told," she said with pedantic formality, "that you spent many years abroad."

"Too many, madam, to please me." He smiled easily at her.

"You wished, then, to return?"

"Lady, it has been my dearest wish." Her eyes veiled slightly with reservation: she had a court full of men to spin her compliments. "Of course—" he laughed, his eyes dropping ruefully to his clasped hands "—one's dearest wish is always to go against one's elders, isn't it? They kept telling me how good it was for me to live abroad, so naturally I hated it." She nodded, thinking of all the hardships of duty. "My delicate health, they said, forbade travel, and my youth required stability." She could see them both, youth and recent illness, still in his face: the fine, girlish skin stretched over highbred bones that had not yet hardened into maturity. "So I studied." He looked at her intently with eyes so blue that for a moment they were all she saw in the pale sculptured face that held them like jewels in a setting. "I resolved to do as much as I could with whatever they gave me, so that—" He stopped abruptly, eyes downcast, his skin colored a delicate rose. "Forgive me, Majesty. It cannot be of interest to Your Grace what—"

"Study, sir," she said softly, "is always of greatest interest to me. Pray go on."

"I read, then," he said, equally softly. "And played the lute. When they told me it might not be healthy for me to be so much indoors, I took up riding, and the bow, and spent hours at sword practice." He shifted in his seat, an unconsciously graceful movement. If he could move that way with a foil in his hands, he must be good.

"Do you plan to continue your studies now?"

"If I can get the books here. I have been through my lord's library, it is woefully out of date. . . ."

She noticed his eyes fixed hungrily on her lap and started, clutching the forgotten volume as she did so. The queen smiled to realize what he had been staring at, and held up the leather-bound book for him to see. "You must look at this, then: my own presentation copy of Dunn's new work on the movement of the heavens. It is only just printed, few others will have it." She patted her skirt. "Come, sit beside me and we shall read it." He rose and settled again, like a dancer, at her feet. All she could see of him now was the light sweep of hair, the dent of a smile partly obscured by the arc of his cheek. "They are all coming to the city now," she said eagerly: "the men of science, the philosophers . . . I plan to lower the taxes on printing . . . Ah, the country is all very well for quiet and study, but you must come to my city for the books and the minds . . . Now, then; here is the Preface."

He fixed his eyes on the page, printed with great carved capitals and woodcut illustrations, and tried not to stray to the marginalia of her rounded fingertips and chewed-looking thumb . . . He knew nothing about Dunn, or books on the heavens. He must study now to seem informed, and to remember it perfectly. He must be perfect. There was still so much to be learned.

Candlelight glowed late into the night in one room of Lord Andreas' manor. The queen's "simple country supper," with its eight simultaneous courses, five wines and attending jugglers and minstrels, had been cleared away hours ago from the great hall, and the court had gone to its well-deserved rest in the various chambers appointed. Only in this small room were tapers lit, their flames polishing the wood-paneled walls to an amber gloss. Despite the warmth of the night heavy curtains were drawn across the windows. It was unlikely that anyone would come wandering down this far corridor and see the light under the door.

The lord of the manor and his lean confederate sat at a round, taper-studded table as the delicate blond man rehearsed to them the story of his day. He struck pose after pose without being aware of it, concluding with one arm outstretched, each finger precisely curled as though to allure his audience; "And so tomorrow I bid you a sweet farewell, and join the royal progress on its way back to court!"

A poised stillness followed. It was broken by the rhythmic thud of flesh against flesh: the fat man was clapping. When echoes began to fill the room, he stopped.

"Excellent," he said. "She'll take you."

"Oh, yes." The melodious voice almost crowed its well-bred triumph. "We are not to be parted, Her Grace and I."

"Perfect!" the lord wheezed. Infected by his enthusiasm,

the young man flourished a royal obeisance. "My humble duty to your lordship. And now, pardon me, gentlemen." The bow extended itself to the black-robed one. "I fear I must retire; the court rides out early tomorrow."

But the fat lord's hand snaked out before he could turn away. Fleshy, surprisingly strong fingers gripped his chin. "No. We do not pardon you."

He knew better than to flinch. He forced himself to meet the glinting, tiny eyes and say politely, "How may I serve your lordship?"

The hand tightened on his jaw. He could smell the remnants of dinner on the man's breath. "You will obey me," Lord Andreas said. "You do not leave until I dismiss you."

"Of course, sir." He made sure the light, willing smile touched his eyes as well as his mouth. But the strong fingers flung his face aside.

"Don't try your tricks on me!" his patron growled. He raised his velvet-clad arm again. The young man spun away from the blow, his hand automatically reaching for a dagger at his hip.

"You are unarmed," the tall man observed placidly from his seat at the table. "Excellent reflexes." He continued amicably, overriding the threat of violence as though he had not seen it, "I was admiring the bow you just made. Would you mind telling me where you learned it?"

The young man lowered his empty hands. A test, he thought; it had only been another test. Lord Andreas, silent now, had subsided into a chair. He steadied his breathing, and prepared the familiar answer. "Abroad, sir, I had tutors—"

"No." The lines of the man's lean face shifted to condescending mockery. "You learned it here, remember?"

"Don't tell me," the fat lord chimed in with interest, "that you're beginning to believe your own stories?"

He held his temper tightly in his clenched hands, letting its heat keep him from the chill of fear. "Forgive me," he said with icy good manners. "I didn't know—"

Their laughter pierced him, striking like hammer-blows inside his head.

"No," the lean man said. "Of course you didn't. You don't really believe all those stories you told the queen?"

"Of course not," he snapped. "I know what's real and what isn't."

"Of course you do." The man's long hand reached out to a taper set on the table near him. For a moment his fingers hovered over the flame as if about to bestow a benediction; then he pinched out the candle flame between two bony fingertips. "So do I." Smoke trailed up from the black wick, dissolving into darkness. "Who are you—really?"

He felt the world lunge away from him in a belly-wrench of blackness—he flung his hands forward, and caught the smooth wood of the table's edge.

"Oh, dear lord!" Lord Andreas' voice echoed in his head. "He's not going to faint, is he?"

"No, of course not." The man stood up, his black robes falling about him in folds of deeper blackness. The young man shrank from his approach. He did not want to be touched by anyone; he wanted only to be alone in perfect darkness, curled in upon himself like a seashell . . . But the other man was only holding out a chair to him. Mutely he sank into it.

"He's exhausted," the man said over his head to Andreas. "He wants to be alone."

"He'll be alone soon enough," Lord Andreas said. "Let him be quiet for once, and listen to me." He heaved his bulk up from the table, and stood before the younger man. "Give me your hand," Andreas told him. He held his right hand up and watched it tremble. "No," said his patron; "the other one." His left hand bore a gold signet ring. It seemed to sink into the flesh of Andreas' fingers as they handled it. The nobleman smiled grimly. "I had this made for you, the day you were born. Do you remember?"

He had to lick his lips before he could answer. "Yes."

"It is yours, and yours alone. Remember. Now," Lord Andreas said, settling back against the table. He kept the young man's hand in his. "I am going to give you the advice any patron would give his ward upon his departure for the royal court. But in your case, it is not mere words—it must be followed to the letter. Do you hear me?" He nodded. "First of all, you are not to touch wine or spirits on any account. It will be noted, but you ought to be enough of a practiced liar by now to be able to make up excuses to fit any occasion. You may gamble with dice or cards all you like—I don't care how much money you run through, but I expect you will win more than you lose. Dress well, but not above your station: you're not to compete with the great lords' sons. They will be impressed with your swordsmanship—they ought to be!" his patron snorted. "You're better than all of them. If one of them should pick a quarrel for the pleasure of dueling with you, for god's sake don't kill him. If you should be wounded, you know you don't have to worry; just keep it covered until people forget so they don't miss the scar." Andreas ran his thumb over the smooth skin of the narrow wrist, which last week had been torn by steel. "I think that's all . . . Oh, yes—the usual warning, lest the ward's head be turned to ingratitude by the vices and splendors of the court: *We made you, and we can unmake you.*" The heavy fingers met sharply around the young man's hand. "Only in this case, my dear, it is not an empty threat."

He pulled together his returning strength to smile coolly up at the nobleman. "A threat indeed. I don't even know how you made me; what precisely should I fear in being unmade? I'm a better swordsman than any of you could set against me, and soon I shall have the favor of the crown. If you d—"

The thin man interrupted the exchange with a mournful sigh. "Bravado," he said. "You must have your little gestures. Appropriate, but scarcely wise." He touched the candlewick with his bare finger, and the flame leaped again into being, illuminating the harsh face from below.

The room was still, even the candle flames rose without a flicker into the hot, dark air. The young man tasted sweat on his upper lip, but did not move to wipe it away. "Ask me," the lean man said. "Ask me again."

The silver-blue eyes fixed helplessly on their creator. "Who am I?"

"Yes . . ." Lord Andreas hissed in triumph, unable to restrain himself from joining in. "Who are you? Where did you come from? How did you gain all that expertise—with the sword, the lute, your own smooth muscles? You have no memory of any life but this—you might not even be human." The fair head jerked upward, and Andreas laughed. "Does that worry you? Does it, my dear?"

The thin man's eyes burned like pale agates. "You must be one of those people who never remember their dreams. But that doesn't mean you never had them. Dream again, my lovely; dream again before you question the gift I gave you. . . ."

The younger man wanted to profess his dislike of riddles, and his distrust of dreams. But the tall one rose, and his shadow rose with him, long and black climbing the wall, along with the candle flame that became all he could see, a pillar of light. Out of it five fingers stretched, long and cool and dark, and touched his eyes, and he dreamed again—the old dream:

He was a woman, alone in a bare room weeping. It lasted only a moment, not enough time to know his name or face, or the cause of the tears; only the misery of being trapped by her own wishes, the four walls no refuge from what lay outside them when she herself was the room and the walls and the kernel of weakness and misery that refused to stop dreaming—

His hands were hot with tears. He opened his eyes to a world of indecipherable light; blinked, and sorted out the nimbus of each separate candle, and the white slashes of the two men's faces.

"It's all right now," the lean man said with alarming tenderness.

His eyes fell to his own hands, clasped on his lap. The gold ring on his forefinger glowed in a setting of tears like crystal. He turned his hand to see the light strike fire first from the tiny silver moon on one side, then from the ruby that was the sun. . . . In the center between them an etched figure danced, alone, one arm flung up toward the sun.

"Lazarus Merridon." He looked up, not sure which of them had addressed him. "Lazarus the Beggar," said the lean man. "Lazarus the New-Risen. A bit of local mythology. *Sol Meridionale:* brought forth at noon. If you're ever knighted you can use it as your motto."

"You see," said the nobleman; "you cannot fail us."

Lazarus rose to his feet, an elegant figure made all the more exquisite by the lineaments of exhaustion. Despite it all his voice was still bell-toned and honey-sweet. "And when I come to court," he asked, "what am I to do, besides gain a knighthood?"

"Anything you please, my dear," they said. "You cannot fail us."

II

Against all previous expectation, the court's return to its seat in the capital that autumn was anything but dull. Little piles of silver were already passing from hand to jeweled hand, honoring strong speculation on the queen's newest study partner. No one could get quite near enough the strange beauty to discover the definite end of his charms; all that could be ascertained was that he did seem to understand whatever it was she was studying. He also proved to be a fine musician and an admirable dancer; and that was really what saved them all in the end from what had hitherto promised to be the most tedious winter in living memory—periods of mourning excepted, of course.

It was the autumn hunt that had suggested it to him, or possibly a bit of exotica from one of her books: after all, she couldn't possibly disapprove of a masque based on a classical theme, and the Hunt of the Unicorn was the subject of innumerable pages of commentary. Odds were ridiculously high that the masque would be approved even before he had played her any of the exquisite music he had composed, since the central role of the captivating Virgin could only be enacted by the court's own Sovereign Lady (*and only virgin*, the snigger went). No one even bothered to wager on who would be Unicorn, and so they lost an interesting gamble, for the composer demurred, and the role went to the young Earl Dumaine—a pretty enough dancer, but everyone knew she had tired of him last year.

On the night of the masque the great hall shone with a forest. Its pillars were wreathed in living greens, while flowery carpets hid the floor. The Master of Revels had outdone himself in fantastical trees of paper, canvas, wood, satin . . . he had wanted live birds, but it was suggested that they might interfere with the music, and possibly the dancers, so he had to make do with elaborate arrays of feathers, with little jeweled eyes peeping out between the leaves.

The sides of the room were thick with courtiers who were not in the performance. Rehearsals had been going on for weeks behind closed doors; except for the subject matter, occasional public bickerings that broke out over costumes and precedence, and the stray tune that would at times escape someone's lips, no one else knew anything about the contents of the masque. They waited in eager anticipation, admiring the decor. The musicians, splendidly decked out in silver and green, were already seated on a dais trimmed with ribbons and boughs. Among them was Lazarus Merridon, holding the lute he would play. His cool eyes swept the audience; then he nodded to the sackbut player, and the notes of an ornamented hunting-call sounded through the hall. Immediately the watching courtiers stopped their gossip-ridden fidgeting to fix their eyes on the center of the room.

First came the dance of the Lovers, then the dance of the Hunters. Then the queen stepped forth, robed in virgin white, her pale hair streaming loose about her, her light eyes bright with excitement. And the Unicorn pranced out, capered with his ivory horn, earning applause for his spectacular leaps, until he danced his way to the seated maiden and, on a burst of cymbals, laid his glowing horn in her lap. . . . Wildly enthused, the hunter-lords broke into unprogrammed shouting as they burst from the undergrowth to slay the unfortunate Earl, whose new silk doublet was actually slashed by a few of the spears. At the center of their dance of death sat the queen with hair unbound, her face flushed, her eyes glittering.

All the nimble of the court found themselves whirling and jumping to the final wild music of victory. The hall was streaked with spinning velvet, silk and satin, the sharp glints of blue, red, green, rainbow jewels flashing from hair and breast, belt and hat and dagger. . . .

Above them, on the musicians' dais, Lazarus Merridon sat playing the lute, and smiled. In his mind, weaving in and out through the wild and measured rhythms of strings and brass and timpani, sounded the voice of the nameless man: *It's all right now.*

Lord Thomas Berowne would have been one of the masquers, being the younger son of a duke and owning an admirable pair of legs himself; but he had only just returned from a foreign embassage on the day of the performance. In the course of the afternoon, however, he had acquired all the gossip to be had about its originator, and he watched the lutenist carefully that night. Lord Thomas had only a rudimentary, nobleman's knowledge of music, but he knew a great deal about courts; thus he was not surprised at the news that followed the next afternoon. Being an extremely well-liked young man, and well-connected, he got it before most others, and managed to be the first to seek out Lazarus Merridon to congratulate him on his success.

Lazarus Merridon smiled, noting the scatter of costly rings on the young lord's hands. "My lord is too generous, truly. Once the music was written, my part was all idleness, while others did the work."

Lord Thomas laughed, as though he'd made a joke. "Oh, the masque, of course! But your real achievement is the royal summons, you know."

Lazarus blinked. He had only just received the summons himself. God, what a place! "Her Majesty's retiring, yes," he said politely. "I shall be deeply honored to be in attendance tonight."

Lord Thomas smiled at this stiffness with cheerful amusement. "You're used to the ways of courts, I see. Never trust anyone who knows too much about you, or who acts too interested. But your own lines of information must not be very well set up yet: anyone here can tell you I'm harmless. My family's too rich to need to make trouble for anyone." His smile sought the musician's eyes. "But I didn't come to gossip with you about the noble Berownes. I only wanted to pass on a little advice." Lord Thomas took his arm, walking familiarly with him down the gallery. It was an easy, comfortable hold. Lazarus tolerated it as he tolerated everything else the court had dealt him. "You see . . ." the young lord leaned his head of brown curls against the golden one—"I thought someone might as well tell you now. You're quite clearly the next royal favorite, and no one grudges you that—" *Don't you?* Lazarus Merridon thought scornfully. "—but you can't expect it to last, handsome stranger. It never does. You haven't been here long, you haven't seen the rest of them come and go the way some of us have."

But, thought the stranger, *have any of you ever seen my like before, Lord Thomas?* A wry smile touched his lips; misinterpreting it Berowne said, "Don't even consider it. The last one who tried to touch her was sent off to command a troop in the Northern Wars, and hasn't been heard of since." There was a tone to his voice that had been lacking before, a sternness underlying the friendly banter. Lazarus glanced at him, but saw only bland amiableness on the round pleasant face. He suddenly wished for an excuse to leave, to escape the company of this friendly man and his enquiring eyes. "Oh, dear!" Lord Thomas cried in mock distress. "And have I managed to insult you, my silent Master Merridon?"

"Of course not, Lord Thomas."

They stopped before a large diamondpane window. "It would be unforgivably clumsy of me to insult a man I admire," said Berowne. The sun struck red lights off his hair as he stared out into the garden. "I do, you know. Ever since you joined us on Progress—"

"Were you—?" Lazarus began. There'd been so many of them then, each a name and a face and a title.

"Oh, you won't remember me," Thomas smiled easily, turning from the window; "I noticed you, though—there was a quietness about you, an otherness, as though you came from very far away . . . you were raised abroad, weren't you?"

For a moment his repertory of lies froze on his tongue. "Abroad, yes . . ." Then he recovered his aplomb, saying ruefully, "I didn't think it showed so much."

Thomas laughed. "Insulting you again, am I? No, it doesn't show, not now. Not that it matters," he added cheerfully. "If I could play and sing as you do, I wouldn't care if

I had two heads and a tail! But I haven't any talent, alas, only lots of expensive clothing. . . ."

Lazarus said, despite himself, "I'm not what—not as good as you think I am."

"Aren't you?" the nobleman asked seriously. "Then I should like to meet your master."

His fair skin gave him away. Thomas saw the flush bleed across the musician's face, and immediately was all contrition, nimbly complimenting him on his fashionably pale complexion and diverting the conversation to his unusual ring.

Lazarus' long slender fingers lay loosely in the other man's soft, well-cared-for ones while Thomas scrutinized the gold signet. "That's fine work. Sun, moon . . . is that a man or a woman there between them?"

"I don't know," he said softly

"It's nice." Lord Thomas smiled, releasing his hand. "You must come see my new paintings sometime; not now, though; you're about to be attacked by some new admirers." Surely enough, a pair of eager courtiers were making their purposeful way down gallery "I daren't stand between you and glory, my dear sir; I might get crushed. Master Merridon, good day—and good luck."

"My Lord." Lazarus bowed briefly, but was interrupted by a hand on his arm. *"Thomas,"* the nobleman smiled. "If you think you can bring yourself to say it."

"Good day, Thomas." For an instant Lazarus met his eyes; then Berowne hurried off in the opposite direction as the two courtiers drew near.

He was relieved when evening came and he could withdraw from public attention to dress for the Retiring.

He arrived at the queen's apartments to find her sitting primly in her blue velvet chair, modestly wrapped in quilted satin and attending ladies. At the door he bowed, and again as he was bidden to enter; a third time before he approached, then he knelt to kiss her hand. When he rose, one of her women went back to brushing out her hair. It was long and fine, and clung to the brush like strands of cobweb. "Good evening, Lazarus," said the queen. She ignored the ministrations, smiling up at him with her pale, weak eyes. "Oh, please sit—there, in that chair; we're not so formal here at close of day. It is a time when I like the company of my friends."

He marveled at the thinness of her voice: one of the world's most powerful women, and she seemed as timid and brittle as a green girl. The fingers of one hand toyed with a golden tassel on her robe. Lazarus answered, "I am honored to be counted among them, Madam."

She leaned a little forward to focus her weak eyes on his face. "You *are* my friend. Your sweet voice and gentle music have lent grace to our court, and our studies together have given me great pleasure. Now I am able to give something to you." A small box was placed in her waiting hand. At a gesture from the queen he knelt before her. She lifted from the box a golden jewel glinting with gemstones, dripping with pearls. It was a unicorn, hung on a golden chain that splashed like water when she raised it. "Wear this for me," the queen said gravely, "in token of our friendship." He bent his head, and felt the heavy chain settle on his neck, weighting his shoulders. It was a princely gift.

Impulsively he twisted from his own finger a thin gold band set with a small ruby. "Madam, I have nothing so fine to offer in return. But if friendship will be content with tokens . . ."

The queen only stared at him.

"Have I offended, Madam?"

"No," she stammered; "no. It is a pretty ring. I—thank you." But still she held it in her hand, as though she feared it might break. Gently then he rose, and knelt down at her side, lifting her blue-veined hand to slip his ring onto her forefinger. "There." He smiled up into her face, his eyes deepened to summer-sky blue in the candlelight. "Now I am ever at your Grace's hand."

When she blinked bright drops stood on her short colorless lashes. "Thank you." She swallowed.

A lady murmured something about retiring. "Yes," said the queen, her voice still thin, "it is late."

Lazarus Merridon rose and bowed. "Then good night, Majesty"

"Good night." As he backed from the Presence, she recollected herself. "Oh—Lazarus. You will come tomorrow night, please—and bring your lute."

The court's attentions were, if anything, worse the second day. On the fourth and fifth they slacked off; those who desired to make their interest known to him had done so, and now they waited to see whether he were truly in. He was, and the seventh day brought him no rest at all from the favor-seekers, and, worse yet, people with long-term goals trying to convince him that they were his friends. He sought refuge in his own rooms with orders to his servant to admit no one, and slept, deep muffled sleep with no dreams. Waking, he would sort through and return most of the gifts the courtiers had left, and dress for those dinners he could not avoid without seeming churlish. He dressed soberly, in tribute to his rank and to the queen's current tastes; the only gaudy thing about him was the unicorn jewel, which had been designed for show and not for taste.

He could, of course, do nothing for them but be graceful and witty at their tables, favoring them with what prestige his presence lent. The queen did not summon him to talk of court positions; she spoke of books and music and, recently, of the fears she harbored: of assassination, of her two sisters, married abroad to kings. "They never liked me—but how they would like my throne. . . . My people love me, I know they do: they cheer as I pass by. But my younger sister always was a schemer—she seeks to suborn our loyal subjects to treason, for if I die her son inherits the throne. . . . she has spies, Lazarus. . . ." Then he would play the lute to her, as she lay back on many pillows in the great velvet bed of state, until she fell asleep, and her silent ladies blew the candles out.

He watched sourly for Thomas Berowne to come along with the rest of them, with more of his good advice and his friendly eyes; but the Duke's son was not among them—Too rich to need a favorite's favor, Lazarus told himself. When he encountered Lord Thomas about the palace, the young man only smiled pleasantly at him, and passed on.

The queen was more than usually melancholy, and did not wish to speak, so he sat and played to her while her ladies brushed and braided her hair for the night. She fretted under their care, turning her head so that her colorless hair escaped in cloud-snake wisps and had to be rebrushed, until she shook it out entirely and snapped to the hovering hands, "Be gone! I can attend myself."

The memories of the only other quarrels he had known made Lazarus nervous of this one; he kept his eyes on his fingers, his presence confined to the humming strings of the lute. Her ladies curtsied. They glanced at the gentleman from long, lowered eyes, waiting for him to stop playing and take his leave. He remained oblivious to their looks, though not to the tension they engendered; at last he looked up, only to hear the queen command, "Let him stay." She raised her voice again in the face of their dumb opposition, but the effect was childish, not regal: "Let him stay, I say! He is a gentleman of my court, he will not harm his sovereign. There is a guard outside the door," she added dryly; "I shall scream if I need help."

He slid his conspirator's grin to her amid the flutter of skirts, good nights and trailing sleeves. When the great door closed on the last of them he said, "Your grace is a very Tartar tonight."

"I meant to be," she pouted. "Let them learn to obey me. I am their queen."

"And mine," he smiled, taking the hand that bore his ring. "How shall I serve my sovereign tonight?"

She pressed his hand, or gripped it, then released it just as suddenly and rose to walk about the dark and lofty room. Tall tapers threw her shadows long against the walls; they crossed and recrossed each other so that the pacing lady peopled the room with smoky dancers. Lazarus waited for her to speak, but she only moved from object to object, picking things up and putting them down, a hairbrush, a mirror. . . . Her long robe of claret velvet dragged sluggishly after her across the polished floor. He picked some random liquid notes from his instrument, but the queen whirled with a tiny cry. He put the lute down gently, knowing that no matter how awkward he felt, his movements would still express nothing but fluid ease. Watching him seemed to calm her. She came and stood at his side, looking down at the soft-fringed head made golden by candlelight, and said softly, "Lazarus."

He looked up. Her eyes were full of tears. The queen's sad gaze fell to where her small fingers twisted his ring around and around on her left hand. "Will you serve me in all things?"

"In all things, Highness."

She shook her head, lips pressed tight. "Not in duty, please, not now." He put up one hand to stop her nervous twisting of the ring, and was amazed at the fierceness of her grip. He asked. "In friendship, then?"

She nodded, full-eyed, not trusting herself to speak.

"In friendship I will serve you all I can." He took both her hands, and rose to draw her gently toward her chair. "Sit down, now, and tell me what I can do." But with a little cry she broke his grasp and clasped him to her.

Under his chin he smelt the clean smell of her hair. He put his arms around her to ease her trembling, but it didn't seem to help. Her hands were little fists, clenched into the small of his back. He felt a tickle of whispered breath close to his neck: "Please. Don't laugh."

"No, Highness."

She drew back enough to view his face fully. "Oh," the queen said softly. He didn't move. Her shaking fingers came up; their tips brushed his lips, then traced the sculpted ridges carefully so that he smiled, and they ran over the new shape as well. She returned him a dewy smile; then slowly, somberly she raised her face, her weak eyes still wide. When her mouth touched his, her body shuddered. He kept his still, although he wanted to smile under her lips' rigidness. His own were soft, pliant . . . she felt them so and slowly let her own relax to meld with them. But when his mouth responded to hers she stiffened, and would have pulled away if he had not stilled it again.

Now her hand traced his jaw, dreamily curled the shell of his ear, parted and smoothed his feather-light hair. One fingertip lightly brushed a delicately-veined eyelid, and arced along the slender wing of brow above it. His eyes were closed. Stiff-fingered, she untied his collar to rest her touch on the base of his throat, where the pulse beat against translucent skin between the rising muscles.

The jet buttons of his doublet gave her some trouble; but when he lifted his arms to assist, her fingers froze until they withdrew. She unlaced his outer sheeves, and he felt the cool linen of his shirt hanging loose about his arms.

He was pure white and golden in the candlelight, almost too perfect to be real: gilded ivory, a confection . . . but his chest rose and fell with his breathing, deep and not so regular as it had been, the only sound in the still room. She kissed the soft mouth again, forcing it taut against her lips. She pressed her body to his, and her throat made a sound. "Highness," his quiet voice said into her hair, "shall I?"

Soft skin brushed her cheek as she nodded. Soon she stood with her feet in a pool of crimson velvet, and her white gown floated up over her head . . . He lifted her at last in his strong slender arms, without words marveling at her frailty, at his own infinite knowledge of her desires and his tender exaltation in them. He moved to her will, and his own thoughts made no difference as the unicorn jewel swung through the air, glittering in the candle flames.

Lord Thomas Berowne strolled down a long sunlit gallery of the palace, on his way to the library. In one hand he carried a scarlet rose: no matter the season, Berowne's wealth and desire kept him surrounded by flowers. Courtiers were clustered up and down the gallery in bunches, their voices hushed and excited. As he passed them people looked up, then resumed their conversation. Thomas lifted the delicate blossom to his nose. Suddenly there was silence at the other end of the hallway. It rippled out before the slender man approaching like some courtly spring tide. Lazarus Merridon walked with a breathtakingly careless grace, courteously answering isolated greetings, ignoring the buzz that grew behind him as he passed. When he reached Lord Thomas, though, he hesitated. The young lord smiled. "Congratulations," he said, and offered him the rose.

"I never thought," she said, lying in the curve of his arm in the dark, "that I would want to marry. Not once I was queen. And it doesn't matter that you are younger, and not of noble blood; I shall give you titles, and we will give my people an heir." She chuckled happily. "How my sister will be furious! There goes her hope of succession."

"You're not with child already!" he said, running his palm smoothly over her body.

She giggled. "No, silly man, how could I tell yet? But if we keep on like this, I will be. . . ."

The queen's chief lady was being rudely shaken. She peered through sleep-gummed lashes at the intruder, and made out the sharp, pale features of Master Lazarus Merridon, her lady's paramour.

"What time is it?"

"Midnight," he responded tersely. "Her Majesty's physician—you must fetch him at once!"

Lady Sophia pulled a dressing gown around her ample form; she was used to emergencies, and even to the ill manners of hysteria. "What is it?"

"I don't know!" He was dressed as scantily—as hastily— as decency would allow. "I don't know, she is in pain—"

"Probably a touch of bad meat," Lady Sophia said comfortably. "Put your clothes on, Master Merridon, and go back to your own bed; I'll see to her Grace's comfort."

But for days thereafter her Grace knew no comfort. It was rumored that her physicians suspected poison. All her food was tasted, and certain investigations made, to no effect. Lazarus remained in her chamber, to sit by her side and play the lute and hold her hand. After a time her pain subsided into weakness, and he came again at night to give her joy.

"Lazarus, if I die . . ."

"Shh, shh, you won't die, you're getting better." But two days later, she woke up screaming again.

"Lazarus." He looked up. Thomas Berowne's hand lay on his shoulder, his eyes full of concern. "Lazarus, you can't sit here before her door all night like a dog. Her Grace is asleep, they say she's resting comfortably. Come up to my rooms."

The eyes crinkled. "My dear father sent me a cask of old claret, I'd like you to help us empty it."

They had told him not to drink, Those Two. But what else had they done to him? What else had they told him? To hell with them and all their mysteries. Just once let him be—let him pretend to be a man like other men, and seek relief like others. Just once. He said, "I'll come."

Around Lord Thomas' polished table, faces were blurring. Lazarus Merridon dealt another round of cards. "Pentacles lead."

"Dammyou, Merridon," a lordling slurred, "you're as fresh as—a cucumber."

"I've been matching you cup for cup," said Lazarus mildly. "What do you bid?"

His head was quite clear. Alcohol, it seemed, had no effect on him. Winning a minor fortune from the cream of the junior nobility did only a little to console him.

"Merridon, put down your card!"

He was putting it down. It was down.

"Well, Merridon?"

What was their hurry?

"Go ahead, pick one."

"Lazarus," Thomas said sharply, "are you all right?"

Of course he was all right. He was fine.

"Lazarus?"

"I'm fine."

"No, you're pale."

"I'm perfectly all right," he said. Why were they all moving so quickly? He reached for his cup, watching the light gleaming on the ring on his hand, bright ruby claret at the bottom of the cup. . . . What was wrong with them all, were they nervous? Tom's mouth moved like hummingbird wings. "Hadn't you better lie down?"

"I am fine," he said. "Look at my hand—" he held it out steadily, "and look at yours."

Earl Dumaine sloshed some claret into his cup. "Keep drinking, then."

"No" Tom said quickly. "You'd better go. You're utterly white. My man will see you to your rooms."

*   *   *

Lazarus lay on his bed, wide-eyed, watching the carved canopy above him. There really was nothing wrong; only it had taken a long time, walking back. When he blinked the canopy went into darkness, then reappeared. This was not drunkenness, this was something else. Those Two, they must have known this would happen. Why had they not told him? Wryly he thought, they could hardly have been afraid he'd not believe them. What did they want? What did they want of him? Fear was forming, a dark, slow tide at the back of his mind. He would give it no room for advancement. Now . . . what, so far, had he done? The masque, where the court had danced to his music—not enough . . . Gifts, favors he had received—not enough . . . He had lain with the queen of course; but she wasn't pregnant, and he doubted that she ever would be, by him: the genius of his black-robed creator could only extend so far. Why would they want him with her, if not to get her with child? Did they think if he wed her, he would strive for their advancement?

The candle at his bedside had burned low. Numbly he realized that he had been thinking for over an hour. Too long. Am I dying? he thought suddenly. Am I poisoned? But none of the other cardplayers had been affected this way; they were just drunk. They might have drunk themselves into a stupor by now. He had heard that you could drink yourself to death. Drink could poison. But I feel fine, he thought, just slow. I cannot get drunk, I cannot be poisoned. . . .

He could not be poisoned. They had known this would happen, with wine, with any potent substance, and they had not told him. The queen was being poisoned, and he was immune. What poison had they taken together? But he had never reacted this way before. Of the poison they took together, he had never received his full share—It had come from him.

Lazarus Merridon turned slowly onto his side. It was ridiculous, a horrible notion. No one could do that, no one. It was unnatural, hideous, impossible. His candle flickered, guttered and went out. In the darkness he fell asleep.

"Master—" Lazarus jumped at the light touch on his arm.

"I wouldn't have woken you, sir, but my lord sent orders the message was to be delivered at once."

It was breaking dawn. He sat up in bed and took the packet his man offered, and broke open the crimson wax that bore Andreas' seal. Several pieces of gold fell into his lap. They had been enclosed in a note from his patron:

My dear boy—
Your timing is abominable. Desist at once, and have the decency to wait until after the marriage, or you will make things very difficult for us. Remember: we made you. Do not fail us.

He looked at the note without seeing it, jingling the gold his patron had sent in his other hand. . . . He had been right. Now there was nothing to do but to fail them.

The gold in his hand would see him out of the country; if he kept on the move he could live for nearly a year on it together with his winnings of last night; by then—God. His winnings. He had left them piled high on the table in Thomas Berowne's room.

Lazarus strode down the halls to Berowne's apartments. Light had just broken, only the palace servants were about. Lord Thomas' man protested that his master was not to be disturbed, but the pale gentleman brushed past him into the inner rooms.

Heavy curtains had been drawn over every possible source of light. Lazarus uncovered one window. He found the bed and pulled back its hangings. The curtain rings rattled on their rods, but the bed's occupant didn't stir.

"Thomas!"

Lord Thomas uncurled just enough to cast one eye up at his visitor. His head was rumpled and stubbled, and he stank of sour wine.

"Thomas, I need the money!"

"Who are you?" Lord Thomas managed to push out from some dimly-remembered area deep inside his throat.

"Lazarus Merridon; I need the money I won last night."

Thomas groaned, closed his eyes and listened to his head throb. "I put it somewhere. . . ."

Lazarus gripped his limp shoulder. "Please, Tom, it's important!"

"Where's the water?" Berowne croaked.

Lazarus cast about the room for it, and found an enameled pitcher and basin. Tom took a swig from the pitcher and poured the rest over his head. He rose reluctantly and limped over to a cabinet, returned to his bedside for the key, and finally presented Lazarus with a knotted linen handkerchief heavy with gold.

"Thank you."

"Not at all," grunted Lord Thomas, sinking back as far as the edge of the bed. "Always delighted to oblige." He pressed his fingers into his eyes. "Now, would you mind telling me why you are calling for such fantastic wealth at this hour of night?"

"It's morning." Lazarus paced up and down the dusky room, nervously tossing the bundle in his hand. "I must ride home at once," he lied. "There was an urgent message from my guardian—"

"Does the queen know?"

"No." He shrugged brusquely. "She'll be all right now."

Tom's mouth opened and closed. "Will she?" he said quietly.

The fierceness of his visitor nearly knocked him over. "Yes! Yes, she will—Tom, you must believe me." The fair man clutched at Berowne's hand.

"Lazarus." Thomas looked at him. "What am I going to tell her?"

The silvery eyes darkened with tears. "I don't know," Lazarus whispered. "Tell her—I could not help it." He lifted the unicorn medal on his chest. "I have it still. I will send it before I come again. Can you tell her that?"

Lord Thomas closed his eyes. "Anything. Anything you like."

"Thank you." Berowne only barely heard the whispered words as he fell back within the bedcurtains. It was early yet. . . . He never missed the fullblown rose plucked from one of his crystal vases, that the queen found beside her on the pillow when she woke.

INTRODUCTION TO "THE STUFF OF HEROES

by Esther M. Friesner

Has it really been almost twenty years since I wrote "The Stuff of Heroes"? Lord, I hope so. Otherwise, all the changes in my life since then never happened and I'm trapped in a bad episode of *Dallas*.

There was only one kid running around the house when I wrote it and now . . . well, there's still just one kid running around the house, but this one is our second-born because the particular tot running around the house lo those many years ago has grown up, graduated from college, gotten a job, moved out, and is currently running around the Big Apple. (Not New York City. He just likes to buy the occasional big apple from the local costermonger, place it on the ground, and run around it widdershins. Hey, he was an English major. That *does* things to a person.) It won't be long before the second kid heads off to college, too, and, we hope, eventual employment. Also we're in a different house now. And besides *that*—

Okay, you get the picture: Time has marched on. (Sometimes it stopped marching and did the Bunny Hop when it didn't think anyone was looking.)

Despite the intervening years I recall distinctly the matchless thrill of getting that first acceptance letter, to say nothing of the exhilaration of cashing that first check. I'm sure that these memories are unique to my own sweet self and that no other author anywhere ever had similar ones. And now let me sell you a bridge in Brooklyn.

So, how came all this to pass? To begin with, almost all of the elements required for that glorious First Sale moment were in place: As the football fans would phrase it, I'd had my game face on for ages, darling, simply *ages*, I knew I wanted to be a writer (despite never having been dropped on my head as a small child). I knew I wanted to be a *paid* writer (having acquired the bad habit of enjoying regular meals. Also due to having been raised by comparison-shopping wolves in Bloomingdale's). I knew I wanted to be a paid *fiction* writer (because anyone can get money for telling the truth, outside of the Congressional Record, that is). What I didn't know was how to get an editor to cooperate.

Perhaps this would be a good time to point out the fact that while I was trying to break into the glamorous and high-paying world of writing fantasy and science fiction, I had already gotten a couple of nonfiction sales under my belt. The first was to *Cats* magazine, a brief feature (with my own photos to illustrate it) on a feline named Annie who lived in our local library. The second was to *Brides* magazine, an article on how to survive the first year of marriage without killing all the people who will give you (read: "force down your throat with a plunger") advice.

But alas, my First Sale of science fiction, glorious science fiction, remained elusive. The worst part was, I was so dang *close!* At the time that I was pummeling on editorial doors, one of those dear and patient souls most often assaulted with my manuscripts was Mr. George Scithers, then editor of *Isaac Asimov's Science Fiction Magazine*. Mr. Scithers did not limit his rejection letters to the cool and distant "We regret that your story does not suit our needs. Best of luck placing it elsewhere." He actually returned manuscripts accompanied by reasons *why* the story just was not working for him. This took the form of a checklist featuring common flaws, faults, and outright gaffes like *Show, don't tell, A vignette is not a story*, and cautions against ending a tale with the only two people left alive on Earth after the Big Kablooie being named Adam and Eve. Alas, I did not keep any of the checklists and am only presenting these examples from memory.

I don't know whether every manuscript that came before him got this treatment. I might have received some form-letter rejections before I started getting the checklists; I can't recall for sure. In any case, the rejected stories were coming home with fewer and fewer errors checked off. Then there were some where Mr. Scithers took the time to write some comments in his own hand. I knew I was approaching that wondrous moment when there would be nothing left for him to check off on the list and nothing to write to me save *Here: Contract. Money.*

But I was approaching it *too* slowly to suit me. The hamster of Doubt nibbled relentlessly at the chewstick of Hope. (Apparently the checklist did not include *You call that a metaphor?!*) Would I ever succeed or was I condemned to be forever a day late and five cents a word short, the eternal also-ran, the plucky understudy in the big Broadway show whose star never has the decency to get food poisoning on opening night? Was there some sort of Secret Handshake after all, mastery of which would guarantee a sale?

I became firmly convinced that what I needed was a gimmick, something to set my work apart from all the rest. It was a very lucky thing that I did not act on this conviction unwisely. I have since heard tales of aspiring writers who, likewise certain that a gimmick is all it takes to break into the market, did things like submit manuscripts with "attachments" like tea bags, or packets of instant cocoa mix, or substances I blush to name, or even—ye heavens!—a bribe.

They say to write about what you know. Failing that, write about what you're obsessing over. How better to work out my ongoing frustration—in a legal and salubrious manner, I hasten to add—than by writing a story about another writer who has discovered the ultimate gimmick for getting her work published. Thus "The Stuff of Heroes" came to be.

I wrote it. I took care to avoid the prose pitfalls previously pointed out to me in past profitless projects (Now why do I think that Avoid Asinine Alliteration was one of them?). I sent it off to Mr. Scithers. I received a contract and a check. Upon opening it I did severe damage to our cat's mental health by shrieking with joy and to our house by doing the Published Author Polka.

I didn't care. I'd made it. All I'd ever wanted was for someone to buy *one* of my stories, just *one* was all I asked, only *one* eensy beensy little fiction sale and I would be forever content—

Now if only someone would buy my novel.

THE STUFF OF HEROES

by Esther M. Friesner

MARGARET poured herself another brandy and, impatient for inspiration, drummed her fingers on the terminal keyboard. It was her third brandy of the evening, but she rationalized her need for it. One brandy for tradition, one for nerves, and one because of that stinking bitch Agnes Frock. The thought of her arch rival enraged Margaret, the third brandy made her careless, and she slammed the snifter down too hard beside the keyboard. Slivers of glass flew, and drops of brandy wet the keys. She thought she smelled something starting to smolder, so with a hearty curse she unplugged the unit. She wasn't going to get any writing done tonight, anyway.

How could they? She still saw the surging crowd of wild-eyed women pressing around the little table where Frock the Gooey, Frock the Saccharine, Frock of the unspeakable rice-pudding heroes, sat autographing copies of her latest novel and first vivipac work, *Wilhelmina's Waltz*. It proved, Margaret thought, that not only did the public have no taste, but they were also as fickle a band of boobs as ever crawled.

Not even heartfelt inner bitterness could drown out the ring of the doorbell. It was rather late for callers. Margaret activated her patented Stopasin Antigrope belt unit just to be safe and, secure in her force-field-shielded virtue, opened the door.

He looked familiar, but how could someone so out-landishly gotten-up look familiar? He was well over six feet tall, strong-featured, wearing pants as tight as his open-collared shirt was loose. He clutched a square package to his hirsute chest. "Your publishers sent me," he announced, and promptly collapsed into tears.

Well, that explains it, Margaret reflected. In her too-short reign as undisputed Empress of Impresses, she had come to expect neither dress code nor moral code among members of the publishing world. Usually, however, Messrs Wang and Loop took pains to communicate with her through messengers who were more conventional and less lachrymose. "Won't you come in?" she said uneasily, and guided him to the settee nearest the Kleenex.

"How could they?" he wailed between sobs. Margaret poured him a brandy, which he downed with a masterful flourish.

"How could they what?" she asked.

"Stab me, but didn't I tell you, lass? *Samantha's Folly* has—has been—" his voice cracked, "—rejected."

So it's come to this, thought Margaret. I should have known it wasn't going to last forever. Damn it to hell, but I didn't think it was going to end so soon!

"They ran the vivipac through the scanner once—just once!" her anguished visitor went on, throwing one immac-ulately booted leg over the arm of the settee and running his ivory fingers through his tousled black curls. "And they used some pudgy chit of a secretary to test the hero. A sniveling brat still drooling mother's milk to test such a man! Such a—such an Apollo, such an Adonis!"

"I take it you liked him," remarked Margaret, vainly try-ing to remember what sort of hero she had whipped up to slake the voracious fantasies of her fans. *Samantha's Folly*?

Oh, yes. Oh, damn! That was the one she'd written when she knew her exclusive patent on vivipacs was due to expire. She had made her hero especially interesting, she thought—mercurial, sensitive yet forceful—in an effort to keep the fans with her even after hacks like Frock started horning in on the vivipac business.

After all, what sane woman would spend an evening wrapped in the wishy-washy embrace of one of Frock's chinless Regency lapdogs when instead she might purchase Margaret Harrow's latest vivipac novel and find herself consumed by the flaming passions and desires of a *real* man? Real, that is, while the novel lasted, but while it did, the viewer was also the doer. And the done to.

"Liked him?" her guest echoed. "*Liked* him?" Tears again rose to his dark, hypnotic eyes. "Bless you, girl, 'twas almost as much as I like—nay, love—you!"

He rose from the settee, and the vivipac cartridge fell from his lap. Secure in the protection of her Stopasin, Margaret bent to retrieve it. There was no way this loony could touch her, and she wasn't going to have the cartridge getting all dusty. Even if she was no longer the only author who could use the vivipac process, still she had invented it and was protective of it. She was no great writer of deathless prose, but as a tech designer with delusions of literary talent she stood alone.

Something was amiss. She looked at the cartridge. She shook it. "It's empty," she said, aghast.

"Yes," the reply rumbled like thunder from his broad, virile chest. "They didn't even have the courtesy to rewind me."

Margaret felt her knees melting. He swept her up in his arms before she hit the floor. The force field of her Stopasin had no effect on a man who was only a supremely perfect, totally tangible holographic entity.

As he bore her triumphantly off to the bedroom, she heard him say, "Don't worry, wench. Nothing's quite so cheering as curling up with a good book."

INTRODUCTION TO "THE ULFJARL'S STONE"

by Mickey Zucker Reichert

"The Ulfjarl's Stone" was published in *Dragon* magazine #141, January 1989. At the time of the sale, the fiction editor position for the magazine was changing. Patrick Price bought the story, Roger Moore discussed the details with me, and Barbara Young handled the contract and the final arrangements. Despite the revolving editors, or perhaps because of them, it was a wonderful experience for a first professional short story sale. This was before TSR, the publishers of *Dragon*, switched to their work-for-hire format.

The excitement was tempered by the arrival of the page proofs, when I discovered the last paragraph of the story was missing. It was an innocent mistake. It was the only writing on the last page, which somehow went missing. I remember making a desperate call from a telephone booth near the highway (I don't remember why I made the call from there, only that it had something to do with time constraints). I discussed the situation with Roger Moore, a remarkably kind and patient man given that I had to repeat myself about eighty-seven times over the noise of tractor trailers zooming past.

I never did get the last paragraph replaced; I was too new and shy at this to insist. I did, however, make some very special friendships that have lasted to this day. TSR is gone, subsumed by Wizards of the Coast, which was subsumed by Hasbro; but Roger and Barbara are still two of my favorite people.

The idea for "Ulfjarl" came from the same source as the five *Bifrost Guardians* novels, which I was working on at the same time (and which are now available in a two-book omnibus from DAW Books): Norse mythology. I loved Greek and Roman mythology as a child but had become tired of reading the same stories repeatedly. I came late to Norse mythology but fell hard for it. I've gone on to many other things, but the Norse myths still pervade much of my work.

This will be the first intact published version of "The Ulfjarl's Stone" with the last paragraph restored. I want to thank Steven Silver, John Helfers and Marty Greenberg for giving me this opportunity.

THE ULFJARL'S STONE

by Mickey Zucker Reichert

CRYSTALS of frozen breath clung to the fur which lined the hood of Anrad Snorrison's cloak. Wind beat against his face, and the tears it drove from his eyes hardened to ice on his cheeks. Swiftly, the rhythmical zigzag of his skis passed miles beneath him, but the bleak, white landscape never changed. He longed for the shelter the pines had provided scarcely half a day earlier. Now, the forest dwindled to a thin black line behind him, separating the snow fields from the cloudless sky.

Anrad knew venturing this close to Jotunheim was dangerous. In a winter so severe the elders claimed it as the first of three which would herald the battle of Ragnarok at the end of the world, his journey seemed sure suicide. Still, Anrad had not been offered a choice. He harbored little love for his father, but Snorri Hardhand was a chief and a great warrior, and he should not have to die in a sickbed. So, the village priest ordered Anrad to leave his father's side and seek the Ulfjarl's stone. Legends claimed its reading would bring new strength to the chieftain.

The ground trembled as a distant glacier marched toward the sea. Anrad felt its movement through feet which had grown wooden from cold. He longed to turn back and surrender to the smoky warmth of the longhouse. But if Anrad returned without finding and reading the runic stone he sought, he would prove himself a coward and condemn his father's soul to Hel, the final rest for men who died ravaged by illness rather than the glories of war.

As a youth, Anrad recalled his mother's tears while he hid behind a thick beam. His father paced angrily. "You make my son into a milksop. He must learn of Odin and the warrior's skill of *klima* as well as the White Christ and books. To control the stallions which wander my fief, his hands must be strong enough to hold their reins. You make him a weakling." His mother had struck his father a ringing blow across the face and had run from the room. His father's voice chased her. "Teach him that, and I'll be pleased."

Anrad sniffed the air, and the cold slid mucus down his throat. Blood filled his hairless cheeks. *I'll not give my father the satisfaction of proving me a coward. I'll read the runic stone, or I'll not return.*

Anrad's pack of provisions, ax, and bow weighed heavily on him. His fingertips burned, and his elk hide mittens stiffened from the cold. The sun paused, half hidden by the blank vista which stretched before him. This night would lay long and bitter across the land. He was ill provisioned for a night on the open ice.

Anrad set his ax and bow on the ice and slid the pack from his shoulder. Its leather flap broke free in his hand. Swearing, he groped through his hard mittens to remove the tent. Despite his efforts, the bundle of sealskin remained frozen to the pack. Anrad had never gone viking or traveled far from his father's garth, but he knew he could not survive the night without his tent and the lantern secured beneath it. *I won't allow myself to die in an attempt to save my father's worthless life.* In frustration, he thrashed the pack until he stood panting and sweat stung his eyes.

The warmth wrestling with the pack produced quickly

gave way to cold. With his woolen underclothing damp, Anrad knew he must find shelter soon or perish. Bitterness welled within him. He pressed his face into the palms of his mittens and cried. *Father was right. Anrad Snorrison is a craven.* He squeezed his hands against his eyes to force back the tears. The rigid leather raked his skin, and a frozen thong from the seam cut his cheek. He jerked his hands away. A drop of blood fell to the snow.

Anrad removed one of his mittens and reached through the cool dampness of his cloak. He grasped the knife at his belt and drew it from its sheath. Wind and particles of ice bit mercilessly into his bare hand while he studied the long, black blade. *There are quicker ways to die than freezing.* He reversed his grip on the knife and stood, motionless, watching a pale splotch of frostbite spread across his thumb.

A gust of wind struck Anrad from behind and drove him a step forward. His ski caught on the pack. He fell, driving his uncovered hand deep into the snow. The crust clawed at the frozen skin of his knuckles. The knife slid from his grip. Screaming with pain, he wrenched his hand from the snow, thrust it beneath his heavy robe, and forced it inside his breeks.

The warmth of his crotch brought new pain to his fingers. As he rolled helplessly in the snow, his skis seemed like shackles on his feet. Cruelly, the handle of the knife pressed into his cheek. Above the blade, the dark form of his pack loomed defiantly.

Anrad struggled with his mittened hand to push himself to his feet. His muscles responded sluggishly. The bitter metal of the knife clung to his face and peeled away painfully as he rose. He stood, hunched forward and teetering in the wind. He reached for the knife. His stiff mitt closed around its handle. Maddeningly, it fumbled in his grasp, but he managed to saw through the thongs which bound his feet to the skis and stagger onto the snow. The crust held beneath his weight, and he collapsed beside his ax.

Wearily, Anrad raised his knife and hacked at the rawhide lacings which closed the seams of his pack. He trembled from the cold as death drew nearer. Suddenly, panic seized him, and he flailed wildly with the blade. Chunks of rawhide fell away, but most of the pack clung tenaciously to its contents. He clawed at the mangled pack with both hands. One of the sides pulled free. He pried his tent loose and unrolled the stiff sealskin on the ice.

The cold conquered Anrad's mind as well as his body. He felt no joy or triumph as he lifted the lantern filled with frozen fat from his shredded pack, crawled across his ax and bow, and slithered between the layers of sealskin. Mechanically, he drew a fist-sized piece of flint from the pouch at his belt and struck it with the spine of his knife. The sparks alighted in the fat and died, unable to ignite the protruding cloth wick.

The drowsiness which crept into Anrad's mind seemed his only reality. Without the heat the lantern could provide, he harbored little hope of living through the night. As the cold numbed his remaining senses, thoughts of sleep replaced those of survival. The cold would disappear once he closed his eyes. He could light the lantern tomorrow. Anrad curled into a ball and surrendered to the chill darkness of the arctic night.

The haze of dream stirred through Anrad's mind. Disembodied, he watched as a great assemblage of Norsemen shouted down a speaker. Strong men with tangled manes of greasy, blond hair crashed swords against their shields. The women spat at the man before the crowd and turned away while children gathered stones. Revulsion at the crowd's treatment of the speaker shook Anrad. He drifted closer to the young man being harried by the crowd.

As Anrad approached, he recognized the speaker's tear-streaked face as his own. Gradually, the buildings and faces among the crowd became familiar. He entered the body which stood impotently before the mob. Anger, fear, and vulnerability wrenched at his soul. This was the gathering to hail him chief after his father's death, but his people would not have him. His spirit and his dream body both wept.

A stone from the crowd crashed against Anrad's side. Growling epithets, the armed men pressed forward and swept him from his feet. They tossed him about like a rag doll in the hands of an enraged child.

A sharp pain cut through Anrad's dream. Dizziness seized him as he tumbled through the air. He struck the ground with a bone-jarring impact. Snow crunched beneath heavy footfalls. *Only one of the white bears would travel on the open ice!* Anrad jolted awake as realization struck him a blow as savage as the cuff from the polar bear. He recalled stories he had heard as a child. One blow from a bear's paw could shatter a bull seal's skull and hurl the body from the water onto the ice. His father had told of two white bears who fought to the death; neither gave quarter. With most of its head torn away, the winner had crawled away to die.

The white bear snuffled and woofed as it circled Anrad's tent. A warm dampness spread through his breeks. He waited, praying to Christ the bear would leave him unmolested. The footfalls stopped near the edge of Anrad's tent. He wanted to burst through the sealskin and run, screaming, to the safety of his father's garth. But terror held him motionless, except for a trembling not entirely from cold.

Suddenly, the tent snapped taut and thrashed wildly. Anrad rolled from the opening and sprawled in the snow. He stared as the bear towered over him, clutching the tent in its jaws. The sealskins dangled half a man's height from the ground. Effortlessly, the beast shredded the tent.

Anrad ran. His boots broke through the snow's crust. He tripped, slid across the ice, and crashed into the remnants of his camp. His pack and bow spun away, but the ax caught beneath him and jerked him to a stop. The bear charged. Anrad snatched up the ax and fled.

The white bear traveled in an easy lope which belied its speed. Quickly, it closed the distance between them. The will to live tore open fear's grip on Anrad. His heart beat faster. Spinning, he raised his ax to meet the bear. Neither he nor the beast hesitated. The ax crashed into its face. Impact drove the weapon from Anrad's grip, and his world exploded into darkness.

*   *   *

Anrad awoke, warm for the first time since he had left his father's garth two days ago. Each breath came with great effort. A weight pinned his shoulder to the ice, and he could not roll far enough to free it. His discomfort seemed inconsequential, compensated by the warmth which enveloped him.

Gradually, the thought-dimming blanket of unconsciousness lifted from Anrad's mind. His situation became clear. The single blow from his ax had killed the bear, but the force of its charge carried the vast body forward and trapped Anrad beneath it. *Even after death, the beast is not vanquished.* Anrad held his breath and pushed until the muscles in his arms and legs burned. Hot blood swept his cheeks, and sparks swirled before his eyes. He exhaled, nearer to exhaustion than escape. He could not move the bear.

It might take days for the bear's carcass to freeze, but once it did, Anrad knew his death would follow. No fate could seem bleaker than helplessly awaiting one's own death. For the first time in Anrad's life, he felt sympathy for his father's illness. He thought he understood the desperation which forced Snorri Hardhand to allow the priest to send his only son on this hopeless mission. Any attempt to fight, no matter how feeble, took more courage than surrender.

Anrad braced his feet against the bear and pushed. The carcass remained immovable, but Anrad slid between the bear and the snow. He repositioned his feet and shoved again. Light penetrated the coarse fur which surrounded him. Hope spurred him on. After another push, his head emerged into the blinding pallor of arctic day. Wind stung his face and brought tears to his eyes. He wondered if survival was worth separating himself from the bear's warmth. A final kick slid him free.

The bear sprawled on the ice before Anrad. Alive, it had stood more than twice as tall as any man. Anrad's ax remained wedged in its skull. Pride for his kill brought an inner warmth and sense of worth he had never known. *Not even Snorri Hardhand can call me, Anrad Bearslayer, a coward!*

To Anrad Bearslayer, finding the Ulfjarl's stone no longer

seemed impossible. He cut strips of hide from the bear and fashioned new bindings for his skis. He pried his ax free, lashed the skis to his feet, and set out to complete his quest. No longer burdened by the heavy tent, Anrad traveled swiftly. Miles passed beneath his skis. At length, he came upon a pressure ridge which drew a jagged line of vertical ice across his path. Beyond it, black cliffs loomed above the fjord where the priest had told him to seek the Ulfjarl's stone.

When Anrad neared the ridge, he removed his skis and drew his ax. Methodically, he carved steps into the ice and climbed. As he inched toward the top, he thought of his father. The image of Snorri Hardhand lying in his deathbed stirred feelings of pity, but no love. Anrad could not respect a man who would wager his only son's life on an errand based on foolish superstition.

Anrad mounted the last step and stood atop the ridge. Only a narrow stretch of ice separated him from land. A triangular rock jutted from the ice at the base of the cliffs. *If God or the Norns graced me with luck, I've found the Ulfjarl's stone.*

Anrad retied the bindings on his skis and prepared for the final part of his journey. Anticipation lent strength to his legs. He glided across the ice to the monolith. A thin film of snow coated the Ulfjarl's stone and obscured the carvings beneath it. He drew his ax and meticulously scraped free every speck of ice before reading its inscription:

> *Ulfjarl went a-hunting*
> *aurochs in the highlands.*
> *Enemies and chieftains*
> *with a host surprised him.*
>
> *Mighty Ulfjarl stood alone*
> *fighting bitter foeman.*
> *Ax and shield and byrnie*
> *splintered all around him.*
>
> *Bravely our Ulfjarl died.*
> *The valkyries attend him.*

> *It is for his living kin*
> *to go out and avenge him.*
>
> *Stone cold will our eyes be*
> *when we refuse the weregild.*
> *Brands into their longhouse*
> *will not soon be forgotten.*
>
> *We tarry carving rune stone*
> *to make the world remember*
> *the vengeance of the yeomen*
> *who loved him as a brother.*

Anrad reread the poem in disbelief. He found no trace of the magic he sought to save his father. The song of Ulfjarl could not help Snorri Hardhand regain his health. Grim understanding seeped into Anrad's mind. *The priest and my father sent me away to die. They never believed a sniveling milksop could find the Ulfjarl's stone.* Frustration, betrayal, and rage writhed within him. *Like Ulfjarl's men, I must avenge myself. And vengeance requires I return to my father's garth.*

The fjord and the pressure ridge quickly disappeared behind Anrad. With the passing miles, his rage dwindled. He knew Snorri Hardhand was a fair man. If Anrad had been a son worthy of his father's attention, the chief could not have helped but love him.

Anrad's shadow stretched before him. After many hours, the remains of his last camp lay scattered before him. A white fox ran from Anrad, dragging the fat-filled lantern across the snow. Without heat from the lantern and, with his tent in shreds, he would be forced to travel through the night. He might still die because of his father's hopeless errand. New anger flared.

The sun dropped below the horizon. As Anrad pushed through the night, his thoughts turned from anger to despair to guilt and back to anger. His emotions seemed like a wheel to carry him across the snow and back to his home, its axle a question for his father: *Why did you try to kill me?*

When the first rays of dawn filtered through the pines,

the low buildings of Snorri Hardhand's stead squatted in the valley before Anrad. Wisps of smoke curled from the longhouse. The sight rekindled rage which sped Anrad's skis on the familiar trail. He skated toward the hall where his father lay.

When Anrad arrived, the priest pushed open the hidebound door. Closing the panel behind him, he approached Anrad. Anrad drew his ax and cut the bindings from his skis, the bear's blood still frozen in scarlet rivulets on the blade. Then Anrad met the priest.

A strand of moist, gray hair fell across the priest's wizened face. He started to speak, but Anrad cut him off. "You sent a boy north to die. I froze. I fought one of the great bears. I found your useless stone. I returned." His knuckles whitened around the ax haft. "Take me to my father before I brush the hair from your eyes, and most of your scalp with it."

The old priest turned and strode along a narrow trail toward the forest. "Your father would see you as well." He beckoned Anrad to follow. "You'll have use enough for your ax later."

Silently, the priest walked into the forest. Anrad trailed him, confused. His reception was not at all as he imagined it. The priest did not seem surprised at his return. He did not cringe from Anrad's bloody ax nor apologize. *And why did the priest lead me away from the longhouse?* When Anrad had left to seek the Ulfjarl's stone, his father could not sit without assistance. For Snorri Hardhand to walk in the woods, Anrad's quest must have brought success.

Anrad trudged after the priest, in awe of the magic he had worked. He tried to picture the Ulfjarl's stone and understand the eldritch craft which made it more than mere rock and words. Consumed by his own thoughts, he failed to notice the small cabin they approached. The priest stopped by its door.

Anrad stared as the old man pulled two large, triangular pieces of cloth from beneath his cloak. "Hel shoes?" *A condemned soul's only protection from Hel's eternal ice.* He reached for the shoes. "Father died? The stone . . ."

"Did its job," the priest finished. "Snorri Hardhand forbid anyone other than his son to bind the Hel shoes to his feet. If you never returned from the ice, he would share your fate." The priest continued. "You were right. We sent a boy to die on the ice. He did, and a man returned." The priest dropped to one knee. "And the Ulfjarl's stone made the chieftain strong. Hail Chief Anrad Icewalker!"

Snorri Hardhand's confidence in his only son overwhelmed Anrad. He fought back tears. *For once, I can make Father proud.* He hefted his ax. "Bearslayer, Anrad Bearslayer."

INTRODUCTION TO "RENDING DARK"

by Emma Bull

I was writing "Rending Dark" on an IBM Selectric at work whenever I could grab the time. Then I quit my job and lost the nice typewriter.

After hearing my complaints about how tough it was to get any writing done, Patricia Wrede, who was in my writers' group and had read the beginning of the story, said, "I'm away at work all day. Come over to my house in the afternoons and work on my computer. You can learn the word processing program by entering as much of the story as you have so far."

I went to Pat's, and found a blank disk waiting to receive my story. I fired up the computer and put the disk in.

It wasn't blank. Pat had already entered the several thousand words I'd given the group. I could start right in telling the rest of the story. She says it was because she was tired of having to wait for the ending. Thank you, Pat.

The beginning of this story is, well, awkward. I was trying to do too much too quickly, trying to make the characters look clever right off the mark, instead of letting the reader warm up to them.

But as I read it, I can see myself learning things as I go, figuring out how to solve narrative puzzles. I want to pat my younger self on the shoulder and say,

"There! See how useful limited third person point of view can be?" My younger self would have hated that. Especially since that would be followed by, "But you're slowing down the action with unnecessary dialogue attributions."

When I started writing "Rending Dark," it was sword and sorcery fantasy. Then a character swore. You can tell a lot about a culture from how people swear, as my courageous writing group, The Scribblies, pointed out. There's a whole ideology behind any swear word. What was the ideology behind "Mother of little pigs," and could I make it more consistent through the story?

Once I addressed the problem, I discovered I wasn't writing a fantasy. I was writing a science fiction story set on a lost colony world. Which wouldn't have been a bad thing . . . if I hadn't been writing it to submit to a fantasy anthology.

This is the real reason why your mom told you not to use swear words.

Sword and sorcery, for me, is still all about the Conan stories. I love that stuff. But even as I read them for the first time, I noticed certain sad tendencies in Conan's lifestyle. He was always alone. There was very little snappy dialogue (possibly because he didn't have anyone to talk to). And the food, in a word, sucked. Conan kept wandering into taverns and inns where there was nothing to eat but roast haunch of thing.

I'd swear I didn't do it on purpose, but this story seems to be a reaction to that. Now that I think of it, all my subsequent work has put a high value on chatty characters and food. And coffee. How did I miss coffee in this one?

Oh, and I'm still fascinated by stories about transformation, and about growing into your destiny.

RENDING DARK

by Emma Bull

MARYA tightened her reins and turned in the saddle, squinting against the snow thickening in the twilight air. She grinned at the short, cloak-muffled figure that rode up beside her. "You know, I thought I heard you swear just now."

Kit snorted. "I said, 'Mother of little pigs!' You promised me that Sallis was two days' ride from Lyle Valley. We are now two days' ride from Lyle Valley. And I am cold. And wet. And getting more of both. And I don't see a town."

Marya laughed. "Why did I ever call you Woodpecker? You scold like a jay."

"Marya, blast it, where's the town?"

"Over the next rise, oh ye of little patience. And if you'll be good, I'll buy the first round when we get there."

"And I'll buy the second and third as usual, so where does that get me?" Kit scowled.

"Oh, quite a way into a drunken carouse. Hallo, there!" Marya raised her left arm, pointing, and snow-reflected light slipped off the gleaming black of claw and tendon.

Below them, barely visible through the falling snow, gas lamps glowed like sparks in a feeble row.

"I'm never wrong," Marya said.

"I could remind you of that pack beast you bought in Hobarth."

"Everyone gets one free mistake."

"Motherlorn wretch! C'mon, let's go!"

Kit booted her mount's ribs, and surged downhill through the piling snow. But Marya hesitated. Had a shadow quaked under the boughs of the pines? She shook her head. *I'm tired. There isn't enough light to cast a shadow by.* The wind wailed behind her as she followed Kit down to Sallis town.

When she reached the gate, Kit was already there, cursing elegantly.

"So use the knocker," said Marya.

"I *have* used the knocker. Twice," Kit snapped and

yanked the rope again. The iron arm boomed against the wood.

The gatekeeper's look-see slid open. "What do you want?"

"*In,* dearie," Marya replied. "What do *you* want when you knock at gates, hmmmm?"

"It's late, and the weather's poor, and—"

"And that's all the more reason to let us in out of it," Kit snapped. "This must be one fine town, if you're afraid of two riders."

"I only meant to say—"

"Here, maybe this'll make you happy." Kit rode close to the look-see and pulled her cloak back, showing the red-and-blue of the Songsmith patch on her sleeve.

"Your pardon, Songsmith, I didn't—"

"Please, just the gate," said Kit, and Marya reflected, not for the first time, how remarkably well a trained performer could make a sigh heard. Ice cracked loudly as the bar was pulled back, and Marya and Kit trotted through.

The large, soft-spoken type, Marya decided upon seeing the gatekeeper. *My favorite.* She pushed back her hood and smiled down at him. "Thank you. And I apologize for my companion's sharp tongue."

Kit blinked and stared at her as the gatekeeper said, "No, no, it's for me to—"

"We've been riding all day, and the weather . . ."

He looked sympathetic. "Early for this," he said, kicking his boot toe through the powder. "The wolves are down from the ridge already, and there's stories of things. . . . It'll be a bad year, I think."

"It's been a bad year for the last half-dozen of them," Kit drawled.

Marya frowned at her, and smiled again at the gatekeeper. "We'd better find an inn, before she eats one of the natives. Is there one straight on?"

"There is only one. Left at the green-shingled house there—" he pointed, "—and down the lane some ways. It's Amali's Halt."

"Thanks. Um, when are you through here?"

"Hour and half-a-turn." He looked up at her.

"Come by when you're through. She'll probably sing something," Marya smiled and jerked her thumb at Kit. "And Give News, of course."

His smile was shy and charming. "I wouldn't miss it."

"Come on, Marya!" Kit called. "If I sit this animal much longer, I'll freeze to the saddle!" She had turned her mount and started down the street.

"Thank you again. Oh," said Marya, "something to get warm with." She drew her left arm out of her cloak at last, holding a coin.

The gatekeeper's face went slack as he stared at her left hand. Marya looked down at it herself, and tried to see it without familiarity: lean bone and tendon and long, curving, cruel claws, all black and shining, cupping the coin like a cage of black iron. Bitterness twisted in her stomach unexpectedly. She watched his face as she flexed the fingers, and saw terror in his eyes when the tap of a talon made the coin ring. He snapped his gaze up to her face. She stared back at him, solemn and silent. After a still moment, she tossed the coin to him. He made no move to catch it. They both watched as it made a little hole in the snow; then she turned her mount and rode down the street after Kit.

"Well," said Marya as she caught up to the Songsmith, "so much for my evening."

"Huh?"

She held up her left arm and wiggled the black fingers.

"It bothered him?"

"It bothered him."

"Creeping, superstitious, Motherlorn provincials." Kit sounded as if she were warming up to something. "Unwashed, unlettered, sheep-screwing, bear-buggering, backwoods—"

"Oh, pipe down," Marya interrupted. "You're only burned because you think if I can't get laid, you shouldn't either."

"That's not true!" Kit shrieked.

Marya grinned wickedly. "If I could get fish to take bait the way you do I could be a rich woman on the coast."

The gatekeeper's directions were good. The inn they

reached was an immaculate little place, and seemed to radiate welcome like heat from an iron stove.

"Bless us all," Kit sighed contentedly.

"I'll take 'em to the stable," Marya offered, swinging out of the saddle.

"You're a dear. I'll order you a wonderful dinner."

"Don't eat it all before I get there."

Kit made a face at her and disappeared into the inn.

Marya found the stable easily. It was clean and well-lit, and the coal-burning Fireproof in the harness room kept the biting edge off the temperature. She looked on approvingly as the stable hand unsaddled their mounts and rubbed them down.

"I'll bet you don't have much to do in weather like this," she commented.

"No'm," said the boy, and flashed her a smile before he bent to brush a long-haired fetlock. He ducked under the animal's belly and stood up. "But we're lively come summer."

"What's your name?"

"Gerry, mum." He looked up and grinned. "At your service." He swept her a road-show bow, the currycomb flourishing wildly with his arm.

"Good," Marya laughed. "If you can get the burrs out of that beastie's coat, that'll be service indeed."

Gerry grinned again and turned back to his work.

She watched him out of the corner of her eye while she wiped down her saddle. She was careful to keep her cloak draped over her left arm. At last she said, "You're very good with the animals. How did you learn so well, so young?"

A wistful smile flickered at his face. "My dad taught me. My dad's Evan Tentrees, and he's the best . . . was the . . . best . . ." Suddenly he turned his face away from her.

"Did I . . . say something dumb?"

His brown hair flurried with the force of his headshake.

"You're lucky," Marya continued. "I wouldn't recognize my dad if he kicked me."

"I . . . gotta get something." He bolted into the feed room. When he came back shortly, empty-handed, Marya looked a question. "Couldn't find it," he said, too loud.

A throttling silence followed. Marya broke it at last with,

"I'm sorry. I guess I did say something stupid. Want to tell me about it?"

He shook his head again, and Marya saw her mount flinch away from the force of the currycomb stroke. Then he said, "My dad was . . . killed."

"Umm." Marya felt as if she'd been holding her breath. "Recently?"

"Last week. He was up on the hills, hunting strays. They went out to look for him the next morning. He was . . . he was . . ."

She heard the quivering in his voice, and headed him off. "Was he caught in a storm?"

Gerry shook his head. "There was something . . . clawed him up, tore him. Something big."

"Wolf? Cat?"

"Bigger."

There's something familiar about this, Marya thought. She finished with the tack, wished Gerry a good evening, and hurried into the inn.

Kit waved furiously at her from a table by the dining room hearth. "Just wait 'til you see dinner!" she crowed, grinning.

"Food always lifts your spirits, Woodpecker. The only time you're ever civil is when dinner's imminent."

"Fingerfish in wine sauce, venison pie, baked squash and apples, new bread, greensprouts, and cider. Ah, here it comes!"

The innkeeper was a big woman, still flushed from supervising the kitchens. She set the tray down on the table and smiled at Marya. "I know what traveling in this kind of weather does to an appetite, dear, which I told your friend the Songsmith. Nobody goes hungry in Amali's Halt."

"I take it you're Amali?"

"That's me."

"Delighted to meet you."

"And your venison pie," Kit added.

Amali chuckled. "Eat it all, dears. And if you fancy it," she went on, suddenly shy, "we'd be pleased to have you in the taproom after."

Marya shot a look at Kit and found her smiling. "I think

we might do that," Kit said. "And if you wouldn't mind, I might even feel like singing a bit."

"It'd be an honor!" Amali beamed. "Enjoy your dinner."

Marya waited until Amali was out of earshot before she said, "Tsk. Another year of this and you'll be spoiled rotten."

"Not with you along to keep me in my place."

"A heavy responsibility."

"Shut up and eat."

Marya obediently forked a mouthful of squash and swallowed it before she went on. "Just heard an odd thing."

Kit looked up, then put her fork down. "That's your 'I think we ought to do something' voice. Spill it."

Marya told her about Gerry's father.

"Bear?" Kit said when she was done.

"That's what I thought, at first. But aren't you Carrying News from Lyle Valley about a bear in these hills?"

"Yeah. They killed one two weeks ago."

"That's what I thought. So, two bears in the same range of hills? And both out this late in the year?"

"Unlikely."

"Very. Then what *is* out there?" Marya stabbed a piece of pie for emphasis.

"How would I know? Look, I'm on my way to Samarty to pick up a manuscript for the Guild. On the way, I'm delivering news. I am not fighting dragons, rescuing golden-tressed idiots locked in towers, or knocking down windmills. What do you want, to organize a hunt?"

"Well . . . yes."

Kit leaned her chin in her palms and looked at her. "Marya Clawfinger, you're hopeless."

"No. Hopeful. You're using your 'I can't reason with her, so I'll have to give in' voice."

"We'll talk it over in the morning. Eat."

The guitar's last chord clung to the air in the taproom, making the listeners reluctant to drive it off with applause. Marya smiled as Kit lifted her head and blinked, as if coming out of a trance. The subtle cue touched off a storm of clapping. *Wonderful thing,* Marya reflected, *the symbiosis*

*between performer and audience. Is that instinct, or does
the Guild teach these things?*

Then Kit set the guitar aside and stood slowly up, and the
room plunged into silence. Everyone in the room had waited
for this, the moment when the Songsmith would Give News.
Marya leaned back to enjoy it.

"From the north and the east," Kit's voice reached out,
enfolding the room. "From silver-roofed Sandyn and the
Firehall I come. I am the voice and the bearer of the past.
What will you have of me?"

Kit's delivery warmed the traditional words. Someone in
the crowd shouted, "Lyle Valley!" and his neighbors murmured assent.

Kit nodded slowly and closed her eyes. The whole room
seemed to tip forward a little with expectation. Then, clear and
bright, tuneless and tuneful all at once, Kit began to chant:

> *Allysum Gredy bore a boy*
> *With the first snow of November.*
> *Ere the snow had come and gone again*
> *Pneumonia took old Francis Berne*
> *And balanced birth and dying.*

> *Etin Yama's grocery burned,*
> *And Etin blamed Jo Hurlisen.*
> *The council fined Jo three months' wage,*
> *And bid him quit cigars.*

> *Protecting flocks on Canwit slope,*
> *Rey Leyne and Winsey Wittemer*
> *Slew a winter-colored bear,*
> *But something still kills sheep and cows*
> *Along the southern ridge.*

> *Nil Sabek and Margrete Durenn*
> *Have sworn the Binding Promise,*
> *And Hary Lil, in his best boots*
> *Walks daily out with Mother Pent.*
> *Life, death, commerce, and love:*
> *Lyle Valley is well.*

The room hummed with talk when Kit finished—neighbors laughing and gossiping over the news. Marya smiled and waited for the next town to be called out, and for Kit to start again.

And the taproom door slammed open. "Hey!" somebody yelled, then stopped.

The boy in the doorway was the stablehand, Gerry; the young woman he was carrying was a blood-spattered stranger.

"Nan!" Amali cried. The tray in her hands hit the floor with a clang, and she ran to catch the woman around the waist. Marya elbowed her way to the door. Someone leaped out of a chair and pushed it toward Amali, who lowered Nan into it. "She's my daughter," Amali said wildly to Marya, who wondered why it mattered.

"Are you hurt?" Marya asked, finding the pulse in the blood-stained wrist, peering into the woman's eyes, noting evidence of shock. Nan shook her head.

"Get her closer to the stove and wrap a blanket around her," Marya ordered. "Give her mint tea or water. No alcohol."

"And then ask her what happened," said Kit, appearing out of the crowd at Marya's side.

"At the gate," Nan said, still breathing hard. "Cal. He's dead. And Jimy."

Marya heard a noise in the back of the room, a little cry.

"How?" Amali asked, her voice tight.

"Cal . . . Cal was opened up from neck to crotch. Just opened up. Jimy's throat . . . was ripped half away." Nan began to sob weakly.

Sudden motion made Marya look toward the door. Gerry had taken a pace into the room, and his lips still held a half-formed word. He clutched at the door frame, his gaze leaping around the room. Then he turned and darted out the door.

"One of you," Amali shouted, "hand me that blanket from—oh." She stared down at Marya with the blank look of panic. "Oh, no. Then someone—something—must have come through the gate."

"What? Why?"

"Cal's the gatekeeper."

"The . . . gatekeeper?" Marya whispered, and looked up, wide-eyed, at Kit. Kit reached out and gripped Marya's left shoulder. The singer's fingers were warm through her shirt, and the contact seemed to trickle strength into her.

"Let's go see." Marya heard her own voice like a grim bell in the silence.

Outside there were two sets of tracks through the drifted snow: Nan's, floundering wildly toward the inn; and another trail, straight and certain, pointing away, toward the gate. Marya scowled and crouched down for a better look, balancing her scabbarded blade across her knees. Then she swore.

The prints were of heelless boots, ridge-soled for good traction on damp and dirty floors, boots for a farmer or stablehand. . . .

"What is it?" Kit asked.

"Gerry," Marya said, dropping the name like a stone down a well. "He's after the thing that killed his father. Come on."

And they ran.

Marya drew her sword as she bounded through the snow. She heard Kit cursing, "Marya! Blast you into darkness, wait for me!" But she was afraid to slow her pace. The gate court was only a turn away. . . .

She made the turn—and stopped, her sword half-raised, dread and disbelief freezing her limbs. Gerry stood in the middle of the court. His face twisted with horror, he held a length of timber thrust out before him with both hands. He might have thought of it, moments before, as a cudgel. Now it was the only solid thing he had to keep between him and the creature before him.

The creature. . . . Black shreds of it seemed always to be stripping away, like black steam, in a wind that blew nowhere else in the street, yet nothing ever fell to the snow, and there was never less of it. It walked upright, and was tall as a bear and gaunt as a half-burnt tree. She heard Kit's voice weak beside her. "Oh, Mother's Pigs. . . . How can I describe that at the next town?"

A dark arm-shape swept out, swift and easy, and slapped at the boy. The timber hit the snow in two splintery pieces.

"Gerry, get away!" Marya leaped at the thing, sweeping her sword in a cut at the dark midsection.

Gerry was screaming and screaming, and suddenly not screaming, falling out of the shadow-thing's embrace with his throat and chest blooming bright and shining red, red bubbling at his mouth where he tried still to scream.

Marya's blade sliced into shadow—and stopped, as if stone had formed around it. Stone was filling the veins of her right hand, calcifying her nerves, brittling her bones, and devouring its way into her shoulder and chest. She wanted to draw a breath, and hadn't the strength. Her sword fell to the snow as she staggered backward, fell to her knees, her human arm limp and swinging wide. She stared at it blankly.

And the shadow turned toward her. The mouth gaped, the eyes glowed with decay—she wanted to shut her eyes, kneel down, and wait for it to go away.

The black arms reached out, obscene parody of comfort, to gather her to it.

"No!" Kit shrieked behind her, and darted past, her dagger a sliver of light in her hand.

"Get back!" Marya yelled, but Kit drove the bright steel up into that thing of tattered darkness—

—and stopped. Kit's mouth opened round with shock. Around her folded the impenetrable shadow of the creature.

"Kit, move it! Get back!" Marya shouted again. Kit seemed to come awake, and flung herself backward. The black thing lashed out. Blood stained the snow where she fell.

"Kit!" Marya slid to her side.

"It's pulling my soul out through the hole in my arm," Kit mumbled.

"What?"

"I can feel it go. Not much nourishment in souls . . ." Kit's head slipped sideways.

The creature leaned like a black flame over them, seeming to swell and pulse. Marya grabbed frantically for her sword. Or tried to grab. Her human arm wouldn't obey her.

She lunged up from the snow, to the being's other side. "Here!" she screamed. "Over here, pigfeed! Short-shaft!" She scrabbled up a fistful of churned-up gravel and flung it left-handed at the dark thing. Its nightmare mouth opened in a hiss that cut into her skull, and it surged toward her. *Wish that hadn't worked quite so well,* Marya thought as she struck out with her taloned arm. Her fingers sank into shadow.

Heat rushed through Marya's bones as the hiss became a sharp and sudden snarl. *I've hurt it!* she exulted. Her skin was hot and prickling. She clenched her claws in the shadow-stuff of the thing, and it slashed wildly at her head, shrieking like steel on stone.

Her body flooded with more-than-fever. *It's burning me*—then her terror was swallowed up in awe. *No . . . I'm burning.* She was not the fuel, but the fire itself; the world lay before her as kindling and coal. Huge with strength, she flared up to scorch the stars, feeding on their power. . . .

The black thing flung backward, howling, leaving flickering darkness fading in her fist. Suddenly she was only a little cold beast kneeling in the snow, and all power had fled. She wanted to scream out for it, to rend flesh, shatter stone, in search of it.

She lunged for the writhing shadow. It swung again at her, missed, then turned and hurtled like some dark driven leaf through the gate and into the night beyond.

The power was gone from her. She looked wildly around the street, envying even the flaring of the lamps. But she had to remain human; there was something a human needed to do. . . .

Then she saw the sprawled red-haired figure in the snow. "Kit!" she cried. "Woodpecker—"

She sank to her knees, cradled the Songsmith in her dark arm, and listened for Kit's breathing. Warm air stirred against her cheek; yes, she breathed. Now the shoulder . . . She searched her clothes and Kit's for something that was neither blood-nor snow-soaked, and cursed aloud when she couldn't find anything.

"Oh, bright Mother. Here," someone said softly above her head, and a clean cloth napkin appeared in front of her face. She grabbed it and made a pad, tied it against Kit's wound with her own sash.

"I need a cloak for her, a blanket, something . . ." Marya

muttered. A bright blue wool cape swung into sight. She tucked it under and around Kit. *Why isn't she conscious?* Marya wiped the hair out of her eyes. Before her the street lamps showed darkened snow, the gate closed at last, and three people she was clearly too late to help . . . Her head hurt, and her body felt too heavy to move.

"Should we take her to the inn?" she heard behind her. She turned.

"Amali!"

"I've been here for . . . a while, but you were. . . ." Amali fluttered her plump hands.

"The word you're looking for is probably 'rude.' " Marya shook off inertia and lifted Kit, letting her snow-sodden cloak swing forward to hide her left arm.

"No harm done," Amali said with a little shrug. "Medics are always odd when they're working."

"Hmm."

"But I hadn't thought a Payer of the Price could take the medics' training."

Marya's foot came down a little too suddenly, and her teeth clacked shut. "A what?" she said.

"A Payer of the Price. I saw your arm, while you tended the Songsmith."

"You did." *Surely,* she thought, *the wretched woman will shut up . . .*

"You shouldn't try to hide your mark, you know. You bear it to show us our Mother's anger at our tampering with Her holy secrets. . . ."

"That's enough!" Marya hissed. Amali's mouth opened and closed. "I'm sorry," Marya said. "I'm not . . . religious."

Amali stared at her warily. "I'll pray for you," she said at last. "Let me go ahead and get a bed ready for her."

Marya nodded, and Amali waded away through the snow.

"She means well," croaked Kit's voice near her shoulder. "Just misinformed."

"Woodpecker? How d'you feel?"

"Like I got hold . . . of the wrong end of a lightning bolt."

"There's a right end on a lightning bolt?"

Kit opened one eye and frowned. "Are you hysterical?" she said faintly. "You're not making any sense."

"You should talk."

"No, I shouldn't. I should rest. If you weren't hysterical, you'd know that."

Marya snorted. "Never try to speak rationally with someone who's lost blood."

"Not blood," Kit shook her head weakly. "More like . . . strength."

"That's what happens when you lose blood."

"No. That's what I meant about . . . about a lightning bolt."

"Huh?"

"Instead of getting a blast of something . . . that—that thing sort of took something out of me."

"Something out of you . . ." Marya repeated. Her right arm had felt that way, as if the strength had been sucked away from it.

"My shoulder hurts," said Kit, almost firmly. "And I'm cold. Don't just stand here."

"Piglets, you're fussy," Marya smiled, and took long strides in Amali's tracks.

Sunlight poured like a liquid through the door as Marya pushed it open a finger's width. "Kit? Are you awake?"

"The place is lit up like the damn Ship come to harbor, and she wants to know if I'm awake," Kit grumbled.

Marya stuck her head into the room and grinned. "Your body I can cure. Your disposition is beyond me." She settled on the end of the bed. "So otherwise, how do you feel?"

"Pretty good, actually. Much better than I ought to, considering how bad I felt out there in the snow."

"Hmmm," said Marya. "Let me look at your arm."

"It was as if. . . ." Kit paused while Marya unwound the bandages, "as if I could feel myself dying—which is ridiculous, since it isn't much of a wound."

"True. It's not. It's also clean, and doing all the things it ought to be doing."

"So I suppose it was just fear. A literal example of being scared to death."

"Maybe." Marya sat back and folded her hands, twining flesh with polished black. "Maybe not."

"Maybe not?"

Marya got up and shot the bolt on the door.

"Marya?"

"I've got something I want to show you."

"My mother warned me about women like you . . ."

"Very funny. Watch this."

Marya crouched down by the iron stove near the bed, and opened the fire-door. "It's lit, right?"

"If it hadn't been," said Kit, "I think we would have noticed."

"Yes, but you can see the flames, can't you?"

Kit sighed. "Humor her. Yes, I can see them."

"All right." Marya stretched out her left hand, through the iron doorway, and spread long clawed fingers over the fire like a black-ribbed net. She felt the heat billowing past—and nothing else. *Am I crazy?* she wondered, suddenly afraid. *Was I crazy last night, when this worked?*

Then her shoulder began to tingle. Fever-warmth swept up left arm, fever-dizziness engulfed her. She was deafened by her own heartbeat.

Between her fingers, she saw the flames struggle, sink; the coals darkened, orange to crimson to wine, then black and ash-gray.

"Urk," Kit said behind her.

Marya sat back on her heels and rubbed her eyes. "That's what I like about you. You always know what to say at times like this."

"Mother at the Helm—"

"It isn't magic, blast it!" Marya snapped. "Calm down. It's part of the . . . the change. You know perfectly well it is."

Kit set her hands firmly on her knees and took several deep breaths. "You're right. I'm calm. Perfectly. Did you know you could do that? Before now?"

"I tried it last night, in my room. I don't think I could before last night."

"So where did it come from?"

"I have a theory . . ."

Kit closed her eyes. "I hate it when you say that."

"You want to hear it?"

"I'm sorry."

"All right. I remember an experiment my mother had me do when I was a kid, with a family of snow hare kittens. I raised half of them in pens outdoors. The other half stayed indoors. The rabbits outdoors changed coloring the way snow hares always do, brown in summer and white in winter. The rabbits raised indoors were never anything but brown."

Kit frowned. "You must have botched it. Snow hares don't do that—and what does that have to do with putting out fires, anyway?"

"I'm getting to that. Pay attention. She explained that my little project showed how living things can sometimes be born with characteristics that don't appear until they're triggered by something outside themselves." Marya flexed her dark fingers. "I think, last night, I had a characteristic triggered."

Kit shook her head impatiently. "You've been cold before. And scared. What—" Her eyes widened. "Triggered by . . . that . . . thing?"

Marya nodded.

"No."

"What's your theory—coincidence?"

"Why should it have any effect on you?"

"Because," and Marya's voice was flat, "that thing and my arm are . . . related."

"That's sheepcrap. A big, steaming—"

"I can use my arm to absorb heat, you saw that. I think the thing we went up against last night can do the same. I think that's why it tears its victims open. It sure as day isn't eating them."

"You're wrong." Kit's face was pale and set.

Marya asked softly, "How do you know?"

"Because you're not like that thing! If you're trying to tell me you are—"

"No, no, no. I'm human—I was, I still am. Just because those rabbits never turned white didn't mean they weren't rabbits."

"Shut up about your Motherlorn rabbits."

Marya wanted suddenly to scream at her. She bit the inside of her mouth instead, and took a deep breath. "All right. I'm just saying—"

"I don't want to hear—"

The door bolt clacked against its socket. "Songsmith?" came Amali's voice from outside the door. "Is everything all right?"

"Oops," Marya muttered, and leaped to unlock the door.

"Is everything all right?" Amali repeated, her plump face full of cheerful concern. She carried a pair of copper-and-brass cans. "Here's hot water. Did you sleep well? Does your shoulder hurt you?"

Kit graciously acknowledged the hot water and followed Amali into the bathing room, letting all the rest of the innkeeper's speech go unanswered.

"Her shoulder's fine," Marya said when Amali came out with the empty water cans. "I looked it over. Has there been any more news?"

"News?" Amali said, straightening the covers on the bed Kit had left.

"Of that thing last night."

"It's certainly not been seen again."

"Certainly?"

Amali frowned and plumped a pillow before she said, "Such things can only walk among us at night, while the Mother sails in dream."

A god who goes to sleep when you need her most, Marya thought. *Wonderful.* "You're sure the Mother herself isn't responsible for little treats like that?"

"The Mother does not create evil," Amali lectured mildly. "Evil comes from us. But She allows evil to walk among us to teach us our errors. When we've learned and corrected ourselves, She will rid the world of such terrible things."

"So all we have to do is be very, very good and the creature will go away."

Amali blinked. "Disrespect doesn't become a Payer of the Price, dear."

Marya clenched her teeth. "Isn't someone at least organizing a hunt for the monster?"

"Wolves come down from the hills in winter," Amali

smiled. "Do you go out hunting them every time, or do you simply take sensible precautions?"

"We aren't talking about wolves."

"There are many dangers this far from the cities. We live differently here."

"And die differently, too, if that creature is any indication," Marya snapped.

Kit strolled out of the bathing room, dressed and drying her hair with a green towel. "What's this about dying?" she asked.

"Nothing to be concerned about, Songsmith," said Amali. "Will you want to travel on today? The weather is good—"

Someone tapped furtively on the door. "Amali?" came Nan's voice, very soft. "Come down quick. The whole town's down there. They're going to go out and—" She'd opened the door and slid through. At the sight of Marya and Kit, she pressed her hand to her mouth. "Oh. Oh Mother."

"I have things to do downstairs," Amali said in a rush, and turned frantically toward Nan and the door.

"And something to do up here first." Marya stretched out her arm, black and shining, and pushed the door closed. Amali turned, and Marya saw that the jolly innkeeper mask had crumbled. The woman's eyes were full of tears. "The truth, please," Marya finished gently.

Nan made a strangled noise. Amali closed her eyes and gulped air.

"Wait a minute," said Kit. "What did I miss?"

"I don't know yet, Woodpecker," Marya replied. "But something out of the ordinary is going on here—" she raised an eyebrow at Amali and Nan, "—and I think these two can tell me all about it."

Amali shook her head. "No. I'm sorry. You should have the truth; you of all people should be trusted with the truth. But not now."

"What? Why not?"

"There are people downstairs who are ready to murder what they should only pity. I may be able to keep them from finding . . . what they hunt."

"The creature," said Marya.

Amali looked away and nodded.

Marya watched her for a moment before she said, "It killed three people last night."

"It couldn't—" Amali began, then nodded again.

"We've go to go!" Nan hissed at Amali. "Downstairs—" Amali's face was set in an anguished stubbornness.

"We might be able to help," Marya said.

Amali bit her lip. "If I tell you . . . promise you'll let it live."

"If we can," said Marya.

"Now, *wait* a minute—" Kit began, but Marya gestured her quiet. Amali looked from Marya to Kit. Then her gaze turned downward.

"The . . . creature we hunt," she said at last, "is my child."

Marya was too stunned to do more than blink. *You knew it was a mutation,* she told herself. *It had to be child to something. But not to this pudgy, red-faced, normal little woman . . .*

Amali continued, "Nan was my first-born. Then I had . . . this one. He was simple, he had to be fed and cleaned—" Her voice cracked and faded, and she pressed her fingers to her lips before she spoke again. "I thought She had judged me strong enough to raise a Payer of the Price. May She help me, *I* thought I was strong enough." She turned to Marya and lifted her head, in pride, or defiance. "Nan and I cared for him for fifteen years. We kept him locked away, for fear the townfolk would do him a mischief."

Or was it, Marya thought, *that you didn't want Sallis to know you had a mutant in the family?*

Amali hesitated, then plunged grimly back into her story. "A few months ago—things began to happen. I was afraid. I . . . Nan and I . . . Mother forgive me, one day we locked the door of his room and went to Lyle Valley. We came back two weeks later."

Tears began to roll down Amali's cheeks. "We buried him after dark, here in the foothills. He was so . . . he must have been dead, he must have! The Mother has brought him back, to punish me for not trusting Her, for my fear, for . . . not loving him." And Amali buried her face in her hands and sobbed.

Kit reached a hand halfway out to Amali's shoulder, paused.

"Could the thing be caught, and confined?" Marya asked finally.

"What?" Kit's voice squeaked a little.

Amali replied, "I think so."

"Why?" Kit wailed.

"Then you have until we find it to convince me that we ought to," said Marya, and started for the door.

"Hold it right there!" Kit said in a voice that rattled the window glass. "Are you going crazy?"

"No," Marya said patiently, "I'm going with the hunting party."

Kit opened and closed her mouth. "Then so am I," she said at last.

"But your shoulder . . ." Marya and Amali said almost at once.

"Where's my cloak?" Beneath Kit's glare, Marya recognized the Last Word.

The foothills were sullen around them, red-washed in the setting sun, thickly clotted with pine groves. Marya squinted in the lash of the bitter wind, switched the reins to her clawed hand, and tucked the other into her armpit to warm it. *Somewhere in all of this,* she reflected, *there's a demon that eats souls. No, somewhere there's a pitiful mutated something that lives on pure energy. Wish I could get Amali to tell me all she knows about it.* She looked down at her black hand. It reflected sunset like a bloody knife. She concentrated on it, trying to draw heat from the winter sunlight as she had drawn from the fire, but it stayed profoundly, fiercely cold, and still.

She clenched her legs on her mount, and it trotted forward through the snow to where Amali was riding. Behind her she could hear Kit's beast surge forward to Amali's other side.

"All right," said Marya. "We've diverted the rest of the hunting party, and we've followed you from spot to spot for the last hour. What are you going to do when we find it?"

"Amali!" Nan's voice rang out. Marya looked up to see

her topping the nearest ridge, around a great plume of frozen snow. "He's nearby! There are tracks here, and a dead—"

Marya flung herself out of the saddle to the ground before she quite knew why. A slight, heavy motion in the pine boughs, a shadow. . . . Her mount screamed, and the snow around her steamed with blood. "Get back!" she yelled, but Kit and Amali had already lunged away from the twisting, dying animal with the black monster on its back.

Marya drew her sword, then realized there was nothing she could do with it. *If it will only stay interested in its kill long enough that I can find a way to stop it,* she thought. But the hell-window eyes turned to her, and it rose and faced her. Her stomach wrenched. *The mind of a retarded sixteen-year-old,* she realized—*I hurt it. It understands revenge.* She raised her sinister arm before her, and thought about death.

The impact of the creature's leap drove her down to the snow. Her shoulder jarred against ice and rock, and she cried out, but her dark arm held steady against the weight, held the nightmare face at bay.

Suddenly her hand coursed with heat, and the creature hissed and struck out at her. She felt a line of freezing pain at her temple and knew it had cut her. The world seemed to be separating into fragments, which in turn began to drift apart from each other. *I'm feverish,* she realized. *My brain's going to cook.*

She heard a thud, and cold showered her face. It happened again, and the demon shadow was gone from above her.

"Marya!" she heard Kit yell. "This way!" A lump of snow whizzed past her head.

She looked wildly in the direction of the voice. "You're throwing snowballs?" she shrieked.

"Come on, will you?" Kit howled back, and grabbed another handful of snow. Amali was crouched at her feet, and seemed to be trying to force both her mittened fists into her mouth. "This won't work—no, here it comes! Move!"

Marya dived for Kit, and reached her side just as the Songsmith fired another snowball. The creature staggered back a step, then came on again.

"Snowballs?" said Marya.

"Well, they're slowing it down!"

"But why?" *The thing absorbs energy,* Marya realized. *Snowballs have energy of motion. Like my sword, and Kit's knife, when we used them last night. But snowballs don't have someone hanging onto them....*

"Snow!" Marya shouted.

"Yes, so what?" Kit yelled back.

Nan was struggling up to them through the drifts. Behind her, Marya saw the towering snow-plume that topped the near ridge, arching in a heavy half-tunnel.

"This way!" She half-dragged Kit toward the ridge. Behind them, Amali and Nan floundered aside as the monster swept forward.

"Take my sword," Marya panted, and thrust it hilt-first at Kit. "You're going to drop this—" she pointed up at the curve of snow, "—on that thing. As soon as I've got it underneath, chop through the ice near the point of the ridge."

Kit looked dubious. "This'll work?"

"I don't know," said Marya. At the corner of her vision, a shadow grew quickly larger. "Go, move it!"

She dodged aside as the creature lunged at her. If she could keep her footing now, and keep moving back ... She could see hints of humanity now in the wild visage—in the shape of temple and cheekbone, in the motion of the gaping jaws—and the terror made her want to huddle whimpering in the snow. She kept moving.

The shadow of the snow-curve cut the ground beneath her into parts of dying light and blue dusk. The black shape crouched, her only warning of its sudden spring. Marya flung herself aside barely in time. She hit the snow hard, and tasted ice and grit in her mouth.

"Kit!" she gasped. "Now!" She rolled fast and came floundering to her feet in the deep snow, ready to leap out of the path of the avalanche of snow and ice ...

... that didn't fall. "Kit!" she yelled again. "Knock it down!" The creature was stalking her once more.

"It won't fall!" shrieked Kit.

Marya spared a glance toward the base of the ridge. Kit was hacking furiously. It was not enough to break down the arch of snow. Marya looked back at the nightshade face all too close to her, and heard a strangling cry she couldn't keep back.

"Jump!" shouted a voice somewhere above her.

"What? Who . . . ?" The monster crouched to spring.

"Jump clear!" she heard again. "Hurry!" Behind her she heard a wooden groan, and a sudden roar. Her mouth and eyes filled with snow.

"Marya?" Kit called wildly. "Are you all right?"

Marya sat up and shook snow out of her face. "I think so. What happened?"

Kit knelt down next to her and looked her over critically. Then she pointed back toward the ridge.

The snow-plume was gone. At the foot of the ridge was a small mountain of snow and ice. Near it lay one of the riding animals, still saddled. Nan was at its head, patting it, talking to it. It tried to rise, and failed.

"Nan saw what we were trying to do, and that it wasn't working," Kit said. "She drove the critter out onto the arch, to bring it down."

Marya nodded, and dragged herself to her feet.

"You're sure you're all right?" Kit asked.

"I hurt all over," said Marya. "A mere nothing." She trudged over to Nan.

"Its leg's broken," Nan said.

"I thought so. I'm sorry."

Nan smiled at her, though the smile was a little lopsided. "It was you or it."

"True. But I'm still sorry."

Nan shook her head, knelt by the beast's head, and took a hunting knife out of a sheath at her belt. Marya looked away quickly, out over the mound of broken snow. Was that a bent, black arm? *No,* Marya realized, *just a tree branch swept down. The creature is buried. By the time it can dig its way out, if it can, it'll be too weak to fight back. And Amali can have her mutant captive back. I wonder how long it will be before she tries to kill it again?*

As if answering her thoughts, Amali appeared at her left shoulder. "Is he dead?"

"I don't think so. It's a hard creature to kill, you know."

Amali looked away. "Even you can't understand."

"I admit, weird, coal-black children who suck the life out of things are difficult to empathize with."

"I loved him at first," Amali murmured.

Marya frowned and looked at her.

"That's so hard for you to believe? Mothers love club-footed children, they love their simple children. My son was no different."

"No different?" Surprise added a squeak to Marya's voice. "A withered, demonic—"

"He wasn't always like that!" Amali shouted. "That's why I thought you could. . . . He was simple, and his left foot was black and twisted and hard as stone. It was only last year that he began to change, and he began to kill things. Before that, he . . ."

Marya felt her eyes ache from staring. Her tongue seemed stuck in her dry mouth. She turned away from Amali, and found Kit, wide-eyed, watching her.

"Don't look at me like that," Marya rasped. "It's not true." But she remembered the wild, blood-thirsty rush of power she had felt in the courtyard at the gate, when she ripped energy away from the mutant child.

"Marya—" Kit reached toward her. But her hand stopped halfway between them.

Marya stared a moment at that hand, before a sob bruised its way out of her throat, and she turned with a wrench and ran.

Her foot caught in snow suddenly deep and uneven, and she fell forward. She stared for a moment at her arms sunk to the elbows in a slope of snow, before she remembered: the avalanche. *If it had just fallen on me, too!*

A little well appeared in the snow before her. Loose powder sifted into it. It grew larger. And suddenly the mass before her shook and shifted, and knotted black twigs, four of them, poked out of the snow.

It wasn't until they clenched that she recognized them.

She wrenched her left hand out of the drift and grabbed the mutant creature's fingers, yanked at them until the arm was clear of the snowbank. Then she scrabbled until she found the face. It seemed even more human now that weakness had shrunk it. It struggled, twisting its head and free

arm. She reached down and plunged her talons around and
into its throat.

The blistering heat that raced up her arm was almost familiar. Under her, the creature bucked and writhed, screaming thinly. She heard a human scream, too, behind her,
before the roaring in her ears deafened her and dragged her
into the dark.

She seemed, after some time, to be waking up. Something about waking struck her as inappropriate; the place,
perhaps . . . Someone was sobbing drearily. Marya felt
something nudging against her shoulder. "Huh?"

"Mother at the Helm. You're still alive."

"Kit! Where . . . what are we . . ."

"Doing here? Never mind, you'll remember soon
enough."

And suddenly Marya did, as she recognized the weeping
as Amali's. "Oh," she said. "Oh, oh, oh, oh—"

Kit's slap stung her cheek. "Quiet. It's all right. You're all
right. Someone would have had to kill it eventually. Can you
get up?"

"I don't know."

"Well, try. I want to get out of here."

Marya nodded. It hurt her head. Kit half-lifted her, and
they stumbled to one of the remaining riding animals.

"We're just leaving?" Marya said. "Shouldn't we help—"

"Right now, neither of us is likely to be much help. Nan
will get Amali home. I want to get back to the inn, pick up
our stuff, and go."

"Travel at night?"

"There's a moon."

Marya shrugged and let Kit boost her up to the saddle.
The Songsmith scrambled up in front and urged their mount
into a fast walk.

For half an hour, Marya watched the moon-cast shadows
of trees deepen and stretch blue-black across the snow.

"D'you want to talk about it?" Kit said finally.

"Well . . . no. Not really. What I want is for it to have
never happened."

"Then it's a deal. It never happened."

"What if that happens to—"

"It won't happen to you," Kit said.

"You don't know that."

There was a long silence. "No, I don't. But what am I supposed to do about it? Hand you over to the peacekeepers? 'Got a dangerous mutant here, Officers,'" Kit grated. "'Well, no, I guess she's not dangerous yet. But she might be, someday . . .' No, thank you. I'd feel stupid."

Marya looked for something else to say, and couldn't find anything. They rode half a kilometer before she murmured, "Thank you."

"Mmm," said Kit.

"For trusting me, I mean."

Kit turned in the saddle, and their mount stopped. "Are you going to keep brooding over yourself?"

"What? No."

"Good. You're a pain when you brood. I don't suppose you brought anything to eat?"

"There's dried fruit in the saddlebag," Marya said.

"Dried fruit. I ask for food, and you talk about dried fruit. The cold has addled your brain," Kit grumbled. "Hand me a Motherlorn raisin." And they rode on.

INTRODUCTION TO "A DIFFERENT KIND OF COURAGE"

by Mercedes Lackey

This story was my first professional sale, although it was not the first professional story I ever had published—the first one published was a Tarma and Kethry story, which sold to a magazine. Since magazines have faster turnarounds than books do—especially anthologies, as I have come to learn!—that story actually saw print before this one did.

I was, I will confess, an ardent Darkover fan. I was absolutely enchanted with Marion Zimmer Bradley's creation, and, in fact, I had the great good fortune to become one of the many, many writers whom she coached and advised and scolded into shape as professional writers.

I had submitted one story to her for a *Sword and Sorceress* anthology, which was rejected on the perfectly reasonable grounds that it wasn't one story, it was two. I followed Marion's advice with that one (which indeed *did* sell as two stories—one to Marion, and the other to that magazine) but while I was waiting to hear about it, I had what I thought might be a good idea for a *Friends of Darkover* anthology that had just opened up.

I'd read the first *Friends of Darkover* anthology with great interest and a little bit of envy, and I had also read a very great deal of Darkover fanfiction, and one thing that I'd noticed was that in the tales of the Free Amazons, the women in question were all very . . .

hearty. Xena the Warrior Princess would have fit right in with that bunch. Now, mind, I very much liked the Free Amazons. I thought they were some of the most sensible women on the planet. But it did seem to me that amidst all the trappers and trackers, the outdoorswomen and huntresses, the caravan-guards and the *chervine*-tamers, there might be a girl or two who, despite being devoted heart-and-soul to the spirit of the Free Amazons, just didn't quite measure up physically.

There's a bit of autobiography there, since I'm not the most graceful creature in the world, and if presented with a sword, I'd probably cut off my own foot. My attempts at archery would make a cat laugh. And as for camping and the Great Outdoors, well, all I can say is I'll see you all at the motel. While I'm by no means as physically timid as my heroine, well, I've met plenty of people who are through no fault of their own.

And in a group that was under as much pressure from society as the Free Amazons were, I could see them being rather harsh, rather than supportive, to girls who didn't exactly match their own stringent standards. Or at least, they would be until something or someone came along that proved to them that the standards they held to shouldn't be used as a means to exclude someone who truly wanted to belong.

I got rather caught up in the idea, and the story took shape quickly. I sent it off to Marion, and to my great joy, she accepted it! My first professional sale!

In fact, I made a Xerox copy of the check and framed it, where it hung on the wall of my office for quite some time.

It was the start of many sales to Marion for her anthologies, and also the start of a long and thoroughly delightful relationship with DAW Books. Thanks to those anthology sales, Elizabeth (Betsy) Wollheim was not entirely unfamiliar with my name when my first novel crossed her desk, and the letters of recommendation from Marion and another fine DAW author, my mentor C. J. Cherryh, didn't hurt! Thanks to all of those things, I'm one of the very fortunate souls who can say that I really *did* sell my first novel to the first publishing house I submitted it to.

So here's to all of us who share the DAW logo. Long may we wave!

A DIFFERENT KIND OF COURAGE

by Mercedes Lackey

RAFI rubbed at the scars on her hand surreptitiously as she sat on her saddle in the tiny, ill-kept traveler's shelter, hoping neither of the other two Guild Sisters with her would notice the movement. Caro, tall, lean and lantern-jawed, moved quickly and efficiently around the walls, stuffing moss into the cracks that the wind continually whistled through. Lirella, smaller than her freemate and much more muscular, had brought armloads of firewood inside and was preparing a hot meal. Both of them had made it very plain to Rafi that her efforts at helping them had only hindered their work.

The scars ached, as they always did when her hands were cold, and Rafi was afraid that if the two older women noticed her stealthy massaging, they'd regard it as one more sign of weakness.

Her hope was in vain; Caro's gray eyes, so quick to detect any movement around her, fixed on Rafi's hands. Caro's long face showed no expression that Rafi could read, but then Rafi had only known the older woman for six months. Rafi froze, and Caro's eyes flickered briefly to her face before looking away again. The glance had been neutral, non-committal—but Rafi wilted anyway.

Neither Caro nor her freemate Lirella had wanted Rafi along on this trip, but there hadn't been a great deal of choice for any of them. "Our orders from Thendara House are to deliver this package directly into the hands of the Keeper at Caer Donn," Guildmother Dorylis had said. "And yes, yes, I know the Domains will have nothing to do with

Aldaran—officially. Like us, the Towers do not always pay any more than lip service to the 'official' policy. That is why they rely on us to run errands like this one for them. The Sisterhood knows nothing of what is in that package, nor do we care, the Keeper at Elhalyn knows that. There is some danger attached to the carrying of it, which is why Thendara has asked that I pick our two best mercenaries to convey it—but there is a problem there. Neither of you are Comynara, nor are you familiar with the protocols surrounding a Keeper. I frankly doubt that you'd be let anywhere near her. Rafi, on the other hand—"

Rafiella had blushed as red as the unruly hair on her head.

"I know, I know. She had Keeper training at Neskaya," Caro had replied, combing her graying brown hair with impatient fingers. "She would be admitted with no questions asked."

But Rafi had heard the words Caro had not spoken. *"Keeper training—which she failed at, as she fails at everything she tries."*

Rafi had tried not to show she'd heard the thought.

The result was that the three of them were sharing the dubious shelter of a poorly maintained waystation deep in the Hellers in the dead of winter. Lirella had made no secret of the fact that she felt Rafi's presence was holding their pace to a crawl, and was the direct cause of their having to settle for this place instead of the shelter of the Guild Hall at Caer Donn they'd hoped to reach this night. Caro had been more circumspect, but Rafi could still feel her disapproval.

"I—is there anything I can do?" she asked in a small voice.

Lirella gave an undisguised snort. Caro's blond partner never made any attempt to disguise what she felt. Rafi had been no help at all in the unsaddling and tethering of the *chervines*—she was afraid of them—could barely control her own when riding, and her fear had communicated itself to the animals, making them jump and shy. She'd barely pulled her own weight in getting their gear under cover. Granted, she had managed to light a fire using her starstone when neither of the other two could coax anything out of the damp tinder that was all that was available. But she wasn't any better at cooking or setting up camp than she was with the *chervines*.

"Patience, *bredhyina*," Caro said in an undertone. "She's only recently out of seclusion. And when, in a Tower or lady's bower, would she have learned anything of rough camping?"

"It's not just that—" the other woman replied softly. "It's that she's such a—a—wet rag!"

Caro stifled a smile with the back of her hand. "Wet rag" was indeed an apt description of their newest, youngest Sister. Lirella had tried, without much success, to teach her both armed and unarmed combat, but the girl had not only shown no aptitude for what was the mainstay commodity at the tiny Guild House at Helmscrag, but had displayed a level of incompetence that Caro wouldn't have believed if she hadn't seen it with her own eyes. It wasn't that she hadn't *tried*—she'd fallen all over herself (quite literally) trying. Lirella finally refused to teach her any more after she'd nearly broken an ankle attempting a simple lunge. And as for the Training Sessions—!

She'd run out of the first one she'd attended sobbing hysterically. Caro was convinced she still cried after each one, but at least now she did it in private. During the Session, she would sit, hands clenched in her lap or constantly rubbing at the scars that crossed them, pale as Lady Death herself. She spoke only when directly questioned, and then in so soft a voice one could hardly hear her. A wet rag indeed!

Nevertheless, she was no less Caro's Sister. "I can think of one thing that would be helpful—" she began.

"Yes?" The girl all but tripped over her own feet, jumping up.

"The only wood here is wet and half rotten. If we're to get any heat in here tonight—well, there must be some deadfall around here. If you'd take the ax and try to find some—"

Rafi took the proffered ax and hurried out into the snow—but not quickly enough to miss Lirella's weary, "Aren't you afraid she'll cut off her own foot with that?" Tears stung her eyes, and away from the critical observance of the freemates, she let them fall.

Lirella was right—she very well might cut off her own foot. She'd come close enough to doing just that with the wooden practice knife at least a dozen times. The knife she wore now was only for show—she had no intention of ever drawing it. If she did, she'd be more a danger to herself and her Sisters than to any attacker. Why had she ever taken Oath?

Don't be any stupider than you have to be—she told herself sadly. *You know why you took Oath.*

That terrible day, that horrible day when the *leroni* at Neskaya had sent her back to her father, saying she hadn't the "strength" to bear further training as a Keeper, and hadn't the nerves for further work in a Tower. She'd tried—oh merciful Avarra, how she'd tried—but the pain, the burns every time she touched someone, every time someone touched her—the limits of her endurance had been reached, and quickly. The shame she'd felt at being unable to bear what little Keitha, a mere child, had taken without a whimper, had made her wish she'd died in threshold as so many had.

Her father had stared at her when she stood before him; his eyes hard and appraising. For as long as she could remember, he'd called her "the useless mouth to feed." She hadn't the prettiness that had made it easy to find husbands for her sisters, she wasn't capable of handling the staff of the castle when her mother died. He'd been openly relieved when Neskaya had asked for permission to train her as a Keeper. And now she was back, useless to Neskaya, as she'd been useless to him.

"Zandru's Hells, you're a dough-faced little thing," he'd said finally, with disgust. "All that time at the Tower, and your looks still haven't improved. And what I'd do with you, if it hadn't been for Lord Dougal, I have no idea. However, the old lecher's lady has gone to her rest, and he wants alliance with our house badly. You're no prize, but you're marriageable, and that's all he wants. He's got no heirs, so see that you give him one quickly. He'll be here within a tennight; we'll hold the *di catenas* ceremony as soon as he arrives."

Rafi had stood frozen in shock and dismay. She'd all but

fainted on the spot. All she could see in her mind was the image of her mother, wrung out with child after child, finally dying trying to deliver her last. Her father's voice, sharp with impatience had finally brought her to herself. She'd curtsied clumsily, made some kind of appropriately grateful comment and left his presence with the uncertain tread of one gone blind.

No one bothered to keep watch on her—no one would ever have expected her to run away. She'd always been so completely obedient, succeeding in that if in nothing else. So no one had stopped her or even questioned her when she left the castle, made her way down to the village, and found the tiny Renunciate Guild House there. She'd known of nowhere else that she'd be safe, for even in her sheltered life she'd heard of Dougal, and the way his wives kept dying, attempting to give him the heir he so desperately desired. To wed him was to receive a death sentence.

She'd not thought beyond taking shelter with them; she'd never had much to do with Free Amazons before. She'd heard tales, of course, some flattering, most not; and had tended to dismiss most of them as midsummer moonshine. The one thing she had been certain of was that no woman or girl who had taken her Oath need ever fear a man's overruling again.

The little world beyond the Guild House doors had taken her completely by surprise. There, it seemed, women were free to be as strong, as clever, as self-sufficient as any man. They were free to order their own lives completely, subject only to the few rules of the Guild. Rafi had been dazzled—she'd never dreamed that such a thing could have existed. She found something else within those walls as well. The Sisters of the Guild *cared* for one another.

She stopped, leaning against a tree, too blinded by tears to continue pretending to hunt for wood. She'd had such hopes that here, at last, she'd find something she could do *right* for a change. She'd wanted to *belong*, to find her place in that camaraderie. After seeing the care, and yes, the love these women had for one another, she knew there was nothing else in the world she wanted more. But she'd failed in the Guild, just as she'd failed everywhere else.

She couldn't have guessed, of course, that the sole trade of women at Helmscrag Guild House was the sale of their abilities as fighters, guards, and guides. Of the eleven women at the tiny Guild House, only the Guild Mother herself never undertook such missions. Unfortunately for Rafi, her woeful lack of physical abilities was as great as her lack of beauty. As a child, she'd always been last chosen in games—in fact her presence on a side guaranteed an automatic handicap—and last as a dancing partner. Learning even to defend herself had been an insurmountable task.

Lirella had decided to give an extra spur to her by being more than usually hard with her. All that had brought was painful bruises and plentiful tears.

Try as she would to keep herself shielded, her *laran* had made the thoughts of her fellow Renunciates painfully clear to her. Lirella considered her to be a sniveling coward. Caro simply thought she was abysmally stupid. Guild Mother was convinced that the root of her difficulties lay in too much self-pity, and that she needed to be bullied out of it. The rest shared those opinions to a great or lesser extent. The overall consensus was that she was completely undependable and a regrettable waste of time. Even her appearance was a faint embarrassment to them. Her clothing always had the look of having been slept in, and no matter how carefully it was cut, her hair never failed to look like an untidy hay-rick. She hardly gave the desired impression of the self-sufficient and self-reliant Renunciate.

Perhaps her father had been right to label her as useless. Certainly her Sisters were sure that she was. And that had hurt worse than anything else that had happened to her.

So once again she found herself the unwanted tag-along, the handicap on the team. The feeling of being left out was made more intense by the special relationship between Caro and Lirella. It was rather ironic that the only thing that had pleased the Guild Sisters (and slightly softened Caro's own attitude toward Rafi) had been her reaction to that relationship. Rafi simply hadn't been the least upset by it, and that had surprised all of them—they'd expected her to react with hysterics when she learned of it. But her only reaction had been a wistful envy.

It must have been thinking of the freemates that brought a shrill of alarm from her *laran*. She was taken out of her morass of tears with a shock. Something—something was very wrong at the camp!

She clutched her starstone and tried to will far-vision, then cried out in pain as for a moment she saw through Caro's eyes, and felt the sword-strike Caro was taking in her own flesh.

Guild Mother had warned them of danger—and she had been right. The danger had been greater than any of them guessed.

Rafi floundered through the snow back toward the little shelter, but she had come farther than she had thought. By the time she reached the camp, the fight was over.

Four dead men lay in the gathering dusk; Lirella was down, unconscious. Caro was bent over her, trying to rouse her while holding an ugly wound in her own thigh in an effort stop the bleeding.

Even as Rafi came into sight of them, Caro collapsed over the body of her freemate.

Rafi did not even pause to think; perhaps it was the absence of critical eyes on her, but she moved surely and without hesitation. Her first action was to tightly bind the worst of the wounds hoping to slow or stop the bleeding; her second to check the women for damage not immediately visible. Although she'd had little training in the use of her *laran* for healing, she had learned to monitor, and she used that skill now.

Caro was in deep shock, and suffering from heavy bloodloss; Lirella was in a worse condition. She'd taken a blow to the head that had broken the skull. Rafi did what little she could to ease the pressure she could sense building there, but Lirella needed better and more expert care, and quickly.

Rafi knew she'd be unable to move the women into the shelter alone; either of them outweighed her, and they'd be dead weight. She stood frozen in indecision, but the urgent need to get them out of the snow and into shelter goaded her on. She thought hard for a moment—then remembered the *chervines*, still hobbled in their lean-to behind the shelter. She did not dare let her fear of the animals come to the surface. She brought the one they used as a pack animal around to the front of the shelter and harnessed him, moving slowly and carefully, both to keep from startling him and to avoid making mistakes that would have to be undone. He snorted at the scent of the fresh blood, but to her relief did no more than that. Tethering him next to Lirella, she ran into the shelter and brought one of the blankets from her bedroll outside. She used her knife to make a hole in each of the top two corners, and fastened ropes as securely as she could. She spread it out on the snow, and rolled Lirella onto it as carefully as she was able, then tied the ropes to either side of the *chervine*'s harness. She took his bridle, trying to project calm at him, and led him slowly into the shelter, dragging Lirella on the blanket. When Lirella was safely inside, and bundled into her own bedroll, Rafi repeated the procedure with Caro.

It was long after dark now—she discovered to her immense relief that Caro had lied about the state of the wood. She soon had the fire built up to a respectable enough blaze so that she was able to administer what little aid she could to her Sisters without fear of them taking a worse chilling than they already had. She stripped them of their bloody, torn garments, cutting them away where she had to, all the time working slowly and thinking out each step at a time. Then she rebandaged their wounds, this time with proper bandages and medication, and rolled them back into their now-combined bedrolls. She knew they needed to be kept warm, and this way they would have the combined comfort of each other's body heat and presence.

But she knew very well that both of them needed more help than she could give them. She didn't dare leave them alone—even assuming she could control one of the *chervines* well enough to ride in search of aid, she had no idea in which direction the nearest help lay. She sat in an agony of indecision, absently rubbing the scars on her hands, trying to think of an answer, when the very feel of one of those scars gave her the answer she needed.

Distance was no barrier to *laran*, particularly not in the Overworld. And there was a Tower nearby, and within it trained Healers, and all the help she needed.

She had no one to monitor her; though it would be dangerous, she'd have to do without. If it had only been her own life at stake she'd never have dared—but it wasn't. Caro and Lirella's lives hung on whether or not they received expert care, and soon. She had no choice. No matter how they felt about her, she was bound by her Oath and by the way she had come to like and admire them to give them whatever help lay in her power.

She bundled herself into what blankets she thought she could spare, made sure the fire would not burn out in her "absence," and checked once again on her patients. When she was satisfied that she'd done everything she could, she settled herself as comfortably as she was able, and forced herself to begin.

This had been one aspect of the training she'd done well at; one by one, she erased all outward sensations from her mind, concentrating only on the starstone in her hand. For one brief moment, her fear returned, and held her back (*I could die out there . . .*), but she mastered it, although it remained in the background, and fell deep into the depths of the stone.

Then she was *out*, and staring down at her own body.

I am a dough-faced little thing, she thought, looking at the untidy child-woman in the heap of blankets, her face tear-streaked, her hair sticking out every which way. At least she was better ordered in the form she wore when *out*—no more attractive; in fact, rather sexless and slender to the point of emaciation, but at least not so—messy.

But this was no time for thinking of herself. Quickly she let her mind move her into the Overworld, the overlight taking the place of the solid world she was leaving behind. Now she stood on a gray, endless plain; she cast about her for the Tower, whose manifestation she knew *must* be here—

And it was. Shining with a light of its own, it called her with the solid familiarity of the one at Neskaya, and she hurried toward it, calling out with her mind and heart, and hoping someone within it would hear her.

A figure suddenly flickered into existence between her and her goal, and from the aura of power she wore, Rafi knew that this must be the Keeper. Her face tended to shift and change within the veils she wore, but the feeling of contained and controlled power was constant and unmistakable.

"Child—" the Keeper said within her mind. "You disturb our work. What possible reason can you have for doing so?"

Rafi did not bother with explanations, but simply opened her mind to her and spread it all out for the Keeper's examination. The telepath exclaimed in sharp surprise, and Rafi felt her add a bit of her strength to Rafi's own, steadying her and supporting her as Rafi felt herself begin to fade.

"I will send help, little Amazon. It will come as soon as may be—but you must keep them alive until it arrives. Thus, must you do, and so—" Like birds returning to the nest, her instructions settled in Rafi's mind; Rafi knew that if her strength held she'd have no difficulty in following them. And, she willed fiercely, her strength *would* hold, for however long it took—

"Now, child, you are unmonitored, and to remain would be dangerous. Hold fast, and remember that help is coming." She gave Rafi a kind of mental shove—

Blue fire sprang up all around her for one instant, and she was curled, half-frozen and cramped, in her blankets by the fire. She was exhausted, and she ached all over—it would be so good just to lie here, and let the cold take her. It would be so easy to slip into sleep; already the cold seemed less. She was so very tired. . . .

Caro moaned, and the sound woke her to her duty, acted like a goad. She disentangled herself from her blankets, moving slowly because of muscles gone stiff, and went to check on her Sisters.

No sooner did she touch the older woman's hand, than the Keeper's instructions fluttered to the surface of her mind. For one moment she shrank into herself in fear—for to do as she'd been told would open her to more pain than she'd ever borne before—but Caro moaned again, and though the fear remained, she knew she could not bear to allow her Sisters to suffer any longer. She tried to summon what little courage she possessed, bolstered that little courage with the words of her Oath, and went to work.

Carefully she eased into rapport with Lirella. The

Keeper's instructions had been very clear and, as long as she worked slowly, were easy to follow. The pressure of the fracture had to be relieved, and the clot that was forming broken up. The rest could be left until more expert help arrived. When she'd done all she could for Lirella, she turned to Caro, and forced the bleeding that soaked her bandages to slow and stop.

All the while, she couldn't help but be conscious of the deep and vital bond between the two women. It was something she'd been aware of for far longer than anyone in the Guild House had guessed—no one with even a touch of *laran* could have missed it—and the extent of their affection never failed to amaze her. She'd never seen anything like it; certainly her father had never shown any such love for any woman, and emotional bonds were forbidden to those being Keeper-trained. Even now, she was conscious of a twinge of envy. She would have given a great deal to have someone care for her the way these two cared for each other. The presence of that bond spurred her on when nothing else could. It would be unthinkable to let something like that die when it was within her power to save it.

It was hard, bitter work. It took every last dreg of energy she had left—and she'd had none to spare after that unmonitored trip into the Overworld. Time after time her fear and the pain she shared with her Sisters drove her out of rapport with them. Each time that happened, she knew she could never force herself to finish what she'd begun. And yet, when the tears of pain stopped, one look at Caro's twisted face or Lirella's gray, pinched one was enough to send her back into rapport again.

When at last she was finished, colder than she'd ever been before and throbbing with weariness, her work still was not complete. The Keeper's instructions had included the fact that both women would need fluids to replace the blood they'd lost, and quickly. So Rafi crawled to the fire, unable to raise enough strength to walk, and set pans of snow to melt there, then carefully spooned the tea and broth she made down their throats. When dawn came, both women were out of immediate danger, and Rafi heard the sound of hoofbeats just outside.

The shelter was suddenly filled to bursting with people; Rafi crawled out of their way into a darkened corner and collapsed into her blankets.

"Zandru's Hells!" swore one young man, whose fiery hair proclaimed him unmistakably Comyn. "How in the name of all that's holy did anyone untrained keep these two alive so long?"

No one bothered to answer his question, which was purely rhetorical anyway. Though their energy made them seem to be many more, there were in fact only four of them. There were two Healers, one of them the young man, the other a gray-haired woman, serene and confident. With them were two girls, a little older than Rafi, to act as monitors; both of them were petite and very attractive, and seemed to be related. It seemed as though the four of them were long accustomed to acting as a team. Rafi learned from their bantering that they had set out immediately as soon as the Keeper had awakened them, and it had taken them all night to reach this shelter. They seemed amazingly fresh and energetic to Rafi, but all four were experienced travelers and had long ago learned the secret of dozing in the saddle.

Rafi watched them from her corner; they seemed to drift in and out of focus constantly, now appearing as ordinary mortals, then seeming to be half transparent, and showing sparkling nets of energy within themselves. She had lost her hold on the passage of time, and it seemed to her that it was only moments before the *leroni* had both Lirella and Caro sitting up and beginning to speak groggily.

Oddly ennough, it was Lirella who thought of her first.

"Rafi—" she muttered, trying to think despite a blinding headache. "We sent her out to get wood—"

"Keighvin, Keeper said there was a third, the one who called us! Where did she go?" the girl who had monitored him exclaimed.

Keighvin's eyes were drawn irresistibly to a huddled bundle in the corner. He rose and in two long strides was peering down at it. A dead-white face looked up at his, seemingly composed of little more than skin stretched over a skull and eyes.

Rafi stared at the young Healer, trying to read his

thoughts. All that she cared about now was that Caro and Lirella were in safe hands; she was far past caring about herself. It was the work of a moment to learn from his mind that all was well with them; with relief, she sighed, and let go—and the shelter and its occupants began to fade away.

"Zandru's Hells!" Keighvin exclaimed again. "Somebody help me!"

"She did all that by herself?" Caro asked incredulously. All three of the Renunciates were sitting bundled in fur robes by the newly mended fire. The *leroni* had brought everything they'd thought might be needful, and it was just as well that they had. Neither Healer had wished to move the wounded women for at least a day, and as for Rafi—she was in no better shape than her two Sisters.

"All that, and more," the second Healer, Gabriela, replied. "I doubt I would have thought of using the *chervine* to drag you into shelter. I certainly wouldn't have had the courage to go out into the Overworld for help without being monitored."

Rafi was finally warm again, and was in a drowsy state of half-awareness where it didn't seem to matter that people were talking about her as if she weren't there. In fact, the conversation was rather interesting.

"And I don't know about you, *mestra*," Keighvin said, cradling a mug of hot tea in both hands, "but to be brutally frank, I don't think I'd have exhausted my resources the way she did for anybody. I'll have you two know that it was touch-and-go for a few moments whether we could keep her from slipping away altogether. She came very close to killing herself by sheer exhaustion in order to save the two of you—she damn near worships both of you, you know. Takes her Renunciate Oath completely literally, we all saw that in her mind. And I'd still like to know how someone with no Healer training managed to keep both of you alive long enough for us to get here."

"That just doesn't sound like the Rafi I know." Lirella seemed baffled.

"I'd say you know her a lot less well than you thought," Keighvin replied with a lifted eyebrow.

"We have a saying in the mountains—" the monitor Caitlin said diffidently. " 'A child lives what he learns.' From what I could see, it seems to me that your Rafi has been told she's useless at every turn. When you're told you're a failure, you tend to become one. And I mean no harm, *mestra*, but she's not exactly suited for the life of a mercenary. Without intending to, you set her one more task she was doomed to fail at."

"That clumsiness, for instance." Keighvin sipped his tea thoughtfully. "It's not something she can help. There's something wrong between *here*—" he tapped his forehead, "—and *here*." He held out a hand. "If you had *laran* I could show you. I'm surprised Neskaya never told her; it might have saved her a lot of needless grief."

"Can it be mended?" Caro wanted to know.

He shook his head regretfully. "Perhaps in the days of my grandfather's grandfather, but not now. We lose more skills every year. It isn't anything incapacitating, in any case. All she needs to do is remember never to move without thinking."

"Which is something a fighter can't afford," Lirella reminded him.

"Who told you she *had* to become a fighter?" he said. "My sister is with the Guild at Elhalyn, and she couldn't fight her way out of a henhouse. She's a Healer, as I am, and a midwife. My father refuses to acknowledge her existence, but we who follow the Healer's path are a bit more pragmatic; I happen to think she does more good where she is than wearing herself out as a brood mare. She's given me a lot of respect for the Guild, by the way. Why don't you send this child there? Rima is constantly sending me letters complaining that she needs an apprentice desperately. From the way she tended you, Rafi surely has the talent for it."

To her own amazement, Rafi heard herself saying quietly, "Please—I'd like that."

Six pairs of eyes turned to meet hers; five with astonishment, one with amusement.

"So, the rabbithorn finds a voice." Keighvin filled another mug with tea, poured in a generous dollop of honey, and brought it to her. "It's not an easy avocation, you know," he said, sitting on his heels beside her. "You spend yourself constantly, often in behalf of people who are ungrateful afterward, and you seldom get to sleep a full, uninterrupted night. You'll see things that will break your heart, sometimes. That will be even more true for you than it is for me, because *you'll* be seeing the battered children, the abused wives, and you won't be able to do anything about their condition except treat the hurts and hope that your own example will show them they needn't live with abuse unless they want to. You'll need strength of spirit the way your two Sisters here need strength of body."

"Yes, but—" she said, a little timidly, "you said I have the talent—and—I did things *right*—you said so!"

"In very deed, you did," Gabriela said warmly. "And there's your answer, *mestra*." She looked full at Caro. "Again, it wasn't your fault, but the way to give this girl confidence is not to try to bully her into fighting back, but to give her something she can *succeed* in. She's no coward, not when it comes to risking herself to save others. She just has a different kind of courage than either of you are used to seeing."

Rafi looked at the scars on the hand that held the mug. "I—I am a coward," she said. "1 can't bear pain. That's why they sent me away from Neskaya."

"Poo." The fourth member of the party came into the conversation for the first time. "I can't take much pain either. That's why they made me a monitor. Some of us just have less tolerance than others. That certainly doesn't make you a coward. You had enough bravery to run away from your father, didn't you? I'm pretty sure 1 wouldn't have dared do that. And you were brave enough last night to do what you knew had to be done, no matter what it cost you. That's a whole lot braver than I am."

"So speaks Gwenna, who dug out the three of us with her bare hands when we were half-buried by an avalanche last year," Keighvin said to Rafi in an undertone.

Rafi stared at the young woman in wide-eyed astonishment. If someone who had done *that* said that *she* was brave—well, perhaps, just perhaps—

"So, what is your verdict? I know what Rima's answer

will be if you offer to send her this young Sister of yours. I have worked often enough with Renunciates to know that the craft of the Healer is as honored as the craft of the fighter. I've met Rima; she's a good teacher. When she's through with Rafi, you probably won't recognize her, and she'll be a Renunciate any Guild Hall would be proud of. What is your answer?" Gabriela asked Caro.

"First and foremost, we have to complete our mission—" Caro replied thoughtfully, as she looked at Rafi with new eyes. "I can't speak for the Guild Mother, but—"

"But?"

"I think, once she hears what we have to say—it *must* be yes."

The *leroni* looked terribly satisfied with themselves—Keighvin grinned at Rafi broadly.

As for Rafi, she sipped her tea in silence, her eyes gone thoughtful and shining, as she contemplated a future that had suddenly become brighter than her wildest dreams—and deep within her, something grew a little stronger.

Confidence, and a different kind of courage.

INTRODUCTION TO "THIRD TIME LUCKY"

by Tanya Huff

The first story I ever sold, "Third Time Lucky"—the story you have here—was not the first story I had published. Although George Scithers at *Amazing Stories* bought "Lucky" in the fall of 1985 (September 13th to be exact; I still have the letter) it didn't come out until the November 1986 issue. In the interim, I'd sold "What Little Girls Are Made Of" to a shared world anthology, *Magic In Ithkar 3*, edited by Andre Norton and Robert Adams. *Ithkar 3* came out in October of 1986, with the result that the second story I'd sold came out a month before the first.

Just so you know.

And as it happens, George Scithers was not the first editor I sent "Lucky" to; it went originally to Marion Zimmer Bradley for one of the early editions of *Sword and Sorceress*. The rejection letter she sent back said, in its entirety, "Dear Sonya: We are not amused. MZB" I still have that letter, too. Then it went to Gardner Dozois at *Isaac Asimov's Science Fiction Magazine* who sent back a form letter with "Sorry, try again." scribbled across the bottom. (Okay, so I didn't actually get rid of any of the letters. It *was* my first story, after all.) The submission to *Amazing Stories* was the third. And was, indeed, lucky.

Serendipitously, pretty much the day I received the news from Mr. Scithers, I took a trip to New York with a friend. While there, manuscript of my first book in hand, I was fortunate enough to be able to speak with Sheila Gilbert at DAW. When Sheila asked if I'd had anything published, I was able to say that although I hadn't had anything exactly published, I'd just sold my first story to George Scithers at *Amazing*. That manuscript was *Child of the Grove* and Sheila not only bought it, she's bought eighteen since, so if having that first professional sale gave me even a little bit of an edge, it also gave me a career I love.

As it turned out, "Third Time Lucky" became the first of six Magdelene stories. Three of them also sold to *Amazing Stories*, the fourth went to *Marion Zimmer Bradley's Fantasy Magazine*, and number six was in *Wizard Fantastic*.

I wrote "Lucky" in the winter of '83 while vacationing with a friend at the Cuban equivalent of a Club Med—where one price pays for almost everything. Fortunately, all I really wanted was a chance to swim and lie in the sun. Fortunately—because that was all there was to do. Well, to be fair, there was also the replica sailing ship they used for a nightclub where Cuban beer was amazingly cheap and the beautiful young men who worked at the resort and spoke no English danced with the tourists as part of the job. But that's a whole 'nuther story—although actually, now I think of it, it turned out to be part of Magdelene's story, too.

I'm not positive where the idea for "Lucky" came from, but I suspect it grew from considering, "what if the most powerful wizard in the world really *was* the most powerful wizard in the world, but all she wanted was a chance to swim and lie in the sun?" I think all writers have a wish-fulfillment character and Magdelene is mine.

I do know the genesis of Silk and the lizard. The Cuban resort was overrun with essentially feral cats used to keep down the vermin population in the adjoining sugar cane fields, and one very pregnant silver tabby hung around our cabana. While sitting in a deck chair one afternoon, I heard crunching and turned to see her with half a lizard hanging out of her mouth. Cats and lizards became a recurring motif.

I wrote the first draft of "Lucky" in longhand in a ring-back scribbler with a picture of Miss Piggy on the cover, sitting on a set of concrete steps knee-deep in the equatorial Atlantic, wearing the last two-piece bathing suit I'd ever own. It was hot, but I liked it hot.

Just think how differently my life would have turned out if I'd been a skier.

THIRD TIME LUCKY

by Tanya Huff

THE lizard had no idea it was being observed as it lay on top of the low coral wall, its mouth slightly open, its eyes unfocused golden jewels. Its only concern was with the warmth of the spring sun—not that the spring sun was much different from the winter sun.

"The real difference," Magdelene explained every spring to a variety of sweating guests, "is that it goes from being hot to being damned hot."

"How can you stand it?" one visitor had panted, languidly fanning himself with a palm leaf.

Magdelene's gray eyes had crinkled at the corners. "I like it hot." And she'd licked her lips.

The visitor, a handsome young nobleman who'd been sent south by his father until a small social infraction blew over, spent the rest of his life wondering if he'd misunderstood.

The lizard liked it hot as well.

Silk, Magdelene's cat, did not. She was expecting her first litter of kittens and between the extra weight and the heat she was miserable. She did, however, like lizards.

The lizard never knew what hit him. One moment he was peacefully enjoying the sun, the next he was dangling upside down between uncomfortably sharp teeth being carried into the garden where he was suddenly and painfully dropped. He was stunned for a moment, then scuttled as fast as he could for the safety that beckoned from under a broken piece of tile.

He didn't make it.

Twice more he was lifted, carried, and dropped. Finally he turned, raised his head, and hissed at his tormentor.

Which was quite enough for Silk. She lunged with dainty precision, bit the lizard's head off, then made short work of the rest of it.

"Are you sure you should be eating lizards in your condition?" Magdelene asked. The crunching of tiny bones had distracted her attention from her book.

Silk merely licked her lips disdainfully and stalked away, her distended belly swaying from side to side.

Magdelene laughed and returned to the story. It was a boring tale of two men adventuring in the land of the Djinn, but the friend who had brought it to her had gone to a great deal of trouble and books were rare—even with that printing device they had come up with in the east—so she read it.

"Mistress, will you be eating in the garden today?"

"Please, Kali. It'll be happening soon; I want to enjoy the peace while I can."

"Happening again, Mistress?"

"Some people never learn, Kali."

"One can hope, Mistress," Kali sniffed and went back in the house to prepare lunch.

"One always hopes," Magdelene sighed, "but it doesn't seem to do much good."

She had lived in the turquoise house on the hill for as long as anyone in the fishing village that held her closest neighbors could remember. Great grandmothers had told little children how, when they were young, their great grandmothers had told them that she had always been there. She had been there so long, in fact, that the villagers took her presence for granted and treated her much the same way as they treated the wind and the coral reef and the sea: with a friendly respect. It had taken them longer to accept Kali and the visible difference of red eyes and ivory horns, but that, too, had come in time. It had been years since it was considered unusual to see the demon housekeeper in the marketplace arguing over the price of fish. It was, however, still unusual to see her lose the argument.

Occasionally it was useful to have Magdelene for a neighbor.

"Carlos, there's a dragon in the harbor."

The village headman sighed and looked at the three heaps of kindling that had been fishing boats a very short time before. It had been a miracle that all six fishermen had survived. "Yes, M'lady, I know."

"I guess," Magdelene mused, squinting into the wind, her skirt and the two scarves she had wrapped around her breasts snapping and dancing about her, "I should go out and talk to him."

"I'll ready my boat." The headman turned to go but, Magdelene held up her hand.

"Don't bother," she said. "Boats are tippy, unstable little things. I'll walk."

And she did. She got wet to about the knees, as the swells made for uneven footing, but while the villagers watched in awe—she'd never done *that* before—she walked out until she stood, bobbing gently up and down with the waves, about five body-lengths from the dragon.

"Well?" she asked.

"Gertz?" replied the huge silver sea-dragon, extraordinarily puzzled. This was outside his experience as well. He turned his head so he could fix her in one opalescent eye.

Magdelene put her hands on her hips.

"Go on," she said firmly. "Shoo!"

The dragon, recognizing the voice of authority, however casual, suddenly decided there was much better fishing farther south, and left.

The villagers cheered as Magdelene stepped back into the sand. She grinned and curtsied, not gracefully but enthusiastically, then waved a hand at the wreckage. Wood, rope, canvas, and the few bits of metal received in trade for fish, shuddered, stirred, then danced themselves back into fishing boats.

Everyone stared in silent surprise. This was more than they'd dared hope for.

"We don't know how to thank you," the headman began, but his wife interrupted.

"Just say it, for Netos' sake," she muttered, knowing her husband's tendency to orate at the slightest provocation. "The Lady knows what she's done, she doesn't need you telling her."

Carlos sighed. "Thank you."

Magdelene twinkled at him. "You're welcome." Then she went home to browbeat Kali into baking something sweet for supper. She hadn't got halfway up the hill before the boats were putting out to replace the morning's lost catch.

Two days later the soldiers came.

"It is happening, Mistress."

"Yes, Kali, I know."

"What would you have me do?"

"I think," Magdelene shaded her eyes with her hand, "you should make lunch for six. We'll eat in the garden."

The captain had been sent by his King to bring back the most powerful wizard in the world. What he and the four soldiers he'd brought with him were supposed to do if the wizard refused to cooperate was beyond him. Die, he suspected. The wizard had been ridiculously easy to find; legends—and the memory of some of them caused him to shift uneasily on his saddle—had led him right to her. He wasn't sure what he'd expected, but it wasn't a forty-year-old woman with laughing eyes and a sunburned nose who was barely dressed.

"I'm looking," he said stiffly, stopping his small troop at the gate in the coral wall, "for Magdelene, the Wizard."

"You're looking at her." Magdelene liked large, well-muscled men with grizzled beards—even if they were wearing too much clothing—so she gave the captain her best smile.

The captain showed no visible reaction, but behind him, young Colin smiled back. The most powerful wizard in the world reminded him of his Aunt Maya.

"I am here to take you to Bokta . . ."

"Where in the Goddess' creation is that?"

"North," he said flatly; worship of the Goddess had been outlawed in Bokta for several dozen years. "Very far north."

"Why does he always go north?" Magdelene asked Silk, who had shown up to see what was going on. "What's wrong with east, or west, or even farther south?"

Silk neither knew nor cared; and as she didn't much like horses, she padded off to find some shade.

Magdelene looked up to find the captain glaring at her and was instantly, although not very sincerely, contrite. "Oh, I'm sorry. You were saying?"

"I am here to take you to Bokta so you may prove yourself to be the most powerful wizard in the world. My King does not believe you are."

"Really? And who told him I wasn't?"

A small smile cracked the captain's beard. "I believe it was his wizard."

"I'll bet," said Magdelene dryly. "And if I don't come?"

"Then I'm to tell you that the wizard will destroy twenty people daily from the time I return without you until you appear."

Magdelene's eyes went hard. "Will he?"

"Yes."

"That son of a bitch!" She considered that for a moment and grinned ruefully at her choice of phrase. "We can leave tomorrow. I'd travel faster on my own, but we'd best follow procedure."

She stepped back and the five men rode into the yard. Suddenly there was no gate in the corral wall.

"Oh, put that away," she chided a nervous soldier, who clutched his sword in an undeniably threatening manner. "If those great big horses of yours can't jump a three-foot wall, even in this heat, you're in trouble. Besides, you couldn't kill me if you wanted to. I've been dead, and it isn't all it's cracked up to be."

The sword remained pointed at her throat.

"Garan!" snapped the captain.

"But, sir . . ."

"Put it away!"

"Yes, sir."

The captain swung off his horse. "Then we are your prisoners."

"Don't be ridiculous, you're my guests. Unsaddle your horses and turn them loose over there. They'll be well taken care of." She turned and headed for the garden. "Then you can join me for lunch. I hope you like shrimp." She paused and faced them again, noting with amusement that they were looking slightly stunned. "And please don't draw on my housekeeper, her feelings are easily hurt."

A small problem arose the next morning.

"You have no horse?" the captain asked incredulously.

Magdelene shook her head. "I can't ride. No sense of rhythm." She slapped her hands in front of her to illustrate the point. "I go one way, the horse goes another, and we meet in the middle. Incredibly uncomfortable way to travel."

As children in Bokta rode before they walked, it hadn't occurred to the captain that the wizard would not have a horse. Or that she'd be unwilling to get one.

"Never mind," she said comfortingly, "we'll stop by the village on our way and borrow Haylio's donkey and cart."

"Donkey and cart?" repeated the captain weakly.

"He's not very fast, but I can sit in a cart with the best of folk." She waved a hand, and the gate reappeared in the wall.

"Mistress—" Kali stood in the garden. "When will you return?"

"How long will it take us to get to this Bokta place?" Magdelene queried the captain who, in company with his men, was eyeing Kali nervously. Garan had his hand on his sword.

"Uh, about three months."

"Then expect me back in about three months plus a day. After all," she added for her escort's benefit, "I don't intend to take the scenic route back. And you," she wagged a finger at Silk who was lying at Kali's feet. "You take care of yourself, and no more lizards."

Silk inspected a perfectly groomed silver paw and refused to answer.

It was a strange cavalcade that moved north along the coast road: five great warhorses carrying overdressed and sweaty soldiers, bracketting a medium-sized donkey pulling a two-wheeled cart and the most powerful wizard in the world.

Magdelene sang loudly and tunelessly as they traveled, her songs usually the type gently bred females were not supposed to know.

"Madam!" The captain had stood it as long as he was able.

A bawdy lyric, in an impossible key, faded to silence. "Something troubling you?"

"It's that song . . ."

"Oh? Am I corrupting your men?"

"No, but you're scaring the horses."

For a moment the captain anticipated being turned into something unpleasant, then Magdelene threw back her head and laughed long and hard.

"Point taken," she gasped when the laughter finally let her talk. "I've no music at all and I know it. Do you sing, Captain?"

"No."

She grinned up at him. "Pity. I'm very," she paused and her smile grew thoughtful as she remembered, "amiable to men who make music."

On his way back to the front of the line the captain almost succeeded in not wondering just how amiable this wizard could be.

The soldiers treated Magdelene with a mixture of fear and respect, fear winning most often, for their King's wizard had taught them to dread the breed; all save Colin, who treated her much the same as he treated his Aunt Maya. Magdelene, who had never been anyone's aunt, slipped happily into the role and Colin became the only one of the fair-skinned northerners to stop burning and peeling and burning again.

"Well, I don't care what you say," growled Garan. "Ain't nobody's aunt can grab a fistful of fire, then sit there tossing it from hand to hand."

"I don't think she was aware she was doing it."

"And that makes it better? Hummph."

They reached Denada in three and a half weeks. Even forced to the donkey's pace, that was two days faster than it had taken going the other way.

The captain sighed in relief; he'd about had it with the perpetual heat of the southlands. Even the rain was warm. He spurred his horse toward the city gate.

"Uh, Sir!"

"Now what?" He wheeled around, narrowly missed running down a farmer with a basket of yams on his head, and was soundly cursed. When he reached the cart, Magdelene removed her small bundle of belongings and was kissing the soft gray muzzle of the donkey.

"What are you doing?"

She grinned up at him. "What does it look like? I'm kissing the donkey."

Colin snickered but managed to school his expression before the captain could look his way.

The captain sighed. "Metros give me strength," he prayed. "Why are you kissing the donkey?"

"Because I'm sending him home." She flicked the animal between his eyes with the first two fingers of her left hand.

Half a startled bray hung on the air, but the donkey and the cart were gone.

"Can your Aunt Maya do that?" hissed Garan.

Colin had to admit she couldn't.

"Why not send us to Bokta that way," demanded the captain, walking his horse through the space where the donkey had been, making sure it had truly vanished, "and avoid all this damned traveling."

"I know where I've been," Magdelene replied gravely, "but even I don't know where I'm going to be until I get there." She shouldered her bag and headed for the gate. The captain and his men could only follow.

The five northern soldiers on their massive warhorses

made little stir as they moved the width of the city, from the gate to the harbor. After all they had been there less than two months before and Denada, a cosmopolitan city with traders arriving daily from exotic places, saved its wonder for the truly unusual. Only a few street whores took any notice of the men, and no one at all noticed the most powerful wizard in the world.

Denada's harbor was huge: twenty ships could tie up, and there was room for another twelve to ride at anchor. Miraculously, the *Raven*, the ship that had carried the soldiers across the inland sea, was still docked and appeared to have just finished loading.

"Two months!" screamed her master, bounding down the gangway. "Two months I sit here since you leave. First, I must clean smell of abominable animals out of my forward hold though still it smells like a stable, then what happens but my steersman—may his liver be eaten by cockroaches—sets sail with a hangover we come up bang on coral and rip off half of keel. It is a miracle—may all the gods in heaven be blessed and I don't doubt they are—that we make it back for repairs. Now at last we are ready to sail." He pounded the captain's shoulder enthusiastically. "So, what can I do for you?"

"I need passage north for myself, my men, and our horses. And for this lady here."

"Aiee, again with the horses!" He didn't give Magdelene, who was dropping stale journey bread into the water to feed the fish, a second glance. "Still, already I have a hold that smells like a stable. Fourteen gold pieces."

"All right, I . . ."

"Two," said Magdelene, her eyes glinting dangerously as she dusted crumbs off her hands.

The ship's master stared accusingly at the captain. "I thought you said she was a lady? Fourteen I say and fourteen it is."

After a spirited discussion, they settled on eight. The captain paid up, and Magdelene deftly lifted four gold pieces from his pouch.

"Hey!"

"You're still up two," she said sweetly. "While you load the horses, I'm going shopping."

"Don't tell me," muttered Garan, stopping Colin before he could speak. "Your Aunt Maya loves to shop."

Hours passed, the ship was ready to sail on the evening tide, and Magdelene had still not returned. Both worried and annoyed, the captain walked to the end of the docks to look for her. He was considering a trip into the city when she came barreling around a corner, a grimy urchin heavily laden with packages in tow, and crashed into his arms.

"Here, take these." She shoved the parcels at him and tossed the boy a silver piece. "Thanks for the help, kid, now beat it before the mob gets here."

"Where have you been?" demanded the captain as they trotted toward the ship. "We're ready to leave. Why are we running an . . ." He stopped. "Mob? What mob?"

Magdelene got him moving again. "I cured a blind beggar. It drew a bit of a crowd. Good thing the kid knew a shortcut."

They sprinted up the gangway just as the leading edge of the mob appeared at the end of the docks. A cry went up as Magdelene was spotted.

"Why didn't you do something a little less spectacular?" muttered the captain, tossing the packages over the rail, then vaulting it himself. "Like raising the dead."

"I did that the last time." She accepted his helping hand, having somehow managed to become tangled in a stray line. "This time I was trying to keep a low profile."

"You've been here before, then."

"Twice."

"Well, maybe next time you can pass through without starting a riot." He shouted to the ship's master to cast off, but it was unnecessary. The instant Magdelene's foot touched the deck, ropes untied themselves and the *Raven* slipped its mooring just ahead of the first hysterical Denadan.

"Why," asked the captain, using the toe of his boot on a package in danger of going overboard, "does the most powerful wizard in the world have to run from a crowd of shopkeepers and beggars?"

Magdelene collapsed on a bale of rope. "I'll let you in on a secret," she panted. "I'm also the laziest wizard in the world. Running was definitely the least complicated thing to do."

The trip across the inland sea had never been done faster. The *Raven* seemed to barely touch the waves and the wind never left her sails.

"I don't like boats," Magdelene explained when the captain voiced his suspicions about the wind. "They make me sick. It's worse than being pregnant."

He stared at her in surprise. He'd never thought of her having a life like other women.

"You had children?"

"Have," she corrected, and it wasn't just the sea that chased the laughter from her eyes. "One. A son. Goddess why I ever let his father talk me into it."

"He could make music," the captain suggested.

Some of the laughter returned. "He could at that."

The ship rolled, and the most powerful wizard in the world turned slightly green.

"Oh, lizard piss!" she muttered and headed for the rail.

The *Raven* docked in Finera in eighteen days. The previous record was twenty-seven.

"Anytime you want to travel the seas, Lady Wizard, you are most welcome to sail with me."

Magdelene smiled stiffly at the ship's master, "Next time I travel, I'll walk." She gripped Colin's arm tightly as he helped her down the gangway. "Sometimes I think he situates himself purposefully so that I have to travel by sea."

Colin looked puzzled.

"Never mind, dear. Just get me somewhere that isn't moving."

"Take her to the Laughing Boar," bellowed the captain over the squeals of the horse being lifted from the hold. "We'll spend the night."

The Laughing Boar was the largest inn in Finera and a favorite with the caravan masters who came into the city to trade with ships from the south. As they crossed the common room, Magdelene counted fifteen different dialects;

one of which, she was surprised to note, she didn't know. Her room was large and cheerful and so, she observed with satisfaction, was the bed.

"This ought to make him sit up and take notice." She winked at her reflection, now clad in a dangerously low cut green silk gown, and went looking for the captain.

Later that night he sat on the edge of her bed, suddenly unsure.

"What's wrong?" she asked, gently tweaking a wiry curl.

He caught her hand. "Did you use your magic to bring me here?"

She smiled and there was nothing, and everything, magic in the smile. "Only the magic that women have been using on men since the Goddess created the world."

"Oh." He considered for a moment. "That's all right, then." And he lowered himself to her lips.

Next morning, as he left Magdelene's room, the captain bumped into Colin in the corridor. The young man executed a parade-ground perfect salute and marched briskly off down the hall, his face a study in suppressed laughter.

"Smart-assed kid," muttered the captain, as he straightened his tunic and stomped off to find breakfast.

"Will we have to camp in this?" Magdelene asked anxiously, watching water stream off the shield she had raised over the entire group. Even Garan was forced to agree there were certain advantages in traveling with a wizard.

"Not for a while," Cohn reassured her. "We follow the Great North Road over half the way, and it seems to be lined with inns."

Magdelene eyed the broad back of the captain. "Good."

"I'd like to see you claim resemblance to your Aunt Maya now." Garan wiped foam off his mouth onto his sleeve. "She's used her blasted magic to bewitch the captain."

"That's all you know," Colin chuckled, finishing his own ale. "My family lives in the capital and the captain has bedded Aunt Maya."

*   *   *

When they reached the border of Bokta, a full division of the King's Guard awaited them, darkly impressive in their black-and-silver armor.

"This is the best you could do?" sneered the Guard Captain, staring disdainfully down his narrow nose at Magdelene in her pony cart. "The King and his Wizard are not going to be pleased."

It had been a long trip, and Magdelene was not in the best of moods. "How would you like to spend the rest of your life as a tree frog?" she asked conversationally.

The Guard Captain ignored her. "Can't you keep her quiet?" he drawled, ennui dripping from the words.

It was difficult to say who was more surprised, the division of King's Guard or the tree frog clinging to the saddle of the Guard Captain's horse.

"Magdelene," sighed the captain, "change him back."

"He's a pompous ass," Magdelene protested sulkily.

"Granted, but he's also the King's favorite nephew. Please."

"Oh, all right." She waved her hand. The Guard Captain cheeped once, found himself back in his own body, and fainted. It was a rather subdued trip into the Capital.

The King's Wizard stirred the entrails of the goat with the tip of his bloody knife. She was here, in the Palace, and when he defeated her he would be the most powerful wizard in the world! Power. He could feel it burning through him, lighting fires of destruction that he would release to obliterate this woman, this Magdelene.

He wiped the knife on a skin taken whole off a stillborn babe, twitched his robes into place, and left his sanctum. Behind him, blood began to drip off the table and form a pool on the carpet.

The King was waiting in the corridor, nervously pacing up and down. He stopped when the Wizard emerged, and his two men-at-arms thankfully fell into place behind him.

"She's in the Palace. We must hurry, or we won't be in the throne room when she arrives."

The Wizard merely nodded curtly. His measured stride didn't change.

"You are sure you can defeat her?" The King, left standing, scrambled to catch up.

"I have studied for over a hundred years. I command the demons of the Netherworld. I control the elements. I can easily defeat one ancient woman."

Magdelene's actual appearance came as a bit of a shock to both men. The crystal had only ever shown her location, never the wizard herself. This was the most powerful wizard in the world? This laughing woman who wasn't even wearing wizardly robes? The King almost chuckled as he took his seat.

Magdelene approached the throne with the captain, bowed when he did, and clicked her tongue when she looked up at the King's Wizard. Thick gray hair sprang from a widow's peak and curled on his shoulders, his eyes were sunken black pits, his nails were claws on the end of long and skinny fingers, and his stooped body was covered in a black robe so closely embroidered with cabalistic symbols that from a distance it looked more gold than black.

"If he'd just once realize that self-control comes first," she hissed to the captain as a herald announced them.

The whispers of the court fell silent as the King's Wizard stepped forward. "I have summoned you to prove yourself," he declared in ponderous tones, blue fire crackling eerily about him.

The captain shifted his weight so that his cloak fell free of his sword. He had always hated this wizard, this scrawny gray scarecrow of a man, and had it not been for the innocent lives that would have been forfeit, he would have never brought Magdelene here to him. At least not after he'd got to know her.

Magdelene successfully fought the urge to giggle. "Interesting outfit, Tristan. Demon-made?"

"My name is Polsarr," snarled the wizard, his lips pulled back over startlingly white teeth.

"Your name," said Magdelene mildly, "is Tristan. I should know, I gave it to you. And now," she turned to the King, "I'd like to be shown to my room, it's been a long trip."

"You are not going anywhere, woman!" bellowed Polsarr. "Until I banish you into darkness!"

"Oh? And would you have everyone say that you defeated the most powerful wizard in the world only because she was exhausted and irritable from four days of bumping over incredibly bad roads?"

The King tugged on Polsarr's sleeve. "We don't want that! There must be no doubt when you win."

Polsarr glowered and muttered but finally had to agree the King was right. "Enjoy your rest," he snarled. "It will be your last." He stalked from the room.

"If he really wants to prove his power," Magdelene muttered to the King, "he should do something about those roads."

The King ignored that. "Captain, take her to the south tower in the east wing. And Captain, you and your men will guard this wizard one more night."

The captain bowed and backed away. Magdelene gave the King her second-best smile and followed.

At the tower—which was as far away from the rest of the Palace as it was possible to get and still be in the Palace—the captain dismissed his men.

"Be back at dawn," he told them. "Even if the King's Wizard decides to attack tonight, there's nothing you could do."

Colin raised an eyebrow at the phrasing but he went with the rest.

The tower was deserted and, judging by the unbroken layer of dust, hadn't been used in years. Magdelene waved a hand at her bag, and it trailed them up the stairs.

"The man's as big an ass as the King's nephew."

There was no need to ask who she meant.

"He's not much like you."

"Thank you. He's not much like his father either. That man didn't have an ambitious bone in his body." She sighed. "Maybe I should've encouraged the kid's musical talents."

The captain threw open a door leading to an old-fashioned bedchamber.

"If I remember correctly, this is the only furnished room in the tower."

Magdelene stepped inside, the bag settling to the floor at her feet. "It's not that bad. The bed looks solid enough for one night at least." She grinned over her shoulder at the captain, only to find him hesitating in the doorway. "What's wrong?"

"I'll stand guard in the hall. "You'll need your strength for tomorrow."

"And I want your strength tonight," she told him gently, drawing him into the room and shutting the door.

Some hours later the captain untangled himself from her embrace and rolled over on his back. "Is there anything," he asked, trying to get his breath back, "that you don't do well?"

Magdelene ran her fingers through the matted hair on his chest. "I'm a lousy mother," she admitted.

Everyone with a plausible excuse crowded into the throne room the next morning. People were packed so tightly against the walls they had to cooperate with their neighbors in order to breathe. Even the Queen, who hated public functions and wanted only to be left alone, was there. The King was almost quivering with excitement, anticipating when he would control the most powerful wizard in the world. Polsarr stood alone in the center of the room.

When Magdelene entered, the room released a collective sigh. She had not escaped in the night.

Leaving the captain and his men by the door, Magdelene walked forward until she stood only three body-lengths from her son.

"Morning, Tristan. Sleep well?"

Polsarr ignored the question. He drew himself up to his full height and declared, "Already I have defeated seven lesser mages."

"Seven," said Magdelene. "Imagine that."

"I banished even the mighty Joshuae to the Nether-worlds!" He saw what he thought was worry in Magdelene's eyes and chuckled.

Magdelene wasn't worried. She was annoyed. "You banished Joshuae to the Netherworld? That was remarkably rude; the man is your name father."

"I HAVE NO NAME FATHER!"

His outraged volume was impressive.

"Well, you don't now, that's for sure. I only hope he finds his way back."

"I WAS BORN IN THE BELLY OF THE MOUNTAIN AND SPEWED FORTH WITH FIRE AND MOLTEN ROCK!"

Magdelene sighed. "And the time before this you were ripped from the loins of the North Wind. The time before that," her brows wrinkled, "I don't remember the time before that, but it was equally ridiculous, I'm sure. Now can we get on with this?"

Polsarr shrieked with wordless rage and blue lightning leaped from his fingertips.

Magdelene stood unconcerned, and the lightning missed.

A fireball grew in Polsarr's hand. When it reached the size of a wagon wheel, he threw it. And then another. And then another.

Magdelene disappeared with the fire. The flames burned viciously for a moment, then suddenly died down. Although the floor was blackened and warped, Magdelene wasn't even scorched.

Polsarr screamed a hideous incantation, spittle flying from his lips to sizzle on the floor. There was a blinding red flash between the wizards . . . and then a demon.

The demon was three times the size of a man, with green scaled skin and burning red eyes. Six-inch tusks drew its mouth back into a snarl and poisons dripped from the scimitar-shaped talons that curved out from both hands and feet. It raised heavily muscled arms, screamed, and lurched toward Magdelene.

Magdelene looked it right in the eye.

The demon stopped screaming.

She folded her arms across her chest and her foot began to tap.

The demon paused and reconsidered. Suddenly recognition dawned. It gave a startled shriek and vanished.

Polsarr began to gather darkness about him, but Magdelene raised her hand.

"Enough," she sighed, and snapped her fingers.

When the smoke cleared, the most powerful wizard in the world cradled a baby in her arms. Polsarr's robe lay empty on the floor, and the wizard was nowhere to be seen.

"Here, hold this." She handed the baby to the King. "I want to say good-bye to some people." She walked to the door where the captain and his men still stood. The silence was overwhelming as the audience tried very hard not to attract the Wizard's attention.

"Colin."

The young man stepped forward, for the first time a little afraid.

"This is for you." She wrestled a silver ring with three blue stones off her finger. "There aren't many wizards left in the world, but should you run foul of one, this will protect you." Then she grinned and everything was all right. "Only from wizards, though: it won't raise a finger against outraged fathers." She pulled a string of coral beads out of the air and dropped them on his palm. "These are for your Aunt Maya." Reaching up, she pulled his head down until she could whisper in his ear. "Tell her I said . . ." Magdelene paused, glanced at the captain, and snickered in a very unwizardlike way. "Never mind, if we're as much alike as you seem to think, she'll come up with it on her own." A kiss on the forehead and she released him. "Come and visit me sometime."

"I will."

She moved over to the captain and took both his hands in hers. "It won't be very safe here for you now. You were responsible for me, and I defeated the King's wizard."

They both turned to look at the King, who was holding the baby as if he'd rather be holding the demon.

The captain smiled down at her. "I was thinking of leaving the King's service anyway."

"That might be a good idea. You can always come and stay with me; young Tristan is going to need a father figure." She gurgled with laughter at the look of terror on his face, kissed him hard enough to carry the feel of his lips away with her, and went to collect her son.

"You really should keep a better eye on him," she said to

the Queen, with a nod to the King who was rubbing at the damp spot on his knee.

And then she vanished.

"Not again, Mistress," sighed Kali as Magdelene handed her the baby.

"Sure looks that way." Magdelene sighed as well, then grinned at a suddenly inspired thought. "See if you can find him a lute!" she called after the demon and went to look for Silk and her kittens.

ON "SING"

by Kristine Kathryn Rusch

I have been a professional writer for more than twenty years. I got my start as a reporter, made my living writing nonfiction articles, wrote radio plays for the Annenberg Foundation, and did a whole bunch of p.r. work for companies in Wisconsin. Then I transferred my attention to fiction, writing several novels and a lot of short stories.

The nasty secret about being a professional writer is that sometimes you forget what you've written. Not how the words go, or the order in which the plot plays out, but you forget entire stories, articles, essays—things you've labored long and hard on. (I have yet to forget a novel, but check with me when I'm 90.)

I haven't forgotten "Sing."

Writers never forget their first professional short story sale. It's a validation—that first step on the long hard road toward a career. But I think I would have remembered "Sing" even if it hadn't sold.

You see, it's one of the few early stories I remember writing.

My home office, at the time, was under the eaves of an old farmhouse. The walls slanted, and the office only had one window. In the summer, the office was so unbearably hot that I couldn't work in the middle of the day. In the winter, it was so cold that I had to wrap myself in blankets just to stay warm.

I was working on an Apple IIe computer, which was already out of date. It had dual floppy drives—no hard drive—and a joystick that I finally hid because my then-husband would rather play games than let me write. The letters appeared on the screen in bright green, and if I worked with the light off, the entire office looked as if it were subject to an alien invasion.

I loved that machine.

In those days, I wrote a lot of stories about music. I'd also been noodling with an idea that was as old as photography—what if the Native Americans were right and a camera really did steal a person's soul?—but I knew I'd read it somewhere before. Somehow, the idea of music and photography blurred in my mind to come up with "Sing."

There's one other thing you should know about me, something that hasn't changed. I love to break the rules. In fact, if you challenge me to a competition, I'll spend more time trying to win while breaking the rules than I will completing the competition. I have no idea why.

So one of my writing instructors told us, in no uncertain terms, that writers should never write in dialect. We debated him, of course. What about Twain? Dickens? Shakespeare?

His answer implied that dialect lessened their books—something which makes me smile even now. Today I would shrug his statement away as silly and uninformed. But then I saw it as a challenge.

For me, "Sing" wasn't about music or souls. It was about voice. I spent days making the voice and the words consistent, almost as if I were composing a piece of music myself.

Then I mailed the story off.

It seemed, at first, that my writing teacher had been right. I got the nastiest rejection slips I'd ever got in my life, telling me to learn grammar and spelling, or to give up writing altogether. I wondered why the editors didn't realize I was writing in dialect.

(Now I know. When I edited, I learned that most new writers don't know grammar or spelling. The assumption is that a new writer is incompetent—not the other way around.)

A new magazine was opening up by the name of *Aboriginal SF*, and the editor, Charles C. Ryan, actually read my story. He loved it, and bought it, making it a cover story.

"Sing" didn't just mark my debut. It also marked the first cover for a hugely popular artist in the SF field—Bob Eggleton. Bob and I have a lot of firsts together. We even won our first Hugos on the same night.

"Sing" means a lot to me, as a first publication, but also as a successful experiment. No matter how many stories I write, I'll always remember this one—not just because it was my first professional sale, but also because it marked the first time in my budding career where I took advice and tossed it, making my writing my own.

SING

by Kristine Kathryn Rusch

WHEN I was a little girl, there was this guy who lived down the road. He was big, but he weren't mean. I don't think he ever hurt nobody before I first met him.

He called himself Dirk and the name fit 'cause he looked like the daggers children use. He was long and thin, with only two arms and two legs. But he was strong, and he moved like he owned the world—or at least a small part of it.

I used to walk past his place a lot. It was the strangest place I ever seen, all shiny and silver, but the lawn was real nice. He kept the flowers well-cropped. Sometimes these strange sounds echoed around the silver and kept me away. But most of the time, he'd sit right outside his door and blow air through a hollow tube. It made the most awful noise I ever heard, but he seemed to like it.

One day he called me over, sat me down and showed me his tube. It had a bunch of little holes punched in it. I thought maybe he wanted me to take it back to my dad 'cause my dad was good at fixing all kinds of things, but Dirk said no, he had something else to ask me.

—Would you, he asked like he was scared I'd say no even before I heard the question, would you teach me how to *sing*?"

Well, I'd never heard the word "sing" before and I told him so. He kinda frowned and said it was the only word he couldn't find a translation for. That word and a couple others he called "related," as if words could share blood like people do.

—I can't teach something that I don't know what it is, I said to him and he started laughing then.

—Child, you *sing* all the time, when you're walking, when you're eating, even when you're laughing. You people make the most beautiful *music*—(one of his related words)—in the entire galaxy. So I came here to learn how to do it.

I told him I sure didn't know what "it" was and I got to thinking that maybe he was a little crazy somehow. Not scary-crazy like some folks can be, but just plain nutty. Wacky enough to make most people uncomfortable.

—Look, sweetheart, he said, back where I come from, I'm one of the most famous *musicians* in the world. But I can't do half of what you people do. You make the experience of two millennia sound like the tinkering of children. I want to use your *songs* the way *Copeland* and *Sibelius* used folk *tunes*. But first I gotta know how you sing.

—You're not helping me, I said. If this *sing* is something I do all the time like breathing or blinking, how come I don't know about it?

—That's the big question. None of you people seems to know what you're doing. It's driving me nuts. Everybody has their own personal *melody* which they play every day with a different variation. It's like *gypsy music*, never the same. And I'm the only one who can hear it.

I got a little scared there when he said he was going nuts. You never know what someone named Dirk would do when he went crazy. So I picked myself up off the flowers and moved away a little, telling him I had to go somewhere when I really didn't.

He said that was okay. I should come back when I didn't have anything better to do.

I went home then and told my dad about the awful broken tube and he said that maybe I should stay away from Dirk 'cause Dirk weren't like other people. No matter what my dad said, I planned to go back 'cause I thought Dirk was pretty interesting even if he were strange. But I didn't get to go 'cause the next day was the day the first dead body turned up outside of Dirk's place.

It was the body of Rastee the sailor. Rastee had been the most romantic person in town. He sailed on air currents and sometimes, if he were feeling nice, he take a handful of us along. Ain't nothing so smooth and fine as gliding along with the breeze, letting the air dip in and out of your pores. But our chance to sail was gone with Rastee 'cause he was the only expert sailor our little town had.

He was lying in the lawn, crushing a nice poppy grouping that the people who lived there before made. The poppies had soaked into Rastee's skin, all the juices in his body had dried up and his wings had gone blue like he couldn't get no breath, but there weren't no broken bones or nothing so even though it looked like he crash-landed, most people was saying he didn't.

But we just picked him up and carried him off to the place of grass so he wouldn't decay and ruin any more flowers. And nobody said nothing to Dirk or to anyone else. We all went home and mourned the freezing of Rastee's soul.

Dirk was around, same as usual that day, and we was all surprised 'cause there ain't no such thing as a murder without a suicide. There's just so much passion and violence going on that the souls intertwine and when one soul freezes over the other turns to ice too. So we all knew that Dirk didn't kill Rastee and 'cause there weren't no other dead bodies around, the town elders went to the place of grass to study Rastee hoping he hadn't flown over another town and brought a plague back with him.

The elders hadn't figured anything out yet when another dead body turned up on Dirk's lawn in the same spot as Rastee. Nobody was too surprised when they found out it was Maggtana. She'd been poisoning herself for years, sprinkling dried parsnips over everything she ate. I admit, I tried parsnips once or twice, and the rush they give is mighty nice, but everybody knows those things are addicting and will kill you if you ain't careful. And everybody knew Maggtana weren't careful.

That was pretty much it until the night Dirk called me over from the side of the street.

—You know, he said, I think I got it all figured out. Your ear can't hear certain *pitches*. That's why you walk around oblivious to the sounds you make.

Like usual, I didn't know what he was talking about so I just nodded and pretended I did.

—But I think I fixed it, he said real excited-like. I jury-rigged the playback on one of my *recorders* so that everything will be in your *frequency*. I can play your *song* for you if you like.

Well, I thought that sounded just fine. It'd been bugging me for days what them related words of his meant and I was pretty glad I was finally gonna find out.

He took me inside his place and it looked as strange as he did, There was wires and metal all over, and more hollow tubes—some made from wood—and hollow boxes with strings. He sat me down on this platform with four legs that he called a chair but it didn't look like no chair to me.

I felt kinda funny in there with all that strange stuff and so I asked him a question.

—You done this with anyone else?

—Sit them in here and make them listen? he asked back.

—I guess. I said, not knowing really what I meant at all.

—No. I put out a directional *mike* and *recorded* them while they were passing by. I didn't think of asking them in. I played the *songs* back on my outside speakers, but I don't think anyone heard.

He was talking kinda oddlike and I remembered him saying how things here was driving him nuts and I kinda got a little scared.

—Whatcha mean, *recorded* them? I asked and he didn't answer, just touched one of those pieces of metal with the wires all around it.

It made a funny little high noise and then I saw Rastee right in front of me, leaning against a metal thing and talking like he always did. Only I knew it weren't Rastee since he was dead. It had to be a frozen part of his soul. I ain't never heard of nobody seeing a frozen soul before and I was afraid it might freeze me, so I screamed real loud. Dirk hit the piece of metal and Rastee went away.

—What's the matter? he asked.

—That was Rastee!

He smiled then and said, —Yes Rastee's *song*. Isn't it lovely? It's one of the best. So free and happy.

—You got Maggtana too then.

—Her *song* has more melancholy in it than all the others. It tears my heart.

Then he sat in one of those odd chairs and looked right at me.

—But yours is the best. My very favorite. So light and innocent and warm. If you just sit a minute, I'll *record* it. It's soundproof in here and I'll get even better quality on you than I did on the others.

—No. I got up out of the chair and ran for the door. —You're not gonna do nothing to me. You froze their souls and now they're dead and I don't want to die like that with clogged pores and no breath and no juices and a soul that can't change when I do.

He put his hand on the door and stood in my way. He looked real upset.

—I'll let you go, just tell me who died.

—Rastee and Maggtana. We found them out in your poppies.

—How come nobody told me?

—'Cause, I said, we thought it didn't have nothing to do with you. Your soul was all right. Nobody murders and lives. Except you.

—But all I did was *record* them, he said. *Recording* doesn't hurt anyone.

I tried to inch around him real slow. —All I know is that Rastee's soul is froze and he's dead and you bring me in here and show me part of Rastee that don't exist no more.

Dirk was staring at his metal stuff. —We *recorded* hundreds of you off planet and nobody died, except. . . .

He went over to one of the metal boxes and pulled papers out from beside it. I moved closer to the door. I didn't want to run in case he turned one of them boxes on me.

—*Playback*, he whispered. They died after *playback*. Oh my god.

He got out of my way. He stared at his metal stuff and water started running down his cheeks. —Oh my god.

I opened the door and let myself out and went running to the town elders to tell them it weren't no plague at all but Dirk and his funny hollow tubes and we all decided that we'd have to make him leave, so we went back to his place in a big group, but he was gone. His place, his tubes, his metal. Everything was all gone. There was just a big flat spot in the flowers where his place used to be.

We searched all over for him, but we never did find him. And Rastee and Maggtana stayed just as dead as they were that morning in the poppies. But the rest of us was all right. And even though I'm old now, I still wonder sometimes what it is about the *sing* that makes one soul freeze without freezing another. The only reason I can think of why Dirk didn't die when he murdered those two is maybe 'cause Dirk could hear the *sing*. And hearing the *sing* meant he didn't have a right and proper soul.

And me, sometimes in the time between twilight and darkness, I miss Dirk and his strange tubes. And I catch myself dreaming about what it would be like to have him turn his metal things toward me. After all, he did say he was going to do me different. I would of loved to see my soul.

But mostly, I just feel sorry for Dirk. He was stealing souls and keeping them in a box. You can't keep a soul in a box. You got to wear it proud, and it's got to be yours, not someone else's. I hope Dirk knows that now. And I hope he learned to use his tubes to block out the *sing*. Maybe that way his soul will come back, and he won't have to run away to strange places searching for it. But most of all, I wish that Dirk would come here so I could tell him I'm sorry. I shouldn't of run away after I screamed. I should of stayed and helped him find out what part of his soul he was missing. And I didn't.

I wonder if that means my *song* ain't light and innocent and warm no more. It bothers me that I ain't got no way to find out.

INTRODUCTION TO "BIRTHNIGHT"

by Michelle West

There are a number of loosely related facts that underpin the writing of this story. First: I love Christmas stories. The story of Santa Claus, the jolly, white-bearded whimsical gift giver, coupled with the certain knowledge that my parents had *lied to me*, deliberately, about his existence, is probably chiefly responsible for the way that love is expressed; there is both giving and losing, gift and loss, inherent on the occasion.

Second: Although I'm not what anyone rational would call a religious person, there's a certain element of Christian myth that I find fascinating, in almost the same way that I find Tolkien fascinating; it speaks to me in a way that resonates, that feels true, and that I rationally would never defend as reality, no matter how much it can inform my own.

Third: When this story was written, I knew almost nothing about the short story market, because my first attempt at a short story was what eventually became the *Hunter's Oath* and *Hunter's Death* duology; my third attempt was what eventually became the *Books of the Sundered* tetralogy. Just for the record, I originally thought that the *Sun Sword* series, of which I am currently working on volume five, would be two novels—so I admit up front that I don't always understand the concept of "length" when it comes to number of words. Mike Resnick, who has written more novels than I, and vastly more short stories than I, and with whom I'm never likely to catch up—and who has also won almost every award known to man for the writing of those—informed me of the anthology for which "Birthnight" was originally written—one which Marty Greenberg was editing. He also had a lot of advice to offer, and if I weren't afraid of embarrassing him with what is admittedly my terrible memory, I'd probably attempt to reconstruct it all. Suffice it to say that if it weren't for Mike Resnick, this story, and most of the others over which he has no direct bearing, would probably not exist.

Fourth: I was working with Tanya Huff when I wrote this story. She had written a story for the same anthology a month or two earlier, and as I pretty much got to read all of her work before she submitted it— which was wonderful for short stories because she handed me the whole thing at once, whereas with novels it was one chapter at a time—and she likes to end her chapters in a way that will "keep people reading," but I digress—I had actually *read* the story in question. It was, of course, excellent, and had all of the earmarks of a Tanya Huff story: It was funny, it made me sniffle in places, and it was completely rooted in contemporary culture from beginning to end. So when I realized that this fledgling story would be in the *same book* as her story, I knew damn well that I wasn't going to write a contemporary piece. She laughed when I told her this. She laughs when I remind her of it. But really, it was true, and it still is; I love her writing, and it is just *so* different from mine that I always feel nervous after finishing something she's written because I know my work won't evoke the same response.

I was living in my first house, and the room that I worked in—which was my office until my oldest son was born—was painted bright pink (a leftover gift from the previous owner of said house—we had always intended to repaint that room, but we had never gotten around to it, and in the end, my mother painted that room pale blue while I was in the hospital delivering my first child because she wasn't going to condemn a child to that despised and loathsome pink), and the story was written on a Mac SE30, and it was many, many months before Christmas, but all of that story came to me in a sitting, in a mad rush of messy words and the emotions that come out of that particular time of year.

I tweaked it afterward, of course, poking and prodding it, and stripping out words so that I would actually come in at the right length, but I was happy with the story as it came out, and it was this story that I chose to read at Harbourfront, when I was—as usual—petrified about having to do anything in a public venue.

I really hope you like it.

BIRTHNIGHT

by Michelle West

ON the open road, surrounded by gentle hills and grass strong enough to withstand the predation of sheep, the black dragon cast a shadow long and wide. His scales, glittering in sunlight, reflected the passage of clouds above; his wings, spread to full, were a delicate stretch of leathered hide, impervious to mere mortal weapons. His jaws opened; he roared and a flare of red fire tickled his throat and lips.

Below, watching sheep graze and keeping an eye on the nearby river, where one of his charges had managed to bramble itself and drown just three days past, the shepherd looked up. He felt the passing gust of wind warm the air; saw the shadow splayed out in all its splendor against the hillocks, and shaded his eyes to squint skyward.

"Clouds," he muttered, as he shook his head. For a moment, he thought he had seen . . . children's dreams. He smiled, remembering the stories his grandmother had often told to him, and went back to his keeping. The sheep were skittish today; perhaps that made him nervous enough to remember a child's fancy.

The great black dragon circled the shepherd three times;

on each passage, he let loose the fiery death of his voice—
but the shepherd had ceased even to look, and in time, the
dragon flew on.

He found them at last, although until he spotted them
from his windward perch, he had not known he was searching. They walked the road like any pilgrims, and only his
eyes knew them for what they were: Immortal, unchanging,
the creatures of magic's first birth. There, with white silk
mane and horn more precious to man than gold, pranced the
unicorn. Fools talked of horses with horns, and still others,
deer or goats—goats!—but they were pathetic in their lack
of vision. This creature was too graceful to be compared to
any mortal thing; too graceful and too dangerously beautiful.

Ahead of the peerless one, cloaked and robed in a darkness that covered her head, the dragon thought he recognized the statue-maker from her gait. Over her, he did not
linger.

But there also was basilisk, stone-maker, a wingless serpent less mighty than a dragon, and at his side, never quite
meeting his eyes, were a small ring of the Sylvan folk, dancing and singing as they walked. They did not fear the
basilisk's gaze; it was clear from the way they had wreathed
his mighty neck in forest flowers that seemed, to the sharp
eyes of the dragon, to be blooming even as he watched.

And there were others—many others—each and every
one of them the firstborn, the endless.

"Your fires are lazy, brother," a voice said from above,
and the dragon looked up, almost startled, so intent had he
been upon his inspection. "And I so hate a lazy fire."

No other creature would dare so impertinent an address;
the dragon roared his annoyance but felt no need to press his
point. It had been a long time since he had seen this fiery
creature. "I was present for your last birth," he said, "and
you were insolent even then—but I was more willing to forgive you; you were young."

"Oh, indeed, more insolent," the phoenix replied, furling
wings of fire and heat and beauty as he dived beneath the
dragon, buoying him up, "and young. My brother, I fear you

speak truer than you know. You attended my last birth—
there will be no others."

The dragon gave a lazy, playful breath—one that would
have scorched a small village or blinded a small army—and
the phoenix preened in the flames. But though they played,
as old friends might, there was a worry in the games—a desperation they could not speak of. For were they not immortal and endless?

"They do not see me," the unicorn said quietly, when at
last the dragon had chosen to land. The phoenix, alas, was
still playing his loving games—this time with the harpies,
who tended to think rather more ill of it than the dragon had.
They screeched and swore and threatened to tear out the
swanlike fire-bird's neck; from thousands of feet below, the
dragon could hear the phoenix trumpet.

"Do not see you? But, sister, you hide."

"I once did." She shook her splendid mane, and turned to
face him, her dark eyes wide and round. "But now—I walk
as you fly, and they do not see me. I even touched one old
woman, to heal her of her aches—and she did not feel my
presence at all."

Dragons are proud creatures, but for her sake, he was
willing to risk weakness. "I, too, am worried. I flew, I cast
my shadows wide, I breathed the fiery death." He snorted;
smoke cindered a tree branch. Satisfied, he continued. "But
they did not even look up."

"And," one of the Sylvan folk broke in, "my people cannot call them further to our dance without the greatest of efforts."

The dragon turned his mighty head to regard the small,
slender woman of the fey ones. And what he saw surprised
even him. He lowered his head to the earth in a gesture of
respect for the Queen of all Faerie.

"Yes," she said, with a smile that held the ages and used
them wisely, "I, too, have come out on this road. Something
is in the earth, my friend—and in the air. There is danger and
death for all of us." She reached out and placed a perfect
hand between his nostrils. He felt a thrill of magic touch
him.

He snorted again, and the fire passed harmlessly around her. "I am no foolish mortal."

Her smile held all the beauty and danger of the reaver of mortal men. "Ah? No, I see you are not, mighty brother." She turned, swirling in a dress made of water and wood, fire and wind, and walked away to where her people waited to pay court.

"She is not without power," the unicorn whispered, long after her presence had faded.

"No, little sister, she is not. Nor will ever be, I feel. But she, too, is worried." He walked slowly and sinuously by the unicorn's delicate path until the sun splashed low upon the horizon; the wound of the sky, and the beginning of day's death. Then, he took to air, that his wings might hide the stars and bring the lovely night to those below.

And in the sky, shining as it had been for these past few days, a star burned low and impossibly bright. There was magic in it, and a fire that the dragon envied and feared. And he had been drawn to it, as had all the immortal kin.

Although they all, in their way, could move more quickly than mortal man can imagine, they chose the road that only they could see, and followed it in a procession not seen since magic's first birth. The harpies became hungry and vexed, and in time even the good-natured bird of fire grew weary of their company. He never landed, although occasionally he elected to skim the surface of grass and tree alike, touching just enough to curl, never enough to singe.

The unicorn and the dragon kept company on the road during the day; only at night did the dragon yearn for, and take to, the open air. For there, hovering by the strength of his great wings, he could see the star that never wavered and never twinkled. Days they traveled, and those days became weeks for any who cared—or knew enough—to mark time's passage, but the star never grew closer, never larger.

Others joined them in their strange, unspoken quest; the hydra with his nine mighty heads, the minotaur with his one, and Pegasus, creature of wind and light—a rival to the unicorn's beauty and grace; a thing of air. Each asked, in whispers, why the others walked, but no one had any answer that they cared to give; immortals seldom speak of their own ignorance.

Last came the Sphinx, with her catlike gait and her inscrutable features. For so mighty, and so knowledgeable a personage, the dragon came down to earth, although it was starlit night.

"Sister," he said, touching ground with a beard of scale.

"Brother," she answered. "What is old as time, yet newly born; brings life to the dying and death to the living; is born of magic and born to end magic's reign?"

The dragon sighed; many years had passed since he'd last seen the Sphinx, and he had forgotten how she chose to converse. Still, her riddles held answers for those skilled enough to see them, and the dragon had lived forever. The game of words distracted him for many hours—well into the sun's rise and renewal, before he at last shook his great head. "A masterful riddle, sister. That is the one you should have asked."

She glared at him balefully, and he did not further mention the single failure that marred her perfect record.

"What is the answer?"

But she did not speak it; instead she looked up and into the daylight sky. There, faint but unmistakable, the aurora of a single star could be seen; pale twin to the sun's grace.

"But what does the riddle mean?" The unicorn asked quietly; she did not have the black dragon's pride behind which to hide her lack of knowledge. "And what was the answer?"

"The answer?" He snorted; he did that often, and the trees bore the brunt of his mild annoyance. "She does not give answers for free—and only mortals have the coin with which to pay her."

"Oh." The unicorn cantered over to the unfortunate tree that had stood in the path of the dragon's fire. Very gently, she laid horn to burned bark—and slowly, the black passage of his breath was erased. "Maybe mortals have the coin with which to pay us all?"

It was a foolish question—one unworthy of an immortal. But as it was she who asked, he thought on it—and when night returned, and the sky beckoned, he was no closer to a comfortable answer than he had been to the sphinx's riddle. But he felt that he preferred the latter's game to the unicorn's open vulnerability.

The night brought answers of a sort, although not in the way that the dragon had expected or hoped for.

As he flew, he watched the road below—and saw, at the farthest reach of his vision, three men on camelback. They were dressed against the chill of the night, and they passed between the trees of the road-made-real by the Queen of Faerie, as if those majestic trees did not exist. They had retainers who traveled on foot; at their beck and call were wagons and caravans fit solely for mortal kings.

Three princes, thought the dragon. *Where do they travel?*

He swept down, outracing the harpies, but his wings did not even panic the camels. The princes did not look up at all from their quiet conversation. The harpies followed; they plunged downward, glinting claws extended, and hit ground before they hit men. Somehow, they had missed, and they rose, shakily, to try, and try again, to make victims out of those who traveled.

But there was no stopping the three and their procession as it came closer and closer to the heart of the traveling beasts. Still, at last, at the break of day, they chose to call a halt to their wandering. Their servants immediately began to set up tents and canvases to protect them from the sun's light.

Only when all was settled and quiet did the Queen of Faerie approach. She wandered, sylphlike but more majestic, into the heart of their gathering, wearing the guise of a mortal maid too beautiful to ignore. Her gathered robe of the elements she disguised as the finest of pure white silks; she looked young, vulnerable—the dream of every foolish youth.

The three princes were seated beneath the largest tent; they drank water from golden goblets, and kept careful watch on the ornate boxes that rested on each man's lap.

Quietly, she approached the most seemly of the men, and ran a gentle finger along the line of his beard. He looked up, his eyes narrowed.

"What is it?" The oldest of the three said, concern and fatigue in his voice.

"I thought I felt something; it must have been the passing wind. It has been a very long journey, and I am tired."

"It has been long, yes," the third man said, "and kings are not used to so arduous a travel—but we are truly blessed, who can undertake this pilgrimage."

The oldest man smiled beatifically. "Yes," he whispered, his hands caressing the inlaid jewel work of his magnificent casket, "we are blessed; for we are mortal kings—but we will see the birth and promise of the king to end all kings—God made flesh." He stood slowly, and walked to the edge of the pavilion. "There—you can still see the star in the sky. We are on the right path, my friends."

If the Queen of all Faerie dared to hold court in such a way that demanded the attention of all the immortals, none cared to complain about it openly. Indeed, when she returned, all ice and cold anger, from her foray into the human encampment, the gathering knew that the unimaginable had come to pass: She had gone, in her own royal person, and failed to call a mortal's attention when she had decided upon it.

The great black dragon lay close to the cool grass, scales in dirt and moss. His head he rested upon his great forepaws; his wings he curled in upon the expanse of his back. His unlidded eyes were fixed upon the fey and delicate fury of the Queen.

"You see," she said softly, in a whisper that might have shaken the underworld, "what we must do, my brethren."

The harpies screeched their agreement. They had passed beyond hunger now, and were ravening; at any moment, the dragon feared that they would begin to attack their kindred.

"We, too, have been drawn onto the course these mortals follow, although we tread the path-made-real at my behest. We, too, have seen the star in the sky—no natural star, nor any magical one that I have encountered before." She lifted a hand, and a ray of light, tinged with an eerie shadow, leaped skyward in her anger. "We are no mortal ephemera, to be called by the whim of a mere godling. Gods have come and gone, and we have remained, steadfast and true, in the darknesses and dreams that they cannot touch."

"Until now, sister," the unicorn said softly. "Can you not feel it?"

No other creature would have dared to correct the Queen of Faerie, and no other creature would have survived it unmarred. But the unicorn was special, dear to the Queen, and earned only a dark frown in return for her question.

"Indeed, dear one, we feel it. But now that we know the cause, we know well what we must do. There is a godling being birthed even now.

"I call for that godling's death." So saying, she raised a second hand and a darkness limned with eerie light also joined her flare in the sky. "This is my curse as Queen undying."

As her words echoed and faded in the near scentless wind, the dragon felt something he had never known before: fear.

They left the three princes—or kings, as the Queen had called them—to the shadows of the mortal realm, with its hot sun, its icy nights, and its endless, barren desert. The star burned brightly, ever brightly, as it laced the sky with shards of cast-off light, and the dragon flew when it was at the height of its brilliance.

He saw the mortal villages pass beneath the shadow of his mighty body, covered now in sleep and silence, now in merriment and celebration, now in mourning and wailing. He saw lives turn beneath him, impossibly fragile, impossibly tiny. He yearned for the breath of fire, for the sounds of their fear and falling bodies—but he knew that until the death of the godling, this grandeur was denied him.

Watching was not.

The phoenix flew beside him in the air, and as the days passed, he grew a little less brilliant, a little less radiant. "The time is coming," he said softly, for the dragon's ear alone, "when the fires will die."

"I will breathe upon you again, little fledgling," the dragon replied, "and you will know new life. You are almost a worthy child to a dragon." It was a lie, of course—no creature would be worthy of that—but he felt compelled to offer it anyway; he did not know why.

"Your fires, I fear," the phoenix replied, all song stilled, "will never again be hot enough to kindle life."

Angered, the dragon roared, startling those below who were in the habit of being taken unaware. He drew a great breath; the wind sailed into his mighty lungs like a storm upon the open sea. His jaws opened wide, and his teeth glittered in the light from the solitary star. Wings flashed black against the sky with so much power the phoenix was driven off course.

The dragon breathed *fire*.

Fire of the firstborn; fire to melt and cinder the very bones of the earth. An endless stream of blue light and heat surged through the air, wilting treetop and grass alike. And when the roaring of voice and fire combined had stilled, the dragon searched the sky for a sign of the phoenix.

It seemed brighter and perhaps just a little renewed.

"That is my fire," the dragon said, with more than a little pride.

"Almost, you give me hope, brother," the magical creature replied.

Satisfied, the black dragon continued to glide, but he roared no more that eve, and although he would not admit it, not even to the gentle one, he was suddenly very weary.

"I have never killed a child before," the unicorn said quietly, as the road stretched on beneath her delicate hooves.

"All mortal men are children," the black dragon replied, equally quietly. "If we sleep, they turn in their season, and wither as trees do. But they emerge into no spring. They are born, they age, they die."

"True," she agreed, but her tone was hesitant.

"What worries you?" The dragon ducked under a playful plume of phoenix fire. He inhaled and returned the volley without changing the nature of the game.

"I remember," she said at last, "when the world was a forest. There were men then, yes, but they were few—and we ruled and played as we desired, teasing their dreams and creating new ones.

"The world is no forest now. Men are harder to reach, harder to touch; instead of seeking us, they have turned away. This invisibility," she added, as she trailed her horn across the air, "is new—but is it so very different? We are already fading."

The dragon thought long on this, but not deeply—although depth was usually his way. "When we kill the child, all will be as it was."

"So you believe the Queen?"

"Of course." He paused. "Do you doubt her?"

"I have never killed a child before."

Starlight trailed down the spirals of her horn like pale, silver liquid. Although he longed to take to the skies, he remained at her side. He felt an odd tremor, a strange desire, as he looked at her silhouette in the night sky. Gold and jewels and magical things had once inspired him—but in time they had lost their luster and importance, and become just another cold, hard bed, undifferentiated from the rocks of his cavern.

She was different, and although he did not desire to possess her or hoard her, he felt something that reminded him of his . . . youth. The star flared suddenly brilliant, and his eyes were drawn to it. Before he understood why, he had opened his great jaws; the sound of his trumpeting filled the quiet night with yearning.

And as he turned the corner of the bending path-made-real, the forest suddenly ended in mid-tree. A blanket of cold, dry sand lay underfoot, and beyond it, so far away that even his eyes could make out no details, lay a small mortal town. High above it, a heart exposed, the star burned in beautiful relief.

They were almost upon it.

There was nothing but for the Queen of Faerie to lead the regal procession through the uncomfortable desert. The cold, of course, bothered no one—but the disappearance of her magically called trees displeased her. She bore the circlet of silver across her flawless face, and her hair, pale and fine, draped from her shoulder to the hem of her magnificent cloak. Her people attended to her in their own way; they played beautiful, haunting melodies on pipes and harps and chimes; they danced and whispered her praises in their soft, fey voices. It did not lighten her mood.

At night, the streets were still; the animals slept away from the cold of the night air in tight little boxes that no dragon would have fit in, had he cared to try. People—and the town had the look of a busy, crowded place—had also disappeared into their dwellings, which were, for the most part, even tinier than those built for their animals.

They treaded the road in silence; even the voices of the Sylvan folk dropped away into a hush. The phoenix hovered an inch or two above the ground, which was as close to earth as he ever came, except for dying; the harpies' endless stream of abuse and obscenities had run dry. The unicorn spoke once, and no one would have urged her to be silent.

"Can you feel it?" she whispered as her hooves did a delicate little dance, "can you feel it?"

There was something in the air; something familiar—a word that hovered close to the tongue without quite being caught and uttered. The dragon shook his mighty head, as if to clear it, but before he could answer, the stable came into view.

It was as the other buildings to the eye; straw strewn about the wood and mud floor; ox and mule within stabled walls, sheep and goat without, in a fenced enclosure. But above it, the star burned bright, burned direct; and there was a tingle in the eyes and heart of any who viewed this humble building that was undeniable. One door, a ramshackle old eyesore, was off its hinge, and it swung in the wind, creaking.

Except that there was no wind. The air was dead and cool.

They had come to kill a child. The child waited. His parents—the black dragon could not think of who else the haggard, sleeping couple could be—lay to either side of him, faces buried in their dirty, tired arms. They slept. But he did not.

His eyes were wide, unblinking—as beautiful and deep as a dragon's unlidded eyes. His face was peaceful; he wanted no milk, no food, no sleep. He stared out upon them, as if they had come to pay him court.

The black dragon lost his breath a moment, as he viewed this perfect, tiny child. No gold, no jewel from the earth's bowel, had ever been so flawless. He felt a tug, like hunger, and knew a pang that he had not felt since his early days in a younger world. He almost rushed forward, to pluck the babe from matted straw and carry it off in a rush of wings to the safety of his caverns.

And then the child spoke. "Welcome."

It was the voice of magic's birth. The babe lifted his hands in no infant's gesture. Palms up, in offering or welcome, he greeted them all from his coarse throne of straw and hay, in his rough robes of peasant infancy. He did not ask why they had come.

"Changeling," whispered the Queen of Faerie, a tremor in her voice.

"No," the child answered. "I am born of a mortal parent."

From behind the ranks of her court, she came. Her face was fair and pale—as perfect and blemishless as his—yet her walk seemed stiff and oddly ancient; there was no grace left in it.

The child looked up at her.

She did not speak of what she saw in his eyes, but she froze; meeting the gaze of the basilisk or the Medusa would have had less effect. She could not move forward, and at last retreated, with just a whisper of forest darkness in which to veil her failure.

And she was not without power; calling upon the green, she whispered a single word as she made her passage. "Sister."

The unicorn bowed her head; her horn touched ground, gleaming in the unnatural light. She approached the child, taking delicate, hesitant steps; the weight of the Queen's request was tangible, terrible.

And because she could not lift her ageless, open eyes, she met the child's gaze, and her horn shuddered to a stop, an inch away from his covered breast.

"Sister," he said, and his delicate, tiny fingers touched the tip of the golden spirals. "We do not war among ourselves."

"You are not of our number," the Queen of Faerie replied, before the trembling unicorn could speak.

"He is." It was not the child who answered, but the Sphinx. She was large, although not so magnificently vast as the dragon, and she could not approach the newborn godling, but nonetheless she made her presence felt by the side of his ephemeral cradle.

The dragon turned an eye to the side to catch her inscrutable profile; he listened carefully, to better hear the word-game that was certain to follow.

For the first time in the Sphinx's long history, no riddle came. "He is the last of our number; there will be no more."

Not even a whisper disturbed the stillness that followed her pronouncement. The star flared suddenly; the sky turned the charred gray of misted day. The godling began to rise, to float in the air as if it were a solid and fitting throne. His fingers still held to the unicorn's horn, and her head rose as he did, until all could see the anchor that she unwittingly formed.

"He said that he was born of mortal parents," the Queen protested. "He did not lie." But she stared, transfixed.

"Mortal parent and endless magic," he answered softly. "I have come to show you rest and peace, if you will have it."

"What peace?" the Sphinx asked.

"There is a garden that waits for you, as new and green and perfect as this world once was. Sister," he said, gazing down upon the unicorn's face, "there are still pools and endless forests; there is silence and beauty; there is a home that waits your presence. Will you walk it?"

"And what of this world?" she asked in a voice so tremulous even the dragon barely heard it.

"It is old and tired, as are you, who echo it. You have become the dreams and the nightmares of mortal, dying men. Wake, and walk free."

She gazed up at him; the black dragon tried, and failed, to catch her expression. "I will walk in your garden."

"Then go," he said, and suddenly, the unicorn began to fade.

Startled, the dragon roared. His breath plumed out in a cloud of red fire and wind. It disturbed nothing.

The godling floated away from the manger, and came next to the Sphinx. "You knew," he said quietly, and she nodded, lifting her face for his infant's touch.

"I have grown tired of riddles and endless questions. My thanks for the final answer." And she, too, faded from view.

To the harpies, he gave the promise of comfort and lack of hunger. To the phoenix, he gave the heart of his star— youth eternal, perfect glory. One by one, the immortals gave ground, until the streets were nearly empty.

The Queen of Faerie stood among her people; the black dragon stood alone. It was to the court of the Queen that the child went.

"What do you have to offer me?" she said proudly, a hint of fear in her eyes. "For this world of mortals is my world, and their dreams are my life. Will you take them from me?"

"No, greatest of my sisters," he said, and his voice grew stronger, fuller; his eyes were the color of starlight. "I am born of mortals, and to them I offer my garden as well. They will dance at your behest, live and love at your side, and know . . . paradise. You will have circles wider and greater than any, but you will never lose these loves to death and decay."

"It is their dying that makes them interesting," she answered coldly.

"It is now; it was not always so. Their death has tainted you."

"And you would give me death to relieve that taint?" Her lips turned up in something that was not even close to a smile.

"Yes," was the stark reply, for no one with mortal blood can lie to the most terrible of Queens. "The choice is yours."

"And if I refuse?"

He shrugged, but his face showed pain. "You refuse. But they will go, in the end, to those gardens—and you will never know them. You will dwindle; the forests will shrink and die at the coming tide of man."

She closed her eyes, knowing as always the truth of what she heard. "I . . . will go."

The black dragon thought her more beautiful, then, than she had ever been, as she preceded her people into the unknown.

"There is only you, now." It was true; but for the black dragon and the godling, the streets were empty, and the first rays of dawn were turning the skies. "Will you go?"

"Yes," the dragon answered quietly. There was no hesitation in his voice. "But why have you left me for last?"

The little godling made no answer. But he seemed frail now, as if the passing of each immortal had robbed him of substance.

"What will you be, when we are gone?"

"Mortal," the child answered, in an oddly still voice.

"Mortal?"

"Yes. But not to other mortals. I will be their light and their darkness. I will give them hope, and I will be the cause of their despair. I will be miracle and mundanity; I will be magic and the law that ends all magic. You have killed thousands, brother—numbers undreamed of will die in my name. The peerless one healed hundreds, and numbers greater will also find healing. You were their dreams; I shall take your place."

"And what will your dream be?"

The child laughed at the gleam in the dragon's eyes. "There will be gold for you in paradise; it was hard to manage." But the dragon was not to be put off by humor, and the laughter faded into stillness. "My dream? Paradise." He looked at his own tiny palms and perfect feet. Shivered.

"And how," the dragon asked quietly, "will you reach paradise? Who will give you passage?" Dragons think deeply, when they choose to think at all."

"You were not listening," the godling said sadly. "I will be mortal, and I will die. My people will kill me slowly." The starlight faded from his eyes, and left a film in its wake. "Will you—will you wait for me there?" It was the first and last time that he sounded like a child.

The dragon took a deep breath, and a hint of smoke curled round his nostrils. "Will I have true fire again?"

"Forever."

"Then I will wait."

The child reached out with a shaky hand, but the dragon shied from his touch. "No, no, little godling. I will wait here."

"You can't," was the flat answer. "When the sun crests the horizon, there will be no immortals left."

"Then you lied to the. Queen!" The dragon's roar was the breath of a chuckle.

"I lied."

"What will happen at full sunrise?"

"You will be mortal."

"Human?"

The child nodded, his gaze intent.

"I will die as you do, then. But still . . . I will wait."

"You will remember me; I can promise that much, but I think I will forget this as I grow." Again fear touched his features, and he spoke quickly; sunrise was almost upon them both. "Remember what it was like to be old and tired—to be only dream, with no reality. Remember that, and when the time comes, do what must be done to free me."

The dragon bowed his mighty head, and the child touched his nostril. Where once a huge, black serpent had towered above the ground, there now stood a very young boy. He caught the child carefully in his arms as the sun came, and gazed up to see the dying, and the birthing, of an age. Then he crept into the manger, kissed the quiet child's forehead, and laid him back down against the straw.

Three decades later, for thirty pieces of silver—a metal he had always disdained—the dragon found a way to bring the last of the immortals home.

INTRODUCTION TO "THE JEWEL AND THE DEMON"

by Lisanne Norman

"The Jewel and the Demon" is the first short story of mine ever published, and coincidentally, it has rather an interesting past to it. It was one of my later attempts at short fiction, and was the medium through which I learned much of the craft of writing. After all, it is far less demoralizing being told your 5,000 word short story should never have seen the light of day, than to be told the same about a 200,000 word novel, isn't it?

I've been a science fiction convention goer since 1978 and by this time, the later 1980s, was well enough known at British conventions to be organizing a program event very dear to my heart. A writers' workshop. I would find a professional writer willing to sit with half a dozen of us hopefuls and chair a kind of round robin of critique. Then an ad went in the next progress report for the convention, asking for those interested in attending a workshop to submit stories to me, and giving them information on how the work should be laid out. The first six stories that reached me would be able to take part in the workshop. I didn't set a topic beyond saying it had to be fantasy or science fiction and no more than 5,000 words long.

The lucky six were then asked to provide me with seven copies of their work to be distributed among us all three months before the convention. Each contributor, and the pro writer, was to read and annotate the stories for our sessions at the convention being held over the forthcoming Easter weekend.

We had two sessions, each about four hours long, during which time we took each story in turn and had two minutes to make comments on it. The writer then had the right of reply, but only one minute long. Then we went around once again with the writer getting the last word. It was exhausting, and the pro writers who took part cannot be thanked enough, but all of us emerged inspired at the end of the sessions. I know I certainly did!

"The Jewel and the Demon" was submitted by me to one of these workshops and in the form it was in then, aroused a little criticism. I shall leave aside the comment that a thief should be built like Arnold Schwarzenegger, not a slim young girl of about fifteen and that of a feminist asking what birth control my young thief used, because they were not relevant. My story wasn't about issues, it was just an adventure story—then. What did come as a surprise was the pro writer asking if I had written it as a homage to Fritz Leiber and his tales of Fafhrd and the Grey Mouser. He then mentioned several other writers, saying my piece was very like theirs and asking me if I had done this on purpose, because if I had, I'd done it well, but should try to be more original.

Shamefacedly I had to admit I had heard of only one of the writers—Fritz Leiber, and had read only one of his books at that time. (Read them, they are great classic sword and sorcery!) At which point, my writer friend tossed his notes on my story over his shoulder and said, "That blows my critique of your story, then!" with a laugh. He then asked me how the story had come to be written.

I had been playing a lot of fantasy role games at that time and had come across several badly written short stories, obviously based on gaming characters. One or two had been so nearly very good, but had been let down by being too obviously written by people who had no real idea of how to use swords, and dark age weapons in general.

I knew I could do better because every weekend from the one after Easter until the middle of October, I would dress up as a Viking, load up the camping kit in the mini bus along with the thirteen other people in our Viking reenactment group, and head off to one of England's historic battlefields to take part in recreating the life and battles of the Saxons and Vikings of the tenth century for the public. These shows varied from small local village fairs to huge spectacles in front of 10,000 people or more at English Heritage sites like Battle Abbey and Old Sarum Iron Age Hill Fort.

At these events I would go on the battlefield with my trusty sword or Dane ax, or sprint around the front lines shooting arrows at the enemy and picking them off for our side. Great fun, and great experience for writing sword and sorcery tales.

As well as all the fighting, there were the evenings round the campfire swapping our own modern tales of derring-do that had happened to us on the battlefields either that day or in the past. And of course, horns of ale were passed generously from hand to hand as the fire crackled and roared, spitting bright sparks high up into the dark night sky. It was a scene straight out of the past, and for many years, I had lived it, so I *knew* I could write a good tale of sword and sorcery.

My main gaming character was an elf called Mouse. Why Mouse? Nothing to do with Fritz Leiber, I said, more to do with the fact she was a gray elf and only 4 foot 8 inches tall—what else could you call a small gray elf thief but Mouse? That raised a chuckle from everyone.

Now my view of magic is different from most fantasy readers and gamers because I see it not as magic, but as natural abilities combined with mental training. Luckily, our games master agreed and had developed magic in his games using a system based on the energy of the character. You got so many energy points based on your race, etc. and could use them on any spells your character had found. Each level of spell had a cost and you subtracted that from the spell points . . . I am sure you get the picture.

I tried thinking through past games that John, his wife Gina, and I had played, but none really loaned themselves to a suitable story so I started taking elements from different games and wove them into a tale of my own. First was the jewel that was to be stolen, and obviously it had to be magical. But magical how? As I said, I have a dislike of the idea of magic being the ability to read a spell from a book and make passes with your hands, so it had to be different. I was working even then on the follow-up to my as-yet unpublished first novel, *Turning Point*. They're now part of the *Sholan Alliance* series about people with psychic abilities, particularly telepathy. They feature Humans and my felinoid aliens, the Sholans. So it was a natural step for me to make the jewel an alien life force based on silicon. There is a reasonable scientific theory still going around that just as we are a life-form based on carbon, it is likely we may come across life based on silicon.

The nature of the jewel had been decided. Obviously, only the reader and I knew the jewel was a lifeform. To a mage on Mouse's world, it would just be a magic talking jewel. Now I had to decide who wanted it stolen and why, and how it was protected by the owner.

In classic fantasy, magic users always want magical jewels, so obviously a mage wanted it, and obviously it was very valuable, so the mage might well send someone with our young thief to see she didn't try to keep the jewel herself—and maybe help her along the way because the jewel would have to be protected by magic, wouldn't it? So the demon was born. Why a demon? Well, his master is a mage, isn't he? What other kind of helper would any self-respecting mage have?

I like my little demon. In fact, if you read more of the stories of Mouse, and there is another of them out in the *Spell Fantastic* anthology, also by DAW Books, you will find out more about this little fellow!

For defenses, I plagiarized unashamedly from the wealth of assumptions of fantasy. I used a fire drake, or a small fire dragon, but with a difference. You'll have to read the story to find out how it is different, though. Then I added guards, as Mouse had to have some humans to fight.

So I had the beginnings of the story, but nothing much about the thief side of young Mouse. Well, I could begin the story with her having just broken into the house and standing at a corridor listening to the sound of . . . guard dogs. Thieves have lots of tricks at their disposal; after all, they are not fighters, so they aim to avoid confrontations. She needed a way of dealing with the dogs that avoided violence. Putting them to sleep was the obvious solution, but this was the dark ages, not modern times, so the immediate thought of dart guns was out. Mind you, after several years of adventuring, nowadays Mouse uses a blowpipe and various poisons or sleeping potions, but we're talking about a much younger person here.

I took an idea from some of the many Chinese martial arts films around at the time—glass balls with a sleep powder in them. I think it was Clarke who said any sufficiently advanced society will seem like magic to a less advanced one. So I was able again to blend technology with the idea of magic as I do in my novels.

As I started writing the story, Mouse came alive as a person for me, and as she did, she wanted to know more about herself and her past. That's where the idea of the heist going badly wrong came from. What if only men could be magic users on Mouse's world? Then the mage would be sure to choose a girl as the thief because she couldn't possibly have the blood of mages in her, could she? But what if she did? What if no one knew her father had been an itinerant wizard? Not even her mother—who now suddenly became a wealthy girl, taken advantage of by this wizard who had left not knowing she was pregnant? Of course, in those times, the girl would be disowned and thrown out. Suddenly Mouse was a thief by accident, not by birth, which made her slightly more glamorous as a character. She had a Past now. And a reason for the heist to go very wrong when she picked up the jewel!

From there it was a small step to deciding what happened to Mouse after the theft of the jewel. All the pieces were now in place, so I was able to finish the story.

When I was asked to submit it to *Battle Magic*, I am pleased to say it needed very little reworking. In the intervening years I had decided, after many talks with John and Gina, and further games using my character Mouse, that she had to have a novel—or two—of her own. So the changes to the original story reflected only this, setting it on the dark age world of Jalna from the Sholan Alliance series and broadening out the characters of Mouse and the demon so they could take off in a series of short stories that would culminate one day in a novel of their own.

That novel has come closer with the publication of the second Mouse story as mentioned earlier in *Spell Fantastic*, and Mouse's life has fleshed out amazingly, as has that of the demon. I am really looking forward to the time when my current schedule allows me to begin writing it.

I hope you enjoy reading this story every bit as much as I enjoyed using my personal experiences on the battlefields of England and the tabletops of suburbia to write it.

With thanks to John and Gina Quadling for many hours of great fantasy role-playing games in their company.

THE JEWEL AND THE DEMON

by Lisanne Norman

"BE still, imp!" Mouse hissed at her tiny companion. "I told you, I can deal with the dogs."

Ahead of them lay their goal, the treasure room of Harra the merchant. She knew its encircling corridor was protected by large hounds, one of which lay opposite them guarding the only entrance.

Mouse reached for the tiny silver whistle suspended on a cord round her neck. She'd won it some time ago in a game of dice from a fellow thief and it had become a treasured and useful possession. Putting it to her lips, she blew gently. Though she could hear nothing, the small but very real demon accompanying her clapped his hands to his ears and grimaced in pain.

The dog lifted its head and pricked its ears, looking around. Pushing the demon back, Mouse flattened herself against the wall. She repeated the whistle—one short, sharp blow. The hound growled softly and, getting to its feet, padded toward them. Releasing the whistle, she transferred several small spherical glass vials to her right hand. The dog had finally gotten a whiff of her scent and its growl rose in pitch, becoming menacing.

The Gods help me if Tallan's magic doesn't work, she thought.

Taking a deep breath, Mouse stepped out of their cover and flung one of the vials at the animal's feet. The glass shattered, releasing a small cloud of white vapor. As she watched, the dog slowed to a halt, skidding on the wooden floor before collapsing in a boneless heap.

"Wait!" she said, as the demon made to rush forward. "We only got one. There's more."

They could hear the rapid click of claws on wood as two more rounded the corner, bounding toward them. It took all her courage to wait until the slavering beasts were nearly upon them before throwing the second and third vials. Seconds later, they lay as senseless as the first.

"Now! Now! While they sleep," the demon exclaimed, hopping from hoof to hoof.

She nodded. The dogs had frightened her more than she cared to admit. Forcing herself to relax a little, she stepped warily past the beasts. Silently they covered the intervening distance to the great double doors. A sturdy hasp, held closed by a simple but efficient padlock, covered the locks.

Mouse spent a few moments examining the padlock before digging in one of her capacious pockets and extracting a lock pick. Cautiously she inserted the wire in the keyhole, twiddling it round and about until she felt it give. Grasping the loop with her free hand, she pulled it open and laid it carefully on the floor away from the door.

"No time for tidy," the demon hissed urgently. "Hurry, hurry!"

"Untidy could kill us if we have to leave quickly," Mouse replied more calmly than she felt as she stroked her hand over the now exposed locks.

There were three of them, and her sixth sense was telling her they must be opened in the right sequence, otherwise alarms would go off in the guard room.

"You hurry," the demon twittered. "Not want you caught. I be safe, but not you."

Mouse glanced down at him. Pretty he wasn't. He looked more like a prematurely aged child of three with his wrinkled brown face and the tiny horns poking through his thatch of dark curls. He stamped an insistent hoof. "Hurry!"

She sighed, turning back to the door. "I need quiet to work, imp. Give me peace."

Once again she ran her hands over the door, trying to sense the order of the enchantment on the locks. She was no magic-user to know how these things worked, but now and then, she was able to divine something of their nature. Her luck had made it possible for her to earn her living after her mother had died rather than end up in one of the city bars or brothels

"Middle one first," she muttered to herself, inserting her piece of wire again. This time she placed her ear to the door, listening for the tiny clicks that told her when she'd tripped each tumbler.

Patiently she worked away until she'd freed the first lock without triggering the alarm.

"Now the top one."

As she worked, the demon shifted impatiently from hoof to hoof, knowing it shouldn't break her concentration. "Dogs wake soon," it muttered fretfully.

"Last one," she said, aware of the building tension. "Not long now. Almost there." She continued working, sweat beginning to break out on her forehead. Her hands were trembling now with the effort of trying to keep them steady. She stopped to wipe slick palms on her pants' legs. Gods, but she was tired already! By the time this was over, she'd have more than earned her high fee. She banished the thought, and bent down to resume her work.

The last tumbler tripped and she turned an exultant face to her companion. "We're through!"

"Open door. Must hurry," he said, urging her forward with his hands.

Gently Mouse grasped the ring handle and, turning it, eased the door open just enough for them to squeeze through. Hugging the wall, she snatched at the demon, grabbing it by its naked shoulder as it prepared to dash forward. Its skin felt hot and slightly uneven, like that of a reptile or an exotic fruit.

"No!" she hissed. "We look around first!"

"You want light?" asked the demon, squirming out from under her hand. "I give." A soft glow began to fill the room.

"Keep it low!" Mouse exclaimed. "We don't know what the inner defenses are yet."

The glow obediently slowed, building until there was only enough light to see the whole of the room. Immediately, their eyes were drawn to the glass case atop the pedestal standing in the center. In it was a gemstone, but a gem unlike any she'd seen before. Now there was light in the room, colors coruscated through it, sending their rainbow hues glancing off the ceiling in tiny patches of brilliance.

"The Living Jewel," Mouse whispered.

"Yes. Jewel for Master Kolin," said the demon.

"What's your wizard want the jewel for?" she asked, unable to take her eyes off its beauty.

"Not know. Just say he want it."

"Huh." Mouse tore her gaze away and examined the rest of the room. The walls were lined with display cabinets containing items of rarity or beauty from other lands. There were even some that must have come from the off-worlder aliens, but none of them compared with the Living Jewel.

"I can see why the merchant doesn't want to part with it," she murmured.

"He refuse to sell it to Master. Say it an item of pride. Reminds him of getting best of enemy," offered the demon in an unusual burst of conversation.

Mouse glanced down at him in surprise, but it was the floor that caught her attention. Her heart began to race as she stopped to examine it more closely, realizing now that since they'd entered the room, she'd been subliminally aware of the warmth underfoot.

The tiles had a faint tracery on them that broadened out as it led to the pedestal at the center of the room. At the base of the plinth, like a spider in the heart of its web, there was a patch of shadow, a darkness. She blinked, and looked back at the crimson lines.

Bending down, cautiously she passed her hand over the pattern, aware as she did so of the variations in temperature between it and the tiles.

"Increase the light a little," she ordered the demon, turning her attention to the shadow again.

As the room brightened, gradually the shadow began to disperse till she could plainly see the shape of a reptile curled around the plinth.

"Darken!" she hissed in fear. "It's a firedrake! These lines on the floor, they're part of its body! If we step on them, we'll waken it."

"I fix with sleep enhancement spell," said the demon. "We lucky you kept light low. Light wakes it too."

He began to mutter in some guttural outlandish language, making several complicated passes in the air with his hands. Mouse began to feel queasy and looked away.

"Is safe now," he assured her a few moments later.

"We still keep off the lines," warned Mouse, listening to her intuition again. "Do you sense any more protections? I don't."

"I say safe," he repeated, tugging at her hand, trying to draw her into the room. "Must hurry now. Dogs wake soon for sure."

Exasperated, she shook him off, motioning him to quiet.

Carefully they picked their way across the network of lines until they stood beside the pedestal. Mouse looked anxiously at the slumbering firedrake.

"Are you sure it'll stay asleep?" she asked, mistrustful of the efficacy of magic spells when they were supposed to be working for her benefit.

"Sure," nodded the demon confidently. "Can't make things sleep, but can enhance it. Kolin only give me little magics. You get jewel now."

Mouse placed her hands carefully on either side of the glass case and lifted it off, passing it down to the demon. She hesitated a moment before reaching forward to lift the jewel reverently off its bed of velvet. Turning it in her hand, she gazed in wonder at the ephemeral flickering hues. One moment it was clear, then the next, every color of the rainbow seemed to glitter within it. At her side, the demon shifted impatiently.

"A moment, imp," she murmured, lost in its beauty. Suddenly, pain lanced through her hand and up her arm to her spine. Arching her back in agony, she let out a soul-wrenching scream as she tried to fling the jewel away from her. It was stuck to her hand; she couldn't let go of it as it seared and burned its way into her very flesh.

She fell to the floor writhing in agony, cradling her hand against her chest, whimpering, the pain now too intense to even cry out. The demon echoed her cry as she twisted sideways, knocking the firedrake with her foot.

He danced around her, for the first time unsure what to do. This was bad. Things were not going according to plan.

Then he heard the pounding footsteps of the guard coming toward the treasure room.

"Lady!" he shrieked, the sound galvanizing him into action. "Lady, you get up! Guards come! You be dead if they catch you." He grabbed her by the arm. "Up! You get up!" he shouted urgently, tugging at her.

It seemed to work, for her struggles subsided and she went limp. Behind them, the firedrake stirred, its wings making a papery sound as it stretched them.

"Up! Up! Firedrake wake!" He was beside himself with terror.

Mouse struggled to her feet, her eyes still glazed with pain. "What . . . ?" she slurred.

"Use sword! Must fight good now," the demon said, letting go of her to pull free the sword that hung on her left hip. He thrust it into her unresisting hands. "Fight guards!" He pushed her round in the direction of the door.

"Guards?" she asked as five of them rushed into the room. She could barely see them so fogged by pain was her vision. How she managed to close her aching hand around the sword hilt she never knew.

Instincts took over and she raised her blade, just managing to deflect the blow of the leading man. Her body knew what to do even if her conscious mind had not quite caught up. She whirled to one side, taking him out with a chest blow as he raised his sword for a second swipe at her.

The firedrake, thoroughly roused now, reared up and belched flame at her back, but she was no longer there, having skipped to one side to avoid the rush of the other four soldiers. Standing them off briefly, she kept her sword at guard and tried to edge round toward the door. She leaped forward, taking out the second man with a deftly turned block that cut him deeply under his sword arm. The third locked blades with her, pushing her back then knocking the sword out of her hands with the sheer force of his next blow. Dazed, she stood there for a moment, her hands limp at her sides. Sure he had her now, the guard advanced more slowly.

Behind them, the firedrake screeched its anger and sent another gout of flame licking at her legs. Mouse wailed at the fresh pain, and flinging her hands up to protect herself, whirled round. She felt a tremendous rush like a tidal wave build inside her—then the room turned dark.

Her wrist was grabbed by a small, clawed hand.

"We go," the demon said, pulling her forward. "Take sword. Leave now, before more guards come."

Mouse's senses returned with a rush, and grabbing the sword that the demon was thrusting back into her hands, she raced for the doorway. She slowed down as the brightness of the corridor made her eyes water and blink. The demon would have none of it and urged her on again. Trusting him, she ran where he led. Within moments, they were back in the little room where they had forced their entry so short a time ago.

Mouse leaped onto the window ledge, reaching down to haul the demon up after her. They scrambled out, jumping down onto the low roof of the stables, leaping from there to land on the dusty ground below. Then they were racing across the yard to the outer wall, praying their rope still waited for them. Up and over they went as all hell let loose behind them. Down the street they ran, slowing only when they left the affluent area of the city to enter the Market Quarter. Finally Mouse felt safe enough to stop and sheathe her sword.

No one was abroad at this hour of night. All the drunks were long since in their beds, save the unlucky ones lying in back alleys with their throats and their purses cut. Mouse and her companion skulked in the shadows, heading deeper into the labyrinth of the Quarters where only those known to be dangerous could safely stray.

Agony stabbed through her head, felling her to her knees. Letting out a strangled cry, she clutched her head.

"What happens, lady? What happens?"

Mouse was barely aware of the demon's distressed cry. Strange alien thoughts had begun to flow compellingly through her mind.

Submit to me. Let me take control. I have the knowledge to make you great. Together we could rule this kingdom. You could be rich, powerful. No ambition would be beyond our achievement. Don't fear this Kolin, we can take him on easily.

"No," she moaned, swaying from side to side where she knelt in the gutter. "Get out of my head! I don't want power!"

But riches. Yes, riches, the voice purred. *I can give you all that—and more.*

"No!" She fought back mentally, pushing against the thoughts, willing them to stop. "Leave me! Leave me alone!"

The demon watched Mouse with a glimmering of understanding as she carried on her one way conversation. He hadn't told her that the reason they'd been able to escape was because from somewhere she'd called up enough Mage-power to blast the last three guards and the firedrake into a smoldering pile of ashes. No, he hadn't told her that—yet.

Obviously the jewel had found a home for which it was not intended. The girl had to carry Mage-blood in her veins like Wizard Kolin, or she could never have made use of the magic. She'd need all her inborn Mage instincts if she was going to control the jewel. As for his master, the only way he could now claim his prize was by killing her, unless she managed to kill Kolin first.

Now there was a thought. Kolin was no easy master, always demanding he do the impossible. Perhaps the girl would make a kinder mistress, if he, Zaylar, could help her. He sighed. The nature of his binding to Kolin prevented that. There would be no release from his punishment until he'd served another six masters. He could only sit back and await the outcome, changing one master for another when his was finally defeated. And defeated he would be, one day. Magical duels seemed to be all these Jalnian mages lived and died for.

He turned his attention again to Mouse, realizing that she'd finally released her head and was slowly beginning to sit up.

"Lady, you all right?" he asked anxiously. All his hopes would come to naught if the jewel dominated her.

Mouse got unsteadily to her feet, running her hands

through her damp hair and pushing it back from her face. "I think so."

She looked at the palms of her hands, comparing one to the other before scrubbing her right one with her left. There was no difference—no lump, no burned flesh. Nothing.

"The jewel, did I dream it or did it really disappear into my hand?"

The demon nodded vigorously. "Is what it does. Lives within the Mage-born. Who win?" he asked, peering closely at her face.

"I did, I think," she replied. Mage-born? *She* was Mage-born?

"Then *you* use jewel, it not use you. You mastered it."

Was that satisfaction she heard in his voice? "Is this why Kolin wanted the jewel?"

"Yes. It make him a stronger wizard. Now you one too." He cocked his head to one side and looked expectantly at her.

"Me, little friend? Not me," she laughed shakily. Suddenly she found herself aware of his hopes for freedom. Frightened, she looked away and the sensation was gone.

"Yes, you. We go to Master Kolin. He find you if you don't. He have to kill you now to get jewel, so you must kill him first."

"Me? Kill Kolin? Who's kidding who, imp?" She began walking in the opposite direction.

"Where you going?" Zaylar demanded, scampering to catch up with her.

"Not to Kolin, that's for sure!"

"Got to! He come after you!" protested the demon, dancing backward in an effort to keep ahead of her. "No place you can hide from a Mage!"

"Why should he? I've taken no money from him yet. It isn't his."

"He think so! Won't stop till he's got jewel," the demon insisted, stopping dead and holding its arms out to bar her way. "Only chance you got is to fight him!"

She ground to a halt in front of him. "You're serious, aren't you? He really will come after me, won't he? Gods, what a mess! Whatever I do, I stand one hell of a good chance of dying!"

"Fighting Kolin is best. Jewel will help you."

"How?"

"Ask it. It protects you now. Maybe it do it anyway without your asking." He shrugged. "It knows what you know. Maybe it want you to live, think you easier to control than wizard like Kolin."

"Wonderful! What I know about magical duels could be written on a pin head," she muttered, resting her hand on the pommel of her sword.

Zaylar hesitated. She really didn't have a clue about what was happening to her. An opportunity as good as this wouldn't come again in a hundred years, he couldn't afford to pass it up. Technically, he couldn't help, but then he'd never been a great one for technicalities, that's what had gotten him into trouble in the King's Court in the first place. Giving her some advice wasn't really helping her, was it? Advice? Had he called it advice? He would only be talking aloud. If she heard him and got an idea, it wasn't his fault, was it?

He looked down at the ground, scraping one hoof idly in the dust. "If I was a thief, wouldn't use magic," he said. "Thief skills be what I know. I'd use them."

"Thief skills? In a magical duel?" She looked at him incredulously.

He tapped his hoof impatiently, drawing her attention to the ground seconds before a small gout of flame erupted from the center of his scratchings.

"Thief skills," she said again as the demon let out a high-pitched scream. Leaping back, he chittered in pain, hopping about on one hoof as he massaged the other.

"Wasn't helping!" he shrieked to the night sky. "Was not!"

Kolin greeted them in his study. He was a somber man, dressed in robes of deep blue as befitted his dark calling. This hadn't bothered Mouse when she took the job; she'd been no threat to him then, but now his garb sent a chill through her right to her bones.

"So, you've returned. You have my jewel?"

"Oh yes, I have it, Wizard Kolin," she replied.

Kolin lifted the drawstring pouch that lay on the desk beside him. "Then give it to me and you will be paid," he said.

"Ah, I have this slight problem," said Mouse, focusing her eyes on the pouch rather than on him.

Kolin frowned. "You said you have the jewel. Where's the problem? Zaylar, does she lie to me?" he demanded.

"No, Master. She has jewel," the demon answered from the doorway.

"Then give it to me," thundered Kolin, dropping the pouch and extending his hand peremptorily. His eyes narrowed suddenly.

"You *do* have it, don't you?" He sat back in his seat, regarding her with curiosity. "How can a scrawny girl, and a thief to boot, have Mage-blood?" he mused aloud. "Were either of your parents Mages, girl?"

Mouse shrugged, meeting his gaze this time. "Not that I know of. My father didn't stay around to find out Mother was pregnant. She always said she got me from a passing fortune-teller."

"Only the Mage-born can carry the Living Jewel," said Kolin. "Without doubt, you're one of us." He frowned again. "Your father broke the law in allowing you to live, but no matter. It is an inconvenience, nothing more." He gestured briefly and a bolt of energy flashed toward Mouse.

Automatically she ducked, lifting her arm and fending it to one side as if it were merely a blow from a raised fist. It sparked and flared against the door, sending the demon chittering for cover.

As shock flooded through her, Mouse felt the jewel stirring within her mind.

Let me fight this battle for you, came the silken thought.

"No," said Mouse. Instinctively she knew that if she opened her mind to the jewel, then win or lose this battle with Kolin, *she* would cease to exist. A sound like the wisp of a sigh, then from deep within, she felt a power begin to build, slowly at first, then spiraling upward till it filled her whole being.

Think of a shield, came the faint thought. *Like the arms-men use.*

She couldn't help it. No sooner had it been suggested than she could see it in her mind's eye. It was none too soon. Kolin struck again and her shield was suddenly suffused with blue fire. It took all her courage to stand her ground.

"So, the jewel helps you," hissed Kolin. "But it's too little, and far too late to save you!"

Ignoring his words, she watched for the gap in Kolin's defenses. As he concentrated on gathering his magical energies, she struck. With one hand, she flung the remaining two vials at his desk while reaching swiftly behind her neck for the knife that nestled there. In one fluid move, she'd pulled it out and thrown it into the heart of the sleep spell cloud.

She saw it strike home, taking with it a bolt of raw energy a hundred times more powerful than anything Kolin had used. As the cloud dissipated, she saw him reeling under the impact, hands clutching the knife that now sprouted from the base of his throat.

Lines of thin blue lightning spiderwebbed from the blade across his body. A silent scream was pinned to his face, and for several moments, his petrified form remained transfixed before he collapsed suddenly into a fine rain of ash.

Shocked, Mouse let her arm fall by her side and stared at the empty seat.

"Where'd he go?' she demanded of the demon, her voice high pitched with shock.

The demon crawled out from under a sideboard. "Dead. He dead now. You kill him, Mistress."

"Dead?" she repeated incredulously. "He can't be dead! He's gone, magicked himself away somewhere!"

"He's dead. You're Mistress now. All this—the house, everything—yours. And me, Zaylar," he added, nodding vigorously.

"I don't want any of this!" Mouse exclaimed. "Neither his house nor you! I'm an honest thief, not a wizard!"

The demon shook its head. "No, you're a wizard now. You're Mage-born, you got jewel. Can't change that."

Mouse looked for a chair—she didn't fancy the one so

hurriedly vacated by its previous owner—and sat down heavily.

"I don't want to be a wizard," she said again.

"Have to be. Power there, jewel there. Lucky this time, jewel helped you. Must learn to control it before it controls you," the demon insisted, concern on its face.

Mouse looked up. "Why should you worry?" she asked. "You're a demon, you don't care about us Jalnians."

"I care because you the Mistress now. We make a deal, eh?"

"What deal?" asked Mouse suspiciously.

"I want be free so no one ever bind me again. You can fix it. I help you."

"What do I get out of it?" she asked, her interest aroused despite herself.

"I live long, long time. Is nothing I stay with you. I teach you, keep jewel from taking you over while learn magic. Then you use this learning, make me an amulet so never bound by Jalnians again. Is deal, yes?"

Mouse arched her eyebrows quizzically. "So you've got delusions of power in your own world. Why can't you make this amulet yourself?"

"Demons can't make amulet, need wizard. You can. Safe for you."

Mouse thought for a moment. Power games she could understand. If the demon was motivated in that direction, then she could be fairly sure he'd keep his word—at least until she'd made the amulet. She sighed, and leaned forward to pick up Kolin's purse.

"Seems like I've got no choice. You've got yourself a deal, Zaylar."

The demon grinned and began cavorting about the room, whooping for all the world like a joyful child. Watching him, Mouse couldn't help smiling. As once more she suppressed the jewel's faint whisper deep within her mind, she cursed herself for breaking her own rules and getting involved with a wizard in the first place. She had a horrible conviction she was going to regret it for a long time.

INTRODUCTION TO "THE RAVEN'S QUEST"

by Fiona Patton

When I was a child, I had a lot of heroes, both real and fictional, but the two which had the greatest and most long-lasting influence on my life were John F. Kennedy and King Arthur. They had a lot in common. Both were leaders with a larger-than-life mystique and the ability to inspire others to strive for a more perfect and idealized society, and both died before that society could be realized.

I had books about each of them and, although my silver-backed picture book on Kennedy and his family is long gone, I still have my Puffin Story Book: *King Arthur and His Knights of the Round Table*, by Roger Lancelyn Green, which my grandmother gave me at the age of seven or eight. Mixed into my favorite stories about "the big guys with swords" were important lessons about honor, valor, and courage, not to mention mythology and English feudalism which laid a strong foundation for the literary genre I chose to go into later.

Kennedy gave me my first understanding about death as I, apparently, sat with my eyes riveted on the TV watching his funeral at the age of ten months old, and King Arthur gave me my first understanding that death was not necessarily the end of the story. Perhaps Jack Kennedy is also merely sleeping with the greatest of his own knights beside him, waiting for the time we need him most. It wouldn't surprise me if there was some mystical connection between Arlington National Cemetery and Avalon, and I certainly won't be ringing any bells nearby.

So, when I heard that Lawrence Schimel was editing an anthology entitled *Camelot Fantastic*, I really wanted to do a story for it. I'd just sold my first book, *The Stone Prince*, to DAW, and although it had yet to come out, that was enough to pitch my enthusiasm, if not an actual idea, to Lawrence at World Fantasy Con. Possibly too polite to say no to my face, or possibly because he liked my enthusiasm, Lawrence said yes.

It was my honor to add my own strand of magic to the multihued tapestry of Arthurian legend, to weave a tale which included another of my heroes: Bran the Blessed, and to mingle with Sir Galahad, Sir Gawain, and Sir Bedivere once again. Maybe someday I'll get the chance to write about Kennedy, but for now "The Raven's Quest" is a small tribute to the king who taught me to strive for the best in myself and the best in my society.

THE RAVEN'S QUEST

by Fiona Patton

IN a cluttered tower room on Bardsey Island, a large, black raven perched on the edge of an iron cauldron and pulled the guts from a dead mouse. Snapping up the grisly meal, it swallowed, then allowed the carcass to fall. The mouse struck the inside of the cauldron with a hollow ping and was reborn. With a brisk, businesslike flap of its wings, the raven stabbed downward, catching the rodent up in its beak. It swiftly disemboweled it again, chuckling at its own cleverness around a mouthful of entrails.

In the center of the room an old man sat hunched over a desk, scrolls of vellum and parchment strewn about him. Without turning his head, he made a disgusted noise in the back of his throat.

"I hardly think Bran's cauldron was meant for such a gruesome purpose, Corvus," he noted.

The raven turned its glossy head sideways, fixing the old man with one black eye. "Did I not serve him well for over two decades?" it demanded, splattering blood across a nearby chessboard. The silver pieces continued to play themselves, oblivious to the gory shower.

"That gives you the right to use the cauldron of rebirth to eat mice?"

With a disdainful toss of its head, the raven flung the empty carcass into a nearby hamper. One hundred mice instantly emerged to scatter over the floor. The bird watched them with interest before taking wing across the room to land on the old man's shoulder. "Was I not the greatest of all Bran's ravens?" it asked.

"Were you not merely *one* of Bran's ravens?" the old man retorted.

"Did he not love me above all the rest? Did he not give me the power of intelligence, and speech that he might more clearly commune with me his purpose in protecting the Realm of Logres?"

"I'll bet he regretted that part."

"What part?" Snapped out of its singsong cadence by the sudden statement, the raven swiveled its head so that one eye regarded the old man's ear.

"The speech part."

Digging through its breast feathers, the bird removed a mite and devoured it before deigning to reply. "Am I not the only one who remembers that he was king and protector over Logres?"

"Logres has a new protector now," the old man answered testily. "Arthur, who was prophesied to be the greatest king of all time."

"Prophesied by who?" the raven sniffed.

"Prophesied by me, Merlin, the most powerful mage of this or any era!" the old man shouted, pushing the raven off his shoulder. With an awkward flapping of wings, the bird landed on the desk, scattering its contents.

"Did Arthur not put the Realm in danger by desecrating

Bran's remains at the White Tower so that he might become the only palladium against invasion?" it persisted.

The old man snatched at a falling scroll. "Insufferable creature!" he muttered, ignoring the question. "Move your great, bloody head!" Smacking the scroll down on the desk, he shot the bird a fierce glance from under his eyebrows. "I will not get involved in a pointless debate with you about Bran and Arthur. I've told you that before."

"But am I not Bran's only raven left alive in Logres? Should I not be told if the Realm was in danger?"

Composing himself, the old man returned to his writing, dipping his quill into a large crystal inkwell before answering. "I'll grant you that Rhian and Calas have joined Bran in death at least," he replied, glaring at the inkwell until the sudden riot of colors returned to their natural state. "But Leanan and Cradel are still alive."

"Have they not gone wild in the Perilous Forest and so lost any chance they might have had to protect the Realm?"

"I suppose."

"And was Nemain not killed by one of Arthur's own archers when she tried to prevent him from disinterring Bran's head at the White Tower?"

"Corvus . . ." The old man's tone held a distinct warning, and the raven hopped back a step.

"Was not Deirdren killed by Lancelot and taken to Avalon in human form?" it asked instead.

"That is what they say."

Eyeing the cauldron of rebirth for a moment, the raven hopped onto the old man's book, smearing the ink. "Will I take human form when I die, Merlin?" it asked.

"No, you are too irritating. You will take the form of a swamp-midge."

"Truly?"

The raven's voice was so melancholy that the old man threw down his quill in disgust. "No, Corvus, not truly, but I will not tell you your future. We've been over this before. Now go away, I have things to do."

He shoved the bird with his elbow, and it rose gracefully into the air to return to its perch.

"And don't put that revolting thing back into Bran's

cauldron," the mage shot after him. "I'm tired of having my workshop spattered with entrails."

"Is it not a revolting thing?" the raven answered reproachfully. "Did I not throw it into the hamper of Gwyddno Garanhir to make it a hundred little live things?"

With an impatient gesture, the old man spoke a word and the hamper closed with a snap. The raven hunkered down into its feathers in a sulk. The old man ignored it, and after a moment it straightened.

"What sort of things do you have to do, Merlin?" it asked in a mollifying tone.

The scratch, scratch of the old man's quill was its only answer.

"Merlin?"

"Writing things," the mage replied tersely.

"What things?"

"Words."

"What words?"

With an exaggerated sigh, the old man set his quill down again. "I'm writing about the future," he answered. "Not that it's truly any of your business."

Recognizing the forgiveness in the tone, the bird returned to its place on his shoulder. It leaned forward to regard the book quizzically. "Why?"

"Why what?"

"Why are you writing about the future?"

"So I don't forget it."

"What will the future be?"

"Whose future?"

"Whose future do you write about?"

"The future of Logres and of Camelot."

"Why?"

"So I don't forget it. Go away."

"Am I in it?"

"Go away, or I'll turn you into a swamp-midge here and now!" The old man threw his quill at the bird who took flight and returned to the lip of the cauldron.

"And why must you sit there? It blocks the light."

The raven obediently hopped down onto the window seat

and looked through the rainy mist to the courtyard below.
"Is there someone coming, Merlin?" it asked.

"I don't know, is there?" Picking up his quill the old man
hunched over his book again.

The air grew warm.

"Is there . . . ? Merlin . . . ?" The raven's eyes grew wide
as the faint image of a woman, hair and eyes as black as the
bird's own feathers, began to form in the center of the room.
The old man seemed not to notice.

"Merlin? Do you not see . . . ?"

The woman reached pale arms toward the old man, and
when she spoke, her voice had the soft sibilance of a serpent.

"Merlin."

He turned, unsurprised. "Nimue."

"You have been long absent from my side."

"I . . . have been busy."

The raven returned silently to the lip of the cauldron,
watching as the mage rose as if in a dream.

"Merlin?" it asked softly. "What are you doing?"

The old man ignored him and the woman smiled.

"Come to me, my love," she whispered.

He moved forward.

"Merlin!" Corvus cried. "Do you not sense danger here?"

The mage swayed and half-turned. Nimue snarled.
Throwing her arms wide, she sent a dozen bands of light
whipping forward to ensnare him.

"Merlin?"

She turned then, her dark red lips drawn up in a cruel
smile. "He cannot hear you, little carrion-eater," she said.
"Keep silent."

Snapping her wrist forward, she sent a ball of fire flying
across the room to smack the bird from its perch. With an
audible crack, it hit the wall and crumpled to the floor in a
jumble of feathers.

Nimue returned her attention to the mage, continuing to
wrap him in bands of light until he was securely cocooned.
Then, weaving her hands in the air, she spun the bands in an
intricate design. A huge hawthorn began to take form about
him. From seedling to sapling to full grown tree it grew in
the space of a few heartbeats, encasing the old man in a

prison of wood. The raven, its one wing flattened against the floor at an awkward angle, its beak smeared with its own blood, watched through a haze of pain, unable to rise or speak.

Nimue leaned forward to kiss the old man's lips. "Sleep, my love," she whispered. "Sleep in the woods of Broceliande until Logres has dire need of you again." She gestured, and the mage and his arboreal prison slowly faded away.

Standing quietly, she watched until the last flicker of his presence faded, then turned to eye the tower's collection of magical and historical items with disdain.

Beside Bran's cauldron the raven grew very still. The pain lacing through its wing made it want to squirm, but it was afraid to draw attention to itself.

Too late. Nimue came forward, her eyes frighteningly luminescent.

"And what shall I do with you, little meddler?" she asked almost to herself.

Its vision swimming, the raven tried to answer, but only a whistle of pain made its way past its cracked beak.

She leaned down and ran one pale finger along its wing. The raven shuddered.

"Broken," she murmured. "Such a pity. Time to die, little blackbird."

She straightened, bringing her foot forward to crush his skull.

Desperation found the raven its voice again.

"Why . . . why would you kill me?" it gasped.

"Why should I not?" she replied, her voice honestly curious. "You are a troublesome detail, more easily removed than allowed to remain."

The pain threatening to make it faint, the raven struggled to find an answer that would deflect her intention.

"Would my life not speak more eloquently of your greatness than my death?" it tried.

"I have no need for others to speak of my greatness, eloquently or not."

"Would you not always feel in your heart that you killed

me because you were not powerful enough to stave off my death?"

"No." Her eyes narrowed. "Must you always speak in questions? It's very annoying."

The raven shuddered as her foot touched its breast.

"Am I not one of the sacred birds of Logres? Is my speech not drawn from the magic of Sovereignty?"

"Is it?" Her voice was cold now. "What do you know of Sovereignty? Do you think that by flapping about Owain and Bran you gained some small scrap of their bond with the land?"

"Do . . ." A trickle of blood ran past its beak and the raven swallowed. "Do my kind not also accompany Morrighan, Badh, and Nemainn to the battlefield?" it asked.

She gave a barking laugh. "So now you share in the divine? You are a fool and your questions are the prattling of a child."

Stung by her words, the raven struggled to meet her eyes. "Do I not know all of the greatest questions of the ages?" it asked recklessly.

"Do you?" She paused. "Well then, perhaps I will spare your life after all if you can find a question that amuses me. Ask."

Dizzy with sudden hope, the raven searched its memory. The pain in its wing and beak was a constant distraction, and it finally blurted out the first question that came to mind.

"Who can remember the coldest winter night?"

"Arawn, Lord of the Underworld, whom you are perilously close to meeting. Try again."

"What . . . what is it that women desire most?"

"You would bring up Sovereignty again? Don't test my patience." Her foot came down to rest against its broken wing and the raven cried out in pain. It could feel the shock of its injuries beginning to cloud its thoughts and it tried desperately to keep hold of the clarity necessary to save its life.

"What . . . what walks on two legs in the morning . . . ?"

"Enough. That is a riddle, not a question. I grow bored with you, little philosopher. Time to join Bran in his endless sleep."

The raven cried out again, unable to think past its fear of

her. "Will you not hear pleas for mercy?" it choked out. "Is not mercy the greatest human virtue?"

Nimue paused. Bending, she lifted the trembling bird up and cradled it in her hands. The pressure against its wing almost caused it to black out, but it just managed to hold on to consciousness as she walked to the window.

"You are a foolish creature," she murmured. "Mercy? What is mercy? For that matter, what is virtue? You tell me, Corvus, Bran's little lover, what do you think is the greatest human virtue?"

The raven tried to hold onto her words, but the pain was throbbing up into its temples and it could not concentrate. It felt the weakness of death creep over its limbs, and its head lolled back against her fingers.

"Does not . . . a human . . . know this better than . . . a raven?" it managed finally.

She gave it a withering smile. "You don't know, do you?" she said, not unkindly. "Questioner with no answers. I think I shall give you the chance to find out, shall I?" She held the raven over the windowsill and it felt the cold rain against its face. It was suddenly reminded of the day, long ago, when it had stood unsteadily on the edge of its first nest and knew it was meant to fly.

"I set you this task," she intoned and the raven felt a sharp tingling all over its body. *"Go forth into the world and ask this question of all you meet: What is the greatest human virtue?"*

She dropped it.

The wind rushed through its feathers and the raven tried to raise its wings, to let the updraft take it away from this frightening woman and the pain she inflicted, but its wings would not catch the wind and it plummeted down to land upon the cobbled courtyard below. The world grew very dark.

He awoke to a blue light flitting past his closed eyelids. The tingling had become an itch. Far away, he heard her voice and knew he was, somehow, still alive.

"Your death is averted for now, little philosopher. When

you know the answer to your question, I will come to you again. Now, awake!"

His eyes snapped open, and Merlin's stone tower loomed above him.

He was alone.

Shivering, he tried to rise. His limbs ached frightfully, and he was so cold. Struggling to sit, he pushed his hands forward to catch his suddenly unfamiliar weight and started.

His hands.

Hands.

His gaze traveled down, to arms and chest and naked manhood to legs and finally to feet. Human feet.

He might have sat there forever, staring down at his sudden transformation, but the cold of the cobblestones finally drove him to make an attempt to rise. Untangling his limbs, he managed to get to his feet, took one step forward, and fell.

After catching his breath, he stared down at his knees, and cautiously flexed the muscles. They bent the wrong way. Slowly his muddled senses began to function again. He'd seen many humans walk and run, but he'd never stopped to study them, and Merlin had always worn a robe. Finally, he called up an ancient memory of Bran the Blessed standing naked on the banks of the Irish Sea as he prepared to swim out to rescue his sister Branwen from King Matholwch. Corvus scrutinized the image and then slowly stood.

It took him several hours to make his way down to the shore where Merlin kept a small fishing craft. By this time he was shaking with cold, but in the bottom of the boat, he found an old, black robe. Wrapping it gratefully about himself, he then studied the oars, turning his head sideways as he was used to doing. He'd often sat on Merlin's shoulder while the old man had rowed out to deep water to fish. He thought he remembered how the mage had done it. Glancing wistfully up at the sky, he climbed cautiously into the boat.

Fortunately the water was calm, and so, with some struggling, he managed to get the craft across to the opposite bank. With no particular plan in mind, he set out walking.

He met no one. At nightfall he curled up in a bed of

leaves and slept, his dreams filled with images of Nimue and Merlin.

In the morning he was ravenously hungry. Pacing back and forth across the road, he searched for mice in the long grassy bank, but his skills as a bird had deserted him, and he found himself unsure of how humans provided for themselves. Their mouths were soft, their hands no good for catching or rending, their eyesight poor. They needed weapons, but he had none. Finally he set out walking again, hugging himself to calm the rumbling of his stomach.

At length he smelled a familiar odor and, looking to one side, saw the carcass of a drowned hare lying in a stream. He didn't question his luck, merely plunged into the water to retrieve it.

Tearing at the bloated body with his hands and teeth, he ripped off hunks of meat and fur, swallowing them without regard to their state. It wasn't until he was almost sated that he heard a noise behind him. He whirled about, dropping the body into the water and came face-to-face with a golden-haired young woman. He stared.

She returned his look frankly, her own gaze traveling from his ragged robe to his blood-covered face. Suddenly aware of how he must look, he wiped his mouth with the corner of his sleeve.

"You shouldn't eat carrion anymore, Corvus," she admonished, her voice low-pitched and musical. "You never know how long it's been there."

Shocked that she knew his name, he made to answer and felt a sudden oddness in his mouth and throat.

"What is the greatest human virtue?"

She folded her arms over her breasts, her eyes narrowing. "From the sight of you, I'd guess I'd have to answer charity," she replied. "When was the last time you had a decent meal; one that didn't involve . . ." She shuddered.

Thinking back to his mice on Bardsey Island, he shook his head. "A long time," he answered and stopped in shock. All his life he'd spoken in questions; the only way he'd known to communicate. He'd always thought that his tie to Sovereignty and the triple Goddess had precluded any other form of speech. But now . . .

"I think I ate yesterday," he tried. "I'm very hungry." He paused, unsure of what to say next.

She gave him an appraising stare then nodded. "My name is Linet. You're to come with me." Without waiting for a reply, she turned and made her way back to the road. Corvus splashed water over his face, then followed, his mind in turmoil.

When he'd scrambled back up the bank, he hurried to catch up with her determined stride. "Why am I to come with you?" he asked when he finally reached her side.

"The Lady of the Fountain requires it. She saw you in a vision and sent me to fetch you to her."

"She saw me?"

Lifting her skirts, Linet stepped lightly over a break in the path before answering. "The Lady had a dream last night that one of Rhiannon's children was in need. She saw the place and sent me there to wait for you."

"But how did you know it was me?"

She shot him an amused look. "Only one who was new to human form would find such a meal as you were eating palatable."

"Oh."

They walked in silence for a time. Finally he glanced sideways at her. "You're very beautiful," he noted. "Are you a queen?"

She laughed. "I am the Lady of the Fountain's servant and guardian, but my grandfather is King Lot of Orkney and my father is Sir Gaheris, a knight of the Round Table."

"So you're a Princess, then."

She favored him with a wry smile. "I suppose. Come, my dwelling is this way."

She led him through a copse of yew trees to a clearing filled with wildflowers where a small cottage stood beside a large, three-tiered fountain. The water sparkled so invitingly as it splashed against the bowls that Corvus found himself desperately thirsty. Linet indicated that he should drink, and when he was finished, he looked up to see a beautiful, unearthly woman standing before him. Suddenly shy, he dropped his gaze, but the woman reached out one slender hand and lifted his chin so that he met her eyes.

"Don't you have something to ask me, follower of Bran?" she asked, her voice the sound of the wind dancing over the water.

He nodded. "What is the greatest human virtue . . . My Lady?"

She tilted her head to one side in so birdlike a gesture that he smiled, free from all fear of her.

"It is different for each person," she answered, "depending on your destiny. For myself it is patience, but for another, who can say."

"Linet says that it's charity."

The Lady smiled in the direction of her handmaid. "And so for Linet it is. What is it for you?"

"I don't know."

"Then you must discover it."

"That's what *she* said. Nim . . ."

The Lady touched a finger to his lips. "Do not speak her name, Corvus. I can see whose geas lies upon you." She straightened. "Go to Camelot. There you will find your answer. Linet will go with you. The children of Rhiannon are innocents, and often come to some harm on their own."

"Will I see you again?" Corvus asked shyly.

She gave him a mysterious smile. "Perhaps." Bending down, she kissed him on the forehead. She smelled of lavender and roses, and Corvus closed his eyes to more fully drink in the scent of her. When he opened them, she was gone. He blinked.

Linet took his hand with a wry smile. "Come, we'll eat first, and then we'll go to Camelot to find your answer."

It took them three days of walking to reach their destination. In that time they talked of many things; his life as companion to first Bran and then Merlin; her childhood on Orkney surrounded by uncles and cousins. She spoke at length of the world of humans, explaining their ways and customs and patiently answering all his questions. By the third day they were walking, arm in arm, like old friends.

But nothing she'd told him had prepared him for his first sight of the greatest city in Logres. As they crested the hill that overlooked the capital, Corvus stopped, awestruck, star-

ing down at the mass of spirals, bell towers, and slate gables
that made up the roofs of Camelot. Birds of every description made their homes in its nooks and crannies. The air was
filled with their song, and the longing to be among them was
so strong that he nearly choked on a sob. Linet squeezed his
hand reassuringly and led him down the hill.

Once through the huge south gate, the streets became
crowded with people. Corvus gawked at every passing merchant or tradesman, overwhelmed by the riot of sounds and
scents all about him. Taking him by the elbow, Linet guided
him expertly down cobblestone streets. But when a herd of
sheep heading for market collided with a company of soldiers, they found themselves flattened against a wall, unable
to go any farther.

She was just about to suggest that they turn back and try
another street when a tall, golden-haired knight, the five-
pointed star of the Goddess prominent upon his surcoat,
urged his mount between them and the crowd.

"Linet?" he asked, looking down with a quizzical smile.
"1 thought it was you. What are you doing in the middle of
this chaos?"

She returned his greeting with a tired smile of her own.

"I've come on the Lady's business, Uncle Gawain," she
answered wearily. "I'm to bring this stranger to Camelot.
He's on a quest. His name is Corvus."

Sir Gawain glanced down at him with an open, friendly
expression. "Well met, Corvus."

Corvus opened his mouth to reply and felt the now familiar tingle.

"What is the greatest human virtue?"

He clamped his mouth shut, horrified at his lack of manners, but Sir Gawain did not seem offended.

"Is that your quest?" he asked. "It's a worthy question.
Valor would be my answer, although some would likely say
love." He turned to Linet. "Did the Lady give you any instructions other than to bring him to Camelot?"

"No, Uncle."

"Does she require that you return immediately?"

Again she answered in the negative.

"Well, Gaheris has gone to Gorre on the King's business

so you must rely on me for hospitality. As for Corvus," he smiled down at him again. "His Majesty is always interested in quests and noble deeds. He holds an open court tomorrow where any might come who have such a tale. How be it if I bring him before His Majesty? Perhaps my fellow knights might be able to aid him in his quest."

Corvus felt his jaw drop. "Go before the King?" he asked weakly. "*The* King? King Arthur?"

"The very same."

"I . . . I couldn't . . . I . . ."

He turned to Linet for help, but she was nodding sagely. "That would be most kind of you, Uncle," she answered.

Gawain now glanced over the street from his higher vantage point.

"This crowd will not slacken off for several hours," he said. "It's market day. Linet, you come up before me in the saddle. Corvus, you take hold of my stirrup, and we'll see if I can get us clear of it."

His heart pounding, Corvus did as he was told and Sir Gawain urged his mount slowly forward. The crowds gave way before him and soon they were past the worst of it and heading for a quiet street. Gawain reined up before a respectable looking hostel.

"I keep rooms here," Linet explained to Corvus' confused expression. "They're quiet and clean. I find that after the peace of the Lady's fountain I'm unused to the bustle of the capital."

Gawain helped her down from the saddle and then turned to Corvus. "I'll send for you tomorrow," he promised. "Don't be nervous. The Court of King Arthur is not so formidable as you might have heard."

He waved at his niece and then turned his mount and clattered away up the street. Corvus watched him go.

"Not so formidable as I might have heard?" he muttered. "Easy for you to say."

Later that night, after dining with Linet, Corvus leaned his arms against the windowsill of his room and looked out across the slate roofs of Camelot. The moon had risen, casting a luminescent glow across the city. A sudden urge to be out in its tangled streets came over him and he gave in to it at once, clambering over the sill and making his cautious way down a drainpipe. Once his feet touched the cobbles, he made off in the direction they'd come from that afternoon.

It wasn't long before he was hopelessly lost, but he paid that no mind as each step took him deeper into the city's fascinating depths. He passed stone houses and timber houses; statues and monuments and obelisks, tiny cemeteries surrounded by stout stone walls, and even tinier gardens with rows of carrots and beets lined up like soldiers. He passed shops and taverns and warehouses, their multicolored signs turned fantastical in the moonlit night. At the door to a particularly well-lit establishment, he asked his question of a woman leaning against the doorjamb who laughed and led him inside.

It was crowded in the main room, men and women lounging about a long, wooden ledge or sitting around small tables. The fireplace to one side belched smoke into the room and Corvus began to cough. The woman beside him said something he could not hear, and then she was gone and another woman was looking down at him, her expression amused. Her hair was thick and black and her pale features and luminescent eyes so reminiscent of Nimue that Corvus paled and began to tremble. She smiled then, the same cruel smile, and drew him to a quiet corner. Once there, she regarded him as one might regard breakfast after a long night.

"I knew I felt my sister's magic," she mused. "I thought it might be she herself, but I see now that it's merely one of her minions." Her eyes roved boldly over his body and he found himself blushing. "No, not a minion," she amended, "but one who's fallen afoul of her, I think. Pretty enough. Too young a man for Nimue's taste, but . . ." she licked her lips, "quite old enough for mine. I am called Morgana." When he started, she smiled again. "Don't believe everything you hear. And do you not have a name? Speak."

Corvus' wet lips were suddenly dry. "What is the greatest human virtue?"

She laughed. "What a stupid question." Dark eyes bright, she ran a hand along his cheek. "Lust."

He took an involuntary step backward. "Lust? Isn't that a vice?" he asked weakly.

"That depends on whose lust you're discussing. Mine is truly a virtue. Now, your name?"

"Uh, Corvus, My Lady."

She regarded him thoughtfully and he felt a power so subtle that he might have imagined it, probing his mind.

"A follower of Rhiannon?" she asked.

"Of Bran."

"Bran is dead."

"Of Merlin, then."

"Merlin has left this world." She placed her fingers on his lips as he made to speak, and her touch made him shiver. "It is of no matter." Giving him a predatory look that caused his heart to skip a beat, she caught his hand and pressed it to her breast. "Have you ever lain with a woman, Corvus?"

His breath ragged, he thought of the various mates he'd had over the years and answered truthfully.

"No."

"How nice."

Tucking his arm in hers so that their bodies pressed against each other, she whispered her intent, then led him, unresisting, down a narrow hallway and into a small chamber.

The morning found him back in his own room, unsure of what to say in response to Linet's innocently asked question of his night's sleep. He found himself unable to meet her eyes, and merely mumbled something incoherent, but before she could press him, the landlady appeared with breakfast and a young man in tow. He introduced himself as Gingalin, Sir Gawain's son and squire, and answered, "love," to Corvus' question. He was here to summon them to the King's court, he explained, but he could join them for breakfast first. He helped himself to a piece of bread, ignoring his cousin Linet's frown.

An hour later, Corvus clasped her hand nervously as they followed Gingalin down some of the same streets he'd explored the night before.

"Linet?" he began, and then fell silent.

"Yes?"

"I'm not sure this is a good idea."

She smiled at him. "You mustn't be afraid of the King, Corvus. He's not at all fierce. He's really very kind and just."

Corvus made a face. "Perhaps to you, but my late master and he didn't exactly see eye to eye on several important matters."

"Bran?"

"Yes."

"Don't worry. The King wouldn't hold their struggle against you. Besides you were in bird form then. How would he recognize you?"

He gave that serious thought. "You're right," he answered finally.

"Of course I am. Just don't mention Bran, and all should be well. If you have to speak of masters, speak of Merlin. That should distract the King, for he was the mage's student for some years."

"I know," Corvus answered testily. "Merlin spoke of him *far* too often."

Linet gave him her wry smile. "You're jealous of the King?"

"No! It's just . . . he was Bran's rival and he dug up his head and . . ." He frowned. "I am not jealous of King Arthur."

"Of course you're not." She squeezed his hand to show she was teasing and he gave her a sour smile. "Anyway, don't worry," she continued. "The Lady of the Fountain would not have sent you into danger and once you meet the King, you will love him and honor him as we all do."

"Don't bet on it," he muttered.

"Hm?"

"Nothing."

Around them, Camelot was awake and beginning the day's trade. They passed through streets of fishmongers, tin smiths, weavers, coopers, chandlers, sign painters, and bread makers. Corvus' head was spinning by the time their path began to rise. Soon they stood above the city and the forest of roofs and towers became evident again. The early morning sun cast a golden hue over the buildings, and Gingalin paused a moment to allow Corvus to stand, gaping once more, in awe of its beauty.

"Have you ever seen the like?" the squire asked, amused. Corvus shook his head. "Never."

"Camelot is first among all cities. London, even Rome, is not so lovely. But come, it wouldn't do to be late." He turned away as the many bells of the city began to toll, filling the air with music.

At the top of the rise, the palace came into view and Corvus stumbled.

If the city itself was lovely, Camelot's Royal Palace was beautiful beyond words. Its delicate, spiral turrets stretched toward the clouds, ending in tiny points of gold. Its towers were made of shimmering marble; its windows of stained glass so perfect that the sun, reflecting off their surface, cast a rainbow of colors across the walls. Within its gates, vast gardens encircled the keep, hosting more flowers and birds than Corvus had ever seen.

He found his eyes filling with tears. "Oh, Merlin," he whispered. "What a thing you have wrought here."

Gangalin led them through the cobbled inner courtyard, past the main doors to a small side portal guarded by two sentinels in the livery of Orkney. He spoke with them and they stood aside as he led them into the palace and down a narrow passageway. At the end was a small door, which he opened and ushered them inside.

They found themselves in a small, richly paneled chamber. Benches stretched along one wall, an intricate latticework screen covered the other. Peering through it, Corvus saw Arthur's Great Hall in all its splendor. More than a dozen knights and ladies took their ease on chairs or leaned against the hall's huge, stone fireplace, which was cold this morning. Above in a gallery he saw a group of musicians, but realized suddenly that he could not hear the music they played, nor the words of those gathered. Linet explained that it was another of Merlin's masterpieces. Gangalin nodded.

"I shall leave you now. Sir Gawain wishes to escort you

to the King himself and shall be along presently." He bowed and withdrew.

Corvus peered through the lattice again and shifted uneasily.

Linet gripped his hand. "Don't be afraid," she said. "I shall make you acquainted with all here before you meet them. You see that man there, the one with the white hair?"

Corvus' gaze followed her finger and he nodded.

"That is Sir Bedivere. He's the King's most trusted councillor. The man he's talking to is Sir Kay, the King's foster brother, and behind him are Sir Dinadan and Sir Dragonet. They have a terrible predilection for practical jokes, so be on your guard if you meet them together." She smiled at the two men fondly. "There is my uncle, Sir Agravaine, by the window. Isn't he handsome? And beside him is my cousin Aleine and my aunt Clarrisant."

"They look very much like you," Corvus noted

"All our family share certain characteristics," she agreed. "Standing by the garden doorway is Sir Lionel, Anna, the King's sister, Sir Sagramore, and Alice, cousin to Sir Lancelot."

"Is he here?" Corvus peered through the lattice anxiously.

"No. He's gone to visit Sir Baudwin at his lands in Brittany. Do you have difficulty with Sir Lancelot as well?" She had her wry smile on again, and Corvus shook his head.

"Not personally. It's just that such men make me nervous. They have a habit of throwing stones. They all do," he added nervously.

Linet frowned, returning her attention to the hall.

"Well, there's a man who would not throw stones," she said, pointing. "That is Sir Galahad."

Corvus stared curiously at the man she indicated, half expecting to see a halo of light shining about him. What he saw instead was a brown-haired youth with an open, pleasant face and the faraway look of a mystic.

"He seems very young to be so renowned," he noted.

"He is young, but they say his purity of heart gives him the strength to overcome all adversity."

"You're right. He doesn't look as if he'd throw stones."

"Nor, I should think, do Sir Tristan or Sir Perceval."

Corvus ducked his head. "I've offended you."

She paused and then gave him a rueful smile. "Perhaps just a little. I've known many of the King's knights since I was a child. I love them all though, yes, I must admit that some of them are reckless and sometimes even a bit cruel. But here comes Uncle Gawain. You must admit that he would never throw stones."

Stepping through the door, Sir Gawain favored them both with his open smile. "You're here, then," he said in a pleased voice. "Are you ready to come before the King?"

Corvus swallowed but allowed himself to be ushered from the chamber by both the knight and the maiden.

The Hall was much noisier than he'd expected, and he flinched, stilling the urge to flap wings no longer there. Linet squeezed his hand, and Sir Gawain gave him an encouraging smile as they led him through the crowd. Silence followed in their wake as the assembled nobility turned and watched curiously. Corvus was suddenly aware of his dusty, ragged appearance and would have run if Linet hadn't kept a tight grip on his hand. Finally, two knights parted, and they stood before a simple, wooden throne. A tall, black-haired man, whose eyes and face held a nobility that Corvus had never encountered before was seated upon it, speaking with a young woman. As they approached, King Arthur looked up and smiled, his blue eyes twinkling.

"Well met, Nephew," he said to Sir Gawain, his voice even and warm. "You also, Linet, but who is this man with you?"

Gawain bowed. "He is called Corvus, My Liege. He is come to Camelot by instruction of the Lady of the Fountain in the hopes we might aid him in a most difficult quest."

The King turned his warm regard on Corvus who found himself smiling shyly in return.

"A quest!" The King said loudly and the gathered turned all their attention toward the throne. "That is always of the greatest interest to us. What is this quest, my friend, and how might we help you with it?"

Gawain gave Corvus a friendly nudge in the back which pushed him a step forward.

"What . . . what is the greatest human virtue, Majesty?" he whispered.

Twirling a ring on his finger, the King considered it gravely. "What do you think it is?" he asked after a time.

"I don't know, Sire."

"That is no doubt why he has been sent, Majesty," Gawain offered and Arthur nodded.

"For myself, my answer would have to be duty, I think," he answered, "the duty of the crown. What do you have a duty to, Corvus?"

The King looked at him with such kindness that Corvus almost blurted out Bran's name for if he had a duty to any it would be to him, but instead he said, "The protection of Logres, Majesty."

Arthur smiled as the assembled murmured their approval of such a word. "A fine answer. The Realm needs many such if it is to remain strong and free."

Again Corvus clamped his teeth shut on an involuntary response. Arthur did not notice.

"But that can't be the answer you seek, for it came right readily to your lips. Come then, you will ask your question of all my noble knights present, and we shall see if any may find the answer that touches your heart."

And so he bade Corvus go to each knight and ask his question. Most gave its personal meaning due thought, and each answered according to his nature.

Sir Dinadan replied humor after a dour Sir Belliese said fidelity, and both Sir Perceval and Sir Bors said honor. Sir Galahad chose faith and Sir Bedivere loyalty, and both Sir Tristan and Lionel chose love as did most of the others. True to his Orkney heritage, Sir Agravaine replied valor as had his brother Gawain.

When Corvus had asked each knight in turn, he found himself before King Arthur again.

"A dizzying array," the King noted.

"Yes, Your Majesty. It seems, if I may make so bold, that it's different for every person."

"That is the fabric of our lives, Corvus. We all have a destiny, and what we value is colored by that destiny."

"But our destinies are hidden in the mists of time, unassailable by all but the most powerful of Seers," Corvus replied, his inquisitive nature drawing him into debate despite his wariness before the King. "How can we then know what we value?"

"Perhaps each person's values influence their destiny," Arthur answered.

Corvus shook his head vehemently. "That cannot be, because then you're trapped in a circle with neither a beginning nor an end."

"What came first, the chicken or the egg?" the King shot back, obviously enjoying himself.

"The chicken."

"Ah, but where did the chicken come from?"

"The Gods."

"And the Gods come from where?" The King's eyes sparkled with mischief and Corvus frowned.

"I don't know," he snapped.

"And what is the greatest human virtue?"

"I . . . I don't know that either." Corvus deflated, but the king gave him another kindly smile.

"Then abide in Camelot a while. I give you free access to any part of our fair city, only you must come before me again should you find your answer."

Corvus gave him a grudging nod. "I will, Your Majesty."

And so Corvus left King Arthur's presence feeling more confused than before he'd arrived.

He remained in Camelot all that summer. Linet and Gawain guided him through the city, stopping noble, merchant, and beggar alike so he might ask them his question. He got so many answers that he lingered through the autumn and winter to spring and back to summer again. Soon he became a familiar sight, many of the citizens taking it upon themselves to bring strangers to him to hear their answers. Linet and he grew closer, until he could no longer remember a time when he did not love her. They lived happily together when her duties at the Lady's fountain permitted, and at other times he stayed at the home of Sir Dinadan, whose temperament suited him very well.

On most days he could be found seated in the palace gardens debating the question with Sir Bedivere or perched in the Palace Hall's upper gallery. Back pressed against a marble pillar, he became the silent witness to all of Camelot's greatest events, and so the years passed swiftly.

He was there when Sir Bertilak, the green knight, challenged Arthur's court to the beheading game, and there when, to his joy and relief, Sir Gawain returned from his meeting with that strange man to remark sourly that humility might perhaps be his answer now.

He was there to watch each newly made knight swear his vows before the King, and there to see which lady caught their attention and which held it. He witnessed the struggle between the Druidic and Christian religions and watched as one by one, each knight chose the way of the cross; all save Gawain who remained the Knight of the Goddess to the end.

He was there when a light so bright that it caused his eyes to fill with tears and spots to dance before his vision marked the appearance of the Holy Grail, and there as each knight of the Round Table spoke of his adventures seeking it. And he was there to grieve with the King when Sir Perceval and Sir Bors came home, bearing Sir Galahad's body and a tale of the completion of the Grail quest.

It seemed to him that something in Camelot dimmed that day, although outwardly it was still as beautiful as ever. Often he dreamed of flying over its slate roofs and common pastures and wondered if his spirit returned to the raven form that, in his waking life, he had all but forgotten.

And so the years passed.

He was still there, although the glossy black of his hair was beginning to gray, as was the King's, when Arthur learned of the love of his wife and the Realm's greatest living knight and with it of the deaths of Sir Colgrevave, Sir Tor, Sir Gareth, and Linet's father, Sir Gaheris.

He watched as, mad with grief, Sir Gawain swore on his honor to seek out Sir Lancelot and make him pay for his brothers' deaths; and he wept as Gawain's body was returned to Camelot to be laid at the King's feet.

He watched with an ever heavier heart as Arthur, his bright eyes and quick smile dimmed, led his few loyal followers to Joyous Gard in France, leaving Sir Mordred to al-

most destroy the Realm. But when Arthur returned to give
him battle, Corvus left his perch and followed the King's
army to Camlan.

Linet went with him. Together they helped carry the
wounded from the field and bury the dead. As each battle
dwindled their numbers, Corvus grew more fearful for the
King's safety, until finally, standing on a rise overlooking
the fields of Camlan, as the last of Camelot's shattered
Round Table fought a terrible battle against itself, they saw
King Arthur fall.

A pain worse than any he had ever felt struck Corvus in
the breast, and he cried out as the Palladium of Logres fell.
Heedless of the danger, Corvus turned and plunged down
the hill.

Running between the few remaining combatants, his eyes
streaming with tears, Corvus stumbled and fell to his knees
before the dying King. Sir Lucan and Sir Bedivere were already there, openly weeping and they did not protest as
Corvus clutched the King's hand.

Arthur's eyes were glassy, but he looked up at him with
a pained smile.

"Have you found your answer yet?" he asked weakly.

Corvus could only shake his head, splattering tears across
the King's face.

"I fear I can no longer help you. You'll have to find it on
your own now, follower of Bran."

Corvus started. "How did you know?"

The ghost of his old smile came to Arthur's lips. "The
king and the land are one," he managed, "and all things are
made clear to him." He grimaced in pain. "I am glad . . . that
Bran and I could be reconciled through you." Spent, he let
his head loll against Sir Bedivere's breast. The two knights
lifted him up and slowly bore him from the field.

Corvus remained, his mind in shock. Already his fellow
ravens were flocking to their feast and a terrible longing to
be among them, with no care save filling an empty belly,
came over him. He raised his head and keened for all he had
lost in both bird form and man form.

He never saw the arrows which flew toward him. One

grazed him across the jaw, the other took him through the arm and pierced his side. He fell.

It was some time before he regained his senses. He found himself lying on a grassy knoll, his head cradled in Linet's lap, her arms about him. She was weeping, and he raised his good hand to catch her tears.

"Lin . . ." He coughed and pain laced through his mouth, making him want to squirm.

"Don't talk," she choked out. "You're going to be all right."

A sharp tingling began to move throughout his body. "But I never . . ." he strained to speak as his mouth filled with blood. "But I never found the answer," he whispered.

"Be still." Linet passed her hands frantically over his face and he reached forward to catch and hold them still.

"Dying," he said simply.

"No. You can't be. We'll get you to a physician."

"Too late. I did . . . so want to stay with you."

"We all want what we cannot have, little philosopher," a voice said above them.

They looked up to see the Lady Nimue standing over them. No longer the terrible presence she'd been in Merlin's tower, she seemed tired and careworn, as if the battle had drained as much life from her as Corvus' wounds had from him. There were fine lines about her mouth and her dark eyes were cloudy. She looked down at him with weary sympathy.

"Have you found your answer yet, Corvus?" she asked.

He tried to shake his head, but it hurt too much to move. "No," he whispered.

"You're almost out of time."

"I know."

Linet looked up. "My Lady, please help him."

Nimue shook her head sadly. "I cannot. Soon I must join my sisters to carry Arthur to Avalon."

Corvus stirred. "Is he . . . is he dead?"

She gave him a faint smile. "King Arthur will never truly die," she said. "He will sleep, the greatest of his knights beside him, until Logres has need of him again." She crouched down. "I cannot save you, little blackbird, but I can bear you to Avalon to lie beside the King."

He managed a weak smile. "Merlin said I would not go to Avalon."

"To the Blessed Realm then, to join with Bran in his endless sleep."

Corvus coughed, and a thin trickle of blood ran down between his lips to spatter onto Linet's sleeve. His heart began to beat laboriously. To be with Bran again. To never be in doubt again. He closed his eyes and several tears squeezed their way between his lids. To never see Linet again. To never fly over the fields of Logres again.

He opened his eyes, and Nimue's face swam in and out of focus.

"Who will protect the Realm," he managed, "if we are all gone?"

"Who, indeed?" She tilted her head to one side. "Would you stay, Corvus, and protect the Realm if you could?"

His answer was easy enough. "Yes."

"Even if it meant returning to your raven form and losing the power of speech? Could you give up all your questions and all their answers?"

"Yes."

"Even if it meant losing all the memories of those who went before you; of Bran and Merlin and of Arthur?"

"Yes."

"Even if it meant losing Linet?"

He paused and she raised her head angrily. "He won't lose me!" she spat out. "Who are you to say he'll lose me?"

"I am a vessel of Sovereignty."

Corvus felt the tears come as he finally recognized her for what she was. He felt like a fool for not seeing it before, but Linet gripped his hand and faced Nimue fearlessly. "I won't leave him," she growled.

"He will not know you."

"I don't care. I will know him."

"Is that your choice then, follower of Bran?" Nimue asked, turning back to Corvus.

He nodded weakly.

"And you will stay with him and aid him?" she asked Linet.

"Yes!"

"Then stay, both of you; stay and protect the Realm; for Bran, for Arthur, and for me, until it has need of us again."

She stood, and between the space of one heartbeat and the next, she was gone.

Corvus lay, feeling the tingling in his limbs and the pain in his mouth and arm growing.

"Linet?"

"I'm here, Corvus."

"I'm so cold."

She gathered him up in her arms as he began to shake. The shock of his injuries made his thinking fuzzy and he struggled to concentrate.

"What is the greatest human virtue?" he asked aloud. His mind moving sluggishly as he thought of Bran, of Arthur, of Gawain and Galahad, and finally he knew.

"Sacrifice," he whispered.

Linet glanced down at him. "What?"

"Sacrifice," he repeated. "Because it's motivated by all the rest; duty, honor, love, valor."

She sighed. "Truly."

"Linet?"

"Yes, Corvus."

"You must . . ." His mouth twisted and found it impossible to form the words. "Will you . . . find Leanan and Cradel in the Perilous Forest?" he croaked out. "Take them . . . Will you take them, take us, to the White Tower?"

"The White Tower?"

He nodded. "As long . . ." he struggled against the encroaching change, fighting to speak this one last sentence as a statement and managed to gasp out . . . "as long as we remain . . . the Realm will be safe."

He fell back, the last of his strength used up in the attempt. The tingling was now all over his body, and he felt himself shrink and his hands grow numb as his arms returned to wings once more.

"Will I . . . will I know you?" he managed through his broken beak.

Linet bowed her head, tears dripping down onto the glossy black of his feathers. "Yes," she answered defiantly. "We will fly together in our dreams, Corvus."

"Will . . . that be enough?"

"Yes."

"Am I not . . . the greatest of Bran's ravens?"

She favored him with her wry smile through her tears. "You are the first of Bran's ravens," she agreed.

"And . . . you will stay with me?"

"I said I would. I will be the Keeper of the Ravens of the White Tower."

The love in her face his last conscious sight, Corvus closed his eyes and slept.

And in the days following the battle of Camlan, a fair, golden-haired woman could be seen traveling toward London, a great raven cradled in her arms. She made her home in the White Tower and called the others of his kind to dwell with them so that England might always be safe against invasion.

And there they still remain.

ABOUT THE AUTHORS

Andre Norton has written and collaborated on over 100 novels in her sixty years as a writer, working with such authors as Robert Bloch, Marion Zimmer Bradley, Mercedes Lackey, and Julian May. Her best-known creation is the Witch World, *which has been the subject of several novels and anthologies. She has received the Nebula Grand Master award, The Fritz Leiber award, and the Daedalus award, and presently resides in Murfreesboro, Tennessee, where she oversees a writers' library and makes time to read and recommend historical mysteries.*

Peter S. Beagle is best known for his fantasy novel, The Last Unicorn, *which has been in print since it first appeared in 1968. His fiction output lessened as he turned to writing screenplays for movies and TV shows like* Star Trek: The Next Generation. *In recent years, however, he has reappeared with the novels* The Innkeeper's Song, The Unicorn Sonata, Tamsin *and* A Dance For Emilia. *More of Peter's short stories can be found in the collections* Giant Bones *and* The Rhinoceros Who Quoted Nietzsche.

*Ursula K. Le Guin is considered one of the most influential authors in the science fiction and fantasy field. Her Earthsea novels (*A Wizard of Earthsea, The Tombs of Atuan, The Farthest Shore, *and* Tehanu*) have been favorably compared to J. R. R. Tolkien's work for their intricate detailing of a fantasy world. Her work in the field has been critically acclaimed as well, garnering her five Nebula awards, five Hugo awards, three Jupiter awards, and the Gandalf award. She has taught writing courses all around the world, and currently lives in Portland, Oregon.*

Nominated five times for the Nebula award and twice for the Hugo, the Edgar, and the World Fantasy awards, Susan Shwartz is a frequent contributor to anthologies and author of historical fiction and military science fiction novels. She lives in New York, which is sufficient justification for writing fantasy and horror. Her recent Star Trek *novel coauthored with Josepha Sherman,* Vulcan's Forge, *made several bestseller lists.*

Charles de Lint is a full-time writer and musician who presently makes his home in Ottawa, Canada, with his wife MaryAnn Harris, an artist and musician. His novels include The Onion Girl, Forests of the Heart, *and* Someplace to Be Flying. *Other recent publications include* Waifs & Strays, *his first YA collection, and* Tapping the Dream Tree, *the fourth collection of Newford stories. For more information about his work, visit his Web site at: www.charlesdelint.com.*

Megan Lindholm has explored many facets of fantasy fiction, from urban fantasy in The Wizard of the Pigeons *to historical fantasy in* The Reindeer People. *She has also collaborated with fellow author Steven Brust on the novel* Gypsy. *More recently, under the pseudonym Robin Hobb, she has written the* Farseer, Liveship Traders, *and her newest, the* Tawnry Man *series. She lives in Washington with her husband and four children.*

Ellen Kushner is the author of the novels Swordspoint *and* Thomas the Rhymer *(World Fantasy Award). Her latest novel, written with Delia Sherman, is* The Fall of the Kings. *She is also the host of Public Radio International's weekly series,* Sound & [sic] Spirit, *and wrote and narrates* The Golden Dreydl: a Klezmer "Nutcracker."

Esther M. Friesner is no stranger to the world of armed-and-dangerous women or warriors having (a) created, edited, and written for the Chicks in Chainmail *series, (b) graduated from Vassar College and (c) raised a teenaged daughter. Her son, husband, two cats, and warrior-princess hamster treat her with accordingly appropriate awe which has nothing to do with the thirty novels she has had published, the two Nebulas she has won, or the over 100 short works she wrote after this one.*

Mickey Zucker Reichert is a pediatrician whose fantasy and science fiction novels include The Legend of Nightfall, The Bifrost Guardians *series,* The Last of the Renshai *trilogy,* The Renshai Chronicles *trilogy,* Flightless Falcon, The Beasts of Barakhai, The Lost Dragons of Barakhai, *and* The Unknown Soldier, *all available from DAW Books. Her short fiction has appeared in numerous anthologies, including* Assassin Fantastic, Knight Fantastic, *and* Vengeance Fantastic. *Her claims to fame: she has performed brain surgery, and her parents really are rocket scientists.*

Emma Bull's first novel, War for the Oaks, *is a cult favorite among fans of contemporary fantasy. Her third novel,* Bone Dance, *was a finalist for the Hugo, Nebula, and World Fantasy awards, and was the second-place Philip K. Dick award novel. She collaborated with Steven Brust on a historical fantasy,* Freedom and Necessity, *and is working solo on another set in Arizona in 1881, called* Territory. *She and her husband, Will Shetterly, sold a screenplay for an animated science fiction film and have had two live-action feature scripts optioned. Emma's band, the Flash Girls, released their third album,* Play Each Morning, Wild Queen, *in 2001.*

Mercedes Lackey was born in Chicago, and worked as a lab assistant, security guard, and computer programmer before turning to fiction writing. Her first book, Arrows of the Queen, *the first in the Valdemar series, was published in 1985. She won the Lambda award for* Magic's Price *and Science Fiction Book Club Book of the Year for* The Elvenbane, *coauthored with Andre Norton. Along with her husband, Larry Dixon, she is a Federally licensed bird rehabilitator, specializing in the care of wild birds. She shares her home with a menagerie of parrots and cats. Recent novels include* Exile's Honor, Take a Thief *and* The Black Swan.

Tanya Huff lives and writes in rural Ontario with her partner, four cats, and an unintentional chihuahua. After sixteen fantasies, she wrote her first space opera, Valor's Choice *(DAW April 2000). Her most recent fantasies are her sequels to* Summon The Keeper, *called* The Second Summoning *and* Long Hot Summoning. *In her spare time she gardens and complains about the weather.*

Kristine Kathryn Rusch is an award-winning fiction writer. Her novella, "The Gallery of His Dreams," won the Locus award for best short fiction. Her body of fiction work won her the John W. Campbell Award, given in 1991 in Europe. She has been nominated for several dozen fiction awards, including the MWA's Edgar award for both short fiction and novel, and her short work has been reprinted in six Year's Best collections.

She has published twenty novels under her own name and sold forty-one total, including pseudonymous books. Her novels have been published in seven languages, and have spent several weeks on The USA Today Bestseller list and The Wall Street Journal Bestseller list. She is the former editor of prestigious The Magazine of Fantasy and Science Fiction, wining a Hugo for her work there. Before that, she and her husband Dean Wesley Smith started and ran Pulphouse Publishing, a science fiction and mystery press in Eugene. She lives and works on the Oregon Coast.

Michelle West is the author of a number of novels, including The Sacred Hunt duology, and The Broken Crown, The Uncrowned King, The Shining Court, and Sea of Sorrows, the first four novels of The Sun Sword series, all available from DAW Books. She reviews books for the on-line column First Contacts, and less frequently for The Magazine of Fantasy & Science Fiction. Other short fiction by her appears in Knight Fantastic, Familiars, Assassin Fantastic, and Villains Victorious.

Born in Glasgow, Scotland, Lisanne Norman started writing at the age of eight in order to find more of the books she liked to read. In 1980, two years after joining The Vikings!, the largest British reenactment society in Britain, she moved to Norfolk, England. There she ran her own specialist archery display team. Now a full-time author, in her Sholan Alliance Series she has created worlds where warriors, magic, and science all coexist. Her latest novel from DAW in the series is Between Darkness and Light.

Fiona Patton was born in Calgary Alberta in 1962 and grew up in the United States. In 1975 she returned to Canada, and after several jobs which had nothing to do with each other, including carnival ride operator and electrician, moved to 75 acres of scrub land in rural Ontario with her partner, four cats of various sizes, and one tiny little dog. Her first book, The Stone Prince, was published by DAW Books in 1997. This was followed by The Painter Knight in 1998, The Granite Shield in 1999, and The Golden Sword in 2001, also published by DAW. She is currently working on her next novel.

MERCEDES LACKEY

The Novels of Valdemar

Exile's Honor

He was once a captain in the army of Karse, a
kingdom that had been at war with Valdemar for
decades. But when Alberich took a stand for
what he believed in—and was betrayed—he was
Chosen by a Companion to be a Herald, and
serve the throne of Valdemar. But can Alberich
keep his honor in a war against his own people?

"A treat for Valdemar fans"
—Booklist

0-7564-0085-6

To Order Call: 1-800-788-6262

DAW 24

John Marco
The Eyes of God

Akeela, the king of Liiria, determined to bring peace to his kingdom, and Lukien, the Bronze Knight of Liiria, peerless with a sword, and who had earned his reputation the hard way, loved each other as brothers, but no two souls could be more different. And both were in love with the beautiful Queen Cassandra. But unknown to anyone, Cassandra hid a terrible secret: a disease that threatened her life and caused unimaginable strife for all who loved her. For Akeela and Lukien, the quest for Cassandra's salvation would overwhelm every bond of loyalty, every point of honor, because only the magical amulets known as the Eyes of God could halt the progress of Cassandra's illness. But the Eyes could also open the way to a magical stronghold that will tear their world apart and redefine the very nature of their reality.

0-7564-0096-1

To Order Call: 1-800-788-6262

Kristen Britain

GREEN RIDER

"The gifted Ms. Britain writes with ease and grace as she creates a mesmerizing fantasy ambiance and an appealing heroine quite free of normal clichés."
—*Romantic Times*

Karigan G'ladheon has fled from school following a fight that would surely lead to her expulsion. As she makes her way through the deep forest, a galloping horse plunges out of the brush, its rider impaled by two black arrows. With his dying breath, he tells her he is a Green Rider, one of the legendary messengers of the King. Giving her his green coat with its symbolic brooch of office, he makes Karigan swear to deliver the message he was carrying. Pursued by unknown assassins, following a path only the horse seems to know, she unwittingly finds herself in a world of deadly danger and complex magic, compelled by forces she does not yet understand....

0-88677-858-1

To Order Call: 1-800-788-6262